more praise for

LONDON BRIDGE IN PLAGUE AND FIRE

"Already distinguished and acclaimed, author David Madden now adds to his tally of titles this inventively constructed, sometimes shocking, imaginative history about London Bridge, its merchants and residents in, mostly, the seventeenth century. Cameos of such as Shakespeare, Milton, Pepys shine a light on stage center, where the cast includes a Poet-Chronicler, rag seller Dropstitch Upshaw, and other vibrant, viable, ordinary characters in extraordinary times of plague and fire, vividly rendered. The novel in due course pitch[ing] into a dramatic, smartly thought-out meditation on good and evil, becoming, in effect, a passion play. *London Bridge in Plague and Fire* is a major achievement, bursting with life and ideas."

—Kelly Cherry, author of *We Can Still Be Friends*

"London Bridge in Plague and Fire is a prodigiously researched marriage of fiction and a sweep of history."

—Janet Burroway, author of *Bridge of Sand*

"Time travel is alive and well in David Madden's book. . . . I mean, in the reader of it. You will be transported to a time and place that is so surprising, vivid, and compelling that you will swear you've been there, with the author by your side."

—Tony Bill, Academy Award–winning producer and director

"Years ago, living in London, I'd amble across the Bridge, singing up its falling down—though it may now, by David Madden, be preserved through *Plague and Fire*. His novel is so vividly impacted in history that if you've never walked, you'll be there, now and multiple thens, through the political, commercial, ecclesiastical, aesthetic history of the Bridge, becoming familiar with its booksellers, merchants, prostitutes, poets, lovers, husbands and wives, and the menagerie of animals with insects mimicking or modeling aspects of its structure, in the chronopanorama of a poetic prose. Around erotic encounters, with London Bridge falling and rising, this novel novel is researched better than most scholarship in academic journals, and all the more poetic for that."

—Herbert Blau, Byron W. and Alice L. Lockwood
Professor of the Humanities, University of Washington

"Madden's novel is written with sensuous and innovative prose. His historic and aesthetic strategy is ambitious and profoundly convincing. Interlaced in the narrative are insightful poems and revealing journal entries. The novel is a superb and penetrating analysis of imaginative truth and arresting facts. It all comes together under the write's artistic gaze, through his sense of harmony, to tell an explosively brilliant story of London Bridge and its fascinating array of characters. This is a winner! Bravo!"

—Clarence Major, novelist, poet, painter

LONDON BRIDGE IN PLAGUE AND FIRE

FICTION BY DAVID MADDEN

London Bridge in Plague and Fire (2012)
Abducted by Circumstance (2010)
Sharpshooter (1996)
The New Orleans of Possibilities (short stories, 1982)
On the Big Wind (1980)
Pleasure Dome (1979)
The Suicide's Wife (1978)
Bijou (1974)
Brothers in Confidence (1972)
The Shadow Knows (short stories, 1970)
Cassandra Singing (1969)
Hair of the Dog (1967)
The Beautiful Greed (1961)

LONDON BRIDGE
IN PLAGUE AND FIRE

A Novel

DAVID MADDEN

THE UNIVERSITY OF TENNESSEE PRESS / KNOXVILLE

A portion of this novel was published as the short story "Thomas à Becket's Bones Are
Missing" in *The Sewanee Review,* Winter 2006, Vol. 114 (1).

The paper in this book meets the requirements of American National
Standards Institute / National Information Standards Organization specification
Z39.48-1992 (Permanence of Paper). It contains 30 percent post-consumer waste
and is certified by the Forest Stewardship Council.

Library of Congress Cataloging-in-Publication Data

Madden, David, 1933-
London Bridge in plague and fire: a novel / David Madden. — 1st ed.
p. cm.
ISBN 978-1-57233-870-8 (hardcover) — ISBN 1-57233-870-9 (hardcover)
1. London Bridge (London, England)—Fiction.
2. Experimental fiction.
I. Title.

PS3505.A3113L66 2012
813'.54—dc23
2012005295

FOR

Robbie
Blake
Kuniko

In memory of Peter de Colechurch,
Master Builder of ancient London Bridge,
started in 1176, finished 1209, four years after his death

What rings the bells of London? Civil War, plague deaths, firestorm winds, child murder.

So who is ringing the bells . . . ? It is *the spirit of story-telling*.
—Thomas Mann, *The Holy Sinner*

The unimagined life is not worth living.

Although light "passes among the impure, it is not polluted."
—Saint Augustine, *Tract on Saint John*

Light is God's shadow.
—Sir Thomas Browne, *Religio Medici*

There is nothing in the mind that did not start in the body.
—Aristotle

Everywhere and always, go after that which is lost.
—Carolyn Forché, *Ourselves or Nothing*

CONTENTS

TO MY READER

I acquired hundreds of books for research into the murder of Thomas à Becket and the building of London Bridge during the late twelfth century, the ongoing history of the bridge, life in the shops and houses on the Bridge, and the events of the plague and the fire. The original inspiration came from seeing in 1944 the haunting image of the Bridge in the credits for Laurence Olivier's film *Henry V.* A more detailed inspiration was *London in Plague and Fire, 1665–1666: Selected Source Material for College Research Papers,* a textbook I used at Centre College in 1960, my second year of teaching.

Among other books, the most useful were Gordon Home, *Old London Bridge* (the second book I read and the best); Frank Barlow, *Thomas Becket*; William Urry, *Thomas Becket: His Last Days*; Walter George Bell, *The Great Plague of London* and *The Great Fire of London*; Samuel Pepys's *Diary*; John Evelyn's *Diary;* Roland Bartel, *London in Plague and Fire: 1665–1666*; and Daniel Defoe, *A Journal of the Plague Year* (a fabric of fact and fiction). A longer, selected list appears at the end of this novel.

Even so, this is not a novel that claims accuracy, plausibility, or credibility in the way a reader would expect from a historian. I imagined the Poet-Chronicler, who imagines the life of Peter de Colechurch, architect of the Bridge, about whom very little is on record, and his building of the Bridge. I share the Poet-Chronicler's passion for researching the facts and his compulsion to overwhelm and transform them in imagination. The Poet-Chronicler and I enmesh the facts in imaginative contexts, a process that began in the first draft.

Reading only in Gordon Home's book about the bridge, I heard nocturnal voices from ancient London Bridge. Every night, just before going to bed, from Christmas Eve 1992 to the next Christmas Eve, I wrote the first draft in brief sessions as if in a trance, facts stimulating almost surrealistic images. Then as I looked at the many drawings and paintings of ancient London Bridge and read about it in numerous other books, I listened to the voice of a young poet living on the Bridge during plague and fire and imagined him listening to voices from the twelfth century when the master builder began his unique engineering feat—the first bridge of stone since the Romans—and writing fifty-six years later his own account of the plague and the fire, drawing upon memory, eyewitnesses, and historical sources in wild combinations. A clear narrative threads through the labyrinthine phantasmagoria.

Since the historical record provides only a few simple facts about Peter de Colechurch, the Poet-Chronicler fully imagines the life of Peter and his relationship with Archbishop Thomas à Becket, murdered in Canterbury Cathedral, about whom an astonishing archive of eyewitness accounts and facts exists. The power of the Poet's imagination enhances the power of his compassion.

Writing this meditative narrative, I mingled the voices I heard with the voices I imagined the Poet heard. During plague and fire, sometimes a "voice," sometimes the named characters, especially the merchants, speak, with variations, lines that historical witnesses wrote, along with the lines the Poet actually hears or imagines. A young seaman writes in his journal and in the margins of his books memories of his childhood on London Bridge, memories he tells an older seaman who becomes his enemy. Speaking, writing, mingling, we three are poet-historians, web weavers, weaving webs of connections out of our emotions, imaginations, and intellects, moving not along a compulsory narrative line so much as from one impression to another. The very mingling of facts and imagination *is* the experience. The flow and confluence of those nocturnal voices, the act of weaving, matter most—not who, when, not even where, not even facts—because when imagination soars, it triumphs, in the end, over facts, if from the beginning, you have been my collaborator.

I trust you.

David Madden

J. M. W. TURNER'S LONDON BRIDGE

Yes. The way the Bridge looks in a certain light,
white, in *my* imagination, framed
by boats, row and sail, in the foreground,
the Tower white, too, in this painting,
at least, all, all under Turner clouds, as
critics are wont to say. Yes, my
clouds. Not God's, this man's, this creator's.
Not ego. Not for a moment. I paint this vision,
but whence cometh the vision? Perhaps
from God. But, I have, like all who praise
or damn this picture, left London Bridge
itself *too* far behind. Let us return.
To 1205, the year Peter de Colechurch died,
having built one of wood that perished and this
of stone that comes to us in modern times,
and was buried at the Chapel Lock under the Chapel.
Return to the almost two hundred
shops, homes above them, the heads, lopped
off, aloft on the Great Stone Gate as warning. All
demolished when my vision arrested me and I stood
on the bank Southwest, above Southwark, above
Shakespeare's Globe, on the dock to paint. Such
a distance from the priest's creation when 'twas new.
Then, as the Eighteenth Century "shot
the rapids," I rowed up to the piers,

close up, to capture from the East, ghostly
in the light beyond the dark arches,
the broken view of Westminster Bridge.
It was then, ladies and gentlemen, as my quick
strokes of watercolour that you see before you caught
the spectacle, that I walked on Ancient London Bridge,
a few steps behind Peter de Colechurch, among
the houses, the shops, in the midst of carts,
animals, my ancestors, *ours*. So, do not
praise this moment's work only, but feel
in your bones the force of high tide, rushing
through the nineteen piers down the Ages,
flooding our mouths.

David Madden

DRAMATIS PERSONAE

BRIDGE BUILDERS
1115–1205

Peter de Colechurch, priest, architect of the Bridge
Thomas à Becket, Chancellor to Henry II, Archbishop of Canterbury
Henry II, friend of Thomas à Becket
Barbra, courtesan, friend of Father Peter de Colechurch and Thomas à
   Becket
Mark, friend of Peter
A Young Woman

BRIDGE DWELLERS
1665–1666

Lucien Redd (Radford Croft), child of civil war, at sea
Daryl Braintree, Poet-Chronicler
Musetta, his mistress
Morgan Wood, child of the Bridge, at sea
Gilda Shadwell, fair lady of the Bridge
Blythe Archer, dark lady of the Bridge

MERCHANT BROTHERHOOD OF THE BRIDGE

Lennox Archer, glover, Blythe's father
Clarke Shadwell, shoemaker, Gilda's father
Phelan Wood, Morgan's father

Arthur Clinkenbeard, goldsmith, leader
Kerry Brooke, fishmonger
Duff Bright, taverner
Burlow Green, necklace maker
Alfred Goodyer, needle maker
Eldon South, haberdasher
Thomas Wright, scrivener
Robertus Allbritton, basket maker
George Gill, spectacle maker
Dropstitch Upshaw, rag seller
Edan Coldiron, master carpenter
Tristram West, apothecary

LONDON BRIDGE IN PLAGUE AND FIRE

1

LUCIEN REDD,
A CHILD OF CIVIL WAR

This Bridge stretched below us—on its twenty piers and arches—is supporting 138 shops, each with a three-to-six-storey house above it, the tallest bridge in England, and eight hundred inhabitants, some such. Quite sick, but not fatally ill, she stands still, in defiance of over two thousand years, time told by sundial, hourglass, and clock, for all of the bridges built at this site over the past are one London Bridge. Chronicled assaults of tides, gale, frost, flood, foreign and domestic bombardment, and the very tension and stress of its own structure fulfilling its function, have taken their toll, aggravated by human and mercantile traffic and royal, municipal, and ecclesiastical neglect.

Come onto the Bridge from London to cross over River Thames to Southwark.

Come on at Southwark to cross over to London.

Built of stone, will she fall?

In time.

Though not of her own free will.

But in 1649, her fatal hour has not yet come.

*   *   *

Oliver Cromwell stood alone in the open space on the long-defunct drawbridge. Looking toward Westminster, he came to watch the sun burn through the mist and shine on a new era, one that his own will itself—"May God's will prevail"—will fashion. He has come to feel the tide race between the starlings under the arches to his left and to his right, feel it in the soles of his boots. The resistance to the tidewater of the narrow openings under the Bridge is an inspiration, tempered only by his memory of the severed heads on pikes above the Great Stone Gateway near the bridge foot at the Southwark end, stuck up there on pikes to warn, he knows, such as he to restrain the fist raised in rebellion.

The marching feet of civil war fall upon thousands.

*   *   *

"Come out or burn with the house!"

As Radford obeyed the soldiers' command, he slipped in his father's blood on the threshold, felt the first of a multitude of blows.

"Stand up, you little shank of Catholic carrion!"

The shouting soldier stood astride him, the toes of his glistening boots becoming clearer as Radford, on his knees, wiped at his tears.

His knees were too weak. He fell on his belly and immediately heard and felt a rushing of cloth that exposed his bare buttocks to the stinging icy wind. A great weight fell upon his back—his body exploded. He screamed, "Mother!" and raised his head, saw his father's face, his head, hurtling through the smoke, heard somewhere behind him an answering scream from his mother, whose stare caught in the same instant the sight of her husband's severed head flying and her son's bare flesh flashing in the smoke. Inhaling the smoke that billowed over him, the boy fell into a searing, painful swoon.

When Radford awoke, the weight on his back was so much greater he could scarcely breathe. Twilight had turned to utter dark by the time he twisted his wounded body, constricted not only from above, he discovered by touch alone, but from below and on both sides by the cold flesh of other bodies. The sharp teeth of mouths frozen open pressed against his back, his sore ribs. He saw faces crusted with old blood, recent blood, and now his own blood. Dirt, snot, food in teeth, pieces of flesh—he imagined human flesh—mud and food in folds and threads, weaves of clothes, a seed, a flower in hair, fresh or wilted, not placed there but caught as a soldier passed through field flowers, then snagged in bristly hair.

He lifted a hand away from his face, shoved an arm aside, pulled his legs out from under the crowns of three heads, a hairy chest, one bare breast whose twin had been hacked away, shouldered through the limbs of other bodies, until he stood up and walked away—his bunghole stinging as if afire, but his buttocks icy from some spilled liquid, his tongue recoiling from the open gashes in his gums, his legs deeply bruised, ribs broken, flesh all over lacerated—into a village that was dead in flames.

Feeling out a narrow pathway through the burning village, mourning his father, calling for his mother, and his brothers and sisters, Radford turned away from the dying but collected from the dead a shirt too small, pants too large and, wearing shoes that did not match, walked out into a world totally different from the one he had enjoyed early yesterday morning as a daily blessing.

On a road strange to him, between the town in ashes at his back and a town yet to come that he envisioned afire, he witnessed, by morning light, the emergence of a new world, a world more of darkness suffused with smoke than of light.

War cries and the detonation of bombs and firearms and screams and curses and Catholic pleas to the Virgin Mary Mother of God and Puritan pleas to Christ Our Savior made that world known to him in its total darkness.

Over Radford's body, at the start ignorant of carnal rapture, the civil war between Puritans and Royalists, Roundheads and Cavaliers, raged back and forth in miniature across four more years. His beauty—"It's them eyes!"—cursed him. Resistance provoked the rage of many men, submission inspired his own shame, and both exposed his face and body to violence so extreme he awoke each time to the wonder that he was still able to breathe. Exposures to extremes of cold and heat, to wind, rain, frost, and sufferance of starvation were enemies as vivid as the men and women and older boys who abused him in every way imaginable, and in many ways he could never have imagined. As balmy weather soothed his body and spirit from time to time, so kindness laid a gentle hand only now and then upon his cringing body, his shivering mind.

An old man once asked Radford whether in all his wanderings he had ever clapped eyes on Cromwell.

"A soldier pointed General Cromwell out to me one day after the Battle of Naseby. I was limping. The General's lip curled in disgust at the sight of me."

Having crossed over many moors and bridges and passed through many towns, Radford wandered into Southwark, responded late that night to the mysterious lure of a narrow street, over which houses hung in mist on both sides like arches, passed under the sign of a fish and anchor, and came to an opening that he took for a dock, saw high above, behind a parapet balustrade, a face he mistook for his father's and on each side the heads of men, eyes closed as in prayer, mouths open as if in awe of the face of God, and then he turned away and stood under a shop sign, Golden Needle, gazing East by starlight upon a vast array of ships huddled together at anchor in harbor. Suddenly, seized, lifted, he was flying out in the very air over swift water toward the ships.

He awoke in the morning on the stern of a ship. He stood up and looked back West up a river nameless to him, at a strange cluster of high houses that stretched over an open space, a sight that passed from view as it dawned on him that what he saw bizarrely resembled a bridge. Out of pure wickedness, someone had tossed him into the water.

At sea a few days later, an old sailor who looked long past ready to go ashore for the final time told Radford that a waterman had plucked him from River Thames and sold him into service on this merchant ship in the Pool bound for Venice.

Prisoner, slave, orphan, Radford realized, two years later, on his fifteenth birthday, that what he suffered among Puritans and Royalists in the civil war had served as a cruel apprenticeship to the miseries of daily life at sea and even days at liberty in ports around the known world.

He told his story once and once only, to a shipmate on that birthday. "I had thought we were fervent Puritans, but I didn't learn until a year or so later that my father had played both sides, but lost his life to the Royalists, and his son—myself—to both scourges.

"Cavaliers raped me one day, Puritan soldiers the next. An asshole on fire, a mouth gorged know no allegiance. Is that a stake he is shoving up my ass or his own cock? First one, then the other, raped repeatedly, until I am so bleeding raw and painful sore, I can't tell the difference. I am cursed with a piercing imagination. As if living on the dark side of the moon, that day I turned to the dark side of my nature and surrendered to the experienced fact that, like all my tormentors and even those who betimes gave me comfort, the soul is a fiction. Soulless, I resolved to take possession of my body and mind. I christened myself with the new name 'Lucien,' to mock God and Englishmen, and I baptized myself in my own piss as Lucifer's very orphan, and was thus reborn, a new being."

Lucien Redd's listener exposed the most enormous erect cock that had ever threatened him. He was the first man Lucien killed, and with his bare hands.

*   *   *

In the secret Chronicles of Old London Bridge, possessor and location now unknown, kept from 1209, the year the stone version opened, to 1831, the year the dismantling of the much-modified bridge began, neither the name Radford Croft nor the name he adopted, Lucien Redd, appears. Nor the name of the boy, Morgan Wood, who suffered Lucien on the ship, nor of the two thirteen-year-old virgins, Blythe Archer and Gilda Shadwell, who survived plague and fire but suffered Lucien Redd on London Bridge. Nor even the names of the Brotherhood of the Bridge Merchants who hired Lucien Redd. Not even the names of the Chroniclers themselves, not even the name of the old Chronicler of the Bridge, Lloyd Braintree, missing during the plague of 1665, nor even his son, Daryl, who had exalted dreams of fame as a poet, but who finally, reluctantly, and then obsessively took up his father's task, nor even the last Chronicler, unknown, if one ever existed, who watched the demolition of the Bridge from November 22, 1831, to August 1832.

The name of the architect of London Bridge, yes. Peter de Colechurch. Mark it well. But no more than the name. No more than a single nib dip into ink.

Not until Daryl Braintree imagined and recorded what he discovered missing.

2

DARYL BRAINTREE, POET-CHRONICLER OF LONDON BRIDGE

Night seeped into every crevice of the Bridge, night crept into the brain of each inhabitant. Lloyd Braintree, reclusive Old Chronicler of London Bridge, the heavy Chronicle ledger in his arms, fear of fading memory oppressing his mind, descended the five flights of stairs, passed through his antiquarian bookshop, into the Bridge roadway and wandered away from Nonesuch House, off the Bridge and into a country strange to him—the City of London—in search of young Morgan Wood among the ships in the Pool, to beg him not to sail away, to confer on him now, before God's terrible voice speaks the word and "fire," "tempest," or "plague" strikes the City once again and even the Bridge at last and destroys the Chronicle, and with it, the venerated task of keeping the Chronicle.

As a child, Lloyd accidentally found his father's secret Chronicle ledger and committed each fabulous line of it to memory, a habit he cultivated even after his father, on his deathbed, handed the book itself on to him, memorizing as he recorded each event. Lloyd's now ill-fated intention had been to dictate events after his father's death, from memory, an act of filial piety, a monument to Memory itself at first, to his son, the would-be poet, but then, certain of Daryl's refusal to carry forward the family tradition since 1209 when the first shops and houses began to appear on the Bridge, his intention had become to pass the Chronicle into the hands of Morgan Wood, who lived on the Bridge and loved it, the events of the Bridge's history in times of war, plague, fire, frost, and glory, that had been his provenance for fifty-four years, from 1611, the year of the publication of another history, the King James Bible.

Forgetting that Morgan Wood had been gone seven years at sea, turning around and around and around on the wrong side of the Bridge for going to the ships in the Pool, Lloyd Braintree recognized nothing, but felt in his very bones that he should be able to. Frenzied, he wandered the streets, searching for a familiar shop sign as for a familiar face and, finding none, still looking up, as if searching now for familiar stars outside his own high window, took one step down, slipped down Old Swan Steps into River Thames—his mind at that moment as blank as the Chronicle's pages for the future—into the mind of God.

*　*　*

The long needle in the Poet's father's hand, pulling up on the thread when sewing book bindings, often flashed in the light that fell just right through the window to catch that long lifting movement at its zenith, the needle flashing in the hand by the light made mellow.

Now that his father was gone—no, only missing!—Daryl Braintree regretted that his own attitude had, in effect, rendered his father gone, missing, far too many irretrievable days and evenings. Why, never having known the mother who died birthing him, had he not turned, even more often than one normally might, to the father? His father, he always knew, was preoccupied with his book binding business, his customers, with history. But his shell was vulnerable. Anyone could see that. Why had he not gently broken through to the man, the father, who was probably waiting inside for him?

And then the rupture, and the sudden substitute—the mere boy, Morgan Wood—not even a month after his father had confided to Daryl that he was the secret Chronicler of London Bridge, that when he must leave off, his fervent last wish was that his son would be eager to take it up.

Remembering his father's hesitant offer to pass on to him the charge of keeping up London Bridge Chronicle and his own contemptuous rejection of a task so mundane and mechanical, the Poet was conscious of feeling something akin to shame.

Expecting to live another ten years, at least, his father had then, the Poet knew, conferred that honor upon thirteen-year-old Morgan Wood, only days before the boy went to sea, originally for only five years, to work off his father's debt to another tradesman on the Bridge, Mister Clinkenbeard, the goldsmith. Gone now seven years.

Daryl knew he would never forget what his father calmly said to him. "This noble task is not for a drunken, whoring, irreligious, cursing young poet, anyhow. I trust a boy's love of the Bridge over the grudging obligation of blood kin such as you."

Having searched for his father for three months, exposing himself to the plague that had begun in April when his father disappeared, having failed to find him, Daryl searched for his father's Chronicle of London Bridge, supposing it to have been hidden somewhere in their rooms in Nonesuch House, considering the possibility his father may have destroyed it, then have left the Bridge deliberately to wander. Lloyd Braintree never told anyone, neither his son nor the boy Morgan Wood, that the last fifty-four years of the Chronicle existed only in his mind, memorized, to be dictated to Morgan Wood and thus recorded in the ancient Chronicle book.

At sea, Morgan Wood wrote in his own journal and in the margins of his books after the journal was full about nothing but London Bridge, and would continue that ritual until Lucien came aboard.

Having failed to find the Chronicle, moved by the disappearance of his father and confined by the plague to Nonesuch, his famous house on the Bridge, the young poet, hung over and reeking of bad whiskey and night-long rutting, with a "Goddamn me for a fool," visited Morgan Wood's father's stationer's shop under the sign of the Quill and Moon across the bridge roadway from the edifice that had been Saint Thomas Chapel until its defacement during Henry VIII's dissolution of the Catholic churches.

As Daryl stepped out of Phelan Wood's shop onto the roadway, the leather-bound book of blank, fresh pages seemed heavier than it ought to have, but by the time he had climbed the five flights of stairs to his father's bedroom, his resolute intention had dissipated his sense of guilt and the book had lost its unnatural weight. He sat at his father's desk by his window on the world and began to write, first "Dedicated to the memory of my Father, Lloyd Braintree," and then:

In the beginning is the Word, but the Word can never, for the London Bridge Chronicler, be his name. We (with this initial act of writing, I am, after all, reluctantly, perforce, one of the legion of chroniclers, ancient and modern, hands moving all over the civilized world as my hand moves) have been, for four centuries, twenty generations, a nameless brotherhood, just as the Chronicle is secret, hidden away, I must imagine, because, I suppose, its scandals are included, with the death of each Chronicler, so that this one may be found somewhere on the Bridge ages hence, or disappear into Irony should the Bridge fall to an act of God. And so, five months after my father's disappearance, I have come to this day. This start. This first crossing on paper. With some fear of inadequacy, certainly.

I must record here for those who discover this Chronicle that my father's own fifty some years' labor as Chronicler may never be found because Father, who is missing, may, if he is alive and wandering, be carrying it to the young sailor Morgan Wood. Mayhap, he destroyed it, despairing of Morgan's return, knowing my lust for fame as a poet. Maybe he wanted to see, at last, much more of the world than a life on the Bridge has displayed to him. I can only imagine the Chronicle's fate and his. I hope he was kidnapped, for a ransom I can afford to raise, so I can rescue him.

Be assured, Reader mine, that what you henceforth read is an act of filial piety. I do not in any wise relish the task of recording mere facts pertaining to the history of London Bridge for the rest of my life. But in truth, my remorse for having disappointed my good father is as bitter as this ink.

Perhaps the young sailor Morgan will return and rescue me. I look down from my high window, hoping to see him step onto the Bridge. My father told me that, in view of my own reluctance, finally declared as refusal, he intended to pass on to a lad who lived on the Bridge this very task. But Morgan's father, Phelan Wood, the stationer, sent him to sea almost a decade ago to work off his debt to Mister Clinkenbeard, the goldsmith.

Because the fate of my father's lifework is so uncertain, I am inspired and finally resolved, not merely to take up events as of this day and forward, but to attempt, in time, to piece together the facts of the past history of this Bridge, to reconstruct, from whatever sources I may discover, among my father's books and records in the Guildhall—neglecting, if it must be, my poetry.

And now to trudge ahead, under the sign of The Open Book Upon Arches that I here and now hang above my Chronicle shop, with the legend "Facts Are the Folly."

*   *   *

Although the date at that moment was May 30, 1665, on a page deep into the blank ledger, leaving pages on which to record events during the centuries since the Romans ruled, since the birth of Christ, the Poet as Chronicler began with:

1665, March 2. Well stricken in years, the Old Chronicler of London Bridge, who, in the tradition of Chroniclers, wore, as I do now, the cloak of anonymity, disappeared without a trace.

The Poet-Chronicler left space enough for dates and events that came between his father's disappearance and the present month.

From his open window high in Nonesuch House, the Poet-Chronicler faintly heard bombardment. Only moments after the uproar subsided, the Poet wrote his first entry after recording his father's disappearance:

1665, June 2. I duly record this fact: War with the Dutch Broke Out again. His Majesty's sailors resident in Southwark crossed London Bridge to go to the Pool to board war ships to oppose the Dutch.

Knowing that fact made him realize that he knew or remembered very little about the historical events that called for the word "again," much less the historical *why* of it all. One thing he did know, he knew what was not fitting for a Chronicle, that King Charles II was rumored to have responded to Dutch insults, "You know the old saying in England, the more a turd is stirred, the more it stinks, and I do not care a turd for anything a Dutchman says of me."

*   *   *

That moment came when the Poet could resist no longer. He introduced, deeper still, into the fresh-smelling paper of his Chronicle book a rough draft of one of his own poems, his first about the Bridge, for readers centuries hence, first in prose lines, then in pseudo-poetic lines so he could see.

My View from the Bridge
From the fifth floor of Nonesuch House
on the Bridge, I gaze eastward down
River Thames, in awe of the White Tower,
in dread of its Bloody Tower,
and the unseen dungeon
of the Little Ease under the Chapel of Saint John
that inspired nightmares in my childhood,
the memory of which now is as chilling
as the nightmares themselves—the fear
of being mewed up in a cramped space.
I see the Tower's most ominous features,
Traitor's Gate, Bloody Tower,
I see the dark brow of Tower Hill
where most executions are still conducted.
I see the Ancient Roman wall that nearly bisects
the grounds within the Tower walls,
just East of White Tower.
How strange that we Londoners,
and indeed folk worldwide, speak
of *the* Tower, when there are, in fact,

twenty towers there, the same number
there are piers upholding
London Bridge. I do not relish
that symmetry of relationship. And consider
that the tower we see most clearly
is the White Tower, not Bloody Tower.
In Bloody Tower—the only tower
that is square—only two were murdered,
the York princes—children—first buried
under Wakefield Tower, then
reburied under a staircase in the White Tower—
or so I have heard tales since childhood.

From the Bridge, the most encompassing view
of the White Tower is from my bedroom window.
Saint Thomas chapel, not Nonesuch House, as now,
was the most prominent feature of the Bridge
that the Duke of Orleans saw from his cell window.
The famous page in the illuminated manuscript
of his poems written in prison
shows him simultaneously
writing poems and greeting the worthy
who bought his ransom after twenty-five years,
and then riding away from the tower. Seeing
the Bridge depicted in that illustration
as being behind the White Tower, not up river westward,
disturbs my sense of my own abode.

Daryl Braintree

The Poet-Chronicler showed a copy of the draft of his poem to his mistress Musetta.

"The Bridge is there only as background to illuminate a volume of poetry and not for its own sake, mediocre poetry—well, one has read Dryden and Milton—by Charles, Duke of Orleans, captured at

Agincourt, imprisoned a quarter century in the Tower, from which he had this view, I suppose. On visits to the Tower with my father, I was often invited to look at it over his slowly stooping shoulder."

The Poet-Chronicler wrote a rough draft of a second poem a few days later.

> **On Resolving to Meditate**
> Until I took up my missing Father's mission as Chronicler,
> this Bridge was to me only the place
> where I happened to breathe, instead of, say,
> Poultry Street, or Bread Street, or Saint Thomas Street.
> I walk the Bridge twice at once,
> as myself and as my dog, Ruff.
>
> Of course, a Bridge has a soul, but not,
> in the case of London Bridge, derived from the spirit
> of its crossers or residents, nor even, perhaps,
> from the spirit of the architect or builders.
> All Bridges have souls of their own.
> But bridges do not sin. They are sites
> of sinning. They may be damned, but
> only by the actions of men, not
> by failure to function or some such state.
> Happy? No. Not even in serving
> millions of crossings, hundreds of years. Sad
> then? Always. Because bridges are not—
> not that they consciously aspire to be
> —human. All that is true of London Bridge. But
> of London Bridge, and only London Bridge,
> many other mysteries are also true. I am
> on those things resolved to meditate.
>> **Daryl Braintree**

June 11. Seventeen more dead of the plague that broke out in April in Saint Giles in the Field.

June 13. Dutch Navy Defeated at Lowestoft.
On the Bridge, the Poet faintly heard the bombardment.
June 27. Plague Deaths: 267.
July 25. A drover transporting plague dead fell dead in Fish Street, and his horses plunged across London Bridge, the corpses rattling in the cart below my window.

*   *   *

Raising his hung-over head from his crossed arms, resting on his father's spacious desk that he had moved up to his own scriptorium, the Poet-Chronicler recalled his father telling him about the Bridge in ancient times.

"No, no, my boy. Shopkeepers on the Bridge did not prey on settlements on each side of the river—the settlements were parasites of the Bridge. First the Bridge itself was a community—small shops, only one or two low dwellings at first, mostly lower-class folk, to catch people going across—then other folk, attracted to it, as to a folkmote, settled on each end of it. Is that not marvelous? I know of no other such experience. Centuries later, people were drawn to the Bridge to live and work on it, to attract customers to it."

'My father ended his days on earth with no source revealing to me any more than the bare facts about Peter de Colechurch, priest architect of London Bridge.' But, to the Poet as a boy, his father's tone of awe and reverence when he spoke of Peter de Colechurch was a living thing in the house, floor by floor.

Peter de Colechurch, too, is missing, the Poet discovered in time, from the histories, and even the other public Chronicles, the Pipe Rolls, the Guildhall, and all other records.

*   *   *

Waiting for Musetta to appear in his doorway, the Poet luxuriated in his memories of the day he first saw his mistress. He had risen late, his head muck-stuffed to the bone, and, squinting against the light,

15

looked out from his fifth-floor bedroom to see what kind of day might be loitering about the Bridge. Then looking down into the open space that the long derelict drawbridge made, he saw a woman striding, solo, toward Nonesuch House on the Bridge, toward the London bank, as if she were the Queen of England. He descended too late to the street to become her solitary entourage.

Doing a week later as he had done then, he saw her appear as she had, and again, his descent was too sluggish.

Came yet a third episode, with the variation that he was certain he recognized her, even from the back, returning to Southwark. But with the same climax.

Aware that she appeared on the Bridge at about the same time of day, he posted himself by the door of his father's antiquarian bookshop, missing her on five occasions.

On the sixth occasion, her flouncing hair brushed his nose and made him sneeze before he saw her back, and followed it. Her mission seemed to be to walk every inch of London Within the Gates, and he feared she would pass through one of the gates into the Liberties or worse, east into the Minories, and go alongside and above the Tower. She was so quick, he lost her, "somewhere in the universe," he later wrote, in an abortive poem.

But found her in his father's shop a week later, head bent over a huge volume of ancient architecture, open in his father's slender hands. Looking up, she smiled, as if to say, "Well, at last." She knew him, Daryl felt.

To deceive his father with this lovely older lady, he left the shop first and waited for her in front of the tavern just off the Bridge on Tooley Street, where one is most immediately in Southwark.

"I will meet you tonight at the theatre in Lincoln Fields Inn." Without breaking her stride she said that.

Turning into the tavern, he tried not to get drunk, to be lucid when he searched the crowd for her.

She never met him anywhere in public but at the theatre, the Phoenix their favorite, where they played the part of strangers, but were intimate, hand to hand, under her dress, cock to cunny. But more often in his rich and poor bachelor friends' houses.

As a young man and as a poet, he reveled in having as mistress an older, sophisticated, worldly woman. But the moment he first beheld her displayed naked body, 'My true mistress,' he told himself, defensively, 'is poetry.'

When she first revealed her body for him, the thought struck him that it was almost twice as old as his own. Even so, he knew the sight of his own could not ravish her as hers ravished him. He could only wonder why one nipple was larger, more succulent than the other. But bliss rendered the question moot.

Still waiting for her to appear, the Poet recalled her first visit to this room.

"Here I am, at last. I hope your father won't regard my visit as a desecration." Musetta exaggerated a grin, quick frown, and a cocked-hips pose.

"Now, now, my beloved, you insisted and I surrendered and here we are. May we let it rest?" He took her uplifted hand.

"I am, truly, happy to be here. But not dressed for the street." She began to unbutton, slowly.

"I am myself only half dressed." Here, he dropped his trousers, kicked them aside.

"Oh, so that is what you've been hiding in these rooms." She feigned a turn-faced blush.

"And more. Having bared my soul in enough amorous poems to reach across London Bridge, tenfold, I have nothing left to bare but this shorter expression of my love."

"You are still talking poetry. Fuck me."

"Indeed, my dear, I shall."

After they had lingered upon and around each other's bodies, they began, less fervently, to voice their minds, she first, at the liquid window, just out of view from below. "That young girl I saw in the street, her face—nay, more her gait—is familiar."

The girl below moved here and there like a discoverer—no, a ferret.

"Blythe Archer has the run of the Bridge. You will have seen her here often at play. I prefer to watch the other one." He searched the shadows among the shops.

"There's another?"

"Very like her—Gilda Shadwell—but not sisters."

Musetta discovered and kissed a cut on his arm that Daryl had taken home from a street fight.

"They sometimes run together. Yes, run. They seem in constant motion in all weathers."

Blythe stopped, vexed.

"I've seen her, I would have thought, in the streets of London."

Her comment seemed as if it set Blythe off.

"Which? They resemble each other, a little." He looked into her face, no longer red from fucking.

"The one we both saw."

"The one with the gait and not the face."

"Yes."

"You will want to see the face of the other. Gilda's. Like a saint's."

"And the other face? Blythe's?"

"Like no other."

"A face like no other is unsettling, don't you think?'

"Yes, but what of *us*?"

"We have, unseen by the public, of course, at this moment, the faces of two who have fucked each other to exhaustion."

"From that, let us move to the question, Is there any hope you will divorce your husband?"

"None. We are not Dissenters, you will recall."

"Unless I become a known poet, King Charles as my patron?"

"That is an another stanza."

"My epic poem is—"

"Unfinished. You seem preoccupied with other matters."

The Poet-Chronicler was not yet ready to plunge her into the Bridge's deep past. "Perhaps I will speak of that in the near future."

"At this very moment, some part of you seems to stand up and speak in terms not quite epic, but certainly dramatic."

"Let the play resume."

At that moment when the Poet's memory was most striking, Musetta appeared suddenly in his doorway, in the very now.

After they had made up for time lost to plague fear, they fell into much talk, much of it at last about what lay upon his mind, the history of the Bridge, with this conclusion: "I was shocked to find so little about the architect and engineer of the Bridge. For almost five hundred years, Peter de Colechurch is missing from the Bridge!"

After his mistress left to make the plague-perilous trek into Southwark home to her husband and children and her charity work, the Poet, smudge pot smoke rising from the roadway to stifle the airborne plague biting into his eyes and nostrils, wrote on a blank page in the back of the Chronicle ledger:

"I feel a compulsion to go back to the start of the very first bridge at the London Bridge site and read whatever I can find among my father's books and elsewhere and record all over again the milestones. How long before the Romans invaded had people lived on the banks on each side before someone laid down the first fallen tree on which to cross over? Perhaps I will find the answer in the books and records. Perhaps the river ran low and they waded for a time, maybe piling up rocks, logs, debris, and when that washed away or the water rose and covered it, they decided to make the effort, somehow, to build a more permanent bridge.

"Modeled after what? What bridges can any of them have seen, or watched getting built, or helped to build, and where?" He asked that aloud, looking from his bedroom window out over River Thames, morning tide rising. "I want to know. The facts, if that's possible. Probably not. Then I will imagine, for my own satisfaction, how it started, when, where. With whom?

"Maybe not even someone who lived at the site, somebody far away who intended to return, or somebody gone forever, until he thought, 'If there were only a bridge there, I would return.'

"Even someone who had never been there, but who had been told there was no bridge there, who feels some obscure urge to build one, only there, not just a bridge, anywhere, somewhere, but there, because someone said, 'There's no bridge across River Thames at London for people coming up to the City from the South.' A bridge is suddenly there, in his imagination, suddenly athwart the river, and he sets out for London, the image of a bridge from Southwark over River Thames to London in his head, urging him northward. He simply wants to see it, a bridge there, and feel it under his feet, walking across. Hence, he builds it, but of wood, some centuries before the birth of Peter de Colechurch.

"So. Now I know how the Bridge got started."

The bird on the sill seemed delighted to hear his declaration.

'Fifty-four years before the birth of the Servant King of the Universe, Julius Caesar conquered southeast Britain. And then?'

In his bedroom, the Poet-Chronicler, by a circuitous route, took a long walk, and concluded, 'A separate Chronicle of my own, from ancient London to Colechurch's London, will help me anchor his Bridge.'

He crossed out the paragraph on the previous page and bought another blank ledger.

Consulting his father's history books and the books of his father's old friends on the Bridge and books delivered from out of the town onto the Bridge—the Venerable Bede, the Anglo-Saxon Chronicle, the Olaf Sagas, Geoffrey of Monmouth, William of Poitier, the Annals of Waverley Abbey, of Florence of Worcester, the Annals of Bermonsey Abbey, the Great Pipe Rolls of the Exchequer, of William of Malmsbury, the Annales Londonienses, Stow's *Survey of London*—the Poet became well armed enough to begin to write as Chronicler of the Bridge from its earlier years.

41 AD. A mere eight years after Christ rose from the dead, Romans under Claudius, once supposed imbecile, but a secret historian, invaded Britain again and settled colonies along the Eastern shore.

43. The naming of Londinium.

50. Roman legionnaires threw a Bridge of wood across River Thames.

About 54 ad, Romans invaded Britain, but Caesar, who called London 'Civitas Trinobantum,' visited but did not linger. Romans built a bridge across the Thames to the new planned city.

*　*　*

"I hear 'Londinium' and 'Longidinum,' after Tacitus, in the mouths of Romans back home in the Forum." Alone, the Poet enjoyed intoning the words, aloud. "And in the mouths of our Britons, Lundayne; in the mouths of the Saxons, Lundenceaster, Lundenbrig, Londennir; in the mouths of strangers, Londra and Londres; in the mouths of the inhabitants, London. Bless you, John Stow, without your *Survey of London*"— of 1598, in the tenth year of the reign of Elizabeth, followed by a revised edition in 1603, the year of the Queen's death—"we would see but not *know* the origin and function of places among which we daily walk."

Even so, the Poet-Chronicler had to admit to himself that he did not know, or remember, assuming it quite likely that his father once or twice told him, the origin of Nonesuch, the unique house in which he wrote those words. Shocked, he turned the pages of Stow in vain for the whole story. Not even a mention.

Eventually, he shucked off his ignorance by coming to know that of all the houses in England, there is none such as this one. Some say the name derives from the Dutch, meaning "without equal, unique." Only eighty-five years old in 1665, it was built in 1579. Henry VIII's Nonsuch Palace (different spelling, same meaning), still standing, was built forty years earlier as a hunting palace and guest house for foreign dignitaries and became a favorite of Queen Elizabeth's ("So golden as I approached that it seemed afire.").

*　*　*

60 AD. The great, fearless, and fearsome Queen Boudicca of the Iceni fiercely defeated the Romans at London and burnt the City and the Roman wooden military Bridge near the site of now standing London Bridge.

120. London afire.

122. Fire destroyed London. Hadrian, poet emperor, visited London on his famous journey and started the erection of his Wall across mountains of Britain from Solway to Tyne.

"How quickly time, four times my own age, passes in a Chronicle."

The Poet's mistress Musetta took a step back and then two steps toward him and struck a pose. "Do Time and our age gap preoccupy your mind of late?"

122 AD. The long rebuilding of London.

"Until 400, the Bridge was the original folkmote—a kind of meeting place of the people." Musetta nodded, threw her shoe at a zigzagging rat, successfully.

* * *

190 AD. In this year began the erection of the defensive Great Roman Wall around London. New waterworks and monumental arch built. Londinium named capital of Britannia Superior.

296. Londinium became capital of Maximus Caesariensis.

367. Saxons, Picts, and Scots conspired, invaded Britain, broke through Hadrian's wall.

400. Saxons began to settle around London.

410. Saxons and others forced Roman retreat from London.

448. Main Saxon invasion.

The Poet-Chronicler rehearsed in advance of his mistress's coming, reading aloud, what he has just written. "Just as warring tribes on the hillsides gathered to trade in the gorge, divided by the narrow, muddy, filthy Tiber River, out of which Rome evolved, so the Celtic peoples gathered on the North bank where the Thames was lowest at low tide. And London was, at first, only the shacks on the Bridge, and, spreading, became parasites of the Bridge, like ticks on a bear. All Roman roads in Britain led then and lead today to London Bridge. Or so the facts suggest and my imagination confirms."

But Musetta's randy, frolicsome mood did not encourage his recital.

* * *

451 AD. Londinium disappeared from historical records. It came to pass that only about fifty people, Saxons, lived in deserted

London—called "dark-earth"—among Roman ruins within the Walls, whilst farms surrounded the City, most of which were situated westward of the Wall.

"Called by the Saxons Lundenwic now, the City became a port. But Britain sank into almost two centuries of historical darkness. Perforce, what is not known, I will know in my imagination."

His mistress, skeptical of Daryl's facts, seemed eager, he was happy to notice, to discover what his imagination would conjure up.

"Roman London was hidden then, in Peter de Colechurch's time," mused Musetta, "under twelfth-century London."

'On the page, as on the bed, she aspires to be my collaborator.'

* * *

Listening to nameless voices, the Poet, seated at his father's desk, taken now as his own, but with hope undiminished for his father's return, wrote, parenthetically, in the margin of his Chronicle book, "From the drawbridge, I looked out over the rushing water at Saint Paul's a-building, meditating upon the prolonged fact that its tower was taking shape as my youth dwindled."

* * *

Wanting to see a map of the town in Peter de Colechurch's time, the Poet visited again Morgan Wood's father, Phelan, stationer and dealer in old maps at the sign of the Quill and Moon on the Bridge.

"Handle that map with especial care, good sir. 'Tis fragile indeed. Creases contaminated with human sweat are invitations to rot. See the separation along old Thames Street? The dearer ones are, of course, more recent and of less interest. Have you examined the prints? Let me show you. Holbein once lived here on the Bridge and died in the plague of 1543."

"Holbein, yes. And other painters live here now, one not long out of Old Marshalsea Prison over in Southwark. A seascape artist, unknown today."

At great peril to himself, the Poet-Chronicler went routinely off the Bridge and into the increasingly plague-ridden city, moving among the dead-wagons and smudge pots to reach the Exchequer, to inspect the Great Pipe Rolls for facts.

From such forays, he always returned, through shit-piles and piss-puddles, light-footed, inspired to open his Chronicle book and to ink entries.

604 AD. Christian King Ethelbert ordered the building of Saint Paul's Cathedral. The bishopric was founded, Mellitas being the first.

610. Saint Paul's was known to be in use.

* * *

After the exhausting thrills of shooting the rapids between piers beneath Nonesuch in a watercraft not yet in use to rescue folk fleeing the plague, the Poet lay on his bed, his dog Ruff at his side, reveling in questions. 'Did the relentless, eternal-seeming sound and smell of River Thames rushing through piers stimulate copulation more frequently on the Bridge than ashore? Projectiles of water, trajectory, through arches, furred with weeds, vines, wild flowers, inspire cock-thrusts into cunnies, counter retrieval, repetitions nightly, but not everybody every night. Maids rear-ended on steep, narrow, dim, or dark staircases. Husbands and wives. Lovers. The Tower menagerie nearby, ravens, rooks, lions, hounds, falcons, dogs, cats, their fucking mimicked here on the Bridge in the maze of rooms above the roadway, the shops. And rats. Birds. Snakes? Snakes *on* the Bridge ever? Wolves wander in from the country-side? Winter, famished? Lustiness and lust enhanced by close quarters contrasted to tide rushes through twenty tight piers? And narrowly fitting watercraft going in? Water, boats thrust in but never, as in copulation, backing out? Such dynamics, hydraulics fascinate me. Parallels, correspondences, I mean.'

He scrutinized the hand that wrote those words.

'The hand, set in motion by the Holy Ghost, is a writing machine, lubricated by coursing blood and lymphatic fluid, Harvey tells us. Such events are seldom, if ever, essayed in literature, except, perhaps, that Francis Bacon has done it.

'But appropriate in a chronicle, my dear?' he would ask his mistress.

'Indeed not,' he imagined she would retort.

He had eagerly waited for his mistress to brighten his doorway, and there she very is. "Look at me, Daryl! I walked all across the Bridge today to Thames Street, defying plague."

He looked at her, scanned her face, and then again. "As people step onto the Bridge and begin to cross, something begins to move and change deep behind the skin of their faces. I see it in yours. What *is* it?"

"Only a poet can answer such questions, m'love." She gave him pause.

"To walk across is to arrive on the other side somehow changed, each time, and forever. To cross a bridge is to be *over there,* different. True whether you do it thrice daily for seventy-seven years or once only. The man or woman or child who crosses only once is perhaps more consciously changed. 'I once walked across London Bridge—when I was a young man,' I heard one of my nocturnal voices declare."

"Yes, having breakfast, knowing everyone else on the Bridge is eating, too, is not the same as *eating,* knowing, in London itself or Southwark."

"Or Paris."

"Time to put Ruff out of the room." His mistress had made her dislike of dogs, even small ones, clear as ice.

After they had romped lustily crisscross and all around his room, first fully clothed and finally newborn naked, she declared, rubbing her shins, "For such an enormous house, your living quarters are too small."

"My living quarters too small? My answer is another question, How many grand houses, even castles, such as Henry VIII's own Nonsuch Palace, have you, like me, on business, of course, seen, in which the room that the master loves most is hardly larger than a dungeon cell, but as cozy, comfortable, and humanizing as a cottage family den? Many, many. Perhaps most. 'Tis the best in mankind as a whole that aspires to size, to match the colossal in nature, but it's the worst in a single man, king, or merchant, that cheats, steals, and kills to erect edifices of imposing size, only to retreat to a fire in a domesticated cave, in the heart of the pile, dark space enclosed in many rooms all around. No, we of the Bridge do not live small. We are big hearts in a little place here."

"Lie down again, spread-eagle." Musetta turned his words into flesh.

"My mind so much on the Bridge, my cock dreamed of making love to you while shooting the rapids under the Bridge, timing the climax for the very moment of entry."

"Your dream is dim-witted, Daryl dear. To fuck *is* to shoot the Bridge."

*   *   *

851 AD. The Vikings stormed London.

886. Alfred the Great (only English king ever named "the Great") recovered and rebuilt London.

950. Two hundred and fifty years before Peter de Colechurch started his stone Bridge, a Bridge House was recorded as being in use at the site and therefore a wooden Bridge however crude.

*   *   *

Everybody
Ruff walked London Bridge with me for thirteen years and will
walk with me many times more, I hope, even though today
she is out of her misery. She wouldn't walk,
she was hurting in her nose. I lay beside her,
crying, talking to her, remembering, explaining,
telling her she was going to be with her mother now,
who my father had to handle as I am now, and not hurt
anymore. I told her I love you and
hit her in the head with a hammer.
Everything that happens to me now happens
on the Bridge. Today—incessant rain and humidity and wind,
sweeping over the Bridge. Only a few days before I began

these nocturnal walks, Ruff lay at my feet. When she came
into the world, people I loved, father, friends, were here,
and now are gone. Everything, everybody
is important. To me. Disoriented
by Ruff's sickness and mine, I forgot last night
to set down my meditations on the Bridge.

Daryl Braintree

*   *   *

961 AD. Great Fires in London, Saint Paul's was burned.

982. The rebuilding of Saint Paul's was begun.

984. A widow and her son, convicted of witchcraft, were executed by drowning at the Bridge.

"I first heard about London Bridge," the Poet imagines someone in the North of England saying, "when I read that in 900 something, they drowned a witch there." The voice sounded so alive in the room, he shut his eyes.

*   *   *

The Poet had a sudden intuition of all the people who ever lived on the Bridge and all those who ever crossed it, throughout London's history, from the first crosser to Musetta, imminent.

Raucously, he shouted, "Everybody onto the Bridge! All at once! Now! *Everybody*!"

Seeing a throng as if from a window, he did not need to *go* to his window.

*   *   *

994 AD. Sweyn led Danish forces, besieged London.

1013. King Ethelred the Unready, and King Olaf the Norseman broke down the heavily fortified Bridge in an attack against the Danish invader.

"Sometimes voices tell me what to write. Listen. 'I survived the Battle of London Bridge that Ethelred fought with the Danes in 1013.' A century and a half before Peter de Colechurch first imagined the stone Bridge."

"The imperfect mole under your armpit fascinates me." Staring at it, Musetta, like a vivacious lizard, darted her tongue at it.

*   *   *

"In flood-time the Bridge piers caused a lake to form." The Poet cannot wait to tell his mistress. "Did you know that the name 'London' means 'lake fort'?"

"I know, dear boy, that some *say* it does. And that others say it does *not*. Geoffrey of Monmouth wrote, I am told, that it was named after King Lud, whose very existence a century before the risen Christ is very much in doubt, Ludgate still standing notwithstanding."

"Oh. I see. . . ."

"And did you know that the name of River Thames, Tamesa, Thamesis, means 'the lagoon'?"

"Of course, I do. I was only just going to tell *you*."

"The source of River Thames is, as I'm sure you know, unclear."

Her bristling mound of Venus and the aroma of her bestirred vagina distracted him from the meager facts.

"The Thames itself has Bridged England with Europe," the Poet wrote, after Musetta was well away, her scent lingering on his fingers, his breath, his still sensitive Thomas, "and London Bridge has united England, all points of the compass."

Returning to Time, the Chronicler felt the mere dates and the terse entries tingle along his scalp, lamenting the brute fact that few of his own verses seem to have that effect upon him.

Eager to give birth to Peter de Colechurch, the Poet-Chronicler took, nonetheless, delight in the march of history.

1015 AD. Great flood in London.

1016. Third siege of London. Canute repulsed.

1017. Canute, son of King Olaf of Denmark, made king of England at age 19, cut off the ears, noses, and hands of his English hostages.

1018. Great fire in London. Saint Paul's burned down again.

1035. King Harold I, Canute's son, called 'Harefoot,' became king.

1040. King Harthacanute, another son of Canute, levied a heavy danegeld upon the folk.

* * *

"Why *London* Bridge?" The Poet's mistress connected his nipples with her index fingers, thumbs touching. "The Bridge spans *both* sides."

"Yes, of course. What's named only London Bridge is, in fact, also Southwark Bridge."

"Then why not Southwark-London Bridge? By name alone, London-Southwark Bridge is altogether."

"Is it not always *three* Bridges—a Bridge for Londoners, another for Bridge dwellers, yet another for Southwarkians?"

"As three different Bridges, is it not always trying to be *one* only? Metaphysically, I mean."

"One day perhaps two bridges will take folks on both sides back and forth. I here and now name the second bridge to come, Southwark Bridge."

Unmindful of his lost footing as expert impressing his mistress with his daily fresh learning, the Poet, wanting to know, hoped she could deliver the answer. "'Wark' means *what*? Obsolete dialect for 'work'? As in military works?"

"I like to hold the word in my mouth—Southoerki—the Dane's way of saying Southwark. You know I've always felt it, how we denizens of Southwark feel differently about the Bridge than they of London and you on the Bridge. How may one express it? The approach to it, to be sure. And the sense that when we leave Southwark to cross it, we are headed for one of the great cities of the known world, while

Londoners heading our way are going, after all, only over to Southwark. . . ." Having addled his intellect with unexpected knowledge, she sincerely wished to know the state of his heart. "And do you miss your father painfully?"

The Poet paused. "I miss his scolding and I miss what he never was. . . . I see Southwark as the site of your cunny, when my cock is not at home in it."

Later that night, having delved again into books strewn over his father's table, newly extended by four feet, the Poet-Chronicler wrote, "Roman coins and other relics have been found in mud under the Bridge. Unaware, Bridge dwellers, ever since the Romans vacated, have built their life stories on a foundation, in some part, of Roman coins and medallions under the gravel, along the line of the Bridge, likenesses engraved upon them of Pompey, Julius, Augustus, Caligula, Nero, Claudius, Antony, Vespasian, Trajan, Hadrian, Faustiva the Elder, Sabina, Aurelius, Tiberius, Valerian, Postumus, Diocletian, Constantine, Julian, Honorius, coins that had passed through hands the known world over—and over again for some few—and medallions that had smoothed the neck skin of men who walked the Roman courtyards that once lay within the ancient walls of Londinium. Among the coins lie the bones of a multitude of folk who drowned about the piers. We cross over their graves unmindful."

As did the Poet himself, in "a cloud of unknowing." For it was near here that his father, having wandered, addled by age, off the Bridge west, along Thames Street, and down to Old Swan Steps, slipped into River Thames, drifted down, settled among the coins and ritual sword washings.

'While the shopkeepers' trade-cards and tokens have moldered away,' the Poet thought, taking change from Kerry Brooke, fishmonger, 'only a handful were known to exist when the Roman coins were retrieved from under gravel by many hands.'

Now looking out his window, he spoke aloud to no one and to everyone. "The Romans came. The Romans went home. The Obscure Ages succeeded them."

*   *   *

1050 AD. King Edward ordered the building of Westminster Abbey.

1060. Historically low tide on the Thames.

1061. Monkish Edward the Confessor, elder son of Ethelred the Unready, the last of the old Saxon Kings of England, was canonized by Pope Alexander.

1065. Death of King Edward the Confessor, called also the priest. First to be buried in Westminster Abbey before the high altar, eight days after the Abbey was consecrated.

1066. Broken down half a century, the Bridge was rebuilt. Harold II was king for only eight and a half months. At the Battle of Hastings against William the Conqueror, an arrow, shot into his eye, slew him. Edith Swan-neck found him and buried him at Waltham Church, which had been built on his command.

1066. William I, the Conqueror from Normandy, invaded Britain and became ruler.

"1067. A fortification was built near a Roman lighthouse. Thus the White Tower there later.

"Saint Magnus the Martyr Church was built by London Bridge.

"1077. Fire in London. It invaded Old Saint Paul's structure once again."

Musetta stood, naked, just back from the window.

"1078. The building of the White Tower—step over to the next window and gaze upon it—was started by William the Conqueror as residence, treasury, prison, stronghold."

Musetta still stood at the window, showing Daryl her back. "I assume you know—if not, now you will know—that in one of those times when the Bridge lay in ruins, only a ferry got folk across River Thames, but not the poor.

"John Overs, owner, had many boats to transport footmen, horsemen, cattle, market folks coming with provisions to the City, strangers, conspirators, and I trust you to imagine what others.

31

"Passing his miserable abode, a body could not imagine the great wealth he possessed, from unceasing toil, frugality, usury. As wealthy he was as some in London.

"His beautiful daughter was pious and well educated, but inaccessible to the eyes or touch of men. One, however, more covetous of the ferryman's fortune than of his daughter, found a way to visit her secretly. On the third visit, she agreed to marry him.

"Pursing the next bit of money, the old ferryman noticed nothing of the lovers, but dreamed up a new way to save. He feigned dead, expecting his servants to fast for a day out of reverence and thus save him the expense of feeding them.

"His daughter reluctantly agreed to participate in the ruse, and he was laid out in his chamber, under a sheet, with a taper at his head and a taper at his feet.

"His servants, of course, danced their joy around his bier, and broke into his larder and plunged into a great banquet.

"In shocked amazement, the old ferryman, having endured this outrage as long as he could, finally rose up, a candle in each hand. The servants recognized him as the Devil himself, disguised as their master. One of them took up a broken oar that happened to be in the chamber and struck his brains out.

"The authorities made inquiry and concluded that the old man was cause and accessory to his own death and his estate fell to the daughter.

"Hearing about his good fortune, the lover rode up from the country with such reckless haste that his horse stumbled and the impetuous rider, who would have made a fit son-in-law, earned a broken neck for his trouble.

"As if the ferryman had earned excommunication with his wretched life, the church refused him burial, but his daughter offered the Friars of Bermondsey Abbey enough money to gain enough dirt to inter her father.

"The Abbot, however, returning from a journey, was horrified at the greed of his Friars and had the old man dug up and tied to his own donkey and turned it out the gates, praying that the donkey would take him to a place where he most deserved burial.

"The donkey carried his burden solemnly along Kent Street to Saint Thomas a Waterings, a place of execution, and there shook off the ferryman's body right under the gibbet, where, without ceremony, some kind soul buried it, assuming it had hung until it dropped.

"Spurning all suitors, the daughter Mary—shouldn't you write an epic poem about all this?—donated her inheritance to the building of the House of Sisters, and went herself into a cloister. It later became the College of Priests. The priests built a bridge of timber across River Thames from there and kept up repairs. Southwark Bridge, soon and since called London Bridge. A bit of my family's history, distantly related, though only just around the corner."

Having just read that account himself in John Stow's *Survey of London,* the Poet-Chronicler wondered at his mistress's independent knowledge of the Gothic past, and relished her fluid way of telling a story, her voice various, her body animated.

'God, I love that woman.'

*   *   *

1087 AD. **A Great Fire destroyed the third Saint Paul's Church, last of the Saxon Saint Paul's, and many other churches, along with the greater part of the City. King William donated Caen stone to rebuild Saint Paul's. Civil strife and a fever epidemic plagued this year.**

King William died of a fall from his horse, which stumbled in Mantes, the town he had just set ablaze.

This year, the Reign of William II began.

*   *   *

Passing a blind man, the Poet wondered what the Bridge is for *him.*

'The foul odors, the smoke, the textures of wood and glass, multifarious voices and sounds, subtle and harsh, the cries of vendors, birds, music, singing, the carts rumbling, clattering, rain.'

He relished writing that so well, he thought he might read it aloud to his mistress, depending upon her mood, girlish gay or matronly sardonic.

Loitering in a silver shop, the Poet memorized an elderly neighbor's reminiscence. "As a little girl, I watched Shakespeare cross many times to the play. I imagined each play, each performance."

The Poet imagines Shakespeare composing as he walked across to the Globe, revising as he returned to his house on Silver Street, near Saint Giles.

*   *   *

1088 AD. Bishop Odo led an unsuccessful revolt on behalf of Robert against his brother Rufus, King William II.

1091. A violent gale and great flooding swept part of the wooden London Bridge away.

The rafters of Saint Mary-le-Bow were sheared clean off and thrust into the ground below.

1092. Fire in London.

1093. Ice and the thaw harmed the Bridge.

*   *   *

On Function and Neglect
Does the Bridge ever wake up
to the fact that it is serving
as a bridge, *know* that
that is its function? Or
is ignorance part of its function?
In knowledge lies rebellion.

Neglect is the wound that awakens
rebellion in the Bridge, as when,
on January 14, 1497, the two arches
of the Great Stone Gate revolted,
collapsed into a single heap,
itself neglected, called, in time, Rock Lock.

Daryl Braintree

1096 AD. The First Crusade crossed London Bridge to Canterbury and hence to Dover.

1097. Flood carried the Bridge away. Rebuilding the Bridge began. And in this year the creation began of a wall and a moat around the Tower, west side, and construction of Westminster Hall in Westminster.

1098. Fire in London.

1099. Westminster Hall finished.

1100. Fire in London. Bow Bridge built over the River Lea in east London, said, in error, to be the first bridge of stone in England, for London Bridge has that distinction. And Bow Bridge is but one arch only.

King William II was slain, accidentally it was said, by an arrow, during a hunting in the New Forest.

Reign of King Henry I, House of the Normans, youngest and only English-born son of William the Conqueror, began.

"His was a reign of the restoration of justice in England and also of war in Normandy to retain the family kingdom, but he was remembered after death as Beauclerc, or the Scholar, for he was more learned than most of the kings of his age. Or did you know that?"

"Of that, I am ignorant." Musetta lidded her large eyes.

*　　*　　*

"Chaucer's pilgrims progressed under this very window." Phelan Wood, the stationer, was showing Daryl a first edition of *The Canterbury Tales* that he had bought from Daryl's father. "Only a month before he did not come home."

"And two centuries of pilgrims passed your window before Chaucer himself was born."

"From which follows what?" The stationer's face, of one bewildered, surprised the Poet.

The Poet recovered composure. "You will be expecting your son Morgan's return from sea at last within the year perhaps?"

"Perhaps, indeed."

That night, Musetta asked, "And did Peter de Colechurch himself go on pilgrimage?"

"I do not know, my dear."

"My dear, Daryl, when, when *will* you know?"

"When I imagine him doing it, the historians being mute."

After Musetta had gone down to the roadway, the Poet wrote, "The tidal rush through the piers turns the mill wheels and the waterwheels round, whizzing, whirring, clanking. The sounds so distract me sometimes from her body, they remind me, when she is absent, of her body."

*   *   *

The Poet, pleased to learn that there had been one bookseller-binder's firm that lasted two hundred years on the Bridge, hoped that it had been his father's family.

'In homage to my father, I must not fail in time to record the names of all the booksellers and describe their signs.'

But he failed.

*   *   *

"The view of the Pool and its ships and the White Tower from the Bridge restores my soul." Arthur Clinkenbeard, goldsmith, sat in his shop next door to the Saint Thomas Chapel, now a warehouse, a testament to the dissolute Henry VIII's dissolution of all English churches, the rag merchant's storage below, sharing space with stacks of paper for Phelan Wood's stationery shop on the west half of the Roadway. "I have witnessed the light on the towers. I seldom take the view to the west. I keep to my own side of the roadway. I always have. Not with any great deliberation, nor with aversion to the bargeman's last view of the Bridge, but because one has one's view, as do you, certainly, a poet's view, from the highest point on the Bridge, master Braintree."

*   *   *

"I have taken on as my mission," the Poet told his mistress, watching her struggle too impetuously with a squeaky pearl button in an eyelet of a new blouse, "to root into the histories and records until I find Peter, unless the plague finds me first."

"If you know Latin in its various forms and dialects. Otherwise, Daryl, it will all prove Greek to you."

'How does she know what she knows, and why does she know what she need not know?'

*   *   *

1114 AD. Very low tide. The Anglo-Saxon Chronicle records the fact that the "ebb-tide was everywhere lower than any man remembered before; so people went riding and walking across the Thames east of the London Bridge."

1120. Tuesday, December 21, on the feast day of Saint Thomas the Apostle, Thomas à Becket was born, in the reign of King Henry I.

That entry forced upon the Poet-Chronicler a choice, whether to include events not known at the time to be significant or to leave them out. Smiling over the entry for that year in the Anglo-Saxon Chronicle—two of King Henry's sons, William and Richard, drowned with many other notables, their bodies never found; supernatural lights appeared in the Sepulcher of the Lord in Jerusalem twice; the Archbishop of York displeased the Archbishop of Canterbury—that it left out the birth of Thomas, ignorant, naturally, of his future greatness, the Poet chose to include the birth in his own Chronicle.

Rethinking this dilemma, he realized that the Anglo-Saxon Chronicler or Chroniclers began with the year of Christ's nativity, although they actually began the Chronicle sometime in the 800s. They, as he, backtracked—they 800 years, he twice that many.

*   *   *

"Tuesdays were fateful for Thomas Becket, child, Londoner, Chancellor, Archbishop. As for the exact year of his nativity, it was,

37

records show, mayhap the year 1115, mayhap 1118, mayhap 1120, mayhap 1126, mayhap 1127, but a Tuesday is certain, or very nearly. I have recorded 1120 as my own best guess—and that of one of his five contemporary biographers, John of Salisbury, his friend, whose Latin is angelic."

"So a chronicle is the record of a Chronicler's struggle with elusive dates?" Musetta squinted, staring.

"Only if the chronicler is not also a poet, who is free to choose among facts and to include imaginings."

"And if you are wrong, will your wongwong wither?" She laughed, charmingly teasing.

Then Musetta collaborated. "Thomas's mother's name was Matilda. Legend insists she was the Muslim daughter of a Sultan. His father was Gilbert Beket [sic], prosperous merchant-citizen of London, a magnate. Both were born in Normandy. Thomas was not a family name, so maybe Matilda was very pious, favoring Thomas the Apostle. His father was perhaps a mercer, dealing in textiles, favoring silk. The house was in Cheapside, a large house in the very center of the City, on the north side of Cheap Street, in the block between Ironmonger Lane and Old Jewry. As you know, there is a Mercers' hall in Ironmonger Lane now, hard by Thomas's house. I like the coincidence that Saint Thomas the Apostle Church is so nearby, on Knight Rider's Street just below Cheapside with direct access to the river bank at Three Cranes." Exposing her knowledge quite puffed her up. "Babe Thomas may have looked sickly, in need of special heavenly aid after many prayers, because he was baptized the same evening in the tiny parish church of Saint Mary Colechurch—"

"Where Peter de Colechurch became chaplain—one of the few facts to survive."

"—which occupied an upper room built upon a wall above ground in the next-door property on the Old Jewry Corner by the great conduit. The chrismal cloth was preserved by his parents, then by Thomas, and went with him, on his head, into the grave, so it is said."

"How do *you* know such things?" The Poet lightly rested his fingertips upon her pudenda.

"Young man, Thomas is a Saint, about whom more is known than anyone else of his time, his having had—I depend upon hearsay—five or more eyewitness biographers, all of whom tell the truth on each and every page, except, of course, where they do not."

3

SHOPKEEPERS ON THE BRIDGE
MEET TO REPORT ITS CONDITION

On a late afternoon when the House of Many Windows, opposite the
Great Stone Gate, crowned with eighteen severed heads impaled on
pikes at the long-defunct drawbridge, a hundred and nine steeples, and
the Tower of London bristled in bright sunlight, in late January 1665,
three months before the plague made folks look up from their daily
occupations and preoccupations, each and every man who owned a
shop and lived on London Bridge responded to a call from the Bridge
Wardens to meet at the Bridge House Bankside, Southwark, to consider
ways and means to repair the ancient Bridge, before February set its
silver teeth into the twenty arches of the ancient, crumbling fabric, and
to brace it against the gales of March.

Their clothes and accoutrements, touching as they strode purpose-
fully in close concourse, set up a fluttering commotion on the Bridge
roadway, where the flow of traffic was now light and the flow of the tide
below was not yet boisterous.

Kerry Brooke, fishmonger, walked to the meeting limping. Clark
Shadwell, shoemaker, asked him why.

"I put my foot through the roadbed, and you see me here in the flesh only by the grace of God, Saint Thomas Becket, and Orville, here by me now."

"Will your daughter marry that wastrel?"

"A girl who will never see thirty again, may never see another man who is not a wastrel, I fear."

Coming off the Bridge, turning left, they processed East on Tooley Street past Southwark Cathedral ("here endeth the mayor and here beginneth the King") to the Bridge House.

The smell of the bakery swelling in the nostrils of men who had not yet had their dinner, between the timber yard and the stone yard, needful in maintaining the Bridge, Anthony Scarlett, the more articulate of the two Bridge Wardens, called for order—more than once.

"We are assembled here to contemplate the many too-long-deferred present and possible future repair needs."

Robert Hussey stepped up to Scarlett's side, thus showing before the assembly the two wardens of London Bridge.

Scarlett continued. "Our request to each of you last week by letter was that you of each lock meet first together, tally up the condition in which you find your own lock, and report here, this afternoon. I will open with our own report from here at Bridge House, simple and to such a point as should prick us all—that the Bridge for which we two are the wardens is in a state of utter dilapidation, as the gale of last night discovered.

"As a reminder of how we are constituted, let us look at the general facts of the matter. The Bridge supports 138 shops, 116 houses, 515 floors, 1,203 rooms. Our last count was 601 souls living in our heaven on earth, but in danger of hell on earth. Supporting 196 men, 148 women, 253 children, not to mention unborn in carriage, and a pack, flock, herd of birds and animals that would defy tallying, this Bridge is overpopulated—as it has been for much of its five-hundred-year history as one built of stone—top heavy, and staggering.

"I shall call by pier number and lock name for reports from each pier and lock in turn, beginning at London side, north, proceeding to bankside Southwark, West side of the Bridge with a bow to Westminster and the King first in every instance, then Mister Hussey will call for reports from those on the East side, overlooking our ships in the Pool. For the sake of good order, let there, please, be no deviations.

"To begin. We beg to hear first from those of you who keep shop and live on London Shore or first Wheel Lock, beginning with Master Horace Butling of the water works below, situated under the bridge, both East and West, of course."

"Not to forget the water tower, too like a steeple for my taste, that competes for attention with our church steeples, including Saint Magnus Martyr, which has no steeple, but a tower, which—"

"Not your turn, Tristram West!"

"—which, if I may finish with a flourish, must bear the burden of a conduit shot up over the roof of that most revered—"

"On pain of ejection from the yard, Mister West! Step forward, Horace Butling, that we may hear of the condition of our vital water works."

"Horace Butling present, to testify. In constant need of repair and rejuvenation for the welfare of all London citizens, save Mister West, who has never known thirst, pissing horses always passing his shop. But my company is fully responsible and fully in control at all times of any and all problems that arise—arise, Tristram West, arise."

"Shops above piers one and two, London Shore wheel lock, East, Tower side."

"John Barnacle, ribbon weaver, at the sign of the Five Bows. When I climb the stairs from my little shop up to my domicile, I feel a sway and hear a creaking that sets my teeth on edge and quivers my guts."

"We are here to tally damage to the structure, John Barnacle, not to inventory every squeak and groan within the house and its master's guts."

Warden Hussey. "Pier two, East!"

"Allen Hazelrigg, mirror maker, under the sign of the Looking Glass. I speak also for Gwayne Churcher, Needle-makers' Guild, under the sign of the Golden Needle and Plus sign, for he is also miscellaneous retailer, here among the finer shops for being closer to the magnates' houses on the Bridge and to the city of London. The bridgehead below us is at present stable."

Clouds passed over. Sun shot through. Clouds passed over, stopped moving, a canvas awaiting paintbrushes of artists.

"It saddens us to pass over pier three, Borough Wheel Lock, pier four, Index wheel lock, pier five, Shore Lock or fifth Wheel Lock, pier six, the King's Lock, pier seven, the little, also called, Queen's Lock, and pier eight, Saint Mary's Lock that Peter de Colechurch named for the Saint Mary of his church, that palisaded space, that desolate open space that keeps our memory of the fire of '33 only too vivid in our minds, for its having diminished the number of shops, houses, inhabitants I otherwise included previous to now. We come then, as we must, to pier nine, Chapel Lock, the original name in honor of whom we are loath to speak."

William Walken, descendant of Saint Thomas à Becket's family, started up from his seat on a rough-cut stone. "Bridge Warden, I do not care to hear veiled references to—"

Warden Scarlett. "Merchants of Chapel Lock, West, what have you to tell us?"

"Phelan Wood, Stationers' Guild, under the sign of the Quill and Moon, speaking for myself and Kerry Brooke, fishmongers' livery, at the sign of the Fish."

"Saint Peter's own."

"I do not wish to move to Saint Paul's Yard where competition is as risky as shooting between the Bridge piers at high tide, but even on this largest pier, owing to the Saint Becket chapel, the name of which we are *indeed* loath to speak, we know our foundation to tremble, not under the weight of tomes of words, nor even of rags and new paper, stored in the old Chapel, not of age alone, but more to the point of our meeting, under the burden of neglect. The roadway is broken up, as if heartbroken over the neglect. Our sleep is most disturbed by the sound of ancient stones falling away from the arches into River Thames."

Warden Scarlett took a sharp step backward. "Lack of funds, especially since the fire of '33 translated one hundred shops and houses into the very air we breathe."

"Warden Scarlett, we are mindful of what you are able to collect of us in rent."

Mister Hussey injected, "Shops East!"

"Dropstitch Upshaw, rag merchant, no livery, no sign, but unmistakable, as the relic of Popery, Chapel Lock, all praise to Henry VIII for turning Thomas à Becket chapel into my warehouse. Just keep the multitudes crossing, for people reach for a rag or so to sell me as they leave their houses. No extraordinary repairs needed at this time. Let it be said that from floors above, we have the finest view of the Tower."

Robert Hussey called for "Pier ten, Long Entry Lock, sometimes called Narrow Passage Lock!"

"Burlow Green, Beads and Necklace Seller, at the sign of the Pearl Necklace, speaking also for Cedric Horne, stiller of strong water, at the sign of the Green Tankard, and Bryce Osborne, woolen draper, at the sign of the Grinning Sheep's Head. In nightmare, I hear a cascade of beads fall into River Thames as a consequence of erosion from the tides of the rubble that fills the starlings."

Hussey. "East!"

"Arthur Clinkenbeard, Goldsmiths' Guild, at the sign of London Bridge Gold, speaking for myself and for Meredith Stirewalt, Scientific Instrument Maker guild, at the sign of the Telescope and Star. Well aware of the fact that the size of the piers and the starlings and the width of the spaces between them are uncommonly irregular, I point out nevertheless that my own is much smaller so that the tides must force themselves between my lock and Chapel lock with loud and quaking power. I dare not make use of my scales when the tide assaults my pier. We must somehow widen the opening or reinforce the structure from the riverbed to the roof top."

Scarlett. "Duly recorded. I am well aware of and deeply grateful for your well-known firm resolve to make the Bridge safe for everyone. Pier eleven, Gut Lock, West. Who speaks?"

"Tristram West, apothecary, at the sign of the Bowl and Pestle—whose piss is as dry as Mister Butling's conduit should be—and for Creighton Freeford, at the sign of the Three Coins, and also for Curran Shelley, Silk Mercers' Guild, at the sign of the Blue Gown. Well, no sign at the moment, for he craves a fresh icon. We must insist that the vegetation, the veritable shaws of bushes, not to say trees, that have taken root in the dirt the storms blast between the stones of our pier be plucked out to prevent the weakened lodgment of more stones and that the fallen stones be replaced—before breakfast if possible."

"The possible is our domain, Tristram."

"The King has remarked that in a certain light our Bridge resembles the fabled hanging gardens of Babylon."

Hussey. "East!"

"George Gill, spectacle maker, at the sign of the Purple Pupil, for I sell wine as well, as each man here knows too well. I speak also for Doyle Langham, Stationers' Guild, under the sign of the Hand and Quill. May I remind you that from 1404 to 1410, sixteen of fifty-seven renters were book artisans."

"How many book renters, George, in 1250 or 1304? I, a mere breeches maker, of the Clothiers' Guild, at the sign of the Green Pantaloons, without whom all London, including book sellers and readers, will go bare-assed into winter, see the progressive repopulating of London Bridge until we are all displaced by booksellers."

One of this company festooned the evening air with something stronger than the smell of bread baking. Frowning, he pivoted a full turn on his toes, pretending to look for the source.

George Gill pushed on. "I expected Esmond Brookfield, wallpaper merchant, under the sign of the Ten Roses, to speak for himself, but he is shy. Tristram West has duly warned us of a menace we should not take lightly. The great many birds that alight on the branches, even build their nests, cause the dirt itself to loosen and crumble, exposing space between the stones for gales to penetrate, weakening the stones."

"Samuel Good, Cough Tincture Seller, graced with a sign known to all—the Red Faced Man. Now is the season of greatest profit for me. I speak also for Barry Armitage, Necklace maker, at the sign of the Red Pearl Necklace, and Emory Ford, tobacconist, Tobacco Blenders' Guild, under the sign of the Three Burning Leaves. I am compelled by circumstances to raise a cry against the shooting of the Bridge, for when the wherries misfire and collide against the starlings, as they do more often midstream where the current is fastest, my shop and house shudder to the very foundations. When a house falls, as we have too often seen, it often brings down with it some part of the shop and house next door on each side and, above all, a significant part of the pier, weakening the arch that like Atlas has the burden of the roadway. One part damned damns several others."

Hussey. "Pier twelve East!"

"Clarke Shadwell, at the sign of the Buckled Shoe. The sound of feet crossing is my doing; a satisfaction not the same were I to hear it in Saint Paul's yard. I speak also for Brian Hazard, toy man, at the sign of the Spinning Top, and for Floyd Grover, at the sign of the Hammer and Awl. Let us be also mindful of the work of the water on the river-bed as the stream rounds the curve after Greenwich and runs headlong toward the Bridge, dragging along its bottom all manner of flotsam, gravel, even stones, hurling them at the substructure, weakening the driven piles all round the starlings. Starlings were built to take that as-sault as a kind of pointed shield. We must inspect every inch of each starling and make sure each is as sound as a drum."

"And now, my own personal favorite, if you will forgive me, Nonesuch Lock, Nonesuch Pier, number thirteen, occupying both East and West sides. We all know, of course, who might speak for Nonesuch House, but the old antiquarian is known to be missing, he who was always so deeply immersed in the past that he may be even now trying to find his way out of some labyrinth or other. We may not expect his son, the young, obscure poet, to speak for him to us, except in rhyme—hardly rivaling Dryden or Milton—or in drunken metric feet, in ac-cents of Bear Tavern. Nonesuch House, we may safely assume, stands firm. Pass on, may we, to pier fourteen, draw lock, West. Speak!"

"Thomas Wright, Scriveners' Guild, under the sign of the Quill and Ink Pot. As the services of scriveners are constantly in demand every-where, I need not keep shop on the Bridge, but it's what I much prefer. To be forced by imminent collapse of the Bridge to vacate would start slow death in me. I speak also for Boyd Finch, Milliner, at the sign of the Blue Ruffle. And Preston Cotton, hatter, Haberdashers' Guild, at the sign of the Cocked Hat. The flow of the river being less tumultuous here, we have instead the rats to combat. They come from ships an-chored in the Pool over there and from Southwark, which—no, I will not stir up that ancient rivalry. Except to say that I wish Southwarkians would pamper their rats at home, forbid visitations abroad. They have, to be more exact, been gnawing into the walls of my shop and house and weak walls make the house lean out over the river."

Kerry Brooke felt a chill. But was it only his imagination that a chill came and went as they stood assembled there?

"Pier fourteen, East!"

"Christopher Benskin, map and print seller, at the sign of the Map of England, here to tell you a thing or two. Here to speak also for Harley Midmore, hairdresser, at the sign of the Silver Wig. I humbly beg Boyd Finch to keep his Southwarkian rats on his side of the street, along with his carpenter ants that are as noisy as the rats."

Scarlett. "Pier fifteen, Roger Lock, West—is *it* in need of repair?"

"Erwin Davis, scale-maker, at the sign of the Scale, speaking for myself and for Radcliff Smithpeters, Salters' Guild, at the sign of the Silver Salt Cellar, a faithful copy of Cellini's. Yes, oh, yes, it is indeed in need of repair, its ailments being almost every one previously identified. Before breakfast would not be a minute too soon."

Hussey: "Pier fifteen East! . . . Is there nobody on Pier fifteen East? East!"

"Robertus Allbrighton, basket maker, at the sign of the Brown Cornucopia, known to be hard of hearing, speaking here, and with me is Russell Noseworthy, hosier, at the sign of the Naked Leg, and Ralph Cutshaw, pouch-maker, at the sign of the Kneeling Cow. Damage to the hautepas that cross the roadway house after house, making a tunnel, occurs usually midstream, but last night's gale chose in its capriciousness to cannonade our pier, leaving the hautepas, as you must have seen in coming here, in such a state that they sway at the oddest moments—from our movements in our houses on either side, of course, and from the foot and wagon traffic crossing, not to pass over whores bouncing their clients up against storefronts. If it falls, it may kill or injure citizens and block the road for hours. Beyond our own personal fears, it should be a concern of the London public."

Scarlett. "To the point, Robertus, very much to the point, and we thank you."

Scarlett. "Pier sixteen West, fifth lock in, from bankside, Southwark."

"William Walken, Mercers' Guild, at the sign of the Overflowing Wagon, and I speak for Yates Dranke, clock maker, at the sign of the Clock-face Pendulum. Not by the way, I wish the fate of Chapel Lock well, for as you all know, it was named for one of my maternal ancestors. And yes, also, I speak for Chancellor Brigges, surgical instrument maker, at the sign of the Scalpel and Bone Saw. Not to mention our splendid view of His Majesty's fleet in the Pool. Should the hautepas fall we may see fewer liaisons between worthless apprentices and our wives. But yes, it is a danger on our pier as well."

"Speak for yourself, William Walken. All the women on London Bridge except one are pure as the day they were born, but several were born already age thirty or so." He swirled his right hand around his belly, satisfied wit had made its point.

"Just then, did you hear a stone fall into the water?"

"I thought I had imagined it."

"Pier sixteen, East! *If* you please!"

"Eldon South, Haberdashers' Guild, at the sign of the Green Hat, and linen draper Jane Wilding, at the sign of the Butterfly, and William Stonefield, Senior, scale maker, at the sign of the Jade Scales. The ship that pulled loose from its moorings and drifted into our lock did damage that thousands of Londoners and Southwarkians have come to gaze upon. I need only repeat here that before breakfast will not do. We must band together this instant and fall to the task."

"Rhetoric will always do temporarily, Eldon. Take what solace you can in that. And may we know what must be done at the fourth lock, West, pier seventeen?"

"Alfred Goodyer, Needle-makers' Guild, at the sign of the Fat Lady Made Slender, and Hugh Christie, a fan-maker, at the sign of the Red Fan."

"Backwards, Alfred!"

"I beg your pardon!"

"My sign is the Fat Lady Made Slender and—."

"Oh, yes. When I want more tea, I . . . And so, here is Jonas Cooke, rope and twine maker livery, at the sign, I am certain, of the Spindle. I am bound to declare, with some sententiousness, as befits the tone of this gathering, that we on the East side have traditionally reported far fewer fears and problems, and I am glad to say that is true today. But we are alarmed for the general welfare of the Bridge. Damage at any point is a threat to us all."

Hussey. "Pier seventeen East!"

"Richard Howard, hair merchant, at the sign of the Red Locks. My shop affords the perfect vantage from which to espy the finest heads of hair from all over the world and hope for a hank of it. But I must account for Lennox Archer, of the Glovers' Guild —not one of the more notable ones, I'm afraid—under the sign of the Hand and Glove, and must not ignore Felton Bouth, Print and Map Sellers' Guild, at the sign of the Globe. The shaking of the Bridge and its superstructures induced by the corn mills, South side, as well as the waterwheels, North side, gives a shock to the structure never dreamed of by its creator. Might the owners of both pay proportionately higher rent—it is only fair—that rent to go to repairs for which insufficient funds exist at present?"

"The Bridge is, of course, but no doubt, let us assume, caution is the word, and henceforth, suppose we, not to say we cannot, but that such will not always be the case. That is my humble opinion."

"Understood, Alfred." All assembled recognized Mister Scarlett's tone as one they all reserved for Alfred's speeches, delivered on the Bridge with neither warning nor an accurate sense of the occasion.

Scarlett. "We come ever closer to Southwark end of our Bridge, with Rock Lock, Gateway Pier."

"James Stedman, Gateway Keeper, speaking under the sign of the Axe and Severed Head, which vary in number from reign to reign. With a view of both Southwark Cathedral and Saint Paul. May I not speak?"

"But of course you may, Keeper of the Heads. Would you were keeper of all heads that speak here this afternoon. My own is quite chocked, not to say toplofty."

"Levity is not my forte."

"As we all well know, sir, as we all well know."

"I rise to ask, May I be allowed to do my work without having to endure jests from the roadway below and windows nearby?"

"Sir, I speak for every man here when I give you my word that henceforth no man, woman, child, or donkey shall regale you with jests and oaths and reproaches and such like."

"Insult noted. As for repairs, the seatings that hold the pikes in place are wobbly from the rusting of the metal and the rotting of the wood in which they are affixed. I require services of the Bridge carpenter to mend this fixture, lest I slip in blood someday as a pike falls and impales my own self, face to face, with master traitor."

"Levity!"

"Levity!"

"Levity!"

Hussey. "We turn from the heads aloft the gateway lock and pier, to the second lock, nineteenth pier."

"Ralph Carr, although I need not announce myself to anyone of you. The ale you all drink when you leave this meeting comes from my shop, hanging precariously over River Thames, like your Thomases pissing it out at the drawbridge or the square, impatient to reach public latrines at the ends of our Bridge. Otherwise, we are strangely content." Ralph noticed a light go on in one of the windows. Then another. He became preoccupied with it. There, a light went out again. Like wind in a cave.

Hussey. "And pier twenty, Shore Lock. What, if anything, must we know? I ask as one who is aware that tavern keepers know more than most of us would have them know—or remember."

"Duff Bright, taverner of the Boar Tavern, under the sign of the Muzzled Bear, with its view of Saint Mary Overies and Saint Olaf's and of the tower—and of George Silcock's house, leaning perilously out over the water."

Scarlett. "Enough. I regret not being content with East and West."

Hussey. "Pier twenty, East! At last!" The smell of new baked bread had been tormenting him.

"Douglas Foster, Painter-stainer, at the sign of the Pot and Brush. You hear me speaking also for Cedric Ward, Leather-Sellers' Guild, at the sign of Boot and Pouch, and Philbert Swires, salter, at the sign of the Silver Salt Cellar. Yes, the corn mill gives the Bridge a case of the palsy on our end, but I do see its worth to Englishmen on both sides of the river and should the Bridge fall, the corn must be ground, but how then? Ergo, et cetera, and so forth."

Hussey. "And beneath piers nineteen and twenty, Borough Wheel Lock, Southwark side, the Corn mill, sister to the London side Waterwheels."

"Basil Softlow, happy to tell you that, like the Water Works in London, we of the Corn Mill in Southwark are ever and always dedicated to grind, grind, grind, our machines latest and best of man's invention, we and those who bring corn from the countryside and those in Southwark and London who take it away, are blessed like Joseph in Egypt."

Goldsmith Clinkenbeard stepped into a clearing and cleared his throat. "May I testify to the fact that we are also in dire need of repairs in our relations to each other as Christians?"

The final issue of this convocation was that goldsmith Clinkenbeard was asked to serve as chair of a committee of fifteen of his own choice to serve with him to devise a plan of action and return before Christmas.

"In solemn expectation that we will not all have to resort to wherries to cross over," said a man no one recognized.

4

MORGAN WOOD, A CHILD OF THE BRIDGE, AT SEA

Morgan Wood stood on the deck of the *Polestar*, trying to pretend that he was within hours of standing on the Bridge. Under his feet, he felt again the Bridge begin to fall. "London Bridge is falling down," he said again, as if to his mother, who had, singing, taught him to sing the song.

At sea for seven years, when that song came out of his mouth, as it often did, he always remembered meeting the ancient Chronicler of London Bridge a few months before he left home to go to sea.

"One day, when you are walking, the very shuddering picture of recklessness, along the spine of the roadway, looking all around and up, as is your wont, I will call down to you from this window and summon you to tell you that the time has come."

Morgan had let his silence stand for the question, "For what?" But as Lloyd Braintree had let his own silence match the boy's, Morgan had faintly sensed the answer, before he finally gave it.

"My own son, as you know, seems convinced that the spirit of the lyric poets abides in him, and that the London Bridge Chronicle, one of the great Chronicles of the civilized world, our legacy, handed down in secrecy from generation to generation—" here he took Morgan's hands and clapped the palms firmly upon his skull—"as merely the recording of facts without fancy, is unworthy of his attention. You, on the other hand, look upon the Bridge as very much only there, there under your feet, under your gaze, and I imagine it one day under your hand, under your command—in names, dates, numbers, facts.

"I have never forgotten what your mother told me a week or so after your family moved onto the Bridge, that when you first stepped out of the London streets onto the bridge foot, you exclaimed, 'Mother, London Bridge is falling down.' Watching you daily from this window, I know in my bones that you were not resorting to metaphor. For you, as for me, the Bridge is actual, and only actual, ergo, for me, you are the heir to the Chronicle. But you must swear to keep even that fact secret."

Morgan wanted to remove his hands from the Chronicler's skull. "May I see it?"

"You are touching it. I have memorized it all, from 1209 to this very day, even as I recorded each fact. And to you, one day, I will dictate it, word for word."

"How long have you lived on London Bridge?"

"Almost a thousand years—fifty generations."

"Yes, I see."

"In the sense that my ancestors have either lived or worked—but mostly lived and, of course, worked here—and that I know that to be true in my very bones. My family history has preserved that fact and I am very proud."

"I don't *know* how long *my* family has lived in London. They never told me."

"Did you ever ask?"

"No."

"*Probably*, they are a new family and came to London from somewhere Without the Gates after their marriage. To start a life together.

"My life work has been London Bridge Chronicler. A Herculean task embraced while yet a boy, willingly, with all my heart. My personal Chronicle nears 69. We are chosen not by any proven skills as scriveners but by the Chronicler's sense that yon youth has a feeling for the Bridge that marks him as one of us. Thus, I have summoned you here."

Feeling so marked, Morgan stepped back, and looked wildly around as if to reach for someone to testify to the contrary.

But Morgan humored the old man, who swore him to secrecy. He had descended—passing Daryl Braintree, the dissolute-looking, stinking, poet son of the Chronicler on the third of five flights of Nonesuch House—passed through the antiquarian bookshop and bindery onto the Bridge roadway, pridefully elated.

A few months later, he was on a ship bound for every port—it seemed now, seven years later—in the charted world, apprenticed by his father to goldsmith Clinkenbeard.

"I was only just able to buy this shop on the Bridge because I promised you to Mister Clinkenbeard upon your thirteenth birthday, and so, my son, you must help pay your father's debt with seven years at sea."

And gladly he would, for so excellent a father, were it not for the Bridge, for having to leave it, and for breaking his promise to the Old Chronicler, that, yes, when called, he *would* climb the stairs again and receive from his memory the Chronicle of London Bridge, writing it all in some huge leather-bound book, thus joining England's many chroniclers, the old man said, from the unknown Anglo-Saxon Chronicler to William Thorne's Chronicle of Augustine's Abbey, Canterbury.

Daily life at sea was in many episodes so horrible—attempted assaults upon his innocence, mind and body—he had turned inward, nostalgic for the Bridge. The horrors of seaport towns contrasted to London—which, for him, was the Bridge.

He longed to return to memory, to his Bridge idyll, a Bridge version of Sir Philip Sidney's *Arcadia* and other pastoral poems he read in the books his father gave him to sustain his mind and lift his spirit during life at sea. He moved in and out of Plato, Dante, and John Salisbury, the Latin his father inspired him to learn at his own pace, not well along as yet, Chaucer in Middle English, and Tyndale's translation of the New Testament. He had written the first entry in his journal, bought in Singapore, July 25, 1661, his second year at sea:

Affection? I can't settle on a single or even a few words. My vocabulary is exhausted in any effort to express my feelings about the Bridge.

When I closed my eyes just now and dug my knuckles into my eye sockets and ruckled them, the Bridge was obscured for a moment by stars and fireworks. And slowly the sky cleared and the Bridge stretched across River Thames, lit by faggots from the bank.

I begin with a steadfast purpose, unflagging, to walk the Bridge night after night until this ship enters the Pool within sight of the Bridge. My pen in hand, I dive into a pool of words. A pleasure unique and always waiting. Glad amaze, the prospect of reading these entries a year from now and, if I grow old, reading them again, having returned and lived my life on the Bridge.

I will give my journal a name: "My Memories of London Bridge." I remember the Bridge most as it was in balmy daylight.

1663, somewhere in the Adriatic Sea.

His journal being full, he wrote in the margins of *The Canterbury Tales:*

Hearing, in foreign ports, my home called a Wonder of the World makes me feel strange, but somehow the contrast makes my own humble memories of London Bridge sharper. But I know it was no ordinary home. Sailors return to farms, one very much like another, or to streets in London and in other cities, one very much like another, but I shall return to a place like no other—I have seen no other, except the fewer houses on the bridges around Notre Dame in Paris and I have heard men tell of Ponte Vecchio in Florence. Gazing in wonder upon the Rialto in Venice made me forget for a moment the 20 Rialtos of London Bridge, but the Rialto's shops span only one arch. Gazing in dread upon the Bridge of Sighs, anchored to the sides of two buildings, the Doge's palace and the prison below the waterline, not to piers in the canal bed, it was for London Bridge I sighed, though it is my fate to serve as a species of innocent prisoner on this ship.

Still, recalling those lesser wonders does not dilute the sense of uniqueness I feel when I recall sights and smells and sounds on the Bridge where my house and my father's stationery shop stands.

I am never *out* of touch. Everything I touch on the ship reminds me at one time or another of the Bridge. I am in touch. I am *touched*. 'He's touched,' one could rightly say of me. I have stayed *in* touch. Many words and their many meanings, and their vulnerability to puns, touch upon the Bridge.

In the Aegean Sea. In the margins of Plato's Republic.

I feel on my neck as I write the breath of the Old Bridge Chronicler, whose name I have forgotten. His breath combines all the sweet and odious smells and fragrances of the Bridge. Sometimes, I hear his voice as a reproachful babble of all the voices speaking and shouting this very moment on the Bridge. But the Holy Ghost, I pray, will tell him that I am not at fault. I will, of course, return some day, and perhaps he will be alive still and I can, as it is indeed my now fervent wish, take up the task of London Bridge Chronicler, which his wastrel poet son declined.

The salt sea air washes over the Bridge, and the water of the North Sea washes under the Bridge. Intervals of fresh water aroma. The seas contend. Between the salt and the fresh, I am water waved and laved and washed.

In port, Constantinople. In the margin of The Merchant of Venice.

Coming and going, we Bridge dwellers were suspended between two busy towns and above a busy body of water—daily life on the Bridge, between moving sky and moving water, heaven and hell, life and death, between beginnings and endings, but mostly continuing, perpetual suspension. From the Bridge's suspension to this ship's, the deck's.

Activity crossing the Bridge in two directions, often clashing, but also suspended. Direct action movement, simultaneous with suspension. Incredible—strange—when you stop, midway on the Bridge, to think about it, as I often do, walking the deck. I suddenly stop, stand stock still, as if I am on the Bridge, and think about it. And every night in my hammock, I take a walk on the Bridge. The ship disappears, my shipmates become shadows. I *am* on the Bridge, walking, and the walk is as memorable as anything that happened aboard ship during the day. Confined almost half my life to a ship, almost as if to the Tower, I go free when I walk on the Bridge.

Approaching the Cape of Good Hope, Africa. In the margins of Sir Philip Sidney's Arcadia.

A certain co-ordination of stormy winds off the Atlantic from the West and tremendous tide force from the North Sea from the East, set up a rhythm that makes the Bridge swing, like the hammocks in the ship's hold. Swinging, I remember the Bridge swaying. Some corner turned on deck, I often see the Bridge that I long to feel under my feet again.

Atlantic Ocean, en route to Lisbon. In the margins of Salisbury's Vita S. Thomae.

My father's shop was situated midway on the Bridge near Saint Thomas Chapel. My parents seldom sent me on errands into the City, Within the Gates, because the Bridge and its approaches provided almost everything. When I did go, stepping off the bridgehead into the city roadway, Southwark or London, I felt cut off, I felt it in my feet, like a mild striking of your crazy bone. They call it that only when you hit it—it's just your simple elbow most of the time. Walking on the Bridge is like having elbows—stepping off is mildly like hitting your crazy bone—the odd feeling that the rest of you—like sneezing, too— doesn't exist for the moment. As the zany throb subsides, you are turning a corner and, at your back, the Bridge is out of sight. Then stepping back onto the Bridge, full of sensations gathered in City lanes and alleys and streets, you suddenly lose all you have gathered there, and then, it's elbows again, only elbows. Ever try to kiss your elbow? Don't try. It cannot be done.

Loom spinning, tale spinning—weaving my childhood on the Bridge. My young manhood on this ship, cook's apprentice, tale spinning. My head spins, overloaded with cargo, and yet I can recall to tell only a few tales, and those tell badly, wanting to be as glib as the writers in the books with which my father lovingly burdened me on my setting forth. Not a burden now, a blessing now. And writing in the margins of my books seems to flow as much out of reading the books as out of my daily life.

*   *   *

Morgan wrote now and then about his muse of the Bridge, a three-year-old girl, now thirteen, singing as she played in her father's glove shop doorway, only a foot or so from deadly human and mechanical traffic. He heard Blythe's voice sometimes on the ship, speaking. Not to him, but to herself, and perhaps to the Holy Ghost.

*   *   *

In the margin of Chaucer, he wrote: Food tastes different on the Bridge. Ever eat Within the Gates and then come home on the Bridge to supper? Salt wind—open your mouth to take a bite and salt wind drifts into the cavity and mingles with the steam and aroma of hot food and down she goes—a Bridge meal, not a London meal. Not even—*I know*—like eating at sea.

At the sign of the Chained Bear. Everything on the Bridge is at the sign of something. Why do I remember *that* sign? So much history goes into each choice, and once the sign goes up, the establishment itself *by that name* begins *its* history. The signs are like repeated utterances—day by day. "I will meet you at the sign of the Silver Salt Cellar." Seen and heard, reinforced effect on the mind, by ear and eye. The sign of the Looking Glass.

On the ship, on the deck, still wearing shoes my father bought for me in one of the shops, I walk the Bridge from sign to sign, conjuring each shop, its goods, its odors and sounds, the voices of its proprietors and clerks and familiar customers.

I walk from pier to pier, calling out the names of each, and calling out the names of the signs. From pier to pier, side to side, the vantage changes. One pier gives off the best view of Old Swan Steps, another of the Pool and its many ships, another of Saint Paul's Tower, Saint Botolph's Wharf, Billingsgate, the White Tower, another of Saint Olaf's, bankside.

After washing pots at the end of the day's work, I sometimes stagger across the Bridge—in the margins of my books. And I have dreamed of flying over it. How do I, dreaming, know the view from the vantage point of birds in flight? Does the mind *create*? Borrowed from the stored perception of birds? God provides?

Simultaneous with Morgan writing, the Poet composed a poem that he thought, as he wrote it, was far more than a rough draft, apprehensive that his lack of interest or agility in the prevailing correct forms, rhyme and all the rest, would impede his progress in becoming the poet of the age, elevated above Dryden and Milton.

A Fit Chronicle

A fit Chronicle records even rain drying on stones,
a bird beating a seed on a stone,
it drops into a crack, where
rocket flowers grow and proliferate. Iron rusts,
bolts, nails in timber, the washing of windows,
into the river East, shit-piss and scraps and cunny rags,
centuries of them, and mold and damp trespass, drawers warp,
become cuss-drawers, not budging to knee-knocks, palm slaps
and jerks that hurt muscles in the shoulder, salt that won't pour
or that clots on the salt spoons in the salt cellars, the rubbing,
polishing of metals, the sip-sip-sip of house shoes, belts
that slowly uncurl all night long on the floor, and hinges
crying from end to end of the Bridge—these *are* events.
Prove to me that they are not. Prove it! You can't!
These things, having happened first, happened
repeatedly when some people, alive then, weren't looking.
And more, much more than I can capture.
Nothing depends on my capturing. Everything happens
anyway. The mice turds studding the pantry, the roaches
making tracks, and snails in the dim damp crevices.
Shreds of tobacco everywhere and books cast aside.

Daryl Braintree

*　*　*

Past the Cape of Good Hope. In the margins of Thomas Nashe's The Unfortunate Traveler, or the Life of Jack Wilton.

I remember every shop, every pillar, every brick, the wood grain of every plank. I know by heart the exact location of everything on London Bridge. And then I met that German in Alexandria who visited the Bridge all of one day and who came away living it still, after 25 years, and as we talked of every shop and pillar and house, I realized that he had gotten some of them out of order, so I corrected him and he corrected me, and that went on for hours, until I had to admit that his facts, after a single day's visit, were more often right than mine, and when we set sail out of Alexandria, I was so happy to have it all restored. Now, I know that it didn't really matter who was right and who was wrong. I had experienced three London Bridges—the actual one of my childhood, the one I remembered, and the one he had reconstructed for me. The correct one was all three as *one,* including any errors remaining.

Arabian Sea, en route to Bombay. In the margins of "Lycidas," in The Poems of John Milton.

I was on the Bridge all day in mood in the Bay of Bengal.

Yes, the sea, in tides, "shoots the Bridge," as watermen risked their lives, shooting their wherries between the piers.

*   *   *

A great tempest broke up the *Polestar,* and Morgan, seriously hurt, was rescued and floundered for over a year in Calcutta before becoming able-bodied again and signing on a newly built ship, *The Sea Rocket*—after the London Rocket, a yellow flower that grows on London Bridge.

Arabian Sea, west coast of India, en route to Bombay. In the margin of The Divine Comedy, *his Italian slowly improving.*

If I were a seabird, I could leave my godfather Clinkenbeard's ship with a morsel he tossed into the air in my beak and fly to England, over London Bridge and look down at where it sets in its place in all creation.

If I were a fish, I would swim along the riverbed and gaze upon first one pier, one starling and arch, and then another and another and yet another until I had swum in and out, like mother and sister weaving, in our garret, all twenty little Rialtos. All God's birds perch on the roofs of the Bridge.

If I were a cat, I would walk everywhere up and down and around and see and smell and feel under every crevice and flower and scent of mice and rats.

I can be a snail, if I wish, and move through narrow dark, damp places and see and hear everything, everybody. How long will it take me to leave my silver tracks on every inch by inch of the Bridge? How near done am I today? Or will it take me forever, snail's time?

God, enable me to *see*, touch, smell, hear *all*, all at once, and forever, even after London Bridge has fallen down.

5

THE BROTHERHOOD OF
THE BRIDGE MEETS TO REPAIR
THE BRIDGE

Following the meeting at the Bridge House of all shop owners on the Bridge, goldsmith Clinkenbeard formed a committee of fifteen merchants, as authorized by Warden Scarlett.

Glover Lennox Archer, eager to be off to the meeting goldsmith Clinkenbeard had called to discuss in more detail ways to repair gale and other damage to London Bridge, was determined first to complete the domestic picture from which he daily hoped, too often in vain, to derive a sense of stability and calm.

"Why has John not come to the table?"

"He is watching the watermen shoot the Bridge." Esther Archer filled her husband's cup fuller with ale than usual.

"He has never seen them before? How long have we lived on the Bridge?"

"His friend Will is to race a bully in a challenge race."

"And John's hope is to witness his friend's drowning?"

"The bully, father." Mister Archer's thirteen-year-old daughter Blythe had lately grown fond of correcting him at every opportunity, with an open sneer more often than not.

Mister Archer shut his eyes to Blythe's mocking eyes, her slightly curled upper lip. His wife wondered why he never reproached the child, but Blythe seemed knowing.

"I shot the Bridge in my youth once, and I praise God each day that I survived to scoff at those foolhardy enough to do it now. A man died that same day on *his* first attempt. Died when he failed to 'catch his breath' under the arch. Shooting the Bridge, like so many others before and after—on a bet, for the thrill of it, to impress a girl, on a dare, or by command, or merely for the show, to impress one's master watching from the bank—died accidentally, or of a suicidal gesture. 'Tis hell mouth when you fail." The thrill, the terror, paralleled the noise and danger on the roadway, contrasted with commercial work beside and domestic bliss above.

Blythe leaned across the table as close to her father's face as she could. "Some do it daily."

"They defy all reason. How does God allow such arrogance? Cirrus overreached himself once only. God was watching."

"The Pagan god of the Norse? At our very own table?"

Taking his wife's question as a mild reproach, Mister Archer gestured for a stop, to say grace, even as Blythe welcomed the presence in spirit of the pagan god.

As he thanked God aloud, Mister Archer simultaneously prayed silently that John would not catch the contagion of daredevil, convinced that 'The devil wins the dare sooner or later,' and prayed that time would diminish Blythe's blame of him for his transgressions.

Below, unseen from the window by those at the supper table, John turned from the open rail on the square and ran across the roadway— sidestepping a red coach—to the West side of the Bridge to see his friend's back leaving death behind.

There! he! Goes! "Will! Will!"

As John stepped back, dizzy, he sensed that little sister Blythe was behind him somewhere watching, a habit that unnerved him.

* * *

Supper over, fishmonger Kerry Brooke waited for his friend stationer Phelan Wood, Morgan's father, to join him at his fish shop for the walk South on the Bridge to Mister Clinkenbeard's goldsmith shop for the first meeting of the committee of fifteen.

"I sometimes feel, shut up in this shop all day, from dawn over the Pool to sunset over Temple Bar, that life, as others live it," said thin-shadow caster Brooke, as corpulent Phelan Wood leaned against the counter to catch his breath amid the mingling odors of fresh and foul fish, "is passing me by over this Bridge—back and forth."

"Life is so close, only your threshold away? Yes, I, too. But look at it this way. They—all those people in motion, that flux of people, are all doing the world's work, each man and woman who passes, just as you are, except their work takes them out of doors where they must cross our Bridge. And, you know, for some, crossing the Bridge, among other narrow passage ways, is a special moment, for being so different."

"And suddenly out here in the open?"

"Except *they* only feel that. *We're* all cooped up inside, you know, in a tunnel formed by the hautepas overhead. It's only at the square and the palisades and the drawbridge *they*—more often than *we*—*see* the openness, the airy rush of the river."

"But you are right. The still world in here is only another part of the world *out there* in motion. I'm grateful, Phelan, for the thought."

"And I for the occasion to think it."

On that shared note, they set out walking South on the Bridge.

Walking South to the meeting, coming up slowly behind Mister Brooke and Mister Wood, full of a sense of purpose yet to be defined by the meeting itself, Tristram West, apothecary, and shoemaker Clarke Shadwell, Gilda's father, were eager to hear the wisdom of Mister Clinkenbeard's recommendations and to assert a few of their own, perhaps.

Mister Shadwell pointed up, "Godward," as Saint Paul liked to say. "I thank God every night that my house has withstood tempest and rot."

"And well you should. Yours is more a leaning lunatic than mine, by far."

"Not *very* far. I look out my window every morning to see whether yours is still only teetering or whether its roof is sticking up out of River Thames."

"Nothing's safe in this world. I'll take my chances, like folks living on the slopes of volcanoes assumed to be extinct."

"So will I, so will I." In company with cynical Mister West, Mister Shadwell reserved the imperative to attribute all to God's will, not his own. "Living on the Bridge poses dangers nothing like those Within the Gates. Wouldn't you agree?"

"Without a moment's hesitation. War-free, plague-free, fire-free, these thirty-three years."

"In '33, those who perished in the fire in the City were too many to bury, while *we* went about our business. Let us never, however, forget the twenty-two or so shops and houses that did burn on the City end of the Bridge, some now rebuilt, but none forever safe."

"I always knew we in the middle of our Bridge were special in the eyes of God."

"And why is that, do you suppose?"

"Because we chose well the houses we inhabit—and where."

"But *why*?"

"It's a mystery, like the ways of God Himself."

"Not to me. Didn't God say, 'In my house there are many mansions'?—and so 'tis with the Bridge—a single house, but with many mansions."

The four men come upon Edan Coldiron, the Bridge's master carpenter, repairing the hole in the roadway by installing a fresh-smelling strut.

"Can you fix it?"

"Hand me that hammer."

"Will it hold?"

"Jump up and down on it."

"What if the Thames freezes and a long frost sets in?"

"From your jumping up and down on it to a hard freeze is a gargantuan leap."

"We can't expect too much?"

"Right. But don't lose faith if after a thousand years you feel the roadway go soft under foot."

"Be serious."

"I *am* being serious. This Bridge is made to outlast several dynasties."

"Is it possible?"

"Have faith."

"Can you name me a Bridge that has lasted that long?"

"No. But I'm telling you about *London* Bridge."

Already assembled at the sign of London Bridge Gold, in Arthur Clinkenbeard's shop with the proprietor were Alfred Goodyer, needle maker, and Eldon South, haberdasher; Drop-stitch Upshaw, rag merchant; Robertus Allbritton, basket maker; Thomas Wright, scrivener; and Lennox Archer, glover. Once Mister Brooke, Mister Wood, Mister Shadwell, Mister West, and Mister Green had joined them upstairs, Mister Clinkenbeard, two more to come, opened the meeting with an almost whispered prayer, then took up the subject around which all were gathered.

"I have a vision of the Bridge's future and a deep and abiding respect for its past." Aware that his talk about that past and the future often seemed to his neighbors more than a little abstract, complex, Mister Clinkenbeard hoped this evening to inspire, persuade, convince. Together, they would repair and maintain. He envisioned a later hand-picked group of seven leading all Bridge dwellers in the achievement of community coherence, just as all the components of the Bridge itself were originally designed to cohere. For him, there was to this mission a religious, although not metaphysical, dimension. Ritual, ceremony, manners meant more to him, at the risk, he knew, of Phariseeism, than metaphysical transcendence. Still, comparing himself to his friend Mister Coldiron, master carpenter, Mister Clinkenbeard felt himself to be somewhat ethereal, although certainly corporeal. "We bear the mark of London Bridge, if not upon our foreheads, upon our souls. At Heaven's Gate, the angels will see us coming, curious specimen, we are to seem to them."

Mister Coldiron, master carpenter, invited only to advise, having no shop on the Bridge, had come in carrying his leather bag full of rattling tools. Well regarded as a man of action, he opened his mouth to speak. "I have little sense or care for the past and no vision of the future. The Bridge must carry its burden *today*. Night must fall on the Bridge. Not the Bridge fall in the night.

"As *you* see bad omen in a fact, *I* direct your attention to the gap in the houses on the Bridge that will save us. The place the fire of 1633 burned many houses, we left open. I worked May 1645 to June 1651 on the new buildings and the two waterwheels beneath them on the north end of the Bridge. We built palisades on each side of that long space between the new houses and the old for fear wild traffic might force walkers and wagons off into River Thames. For six years, people crossing watched us build several new shops and houses where fire had been. So, the fire next time will not, God willing, burn those new houses, then leap over the vacant space to all the other shops and houses, and on across to Southwark."

"Did not the act of 1621 require all new houses to be faced with brick or stone—except those on London Bridge, making the north end a burning exemption?"

"I am bone-weary." Edan Coldiron sat still as stone dropped in river water. "At work all morning replacing broken windows in the House of Many Windows and repairing the damaged starling under the old drawbridge and a hole in the roadway. The tempest thrust debris against the starlings with such violence last night—I saw it myself—we were twenty strong up on the starling and in boats all around with stones, trying to prevent further erosion from tides and flood waters, the sky above as serene as Madam's shoes parked by the hearth. Recall the singing game we played often and often on the roadway? 'London Bridge is broken down!' Well, not while I am on the watch.

"With a claw hammer and a nail, I have kept London Bridge many a time from falling down. The arch never sleeps, but a fallen arch is a nightmare for London Bridge. My mission is to repair Time's ravages, restoring where weather, war, or collision of barge or ice do damage, adding on new parts, and with the claw ripping down and carting off old parts of it. Nails keep parts married, the claw divorces them. That's how I've always viewed my trade, my occupation. With a hammer in one hand and a nail in the other, I have perfected an engine that drives nails deep into what we call a Bridge. *You* can walk across because *I've* been there before you, and others of my ilk have been there before me for almost five hundred years. But *live* on the Bridge? I never cared for the idea of it. When I leave the Bridge and enter the streets of London, I leave that old lady behind me, as if stepping across an invisible line in the desert into the forest."

"Did you ever bounce on a bed on the Bridge?" Eldon South thus kept up his reputation as master of the *non sequitur.* "You step up off the roadway itself into your house, bone-weary, too beat down to speak to whoever that woman mending a sleeve over by the window is—and climb the narrow stair, barking your elbows from side to side, and you stagger into the bedroom and over to the bed, spread out like a plump lady with a pillow for a face, and you pitch yourself suddenly with a giggle of ecstasy over onto the flock mattress and commence to bounce yourself up and down like a kid on the bed ropes, and there's the moon over the water, and down and bounce up and, oh! there's Saint Paul's dome, and down and bounce, oh! the moon . . . and sag down, and softly off, into Dreamland."

Restless, Tristram West, rose, walked about. "More pertinent to the purpose of our meeting—the problems that trouble the Bridge— setting aside for the moment, the ugly water conduit sky-high over Saint Magnus Martyr steeple—may I introduce into our deliberations the bawdy woman we have complained of these many years and who plagues us still with her flagrant disregard. A cabal is needful to be rid of her. She is not, as some contend, crazy. She lifts her skirts fore and aft with a clear head. Unlike our mute Bridge, she can tell you exactly who the traffic over her has been throughout her three score and seven."

"Gladly." Mister Green nodded.

"She makes no bones about them." Mister Upshaw clapped his hands. "They are legion. Some die for her cunny."

"Some," Mister Brooke interposed, "die *of* it."

"Filthy creature that she is," waxed Mister Upshaw, "she will aston- ish us betimes with a display of finery befitting a lady of the court."

"Once even from a barge, alighting—as if in mockery of Queen Elizabeth's old habit—on Old Swan Steps to avoid walking on the Bridge." Mister Wood saw her plainly, remembering what someone told him. "But once she shot the Bridge, was dumped, and came up laughing, as we watched from our windows, hoping she would drown. And laughed as boisterous as ever throughout the days and nights we kept her in the cage at the south end of the Bridge."

"Fornication, adultery are not rare on the Bridge." Mister Coldiron was often a spectator.

"No one would so pretend." Mister South wondered what he had just now meant.

"But the loud mouth!" Mister Upshaw cringed as if his own words conjured her up too close. "The roaring farting in the roadway by way of defiance! and mocking our protestations and prohibitions!"

"And the raucous laughter!" Mister Green heard himself giggle and stopped.

"And screams of ecstasy, that affright our women's and children's sweet dreams." Mister Gill tamped the embers of his own remembered ecstasy on hearing her.

"Abhorrent!" Mister Archer jumped up as if lifted up on his up-lifted finger. "We must be rid of her before she infects us all."

"Her quim—" Mister South was the only person in the room un-aware of the spark of delight in his outcry "—is without qualm!"

All turned toward the corner to look at him.

"And, then," said Mister Gill, happy to be of further use, "there are her sister scourges, the gossips, who conspire with common rot in the piers to set our daily life atremble."

"Not alone," said Mister Upshaw, seeing the images as clearly as he saw his audience, "among the many undesirable types who make a hell of our heaven and steady work for the street caricaturists, who love to limn them all."

And by the waning light through a window of his cupola in Nonesuch House, the Poet read aloud to himself the first rough draft of a poem he had just written.

Wisdom Teeth

Piers and their starlings
go deep, like roots,
like molars, wisdom teeth,
keeping this exotic plant,

London Bridge,
from floating down river,
keeping it buoyant.
Like a water plant,
it moves, gives,
is never totally still—
a ship at anchor,
moving *in* its berth.

Daryl Braintree

By the same waning light that fell upon the Poet's page, the meeting of merchants moved haltingly along.

Mister Coldiron interjected. "I assure you that I am mindful of my role in this meeting, as advisor only, based only on my craft as Master Carpenter, even so, as such, I mind that we have drifted off our course, from necessary repairs to the Bridge, which we all have agreed is falling by increments, to regrettable manifestations of human nature, fallen long ago in the Garden."

"Would you not concur in this, Mister Coldiron," said Mister Clinkenbeard, "that *drift* itself in a body such as this is in itself a manifestation of our imperfect human nature?"

"I do indeed, but might we strive to have less of it?"

"May we agree, however, that safety is our paramount concern?" Mister Clinkenbeard swung his gaze left to right several times. "Nothing on this Bridge is safe. If you will allow me to enumerate the perils to life and limb: traffic crossings, crashings, maimings, kidnappings, houses leaning, swaying in tempest. Fire hazards."

"Night robbers." Mister Green felt useful.

"Piers and starlings crumbling." Mister Coldiron had already silently, stoutly resolved to solve the problem. "On the verge of falling away from the Bridge."

"Falls from the Bridge tower." Mister Allbritton remembered his narrow escape from death when, as a daredevil child, he tempted fate with a swan dive from up yonder that left his belly blistered with shame.

"Shooting the Bridge." John's father, Mister Archer, wanted Mister Gill to recall that he had been a witness to his childhood foolishness, after which Gill himself had successfully shot the Bridge.

"Poisoned food and drink." Mister South had dinner on his mind.

"Plague perhaps." Mister Gill did not wish at this time to take note of the rising number of cases in the environs.

"Dog and cat bites." Mister Brooke felt he had scraped the bottom of the barrel of possibilities.

"Wreckage on the Bridge often, often slowing, often stopping all traffic for hours," said Bridge Warden Scarlett, coming in late, invited as a silent observer, unable at last to keep his mouth shut. "Like flood or tempest debris between the pillars. People suddenly pressed back against walls and windows and railings to avoid the vehicles. As he feared, Samuel Good's house fell into the river last evening suppertime. He and his are all in Saint Bartholomew Hospital."

"Have we drunk all the tea then?" Mister Upshaw had not nearly his fill of it.

"Some called London Bridge the Great Weir because of its fluid-dam influence on the water, creating the Pool." Mister Gill farted with alacrity.

"Is that not—like the story the Bridge is built upon wool—only a legend now?" By happenstance, Mister Wright had a Bible opened on his knee to Jonah.

"By walking across the Bridge, a citizen is himself a Bridge between London and Southwark." Hat-maker South realized he had made that observation various times before, to each man assembled. He ventured to expand upon it. "The Bridge is covered. Wigs, hats cover the heads of the Bridge crossers. They say the builders padded the starlings with great bales of wool."

"That this Bridge was built upon wool is a legend. Not really wool, but the tax on wool."

"I, however, embrace the legend. I sometimes feel it, as I handle wool, making hats. Wool comes to me by water, unloaded on the starlings, hoisted up to my window." This thought was original to the present occasion, Mister South realized, and waxed upon it. "The hats shaped in my hand go out of my shop and cross the Bridge on my customers' heads. And I like seeing them go by, each day, one of my hats, at least. Oh, yes, I know my own from my rivals. And I imagine how others see mine and his as they go by, as they descend the slope of the Bridge roadway into London or Southwark. Knowing the Bridge is built on wool makes me enjoy the sight of nice wool handiwork even more than 'twould be otherwise."

"Did Canute the Dane, in fact, six centuries past, divert the river through a canal so that he could get his great navy around the Bridge and besiege London?"

"I can imagine so."

"Does anyone in this room recall what attitude toward the Bridge influenced the separation of city from Bridge by the refusal to consider Bridge Street and Bridge Road the same?"

"Last night, I lay awake listening to a dog on the bank barking in the rain." Mister South, aware that he had held their attention, reached for it again. "This morning I found a rat, trapped, dead."

"And yet, and yet, who has spoken here of the plague?" Mister Shadwell had had little else on his mind.

"Need we?" Rag Merchant Upshaw was cheerfully convinced that they need not. "Congested though we are, as much as the most congested streets in London, we live over water where breezes, winds cleanse us daily as a wife wipes clean a baby's bum. No one from the streets of London or Southwark pass over without our consent."

"And yet, what might lurk in the rags you collect and bring onto the Bridge?"

"It's the damned not-knowing." Mister Clinkenbeard felt a certain profundity ought to mark the closing of the meeting. "We know everything a human being *can* know about this Bridge as it stands today. But there was one, not among us but missing, our neighbor on the Bridge, who knew everything within memory and record of the Bridge from its birth. You all know the rumor that he may secretly be the keeper of an inherited Chronicle of the Bridge. It has become known that his son the wayward poet has been searching out books and records in the Guildhall and elsewhere about the building of the Bridge by Peter de Colechurch, warden of the Brethren of the Bridge. His identity has always been a secret, although the existence of this Chronicler is fairly certain. But it's the future we cannot know. The future of this Bridge for us and our descendants—*that* we cannot know. It's the damned not-knowing that torments us all tonight, that draws us together like a living question mark. We are damned not to know and we are damned in what we do know about our answer to questions of the future. The damned not-knowing must torment us into knowing."

Kerry Brooke leaned forward in his chair. "By what name shall we be known to each other?"

Mister Archer rubbed together the gloves he had made himself. "Well, *I* feel comfortably a member of—the Brotherhood of the Bridge. We are the Brotherhood of the Bridge, are we not?"

"Excellent." A chorus of agreement followed that climactic remark.

Clinkenbeard adjourned the committee until the same day, time, and place next week. All gone, Clinkenbeard prided himself on his restraint, observing, as he had intended, the serious folk from the not-so, enabling him to choose before the next meeting a smaller working committee of seven.

6

FATHER PETER DE COLECHURCH STEALS THE MURDERED BODY OF ARCHBISHOP THOMAS À BECKET

Weary of research as Chronicler, the Poet lay, eyes shut, in fitful reverie. 'Cats on the Bridge are, like the cats of Venice, cared for, adored. London town cats venture onto the Bridge seldom twice. . . .

A favoring wind: Weather of the soul. Food of the spirit. Love of mankind on the Bridge. . . . Exclusive, yes. Like Calvinists. Proud. Wealthy.'

"How else live on a Bridge?" He spoke aloud, to wake himself, saw suddenly Musetta at the foot of the bed, taking off her hat, smiling at his odd behavior.

"Don't forget the fog in our time, the time of plague and fire, and how it affected all our sufferings and fears, the very look of things. Fog as the watery grave of the dying, a street-stream, London as Venice, carrying off the night's dead. Walking among that, seeing that from various angles and from various apertures from the Bridge." He saw sudden depth in Musetta's eyes. "'To have seen what I have seen, see what I *see*.'"

Daryl turned from her stony gaze. "I suppose for some of us, love of the Bridge has become almost idolatrous, the Bridge an altar on which our daily life rituals are a form of worship. Troubles of Kingdom and neighborhood, natural disasters, acts of God and man, notwithstanding, such people look off the Bridge, out and down River Thames toward the Pool or up River Thames toward Westminster, and breathed deep in thanksgiving and praise for merely being there on the Bridge."

"Better you should worship the gods of love, or shall I say, the incarnation closest to you, each visit another phase of Venus."

"Quietly read, will you, my new poem? That is to say, a draft, mind you."

> No life so lived can be a waste
> or misspent. Lived in the imagination,
> where I have walked every night
> while war and plague prowled around me.
> This Bridge grows stronger as the historical Bridge
> erodes at its foundation—nineteen starlings.
> It grows by nights, by lines and pages,
> as stones decay and the Bridge grows old.
> Mine is not the only life so lived. Imaginations
> All over the rounded surface of this seemingly flat planet
> Are building as the world implodes minutely, as the cells
> Break down in the brain, more slowly
> Signaling the hand that writes. Flights of fancy.
> Ahead of the articulation of death. These plagues
> May one day burn out—but they are only
> As the reflections of the everlasting Bridge
> Upon the flowing, transient surface of River Thames.

Musetta looked up from the page. "Are all your poems about the Bridge?"

"I wrote my first poem about the Bridge, but nowhere in it do I mention the Bridge itself. I wrote it about my roving youth in London, before I returned to my father's house on the Bridge. But bridges rise in many of my poems now, and one of them is London Bridge."

"And none," she murmured, suddenly showing her right breast, bold as a face, "are about me?"

* * *

1130 AD. First time a name and money were associated with the Bridge, but in its wooden avatar, as when Geoffrey Ingeniator rebuilt two of its arches of elm.

"We Londoners are blessed," wrote the Poet-Chronicler in the margin of a page in the Chronicle, "to have John Stow's *Survey,* even though only two pages are given over to the history of the Bridge from the New Millennium to Peter's death in 1205. Having told us about Peter only his name and that he was a priest of Saint Mary Colechurch, Stow leaves us to answer other fundamental questions. And to imagine all else."

The Poet will end his days on earth without ever discovering a source that reveals to him any more bare facts than those.

'Stow is silent and I am tormented. But my torment is even more profound. In other words—thousands of words—what is the answer to such fundamental questions as, Who was Peter de Colechurch? What was Peter de Colechurch's real first name? What was his father's name? What was his father's profession or occupation? What was his mother's name? Where was he born? Where was he reared? Who were his brothers and sisters, if any, and other relatives of likely note? Was he, as is most likely, named after Saint Peter, and if so, for what reason? Where was he trained to the priesthood? What is the story of his priesthood? Why was he assigned to the small, nondescript, nevertheless architecturally unique, Saint Mary Colechurch in Old Jewry?

'Above all—or perhaps not—how did he become a Bridge builder, and why, of all the priestly Bridge builders in the church, was *he* given the task of repairing the ancient wooden bridge, and later of rebuilding London Bridge in stone? The records are mute.'

Three weeks later, the Poet wrote, "For answers, I am compelled to venture once more into realms of the imagination."

Three weeks after that entry, he wrote, "On the Bridge, in my scriptorium from this cupola, the highest vantage point in Nonesuch House, I will build a Bridge in words between past and present. The Bridge is, after all, a thought turned to stone."

*   *   *

Mesmerized by the bills of mortality, the Chronicler dared not set forth in search of more records and books about the Bridge.

So delving into imagination, Daryl wrote:

In the kitchen, Peter, not yet a priest, delivering bread to the Becket household from his uncle's bakery, was surprised to discover Thomas of London, sharpening a hunting spear. They recognized each other immediately. Thomas of London introduced himself as Thomas à Becket.

Peter had known by the look on Thomas's face when he gazed in his direction that Thomas had known that he admired him as a young man about town, and he imagined that that was why Thomas felt at ease asking him to lend him a hand.

"I'm meeting a man outside Aldgate. Hold our horses and stand watch, will you?"

Knowing only that and not asking to know more, Peter met him at the gate of Thomas's family property hard by Saint Mary Colechurch.

He rode double behind Thomas on a fine horse.

Thomas's friend joined them on a much finer horse.

They rode East across the town and through Aldgate and onto Windmill Hill.

"Here." Thomas handed Peter the reins of the two horses. "Sit mine, and hold his, and watch, and if anyone comes to the door, scream, 'Thief!' to disconcert him, loud enough for us, inside, to hear. See that window? Like arrows from a bow, we will shoot through the shutters and into the street, masked. Be not afraid. 'Tis your apprenticeship of sorts, my lad."

When Peter later heard moaning come from behind the shutters, he wondered, 'What trade?'

Riding back after that first adventure, which passed without his having to raise the alarm, he had questions for his mentor, such as, "Why was that woman moaning and groaning and emitting those fitful little, startled cries?"

"In time." Thomas's tone was philosophical. "In time." He smiled mysteriously.

Next time, Peter did raise the alarm. And asked more penetrating questions, in the nature of, "Why did that red-faced man going in the front door eject you and your friend out the window above?"

"When you are ready, my boy." Thomas laughed at him. "When you are ready."

He felt far from unready.

On the road, moonlight discovered to him a sword.

Thomas reached down and handed it back to Peter. "Pretend it has been to the Crusade and cherish it all your days."

To watch construction of the nave, now two years from scheduled completion, Peter returned often to Saint Paul's, where, before studying at the Abbey founded by the founder of the church in England, Augustine, in Canterbury, he had had early informal training, from learning to read and write to some scattered theology, always aware that Saint Paul's had been under construction since before his father's birth, and his own, and following his father's accidental death as stone mason there.

*   *   *

One night, Thomas stood watch with Peter while his friend swived his favorite married lady.

Riding back into the City, Peter said, "When I waited alone, I was stone bored."

"Boredom is a deadly sin. Like sloth, ennui, accidie."

"My friend Mark poses hard questions like that to me. 'Jesus is the son of David, but with what difference?'"

"From such questions, turn away for a while, until you have understood that we must perforce endure a war within: the old Pagan nature and the new Christian, which is the Holy Spirit, not a nature, as such. It is in the spirit that we 'move and have our being.'"

"Why use the word 'Spirit' instead of 'Ghost'?"

"God above, below, our ambience. The ambient Holy Spirit."

"My friend, Mark, seeks freedom from all that is not Spirit."

"Freedom from the very tongue with which he speaks of such things? Christ said, 'This is my body, this is my blood, whenever you break and eat bread or pour and drink wine, remember me.' Blood beats in the body of both the Old and the New Testament, even in the body of the Gnostics who loathed the body and all its functions and ills. Is not the body a temple, and are not temples built by bodies? No, my young friend, no, your young friend, no, cannot be free of the body, the brain that thinks, for intellect is as real as emotions, as a stiff cock. True freedom is a hovering, or quivering, on the margins of limitations."

"Thomas, please tell me, would you rather think or fuck?"

"It is my aspiration to think while fucking."

The Poet now imagined Peter and Mark studying for the priest-hood in Augustine Abbey at Canterbury.

Peter and Mark both aspired to be monks, but both finally realized that they wanted to get out into the world, "Peter to serve, Mark to observe," Peter and Mark, often said, the phrase having come up just as their adolescent rhyming mania was running its course.

The Abbot chose the name Peter as a gift commemorative of the early stages of the church. "I remind you—I'm not sure why—that Simon is the only disciple to whom Christ gave a new name, which in Greek means 'rock.' 'And I say unto thee that thou art Peter, and on this rock I will build the church; and the gates of Hades shall not pre-vail against it.' Matthew, 16:18."

*   *   *

As he was reading an ancient Chronicle, the Poet-Chronicler was delighted to come across a marginal comment, rendering his own mar-ginal transgressions not so unique. "This hand chronicling the dates has always been crabbed, some infancy deformity—not at very birth, Mother told me—so that you are reading my record only after some monk or monkish man—or woman—has deciphered and copied it over for me, you, posterity. A New King was tapped tonight—that's why I have opened my tome at this early hour. Chroniclers, I have always imagined, do it at night. I do. I am not typical of the tribe, however, for did I not speak to you in my own voice? Who I am, however, is only the Chronicler."

The Poet felt an ironic fellow feeling with that ancient, nameless Chronicler, for his own writing hand has been somewhat crippled for five years from that time he shot the Bridge, got his hand crushed between boat and pier. The hand that wrote:

In the confessional, Peter listened to the lovely voice of a woman.

"This sin you have come to me to confess is by any measure minor."

"I watched you direct work on Wolbrook Bridge, and felt drawn to you. I was thinking one day, *my* work is done. I want to watch *his* work year by year."

"And what is your work, my child?"

"Courtesan."

"Your voice has a familiar tone, and you speak to me as if you have known me."

"I confess, Father, that we have known each other, in time past, as Adam knew Eve."

'God, I must step out.' "Go in peace, child. Your sins are forgiven."

He waited for her in the shadows a few paces away from the confessional.

She looked eager to explain how she came to this obscure little church. "Thomas told me where to find you. You will not find Thomas with me in the way he once was—he and young prince Henry, who as king still visits me. But I remain interested in all three of you. Together with others, of course. Out of sheer curiosity, but not without affection."

"I have not forgotten you, Barbra. My first, my only."

"May we talk again some day?"

"I look forward to that day."

"Perhaps you will see me walking near Wolbrook Bridge and we can talk nearby."

*   *   *

One for hours, Daryl and Musetta rolled over on their backs as two.

"Imagine the irony of Peter's not knowing much about the Bridge's history. Bits and pieces, like flotsam and jetsam."

"And marmalade."

"Free though he is—was—of women."

"Your memory of Barbra is dimming?"

"Oh, yes. Thank you. I can smell her, she is so real." Daryl turned over on his belly again and rose up on his hands and knees.

* * *

"We can only imagine what the wooden Bridge was like across the Thames, which was shallower then. And imagine how gales, tempests, fires destroyed it over and over, century after century. About ten years after the crucifixion of Christ, a Bridge of Celtic workmanship is said to have been built there. Had Saint Paul in his travels reached London— and my imagination proves that he did indeed—he would have walked across this Bridge in one of its primitive avatars."

Musetta, her head still enshrouded in the dress she was pulling back on, nodded.

1162 AD. Chancellor Thomas à Becket was elected Archbishop of Canterbury.

* * *

When he began to think about this task of rebuilding the Bridge of elm, Peter said to Barbra, "You are my muse, God is my sustainer."

Out of her languor, she smiled for him. "My name is stranger. In Greek."

"Surely, it is God who saves me. . . ." Peter thought his courtesan friend had the voice of an angel.

"I wish I had sung that hymn and others to my mother, before she died. In the fire."

"Yes, you told me. More than once, poor boy. And then your father falling in the ruins of Saint Paul's. Stone mason?"

"Yes. Stone mason. During the great rebuilding."

Peter watched Barbra shift her body to a different position altogether, as she always did when shifting to a different subject. "Do you know John of Salisbury?"

"Yes, but mainly for Mark's sake. He craves conversation with that saintly man."

"Am I ever to meet this Mark fellow?"

"Living in the Word far more than the flesh, he may be tongue-tied in the presence of the flesh made word."

"I can only hope you will help me put him to the test one day."

"Function as a kind of divine pimp? A devilish prospect."

Daryl turned from Barbra of his imagination to Musetta. "Early May, watching Thomas à Becket cross the Bridge, still of wood, elm, as dubious Archbishop, remembering him whoring in lewd disport, though probably unknown except to Peter, Henry, and a favored few, then as consummate Lord Chancellor, affected Peter as an act symbolic of the progression of man from one station in life to another. Just as God saw Saint Paul in Saul the persecutor of Christians, Saint Augustine in Augustine the libertine, he saw Archbishop Thomas Becket in Thomas of London. Much to the chagrin of many, especially Becket's arch enemy, Gilbert of Foliot, once Sheriff of London, later Bishop of Hereford, a good but difficult man.

"Peter followed the procession to Westminster, where he watched the election Wednesday before Whitsun. Thomas had passed without transition from the realm of secular glory into the realm of sacred glory.

"Early September, he followed the procession to Canterbury, through the gates of the Priory, into the nave of the Cathedral, familiar site, and witnessed the consecration ceremony."

"So far, so good."

"But good enough?"

"For the nonce."

"Musetta, you are the goddess of measured tones."

1163 AD. Peter began, at age 30, rebuilding the elm version of London Bridge. Gilbert Foliot became Bishop of London.

Eager to sit Peter down with Barbra, the Poet wrote, "One of those minor private events that set major historical events into motion occurred when an ecclesiastical clerk murdered a knight. When the church exercised its lawful authority to acquit the man, Archbishop Becket approved. The King took offense, declaring such a trial to be within Royal Customs. Archbishop Becket declared the case clearly and strictly a church matter."

"I agree with Archbishop Thomas," Barbra said, "but some in the church do not. I know what his enemies do not, that his thomas is smaller than their thomases."

"We pissed on a rock once, but there was no moon." Peter turned from the past to the present. "The King is hurt to see his old friend oppose him. 'Think of hell as God's broken heart,' Henry is said to have said to Thomas."

After three more instances of Archbishop Thomas's contradicting royal will, the King, urged by others as well, summoned the bishops into council at Westminster to inform them that clerks would henceforth be punished in secular court and that bishops must support and obey his "Royal Customs."

Archbishop Becket forcefully argued that the church's power in such matters must not be diminished. Henry's solution—share power: let church judge, let state punish—seemed to many a friendly gesture. But Archbishop Becket saw it as an attack on the church, to be followed, he feared, by another and another, until Henry would, he knew, as aspirant to total power, achieve his goal, mainly for his son, Henry, heir apparent, who would be set upon by many and powerful enemies after his father's death.

"Be missionary into your own family," Archbishop Becket told King Henry.

1164, January. King Henry summoned both bishops and barons, knights, to Clarendon Castle where they were to give public assent to his list of "Customs," drawn up in constitutional form.

The many facets of this list Archbishop Thomas à Becket reduced to a bold declaration that thrilled Peter's soul, when he heard it reported, to the very quick. "I declare, by God Almighty, that no seal of mine shall ever be fixed to constitutions such as these."

"They say," said Mark, as he and Peter strolled along the west bank of River Fleet, "that his cross-bearer, Alexander Llewelyn of Wales, was even more uncompromising. The Archbishop had attempted to soften the blow to Henry with conciliatory words on minor matters. Alexander shocked his master and all his entourage by berating Archbishop Becket in stinging flourishes of rhetoric for betraying his conscience and his fame. His exact words spring readily from my tongue, to wit: 'You have left to posterity an example hateful to God and contrary to justice. You have stretched out your hands to observe impious customs and have joined with this wicked minister of Satan to the destruction of ecclesiastical liberty.' I relish his phrase-making power: 'The public power disturbs all things. The synagogue of Satan profanes the sanctuary of God.'

"The Archbishop became suddenly plain old Tom and wept.

"The Archbishop's words too I have committed to memory: 'I will sit silent in grief until the Day Star shall visit me from afar, so that I may be worthy to be absolved by God and my lord the Pope.'

"Then he went into penance, fasting, wearing rough attire—short of a hair shirt, to be sure—promising not to celebrate mass until he had removed the stain from his soul."

*   *   *

'What I wrote in the back of the Chronicle Book last night was a kind of event, a nocturnal meditation on London Bridge. Tonight, I begin nightly meditations on London Bridge. Just before I go to bed, I will enter in this diary, my own thoughts, feelings, imaginings about the Bridge. No rules. Go as you please, with or without baggage. More baggage, history, perhaps later. Gladly. Time. *Make* time. Read. Reflect. These meditations of ten minutes or so will be my own personal contributions, as a Poet, so to speak, to the history of the Bridge. My nocturnes are events. Are they Poetry? Time will tell. Or my mistress, Musetta.'

*   *   *

1168 AD. As the stain of history passed over the new Bridge, Peter's inspections revealed structural and specific weaknesses that remained untested by severe weather or fire until the night of November 2, 1168, when a fire of mysterious origin broke up two piers.

* * *

1170. Having lived and toiled self-exiled in France as a simple monk, leaving Canterbury without an Archbishop in residence and England without its Mother Church primate for six years, Becket reconciled with his friend and King in a meadow in France between Fréteval and Vievy-le-Raye—without the symbolic, almost sacramental kiss of King and Archbishop that friends of each had desired and all had hoped to witness. Tears in his eyes, Becket had started to dismount, but King Henry caught his stirrup and signaled "no" by his upraised hand.

* * *

Tuesday, December 1, 1170. Returning, now fifty years old, uneasy but determined, the Archbishop embarked from Wissant for England, disembarking at Sandwich near Dover.

In an attitude of vengeance, Archbishop Becket had sent ahead papal letters sentencing the Archbishop of York and two bishops, and rejoiced when told they had been received, quoting Psalm 58, one of David's, which ends, "He shall wash his feet in the blood of the wicked."

"After a few weeks at Canterbury, Thomas plans," Bishop Foliot, excommunicated by Thomas, absolved by the Pope, re-excommunicated by Thomas, told Peter, "to cross the new Bridge and attend Mass at Saint Mary Colechurch and visit his family in Becket Hall next door."

Having prepared the Bridge, the church, and his spirit for the coming of Archbishop Becket, Peter stood on Saint Botolph's wharf to gaze upon the Bridge. They had come a long way in the flesh and the spirit from the nights when he held Thomas's and Henry's horses and stood envious watch to this imminent occasion in the broad light of God's day.

But it came to pass that Archbishop Thomas à Becket never crossed the wooden Bridge he had, as Chancellor Becket, commanded Peter to build and that Peter had finished five years ago.

Gazing at the Bridge, Peter saw a gale start in the ribbons at the breasts of a girl who, crossing from London to Southwark, had stopped at the middle of the Bridge to gaze at the ships in the Pool.

The Poet-Chronicler, having reached the key episode in his imagined life of the master-builder of the Bridge, Peter de Colechurch, wrote as in a trance:

Early morning after Christmas, too cold, Peter awoke in his cell and got up to walk himself warm, kept walking until he was on the Bridge, stepping, sometimes leaping, over the storm-broken places, glad the sun had not yet come up, when he heard at his back galloping hooves. A unicorn, he hoped. A satyr, perhaps. He turned, saw a white horse, like a sculpture about to spring to life, then vibrantly alive, running toward him, not panicked, just running as a horse, turned loose, runs across a moor, solitary from other horses, no human rider, past him, razor close, rush of air and stinging flick of mane, its breathing as loud as its hooves, on across the Bridge, leaping over the tempest-broken places, disappearing into Southwark.

I must not doze off, lest I wake and think this beautiful horse the figment of a dream.

Spitting off the Bridge as the sun's first spark lit the river between two ships in the Pool made him feel certain he was not sleeping.

He stayed on the Bridge talking to God, Christ, and the Holy Ghost, severally, until the first Bridge crosser appeared.

After the noon meal in Saint Mary Colechurch, he felt drawn again to the river, to inspect the Bridge's defects from Old Swan Steps. Not to be distracted, he pissed where he stood, on the bank. Distracted by the movement between two shops of a woman walking on the Bridge, Peter watched for her to appear again in the other open spaces.

When the young woman appeared in full view, he realized he had been hoping she would be the girl who had appeared on the Bridge, like a vision, just before the tempest. His pissing cock leapt in his hand. Like the white horse of the morning, she seemed sculpted of stone, this moment come alive, but unlike the white horse, she moved slowly, with such grace, even as she avoided the broken places to walk the planks laid down across, she set off in his body a sense of movement confluent with hers.

'Had I not built this Bridge, I would not be watching her walking. I may never have seen her. She is here because my Bridge is here.'

As she passed the candlestick shop, one of the few shops on the Bridge not damaged, she disappeared—but not her image from his mind—then reappeared in the spaces the storm broke open between the shops, as if framed, picture after picture. When at the Southwark bridgehead she entered the crowd and disappeared, his guts felt the certainty that he would never see her again.

Refusing to let her pass out of his life, he climbed Old Swan Steps and set out across the Bridge, in pursuit of her, not as a vision of beauty held at a distance to preserve its purity—as before the gale struck—but as an angelic body he must delicately embrace. He watched her step off the Bridge into the morning crowd gathering at the markets and around Saint Mary Overies Church in Southwark.

Even deep in the crowd, she stood out.

'I am a body, wholly body, God, lusting for a young girl's body.

'No, Jesus, I am a priest lusting for a young girl, I am the body following the thought.'

For a moment, he lost her.

'A sign, Holy Ghost, to turn back?'

Guilt failed to rein him in, lust spurred him on. Then her head bobbed above the crowd in a narrow street, on a horse that he could not fully see. White. Then he saw it, not all white. White and black, mostly black. Pushing past another young girl, he smelled her. An ordinary woman smell. How would *she* smell, if he got close enough? Now *her* smell, imagined, drew him closer.

Passing out of Southwark, she entered Canterbury Road.

He turned back into Southwark and rented a horse from a stable where he was known. "I must to Canterbury on church business." The lie caught in his throat like a nostril hair, sharp.

"Yes, Father, the Archbishop is expected there from Dover."

"Yes, I must be there to greet him."

"If *I* could, I would, but the day's work keeps me rooted to this spot."

Peter followed the vision made flesh.

What's your name? He had not wondered before. Now he wanted to hear her name and to kiss the mouth that said her name and to say her name. The movement of the horse set her body swaying, her hair, her shoulders, her hips, silk on leather. Now the movement of the horse's ass, even though it was a gelding, participated in the sight that affected him, then the very lifting of its hind legs. When the horse pissed and then shat as it walked, he felt bereft of spirit, transfixed in the body.

My feet are cold, her feet are cold. My cock is on fire, her cunny is calm. If I draw up beside her, I shall be doomed. Seeing me, *she* will remain as she was, unchanged.

She never looks back. She is weaving a story of herself and her lover. No, she has been in an attitude of prayer ever since she came into view. Perhaps, she has reached that point at which she must decide whether to become a nun. Peter followed the young woman out of Southwark and through Greenwich and along the Canterbury Road for twenty miles.

Twilight, she turned her horse into the yard of a hospital for wayfarers.

Eating, drinking, shouting men, women, and a few children filled the hall, where she sat at a small table against the wall, the smoke and smell of mutton, rosemary, and ale, and sweat, and farts, made such a swarm she, sitting still, seemed animated from within, her eyes darting about the place, catching the fire and the candlelight, igniting in Peter from toe to crown, from fingertips to his guts, from tongue to nipples, from ears to nostrils, a total body resonance, existent in the instant only, without thought, hearing, vision, smell, touch acute, mouth dumb.

He sat. "There is no other place."

As she looked around, he followed her gaze to where it fell upon the two or three vacant places at tables here and there about the low-ceilinged hall. "The road to Canterbury." She seemed to think that explained the elbow-to-elbow clutter of wayfarers.

She's very hungry. He bought mutton and ale for her.

She did not look as young as she had seemed from a distance. Body of a country girl, eyes alive, a cat not quite domesticated. Her breasts heaved as she ate and when she talked, her voice was not that of an angel, nor her words, crude but not vulgar. Her odor was that of a country girl who had traveled several days. She was everything that, as a young man holding horses for Thomas Becket and Henry when he was prince only, he had wanted for his first fuck. Not that wondrous whore Barbra, but at last the body his body had yearned for.

From lust look away.

He watched her wipe grease from her mouth with the back of her sun-browned hand. "Goodnight."

She smiled and nodded.

In the room next to the hall, where travelers, male and female, slept on rushes on the floor, Peter listened to the rats and the mice, scratched where fleas and other vermin bit, unable to sleep, until he woke to her voice warm in his ear. "I am going to sleep with the animals."

He followed her. "Yes, better horses than fleas and rats."

"My feet are icy."

Kneeling upon the fetid straw, Peter blew on her feet.

She knelt and blew on his feet. "Let's fuck each other." As if that were another way, a better way, to get warm.

Fucking her, he was mindless, spiritless, wholly body.

Hooves pounding, harnesses jingling, iron clanking distracted him. As the riders drew nearer, he was about to cum and all her movements declared that she was about to cum. Trying to figure how many riders were passing, he became more mind than body, remembering rumors that some of King Henry's barons might ride from any and every direction to Canterbury to do Archbishop Becket harm. From where they lay, he looked out at the moonlight on the road.

"Who are they, God?"

Three knights shattered the stream of moonlight on the road, their armor clanking ferociously.

She did not look. "It's only the four horsemen of the apocalypse our priest is always threatening our village with. Come finish fucking."

"I must go to Canterbury." Peter slipped his cock out of her cunny and turned to his horse.

"So must I, but first, I must get my fucking."

"Forgive me. I must warn Archbishop Becket!" Peter prepared his horse for mounting.

A victim of the pain of engorged cods for the first time in a long time, he mounted his horse.

She stood up. "Father, will I go to hell for fucking a priest?"

"I don't know, my dear, but if you go, it will not be as hot for you as it will be for me." Having thanked her in French, he realized too late Saxons refuse to learn French.

He followed the three knights down the Canterbury Road, through Crayford, where they stayed the night, while he went on as far as he could.

He asked whether anyone had seen the knights pass through Gadshill. "No" meant, he prayed, that he was still ahead, so he slept outside the town in an obscure corner of the stable in an inn.

While crossing the bridge over River Medway after Rochester, where he had slept in a monastery, he learned from passersby that three royal knights had crossed earlier.

Desperate, he did not stop in Faversham, but pushed the horse in the harsh December cold until she was so exhausted he had to rest her and himself.

Crossing the bridge in Canterbury over the Great Stout River [here the Poet's imagination fell back upon his research into what "really" happened, compelling fact and fancy to move more slowly, hand in hand], his nose and lungs full of the dust of the rushes upon which he had lain, he passed through the West Gate past Holy Cross Church at four o'clock, growing dark, of the fourth day of his journey, eager to be the one who would warn the Archbishop.

As he passed Saint Peter's church and rode onto the Bridge over the little fork of the River Stout, he was aware that the villagers seemed joyous that the Archbishop had returned to them and was in their very midst.

But he heard one say, "The dog turned to his own vomit again."

He imagined more royal knights converging on the town down the roads from Whitstable and Machinton, up from Wye and Dover, and east from Sandwich. Passing East Bridge Hospital and the King's Mill, he turned north on Palace Street past All Saints' Church and then past the church of Saint Alfeah, the martyred Archbishop of nine centuries past.

He rode through the gate into the courtyard of the Great Hall of the Archbishop's palace, full of soldiers in postures of aggressive alert and, having tied his horse loosely to a mulberry tree, approached the Great Hall in darkness. Turning to see whether the men in the court-yard were stepping off to oppose him, he saw that his horse had got loose, wandering away from the tree, stroked idly by one of the men as it passed. But a trembling sense of urgency sent him through the door and into the Archbishop's Great Hall and into the Archbishop's chamber to warn Thomas, as he had many times almost two decades before when he held his horse as he and his friend the prince fucked a girl in a room above the street. But the hall was empty. The chamber was empty.

'Where is he, God?'

Shouting, crying, moaning, lamentation echoed down a passageway between the Great Cloister—soldiers were striding up and down as if about to spring like hounds—and the nave where the townspeople would be assembled for evensong services. Hoping to find the Archbishop in the chambers reached by the circular stairway, he thrust himself into the stairwell, familiar from several visits over the years. Tools of carpenters repairing the stairs lay about.

Suddenly, the stairway reverberated with the same sound, but echoing, of clashing armor he had heard on the open road.

One knight, sword drawn, descended toward him, behind that knight, three more heads encased in mailed iron. "*Reaus*! Royal knights! King's men! King's men!" A metal encased forearm pushed him aside, and a broken sword struck Peter's own forearm. Each of the others deliberately elbowed him, sharing the assault. Their mailed hauberks and helmets that covered their faces and the shadows made their armor a convulsion of clattering, clashing metal.

Four knights, God, not three. Did I follow the wrong knights?

Face to face, he recognized the bare face of Hugh de Horsea, alias Mauclerc, an unfrocked priest who was known to hold a grudge against Thomas.

'He does not know me, Lord.'

The metal clamor descending and diminishing behind him as he ascended the steep stairs, he heard lamentations in the nave and the chapels. By dim light from an unseen source, he saw blood on his arm, but felt no sharp pain, only a numb ache that the blade of the sword had raised. "*Your* blood, Thomas?"

He passed a monk reeling from a blow and, further along, a servant, moaning and muttering in French.

Peter walked rapidly along the south colonnade of the cloisters. The second door opened into the chapel of Saint Benedict, creator of Becket's order, where Becket had once seen a vision of himself crucified.

Many monks and priests and clerks filling the chapel, he hung back in the shadows behind the flung-open door.

All voices, sounds, movements seemed the issue of violence.

Up by the chapel altar, a stranger leaned against the wall, holding his arm, profusely bleeding, his face expressing jarring waves of pain. 'He seems to be looking over the heads of the others into my eyes, Lord.'

As monks in black leaned or knelt down and others rose and moved aside or hovered, Peter looked down, saw by fitful candlelight, a foot, a hand, a bloody piece of cloth, a pool of blood on the stones. Fragments of voices from men he saw only in a confusion of fragments spoke of what the four knights had done to Thomas, whose body he saw only in shifting fragmented views.

"—four knights, not five—broke in just as Archbishop Becket was climbing the short flight of stairs to pass alongside the choir to the north transept and the high altar."

"To avoid desecration to the altar, he had turned back to the chapel of Saint Benedict to hear the knights and stay them."

"Where did William of Canterbury go?"

"Where has Benedict of Peterborough hidden himself?"

"Here's Robert"—canon of Merton—"the whole time."

"But where is William fitzStephen?"

'One monk only, *you* see him, God, back here behind the door, but here, nonetheless.'

"And above all, where is good John of Salisbury?"

"After the first blow, I went to my brethren in the choir."

"—foot on Thomas's neck."

"—stamped out his brains and stomped about in his blood."

"—and cried, 'Let us away, knights. He will rise no more.' Hugh of Horsea"—'the unfrocked priest, Lord.'"

The maimed stranger must have stayed with Thomas, raised his arm to ward off a blow, perhaps the first. 'And I too late, O Lord, but just in time to take the same blade and his blood on my own self-protective arm?'

Only a few candles and lamps in Lady Chapel across the passageway from Saint Benedict chapel, Peter was aware, and the nave and the choir.

Peter watched a bloody hand pass something back to any reaching hand, saw a hand reach to take a bloody piece of cloth. And then another hand.

"—called one of them a pimp for all the whores in the king's court."

'Wait. What? They jump around in the telling.'

"—knights and soldiers out in the courtyard and the orchard."

'Yes. Listen.'

"We had to use force to get him to the safety of the Cathedral."

"—said, 'Do not bar the door of a holy place.'"

"—monks pleaded with him again to bar the door."

"The knights broke in, shouting, 'Where is the traitor? Where is the Archbishop?'"

"—came back down the steps, declared, 'I am here, and no traitor!'"

"'You will absolve the bishops you have excommunicated!'"

"He could have slipped away so easily."

'So many places to hide, Lord, in your darkening house.'

"But, no, he said, I will not."

"Again and again, he said it."

By the dim light of his imagination, Peter watched Thomas's black cloak moving among the black robes of the monks.

"That one is the only man who never left the Archbishop—a stranger."

"Edward Grim is my name, Archbishop's new clerk."

"—most of us watched from a safe distance."

"And what did we see? Very little here and there."

"But too much altogether."

"Who were those barons?"

"Thomas knew them all."

"Called one of them Reginald."

"Seemed ready and even eager for martyrdom."

"He could have moved secretly from one town to the next."

"Would he? Not he."

"A legacy of courage, thick as blood."

"He would not even let them drag him to prison, like Peter and Paul."

"We knew that once they got him away from the Cathedral, they would kill him, kill him."

"Not prison-minded, but perhaps murder-minded."

"Did you hear the monk who said he heard them demand that he repeal his sentences upon the bishops?"

"Only the Pope can do that."

"And that, they say, is what he said. 'Only the Pope can do that.'"

"It was then they threatened to kill him."

"'I am prepared to die! But you must not hurt any of my clerks or any member of my flock.'"

"That was when—"

"Yes, one of the knights swung his sword at him, knocked his cap off."

"They took hold of him by his cloak and he struggled to pull loose."

"One of the knights tried to carry him off on his back."

"'Thunderous shameful!' Thomas yelled at one of them."

"That was William de Tracy. Or the one he called Reginald."

"Reginald. Pimp, he called him."

"Shook himself free with such force the knight fell upon the stones."

"That one, Edward Grim, held onto the Archbishop so firmly, the knights could not budge him."

"More townspeople come for evensong gathered around, so they must have feared a rush to rescue."

"Ungrateful Reginald struck the first blow."

'Was that Edward Grim's voice?'

"Then each of the others struck."

"Like Christ, he bowed his head—"

"—to God's plan."

"Those strong arms held low, those strong hands together in prayer."

"I wish I had been a witness to hear his prayer."

"Hear it now, for I heard it then. 'I commend myself to God, the Blessed Mary, Saint Denis'"—'beheaded by the French nine centuries ago—' "'and the patron saints of this church.'"

"I saw one of them raise and aim his sword and I raised my arm"— Grim held his arm, his hand a tourniquet. "—and the sword came down and cut off the Archbishop's scalp and on down into my arm. To the bone, I fear."

"Struck and struck, over and over again. The light in here is too dim to see who—just four aging knights."

"Archbishop fell to his knees, saying, 'For the name of Jesus—'"

"—forward on his hands—"

"'—and the protection of the church—'"

"—face down upon the stone—"

"'I am ready to embrace death.' Yes, that familiar face against the stones."

"As he lies now."

"As he lies now."

"Too dim to see who struck the last blow—"

"I think I know."

"That blow to his head, screaming, 'This is for love of my lord William, the king's brother!' cutting the crown away from the Archbishop's poor head, and his sword, may it be damned, broke in two on the pavement."

"That's when Hugh of Horsea stepped out of the crowd and jabbed his sword into Archbishop's open skull and cast his brains about."

"Some of it here."

"And there."

"Step back!"

"Step away!"

"Mind the blood!"

"He yelled, 'Let's be off, Knights! This fellow won't get up again!'"

"Only one among us tried to shield him—a man none of us know."

"Your name is Edward Grim?"

'Archbishop's clerk Grim sprawls against the wall, in a faint, Lord, no longer strong enough to clutch his arm to stem the blood.'

"The Knights are looting and the people come behind them, looting!"

"All out but one or two to stay with the body."

"We must gather in secret to decide what to do. Follow me into the Chapter House."

Each priest and monk seemed to turn several different ways, brushing against each other, then each headed for the archway of the chapel, slowly.

As men left the chapel, reluctantly, Peter lingered, and finally ducked around a pillar and waited. 'They have left no light, Jesus.'

"I will watch for thee, Thomas."

As he watched, Peter was all the while aware that this ancient fabric within which he moved was more than one of the great Cathedrals of the Western World, more than a fabric of stone and wood and metal, but, like other Cathedrals of great magnitude, like Saint Paul's, though it was not yet complete, Canterbury Cathedral had been, since 600 or earlier, a fabric of terminology, within which a great swarm of ecclesiastical terms had been spoken or enacted thousands of times. This profanation at the altar of Saint Benedict occurred within sight or sound or keen awareness of a place of many parts that Peter held sacred—Trinity Chapel, the high altar, Saint Alphege, Saint Dunstan, North transept, South transept, the Choir, Lady Chapel, and five other chapels, the nave, cruciform, guildsmen made from floor to ceiling with piers and capitals, forming the apse above the high altar, arcades, with triforium above, clerestory, tracery, ribbed vaulting, buttresses, stained glass orifices. Tombs of Saint Dunstan and Saint Alphege. Dank undercroft, where two Saxon Archbishops, Eadsin and Ethelred, are buried. Surrounding lay the Great Cloister, Cellarer's Range, Chapter House, Great Hall, chamber, chapel, kitchens, all, all a complete design, as when engineers first conceived it, laid out in the minds of Thomas, Peter, all the ecclesiasts, and the four knights.

It cannot, cannot, must not, be said, then, merely that the assassins entered simply a place called Canterbury Cathedral. Monks and priests and Archbishops, Augustine, Anselm, Theobald, and laity had filled all these spaces often in nine centuries, and the men of this moment had abandoned all to stand in the choir or near and beside the high altar where blood was congealing and the body's blood was from within itself turning cold, where lay, askew, the cloven head, once a cathedral itself of intricate intrigue and rapturous intuitions, perhaps visions. Fabrics within fabrics, the complicated fabric of theology, and four instances of simple military fabric—intent with "noble" purpose upon slaughter—within the simple fabric of stone, wood, and iron. And there in the midst, Peter, who, original purpose a bloody failure, stood poised on the lip of impulse, rain on the roof, thunder resounding in the nave.

"'I beheld Satan as lightning fall from heaven,' so saith Luke, in the gospel." Peter spoke to Thomas, if to defy the brute fact of this death. "What commandments have we broken? Of which beatitudes have we proved unworthy? God, let Thomas speak to me, let him answer the tormenting questions. Thomas of London, you committed a multitude of sins. Did you repent? Thomas Royal Chancellor, what evil did you mingle with the good you wrought? Jesus, I fear this thunder and lightning, as both sinners and saints must have feared it when you died on the cross. Thomas Archbishop of Canterbury, your love made the poor for a time less miserable, while you wrought havoc in court and church. And yet, I held your horse and you were my sometime mentor, less by instruction than by example, in all things good and evil. Holy Ghost, does Thomas's spirit move among us and forever, or is this flesh flesh only and are these bones to be forever mute? Abba. . . ." Peter wept.

Soon, too soon, the monks returned.

Archbishop Becket rose up, no, surely, *seemed* to rise up, and bestowed upon all those in the murky light and deep in the shadows the sign of the cross, and upon himself, it seemed to those who gasped, Peter in concert with all the others.

A long pause having passed, one monk stuck his finger in the wound, another dipped a rag in it. Some monks and townspeople captured blood into vials, some stroked blood around their eyes.

Peter heard the ripping of cloth. Osbert, the Archbishop's chamberlain, seemed to be using a piece of his own shirt to tie Thomas's severed crown to his head.

Lifting Thomas's body to place it onto a bier, they uncovered a hammer and a double-headed axe.

Someone found and held up for all to see the pointed half of the Knight's broken sword.

"We are obliged to keep this as a relic for the shrine."

"Let us carry the body on the Cathedral bier out of the chapel and along the choir, the way Thomas had been walking when the knights broke in."

Seeking the shadows, Peter, failed messenger, followed.

The clerks, monks, and servants were re-assembling, the townsfolk were crowding into the nave.

"That man charged that I was illegal prior of Christ Church. Beckoned the Prior of Dover and the Abbot of Boxley to deal with me. Thomas Becket will not replace me now. Odo. May your last thought be of me. Odo, Prior of Canterbury."

"When he was royal chancellor, he was positioned well in time to dispossess us of much of what we own."

'Yes, God, that was a fear many harbored.'

"Declared we are too fearful to challenge the king. Yes."

"The city is occupied by soldiers. How can we resist?"

"He demanded too much of mere monks."

"Did not the knights call him a traitor to the king and to the kingdom?"

"Thomas and his clerks are not liked in Canterbury."

"Some say, some say."

'They were so long without a leader, Jesus, without unity, spiritless. And now this uncertain future.'

"Only fifty years old."

"Becket wanted the power of a king. Becket wanted to be more than a king. Let Becket be a king now."

'Some onlookers are saying negative things now, Jesus.' Peter began to pay attention to the tone and qualities of the voices.

"His stubbornness killed him." 'That hoarse voice.'

"Thomas was vindictive." 'Hissing high-pitched voice.'

"Scornfully proud."

"Greedy for glory. Glory, glory, glory." 'Like a duet, hoarse and high-pitched.'

'Yes, God, I must concur.'

"He disturbed the very life of the monastery."

"—rampant disorder."

"Stagnation."

Peter looked toward the high altar. Thomas's body lay on the bier before it, a bandage tying his crown to his head, a little cap covering it. On his face, in the flickering candlelight, only a trace of blood from his right temple, across his nose, down his left cheek.

He watched them strip the bloody outer garments from Thomas's body and set them aside. 'For the poor, Lord, as when noblemen are beheaded in London.'

The monks in unison uttered a sound of awe.

"Look, he's a true monk!"

Moving closer, risking discovery, Peter just barely saw that Thomas wore a monastic cowl and shirt.

Peter recognized Robert of Merton kneeling and delving into Thomas's undergarments. "He is wearing a hair shirt and breeches! He has been a monk in secret all along, one of us!"

"Look!"

Peter saw without looking that lice and worms swarmed in the hair shirt and breeches. Penitent like a common monk.

"Astonishing!"

"No one could have known about this."

"Let it be known that he has been a true monk all along."

"No furs of gris and vair—"

"—and no garments of rich samite and silk!" The hoarse high-pitched duet again.

"Sop up the rest of his blood! Wring the blood from his clothes and from the cloths you have used to soak up his blood."

"We do not have time to observe ritual, to wash and embalm the body."

"The body of the Archbishop Thomas à Becket of Canterbury," whispered Peter, "has been anointed in his own blood, Jesus."

"Rush to his trunks, bring out the vestments he has already designated for this moment. You will find the very garments in which he was ordained eight years ago, the alb, the superhumeral, mitre, stole, maniple, and the charismatic that caught the sacred oil at his anointing, a comfort to know, and a comfort to see them all again upon his body."

"Yes, we must bury him before day breaks."

'This raucous thunder and rain stirs up their fear again, God.'

"The knights may return with more soldiers."

"They will seize the body."

"They will drag it in the mud through the town tied to the tail of one of their war horses."

"They will hang his mutilated body from a tree limb."

"Toss it on to a shit hill."

'That single-minded duet again.'

"Chop it up—"

"—throw it to the hogs."

"Because the church has been polluted with murderous violence and blood—" 'the voice of Richard of Dover, Thomas's friend who had traveled with him recently, assumes leadership—' "we cannot give him a funeral Mass, we cannot give his flock the comfort of a service."

Watching, listening, aware that in their confusion, the priests had neglected to post a guard. Peter hoped for his opportunity. 'To do what, Jesus?'

"Down in the crypt, Richard, there happens to be a sunken marble sarcophagus previously prepared for a burial."

"Archbishop ordered it several days ago, as if with foreknowledge." 'Who is that chiming in?'

"Let us bury him beneath the Trinity Chapel where he so often prayed—" 'that's Richard again—' "behind the High Altar, at the end of the crypt. He will have the altar of Saint John the Baptist on his left, and on his right, he will have the altar of Augustine of Canterbury."

"Let us go down and look."

"Yes, but quickly."

All gone below now, Peter stepped briskly to the bier, lifted Thomas's body, naked except for the vermin-swarming hair shirt and hair drawers, onto his shoulder and turned with a rasp that sounded to him very keen and loud, and ran, crouched, out of the faint candlelight, into the shadows, into the total dark, back the way they had brought the body, past the blood-smeared site of the murder, and down the narrow, steep staircase, where the Knight had struck him with the broken blade, making his shoulder scrape the stone wall to guide him down in the dark, three times almost falling, falling off the bottom step. Rising, he struggled to take hold of the body. "Lord, may it be thy will that my horse will have returned to the mulberry tree and tarried there."

The Poet-Chronicler, writing at his work table high in Nonesuch House, surrounded by the biographies of Becket by John of Salisbury, Edward Grim, William fitzStephen, and Benedict of Peterborough, who witnessed the murder, and his friend, John of Salisbury, William of Canterbury, Herbert Bosham, Alan of Tewkesbury, Anonymous I and II, and the Icelandic Thomas Saga, among several others, most written within a decade of the murder (another rumored to have been written by a woman), suddenly smelled the blood of a woman with the curse, and the next moment heard and felt hot breath panting on his neck and turned and looked up into the face of that girl, Blythe Arden.

"You put a fright on me, child. The shop is closed, given the plague."

"I've come with a message from a lady of Southwark."

"And also from hell, a touch of the plague?"

"That's me monthly. On days when I'm not cursed, I carry on me the bloom and aroma of heath flowers."

"Old enough to bleed, too young to—I'll have the message, child, hoping it has not picked up plague."

"She does not write to you, sir. 'Tis a mouth-to-mouth message."

"Then spit it out and be gone with you. You've broken into my workroom as well as my shop and my domicile."

"I've never been in Nonesuch House, nor this high above the world before. Look at the Pool from here, the great ships all assembled."

"May I know the lady's message?"

"It makes no sense."

"I will be the judge of that. If you ever speak it."

"Oh, I will, I will, I promise."

He watched her circumnavigate the room, touching everything within reach. "Don't touch."

"They all say plague's in the air, not on our fingertips."

"Have you not touched your lips?"

"Aye, and many others besides."

In a rush, he intuited many hands up under her dress and blushed. "You must not—"

"'Must not?' I like not 'must not.'"

"Must I wring your neck to get you to squawk my message out?"

"Though it makes no sense, I am here to transmit it. It is simply this: 'I cannot raise the drawbridge until the plague has passed.' Did I not tell you, it makes no sense?"

"You did indeed, child. Now go home."

"Why?"

"You should be abed at this hour. Your parents."

"Listen! You can hear them snore from the London end of the Bridge."

"So you have sneaked out to explore the world."

"First London, and then the world. I shall hide in the hold of a great ship one night and step ashore in the Orient."

He looked into her eyes and nodded. "I have only to shut my eyes."

"I crave also to touch every *thing* in the world—and every one."

"Will your friend go with you?"

"Oh, yes, as far as the staples at each end of the Bridge. Only so far will she stray from her parents."

"Unless you can prevail? I see it in your eyes."

"Gilda sees something in my eyes that gives her pause."

"A good long pause might save your own life, child."

"Say you 'child' to put me off or to lure me in?"

She spoke, he sensed, from experiences he dare not imagine—not while she was still in the room.

"You must sneak back into your bed now. And wake in the morning resolved not to venture into London until the plague has passed."

"I know how to get in."

"Don't tell me you broke my window."

"Glaziers need work these days."

He gave her money. "Go."

"I've seen you watching us. Why do their looks linger longer upon Gilda than upon me?"

"They? Men? *I* do not watch you."

"I look up and there you are at your window."

"I am thinking."

"Say it."

"No, I am thinking of the next line perhaps. I am a poet."

"What did she mean, 'I cannot raise the drawbridge?' It has been broken since before I was born."

He was certain she knew exactly the meaning of the riddle. "Go. Go."

"You are the least friendly man I have met in the whole world."

He left his work table where his writing lay, in the company of Becket's biographers, and walked to the door of the scriptorium, beckoning her to follow. He opened the door, wide. She stood so close to him in the doorway that he smelled the bad blood again.

"Be careful going down. The stairway is dark. Feel your way down along the wall."

"You provide no candle to light my way?"

"You are a bloody nuisance, child." Both the message and the messenger were severe interruptions to the Poet-Chronicler's effort to imagine and express Peter's own thoughts and actions in Canterbury Cathedral. He jerked the candle off the table so quickly, the flame sputtered out. Suddenly, the blood was upon him again, the stink so rank he tasted it faintly upon the tip of his tongue. He pushed her body aside and fled down the steps in the dark, feeling Peter brush past him going up the stairs to warn Archbishop Becket.

Somewhere near the second landing, he fumbled in his pocket for a match and reached for the tinderbox and lit the candle, saw sprinkles of blood going up—or down?—the stairs and felt his cock springing hard against the fabric of his trousers, crying to get out. The drawbridge is raised, a strangled laugh, as he heard her above, coming down. He whirled and continued down, to reach the door before she could breathe upon his neck again.

Panting, she staggered down and across the bookshop into the circle of the candlelight where he stood at the open door. Like an obedient child she passed him, then from the street, the face that looked back at him over her shoulder was that of a wanton woman.

Not looking, but knowing the trail of blood was beneath his feet, he climbed the stairs, doubting but with no certainty, that his mistress had entrusted that message, however seemingly senseless, or any other, to such a creature. Peter brushed past him going down the circular stairs, Becket's body his burden.

As Peter staggered out of the Great Hall, the echoes of cries of shock and consternation drifted from the altar down the stairs behind him.

His hired horse was gone, but a soldier had tied his own horse, unattended, to the mulberry tree. Peter placed Thomas's body across the horse's neck and mounted behind it and rode out of the courtyard and through the town gate.

The moon was clouded over, but he was able to keep to the street until he could conceal the body and himself and his stolen horse under the Bridge over the little fork of River Stout. Then he rode all night and hid himself and the body all day in a shaw full of thorns and dead branches and rode all night again, back through all the towns.

In Rochester, he was seen, and he was believed, when he said, "A monk of my monastery in London, to be buried at Saint Paul's."

Fleeing with Thomas's body, Peter imagined the search for the body throughout the fabric of Canterbury Cathedral.

'Why did I take up the body, Holy Ghost?' As he rode, Peter settled into a sense of God's purpose for his impulsive action, to prevent the Barons who were very likely to return from mutilating, desecrating the body of a man in whom good and bad faith were divinely mixed.

When at last he rode past the hospital when he had spent the first night in pursuit of the girl, he saw her in a sort of delirium of fatigue, grown even older, haggard now, rush into the road, her dress up over her face, naked, in "lewd disport," a phrase he heard in his head, and rode on until, just before God's light, he was approaching the Bridge he had built of elm across River Thames, the Bridge he had been preparing for the ceremony of Archbishop Thomas à Becket's triumphal entry into the city of his nativity. Midway, he reined in the horse and said, not to the body slung across the horse's neck, but to Thomas's spirit, "I will build a chapel on this bridge in your honor, Thomas, and devise a way some day to bury your body there." His own voice woke him to the stench of the body.

A chapel on the Bridge. Yes. But, God, do you want me to name it in honor of Thomas?

He had stolen the body in a state of revulsion at the prospect of its desecration, every piece of clothing to the last thread, every drop of blood, piece of flesh, and every bone down to the little finger's three separated joints, from his enemies trying to humiliate his remains and eliminate all trace of his existence on earth to prevent him from becoming a saint.

Peter spurred the military horse on, simultaneously imagining places where in London he might conceal the body—under the Bridge, in Saint Paul's, in the house of Barbra the courtesan—and having a vision of Thomas's chapel, taking shape in his head, blinding him to the sight of London that finally stretched before him as he rode over the broken Bridge.

In the night, Peter dug a narrow grave in Saint Mary Colechurch's little bone yard, between his father and his mother, interring Thomas lying on his left side, aware every minute and with every exertion of Thomas à Becket's nativity, of the wall under the stairs that Thomas's parents, fearing the frail infant might die before daybreak, had climbed to take him into the church to be baptized only hours after his difficult birth. I will move him, Holy Spirit, at another time. To where? Under the weight of the question, he sank into sleep.

*   *   *

Night Meditation
Pervading the lives of Bridge dwellers is their sense of being
under water, waking to reflections of River Thames
through wavy imperfections in window glass
upon the floors, walls, ceilings—and all day
in the shops—and in twilight up stairs in the domicile.
It is almost always at night
that I meditate on the Bridge, breathing
the mingling airs of city and river.
The Bridge is then for me an experience of night.
Does darkness pervade these pages thus far? I inhabit
my subject as sleep inhabits mind, lung, and blood.
                                        Daryl Braintree

*   *   *

The Poet-Chronicler felt the key episode in his factual, imagined life of Peter de Colechurch needed an added touch. Peter's friend Mark would provide it: "They let the body lie where it fell, before the High Altar, and buried it in the crypt beneath on the next morning."

"Your news is as fresh as the dew on this stone."

"I was there, in the vicinity, though too late to see with my own eyes."

"Not that you doubted?"

"Doubted what?"

"That the body—No, why should—?"

"Why should I, indeed?"

"The four knights crossed the Channel from Normandy in separate ships, landed at Sandwich, above Dover, maybe a few at Dover itself, rendezvoused at Saltwood Castle, near Hythe, below Dover, then took the road north, I suppose, to Canterbury from Wye or from Dover. Four first interrogated him in his palace, then one stood guard, while the others executed their mission. Stories contradict, human nature being what it insists upon being, but all strike this one note in concert: that Thomas made no effort to avoid seeing the knights and later to flee from them, and made a great effort to offend and incite the knights and then, when attacked, made no effort to defend himself."

"To fulfill the prophecies, Christ had to nurse events along by provoking the priests, declining to answer Pilate. That is only one possibility, that Thomas followed Christ."

"It will all come out in time."

"Meanwhile, I must direct repairs upon the Bridge."

Over several months, Mark amended his report several times, one version of the supposed facts being that the body was discovered missing. "Thus, they knowingly buried in Canterbury Cathedral a false Archbishop."

Peter's imagination, as the Poet-Chronicler imagined it, anticipated each weaving and unweaving of the legend as it came from Mark's gap-toothed mouth.

*　　*　　*

It is a matter of historical record, which, I must confess, has been lost to posterity, that two monks, having discovered the body missing, conspired to place another body in the crypt, its face and scalp disfigured a little more than Thomas's had been, then later on, one felt obliged to kill the other, a known gossip, leaving the secret safe with the other monk until he died of the plague in the course of his penitential wanderings disguised as a goliard.

7

LUCIEN COMES ONTO MORGAN'S SHIP

As the Poet-Chronicler imagined Peter de Colechurch building London Bridge, Morgan, a son of the Bridge, continued recording his memories in the margins of his books.

At first, Morgan took little notice of two of the three men the Captain had hired in Surinam to replace men who perished in a typhoon, but the third stepped up to the door of the cabin as sudden as the shadow of a seabird swooping across the deck. He gave out his name as Lucien, which seemed to explain the strange aura Morgan felt, more than saw, about the man.

Tall and sinewy, he was so thin that, standing sideways in a certain light, he seemed to be there and not there. His eyes cobalt blue and cold as the air just before a typhoon became soft when his sad mouth reshaped into a saintly smile.

In Morgan's first steady look at the man—from which the man did not flinch—it seemed that he had come somehow to the rescue, to take him home before he had served out his father's debt.

On deck, as if etching his portrait in stone, Lucien seemed to limn Morgan from crown to foot. The look, when Lucien turned away with the rope he had given into his hands, seemed to take Morgan away, leaving only something suspended in the space between him and that tall, reed-like back.

The hammock above Morgan's, that the typhoon last week had emptied, Lucien now filled, at length. Swaying in perfect rhythm with the ship's response to the agitation of the waves that made Morgan stagger, Lucien had tightened the thongs to the iron ring in the bulkhead, making a canvas drum of the hammock. Morgan looked up, before the lamp was snuffed, at little sag.

The voice, neither fetched from a depth of chest nor pitched high in the nose, was thin as a taut wire and sent out as its basic timbre a tremulousness that created a zone inclusive of Morgan himself.

"You may call me Lucien."

"Lucien is a French name, but you are English."

"It means light, as does Lucifer."

"So does Luke. May I call you Luke?"

"If I may call you Morg."

"But that is the opposite of my name, which means Sea-dweller. Morg makes me a small farm."

"Tell me, little brother, who you be and from whence you come to be here?"

"This is my story." Morgan told him a brief version of his short life. ". . . And so my father went hunting for shop space. When one searches for a shop on London Bridge, one always also finds a house. Everything is 'at the sign of'—one enters under a *sign* into a cool, dim cave, a shop. The salt merchant, five doors south of our stationer's shop, keeps a parrot that repeats 'my fair lady,' a voice so strident it carries across oceans into my dreams and nightmares."

*   *   *

'I imagine stars seen from the rumored skylight of Nonesuch House mid-Bridge. I do remember the look across the roadway of a shop and house half-finished between older shops and houses, stars between.

'I feel the roadway underfoot now, foot shod—barefoot before.'

* * *

Fort Saint George on the Coromandel coast in the Bay of Bengal.

"We are privileged, living on the Bridge, not in the City," Morgan whispered to Lucien, in the dark of others' sleeping. "We do all the things of daily living that others the world over do, but for us, those things are different, however intent we are, oblivious—even so, it always brings us back to it—the smells and noises, the tingle in the soles of our feet, walking on the Bridge, that's always a sort of trembling."

* * *

Indian Ocean, en route to Malacca.

After several days of a silence like an unbroken dialogue, Lucien spoke, drawing Morgan back from the verge of sleep. "I want to hear you tell again about this Bridge you lived on and that you're going home to, this Nosuch House, little brother. Me, if I ever go back, it will be to the self-same pile of cow shit I left behind and sour apple trees. Even my name—Radford—I pissed into the ground, turned my back on it, and walked and sailed away from it as Lucien."

1666, Java Sea, approaching Sundra Strait and port of Batavia.

Lucien listening, Morgan described the Bridge down to the last nail and block of stone.

"When my father pointed out the window one day—when we were still newcomers to the Bridge—toward a warehouse, he said, 'Look. There's where the builder of our Bridge—Peter de Colechurch—is buried,' I thought it strange that a person could be buried on a Bridge, a priest under a warehouse. I did not know then that to live and conduct one's business on a Bridge, among many others, was indeed unique in human history. Sometime later I got it fixed in my head that others, too, were buried there, as in any cemetery, and that when I died of old age, I too would be buried on the Bridge. But now I know that Peter de Colechurch—who folks say never lived as we do on his Bridge, never even said Mass in the chapel he designed, for neither Bridge nor chapel was finished when he died—is unique in his own way. He is the *only* person buried on the Bridge—in the undercroft of the old Saint Thomas Chapel, a warehouse, since Henry VIII did what he did."

"Does Thomas à Becket not then watch over it?"

"He is our Christian guardian."

"Yes, of course, but you do know, do you not, that only the sacrifice of a female virgin child can appease whatever pagan gods still exert influence over the fate of Bridges everywhere on earth? It is in the song, so it can't be false."

"I cannot believe that."

"Then am I to imagine that you cannot believe that when you walked on the Bridge and that at this very moment the bones of a girl child tremble all day and all night long as people, horses, wagons cross the Bridge and tides assault it as they have for over four centuries?"

"You tease me."

"Perhaps so, but that is part of your memory of the Bridge *now,* isn't it?"

Three or four days later, Morgan's silent answer, "Yes," had sunk in.

Wondering where Lucien had come across that dark knowledge, Morgan supposed one of his voyages had taken him to an exotic country where the primitive ritual was still practiced. But why had he retained such knowledge and why had he passed it on to Morgan, perhaps alone of all the men on the Rocket?

'I am, after all, still but a child.'

1666, South China Sea, en route to Zeelandia.

"Gaze upon the exquisite gardens on London Bridge. Wild flowers and flowering weeds carried by winds and birds to dirt-filled cracks and crannies. They are the smallest but most decorative in the world. Sometimes a stray flower or a weed in sudden bloom inspires the householder to create around it a flowering gesture only the gardener and God can see."

"Trees?"

"Small ones, unreachable, growing up out of a pier or out of a star-ling, or window frame of a derelict house, or up out of a roof, attracting crows, ravens, doves."

East China Sea, destination undeclared.

Morgan's nocturnal reverie often stirred him to bring Lucien into the flow of his memory. "Another neighbor keeps a large, live camel in his house on the Bridge. And other exotic animals transported from faraway places live on the Bridge. A child's cargo for delight.

"And exotic folk appeared on the Bridge. Gypsies. Jews. Ethiopes. Pirates. Even Dutchmen. Even Erasmus and the Duke of Saxe-Weimar. Londoners returning from America with painted savages in costume. Sailors from the four corners of the world anchor in the pool and come ashore in wherries. Speaking in foreign tongues, travelers from all over the civilized world walk onto the Bridge. In only the short time I lived there, I saw many. I heard what they said, looking up and down and about, but understood nothing, except the amazement in their eyes and awe in their open mouths. They walked haltingly along the street of this town on a Bridge, as if deep in awe, taking possession, for telling tales back in their country, for memory in old age, I must imagine."

In port, Nagasaki.

"Sometimes, but rarely, a hay barge would shoot the Bridge and I smelled the hay as it shot out from under my window, and all the coun-tryside flooded my bedchamber.

"The wherries carried people back and forth, and barges, plain or ornate, carried carriages and horses that did not want to brave Bridge traffic.

"My father told tales of the picturesque Frost Fair on River Thames when it froze over—sledding, ox roasting, football playing and nine-pins, double lines of shop tents mimicking London Bridge, even a booth for printing folks' names on broadsides—so painters left canvasses."

* * *

"How do we appear to people who are standing on the stairs at the water's edge," said the Poet to his mistress, "looking over at us? From the ends of streets at the river? From windows opening onto the river?"

Musetta sighed, crossing her naked legs. "Makes you wonder, doesn't it?"

After his mistress had gone home, the Poet, wishing she were as much a muse as amusing, turned to poetry, as Morgan turned to Lucien.

Questions at Random

I often question the Bridge. Not really
an interrogation. Random questions, arising
in broad daylight or in night
reveries or dreams or daybreak reveries.
On moonlit nights. Life's questions,
sometimes. But mostly logical questions.
Man may live by questions and bread alone.
Bridges make twin cities seldom. Folks
go through Southwark to reach the Bridge foot
so that they may cross over into London.
Why do so few bridges, in all history, connect
two about equally large and powerful cities, even
from country to country or province, or parish?

Daryl Braintree

*   *   *

Approaching the Cape of Good Hope.
In the margins of Martin Luther's *On the Babylonian Captivity of the Church*, in need of some privacy of memory, and feeling that he talked about the Bridge too often to Lucien.

This is one Bridge you cannot glide under—as on Venice's tranquil canals—and gaze above at the light playing over the mossy, moist underbelly of the roadway.

In the Atlantic Ocean, bound for Lisbon.

Morgan adopted a tone meant to beguile Lucien. "On the Bridge you *see* and feel weather wonderfully. Blows, bluster, fog, twilight smoky, gales, ice, damp, chill, wind. In heat, odors and wafting air conspire. On cold days, simmering stew borne on the air. Balmy breezes. Mold. Mildew. Floods. Hail. Sleep. Mist. Fine Rain. Gentle rain.

"At sea, constantly aware of weather, moving into it, away from it— sensitive to it, expecting it, fearful, apprehensive. Grateful. Hurt. Rheumatism. Old wounds and fractures.

"And all my senses are always over-activated. I must suppress them at times—other times I leave myself open to every source. A great stink, of course, most of the time, but as the weather plays upon it, the Bridge gives vent to an oriental bazaar of stinks and aromas.

"Rain drove us off the Bridge or bunched us up under the hautepas that extend from house to house over the roadway, or under the Great Stone Gate, where sometimes thirty severed heads above look down from pikes. Caught in the first dash of rain on the span opened up to the air by fire at the north, London end, you have to run for it, home inside London, or back where you started from in your shop and house on the Bridge, or if it was not too cold-wet, back to Southwark. Rain sluiced down the back of your neck from the roof or leapt up at your ankles from puddles or gutters. But watching one curtain of rain blow toward the window from the West, followed by another behind was lovely—even when, coming in out of the rain storm, you stood dripping on the Persian carpet."

Lucien listening, Morgan became aware, drew out of him more poetic details and descriptions than when he only wrote in his journal.

In the Atlantic Ocean, en route to Lisbon.

"Lovers carved their names, enemies carved their threats, idlers carved chaotic gashes in the wood on the Bridge, on the substructure, the superstructure, and inside the gateway. I love Dilsey till the Day I Die, Bill. Death to Toby Siler. Some were hieroglyphs—neither Greek nor Cantonese nor Russian, but just as strange to the eyes that scrutinized them. Runic, some were. Others obscene—'fucked her *here.*' Braggarts and liars. Sometimes, over the centuries, turners of phrases, such as the young man who lived in Nonesuch House, as if they were poets."

*   *   *

"The flow of commerce from ships like ours on the river rises up to the Bridge and flows across it. A spectacle. Cargoes crossing: grains, meat, fruits, vegetables. In every street, carts and coaches make such a thundering you wonder if the world runs upon wheels.

"Threefold worse noise on the tunnel-like Bridge. I hear even now the waterwheels and the mill wheels and the river roaring, but not like the sea that we hear now just on the other side of this bulkhead."

*   *   *

En route to Calcutta.

"Nowhere else in the world are houses and shops so tight and people nowhere else move within such small compasses, though quite contentedly.

"As you enter, your blood starts pumping a little faster. It's never really routine. Even out of a market throng, headed for the Bridge, you feel the blood pressure rise. All that sprawling market activity becomes funneled, tunneled."

*   *   *

Approaching Calcutta.

In the margin of John of Salisbury's *Vita S. Thomae.*

Wrote nothing last night, *but* devoted an hour or so in the crow's nest telling Lucien all about the Bridge—in my head.

*   *   *

In Calcutta, a new, young seaman came aboard. "I bring you word of plague in Amsterdam, likely to spread to London in ship rats. My own ship brought it in, I surmised, and deserted, and shipped out again from London Pool and shipwreck put me ashore here."

Someone threw the young seaman overboard.

*   *   *

"I am listening."

"The light. No light like the light that laves or strikes the Bridge. Dawn, noon, twilight, moonlight, starlight, even wavering torchlight, as when light originates on the Bridge itself, within doors, showing itself at windows and throws itself out upon the water and over thresholds onto the roadway. Slanting light from above, or at narrow breaks West and East where houses do not quite lean against each other, and at the square, the drawbridge pier. Morning light of the night watchman, torchlight fixed above the gate, colored light that has fallen through stained glass, light flashing from water upon windowpanes. Light reflected in eyes, aslant a cheek, light cupped in the mouths of shouting watermen in their wherries. Dappled light rests my soul. I seek it. It laves me."

"One day, I will walk in that light."

Morgan could not decipher Lucien's strange tone.

8

VOICES IN THE GREAT PLAGUE
OF LONDON

In advanced old age, the still-unpublished Poet returned to his erratic research and personal impressions to write, as Chronicler bedeviled by Poet, a bizarre account of the plague and the fire and of some meetings of the Brotherhood of the Bridge.

Still living in Nonesuch House on the bridge, the money his missing father left behind dwindling, he was forced to sell some of the shop's rare books, one by one, divide the shop to rent, and to fill the many rooms with lodgers, transient and long-staying. Like the Poet, Nonesuch was falling into dilapidation.

He never stopped hoping for his father's return, never stopped searching for Musetta, long missing.

Plagued with skull-shattering headaches from a blow fishmonger Kerry Brooke inflicted in a nocturnal attack that left Brooke dead, the Poet, his vision blurred, gathered fragments of the events of the plague and the fire from faulty memory, imagination, dreams, and from actual oral and published accounts. Writing his own accounts, he adeptly secured, by fair means and foul, access to accounts not yet published.

To create "an echo chamber of communal voices," a phrase he often repeated, meshing fact and imagination, he sometimes accidentally, often deliberately, put into the mouths of merchants and anonymous bridge dwellers, Londoners, and Southwarkians some published and unpublished phrases and sentences, especially those of Samuel Pepys, John Evelyn, Nathaniel Hodges, William Boghurst, William Sancroft, Symon Patrick, John Graunt, W. Sandys, the Earl of Clarendon, Daniel Defoe, and official documents and newspaper accounts. One voice on record inspirited another of imagination.

His love of the facts and of the words of writers of his time enthralled his imagination. Hearing their words and sentences coming out of the mouths of other people, mingled with their own words, so delighted him that he could not resist the compulsion to weave them into his accounts. He so loved the very thumping sound of his father's friend Pepys's account, for instance, that he sometimes quoted him directly but sometimes put his words into the mouths of other people he knew and the people he imagined as if the words were their own. Listening to voices so commingled and imagining those voices speaking to the thousands of readers of his deliberately strange account not only delighted but often thrilled him. That this mad "method" was, he assumed, unique among poets and Chroniclers gave him a sustained perverse pleasure.

Referring to himself in the third person, here is what the Poet-Chronicler wrote:

Brothers and sisters in Christ had called on God to destroy each other in a long civil war over disputes centered upon sacraments. Common belief is that the victors, first the Puritans and then the Royalists, had purged the vanquished of their respective impurities. And now in Restoration London in April of 1665, the cry again was that London had made a great turning to sin, and the body of Christ had grown thin, almost emaciated. God's punishing voice spoke at first in a whisper so faint, few beyond two families in Drury Lane heard and took heed: "Two dead of plague."

Within memory of Londoners, only a few yet lived to remember the plague of 1603, the year Queen Elizabeth died a more ordinary death, while Thomas Dekker recorded in *The Wonderful Year* that 33,347 perished, but many more survived to remember the scourge of 1625, when 41,313 perished, and the Long Plague of 1640–1647, when 14,420 were enlisted in the naked legions of plague dead, inspiring some folks to imagine London to be a vast bone yard on top of the buried Roman London.

In April 1665, God raised His Voice to an audible whisper, but still no one on London Bridge, the only bridge over River Thames in London, heard it above cries of vendors, rattle of iron wheels on stone, mill wheels and waterwheels under the bridgeheads, hammers of craftsmen, shouts of the tides through the arches, laughter and singing of children at play, myriad voices along the Bridge roadway and inside the shops and up inside the three- or four-storey domestic rooms, not even when God cleared his throat and uttered a shouting whisper: "Look upon these ten dead gathered Without the Gates this morning in the Liberties."

'We fear. Sometimes "terror" is the word—when we feel in our bones transgression. Oh, it's the usual array of superstitions that afflicts all England and Europe. Bridges bring it all out and add more. Bridge superstitions give us distinction compared with Londoners in the Liberties and Within the Gates.

'Alleys conjure, too, I suppose. But the majesty innate in bridges endows bridge superstitions with greater visibility and force. I live on the Bridge and in my imagination simultaneously, but not enough on the Bridge to remember readily a single superstition. So I must, I will, when I can, turn to resources.'

1665, June 13. A Day of Victory over the Dutch Fleet at Lowestoft. Reports of plague in Drury Lane environs continue.

Conditions were conducive. After the black frost of winter, summer was a baker's oven, flies blackening walls, ants swarming over the roads, frogs overpopulating ditches. The worst winter, the worst summer— then plague—then River Thames frozen—then another summer of roasting misery—then fire inevitably to come again. Signs, paramount being the blazing comet that appeared for several months, foretold.

*   *   *

A voice. "Only one pest-house, built to serve 500, tries to deal with the swarm of 10,000."

Imposthumes, abscesses seen for centuries on the bodies were not in dark centuries earlier suspected as signs of plague, but in time, became alarmingly suspicious.

The violent infusion of the distemper was invisible to all, but the effects were everywhere visible, when not concealed behind doors marked with a quick down and cross slash of red.

A voice. "Too few remain now untainted to tend to the sick or to bury the neglected sick."

But three men dug a pit, and looked at it. The hole exposed the philosopher in one of the diggers. "This pit is a gulf between our life yesterday morning and our life tomorrow morning."

The reach of the "communication" did not reach London Bridge.

Warnings went out that to regard the plague as gone entirely is almost as deadly as to be infected, but the authorities might as well have talked to the still-infected air itself.

*   *   *

Gilda, ignorant of the Celtic origin of her name, "servant of God," heard the gentle voice of Christ each night respond to her prayers of thanksgiving.

One morning, on the stair, she overheard her father's deep voice in the shop below whispering to her mother, "Oh, my dear, London's hour of retribution has come at last. Word has come onto the Bridge— Twenty dead Within the Gates." God's own anger, stirring like turbulent water in father's voice, made Gilda tremble.

That her father, Clarke Shadwell, shoemaker, whose voice usually filled the shop with good cheer or friendly disputation, had whispered for her sake, made her feel his protection, in league with her mother. Unlike some of her friends, she never had to turn from mistreatment by her father or her mother to comfort in Christ. She descended slowly, into an image of mother and father holding hands, en-ringing her in light, the evils and calamities of the world ashore inside London and Southwark receding into the shadows.

Blythe Archer, always delighted to know the ambiguously ironic root meaning of her name, "the joyous one," stood already in the open doorway, holding her hand out to Gilda, her eyes aglow with the day's promise, her body vibrant in arrested motion.

Kissing her father and then her mother, Gilda ran to Blythe, eagerly reaching out to take her hand. "To London or to Southwark?" Blythe asked her, their arms around each other's shoulders, hips bumping, turning this way, that way, eager with one accord to plunge either way.

"You say."

"I say Southwark. No, I say London. You say."

"I am content either way."

"Then—" Blythe propelled both their bodies North toward London, away from Gilda's house on Pedler's Lock east, but on the fifth step whirled them around, hair flying, toward the Southwark end, and many whose eyes fell upon the roadway were glad to see those two girls pass.

Two carts colliding forced a pause in their exhilarated plunge into the new day, Gilda patient, interested in the mechanics of this familiar event on the Bridge, Blythe still in motion, running in place.

Passing Nonesuch House, Blythe looked up. Following her gaze, Gilda saw the poet Blythe had pointed out at his window weeks before.

Darting into Bear Tavern, Gilda indulged Blythe in her ritual announcement, "We're looking for our husbands!" The known and unknown faces turned to them where they stood entwined on the threshold.

"We're only just looking!" Gilda revised, ducking out of Blythe's tight embrace, turning with a giggle to return to the roadway, stepping back a moment to avoid a careening wagon and the showering spittle of the drover's curse.

They waved to folks entering and leaving Bear Tavern. The girls' last stop was the staples. "Here the Mayor endeth and the King beginneth!" Both having ritualistically touched the two staples, Gilda the one on the East side, Blythe the one on the West side, connected by a chain at the bridge-foot when conditions required, Gilda played her role, stopped suddenly, leaned forward, her arms rolling in a circular motion, as if she stood on the edge of a Dover cliff, seen only in etchings, while Blythe played out her part, in wild abandon racing on ahead into the mouth of Southwark's Tooley Street and on up High to Tabard Inn, last stop for pilgrims a-going to Canterbury to touch Saint Thomas à Becket's shrine even since before Chaucer's time.

"Nothing's on the Bridge, Gilda! It's all over here!" Blythe made exactly the same claim here as when she would turn in Fish Street, waving her arms like a windmill, between the staple posts on the London end of the Bridge.

Gilda was aware that Blythe never knew that what caught her attention more than Blythe's voice and antic gestures was Southwark Church Bell Tower behind her here, as it was Saint Magnus the Martyr's bell tower at the London end, Blythe's voice submerged in the wordless voice of Christ that was the sound that pervaded Gilda's waking hours and made her readily sleep, free of nightmares.

Blythe always came back to where Gilda stood by a staple post, stepping aside as coach and cartwheels rushed raising a loud clatter toward her onto the Bridge. Then together, they walked at a more sedate pace back toward their fathers' shops.

Gilda looked back and up with Blythe at the severed heads of traitors stuck on pikes over the Great Stone Gateway, hoping no new face looked down at her, wishing she didn't know that Blythe's hope was to see up there against the morning's gray light a new face, a face they had probably once seen pass alive over the Bridge.

As morning foot and wheel traffic became rapidly more congested and heedless, they ducked into doorways more and more frequently.

Blythe withheld from Gilda—for revelation on a later day to shock her senseless—the fact that some of the faces they greeted in the early morning on the Bridge she, wearing a mask, had, sneaking out of the house in the middle of the night, breathed upon in the sooty dark several hours before.

*   *   *

As she began drawing, in secret, because her mother said artists were cursed for imitating, even competing with nature and therefore God, trying to take His place, Gilda pondered, 'Where has this snail been, I wonder? All over the Bridge, of course—oh, yes—and here by dawn's first light it slowly *is*—on my windowsill. Thank you, God, for the attention. All around and around, under and over, every inch of its life—this Bridge—so that it would appear here, as I do. At my window, sun on the sill, lapping over its shell and my hand as I reach out to stroke it. And now through my window across my lap as I write this about it in my sketchbook, and as, of course, the snail lays down a trail of silver embarked upon and around total, absolute coverage of this ancient Bridge, as slowly as a ship sails around the world and may now be homeward bound. I wish I had a brother on such a ship, home at last. Come in to wake me to this new day on the Bridge, he places his hand on this same windowsill.

'No, mother dear, I do not compete with God. Drawing is, for me, one more way of praying.'

*　　*　　*

"When she comes in the morning," said Gilda's father, "you must tell Blythe that you are forbidden the roadway."

Sorry indeed to miss the early morning ritual with Blythe, Gilda was even more willing to obey her father.

"God's wrath has marched from street to street in the Liberties and is now Within the Gates," Father declared. "He will visit the Bridge," Father prophesied. "We must keep within doors and have commerce with our fellow citizens only as they show sore need for our services."

Imagining her father's shoes on thousands of feet in the plague-infested streets made the smell of Leadenhall leather and dye even stronger in her nostrils. 'Men and women and children of high and low degree will step into the streets of London, bent upon the Bridge, and some will stop in their tracks, in shoes my father's hands fashioned, and more will step over the threshold of the shop and breathe into my father's face, and some of those will step off the Bridge and drop and wake in agony to look up one last hour into their loved ones' faces.' Gilda shuddered for them all, feeling secure in the assurances her father made to her and her mother and her little brothers and sisters, safe on the Bridge for yet a while.

Gilda carried into her bed a prayerful attitude, conversing with the Holy Physician, mindful, without knowing why, of Blythe's special need for God's mercy, in Christ's name. "Amen."

In the evenings, above the shop, tightly shut, Gilda's father hovered over them all, praying that it be God's will that he and his family survive, for the souls of those whose names had appeared on the mortality bills, perished that day, and for all to whom health would return but who would face an uncertain tomorrow. Clarke Shadwell prayed the citizens on the Bridge would be spared, God willing.

*   *   *

Gilda's father wrote in the back page of his business journal, where it had long been his habit to keep only the names of all men, women, and children in London and Southwark who wore the shoes he made and the cost. "We are always so extremely watchful for Bridge crossers who might fall off, as sailors on ships at sea fall, or boatmen who might fall out of their boats shooting the Bridge, or people intent on throwing their own lives into the river. Shocking to see folk from our windows on the bank quite far above and below the Bridge rush headlong into River Thames, tormented by plague or fear of it—of the red rose, the bubo, the plague token—or suffering intolerably the pain of the swelling of the buboes. Escape into the river water from their own bodies—not their own any more, now that I stop to think about it, because the sickness usurps ownership rights, not rights, 'the *wrong* of ownership' by disease. The sick man is displaced, evicted but also *held* in place, locked in. Locked in his house, he is locked inside a body quickly becoming vacant in death. Lord, in your mercy hear our prayers."

As her father was writing, Gilda took his place, setting a young man's shoes upon the counter, one toe forward, one toe backward.

"I am not yet visited." His tone conveyed a conviction that the day would come soon when he could not say that to her.

She pivoted the toe aimed toward herself so that it pointed with the other shoe toward him.

* * *

Rag merchant Dropstitch Upshaw, scouting for clothes left in the wake of the plague, looked down on his cousin, saw rue in his open mouth.

"He is quite dead even now."

His cousin's wife opened her arms to him for comfort. Pulling a rag off his shoulder, Dropstitch flung it across his nose and mouth, backed away from her, as from Hell-mouth.

* * *

Two men lifting corpses into the dead wagon smoked pipes. The plague had inspired almost everyone to smoke pipes and to set out smudge pots to distract the disease. One man lay curled up in a ball, a pipe clenched in his teeth, the plague snug in his guts.

* * *

A voice. "Everyone suspects casks, salt butter, Cheshire cheese, flesh meat from slaughter houses, market people, butchers of White Chapel especially, for inward gangrene affected their vitals."

* * *

Even as poems, like discarded handbills, littered his scriptorium floor, the Poet persisted.

On Silence
That hour on the Bridge of tomb silence.
That hour when silence so sets its gentle teeth
into the Bridge that the wheels, axles, rigging
of a single carriage make me hear and feel
noise louder in my bones than when the racket

is greatest at midday. Musetta,
my mistress, is at the door.

Daryl Braintree

"I darken your door, untainted, my ink-stained love." The Poet's mistress announced herself, ending their separation. Neither Londoners nor Southwarkians had been allowed onto the Bridge to mingle with its 600 residents, more or less, except on urgent business. Mainly, her husband and little girl, she tells him, and volunteer work at Saint Thomas Hospital in Southwark have kept her away.

"Not even mistresses who minister to the sore needs of young poets."

"You may mock my poetry, only to marvel at my future renown."

"I marvel very now." She put her untainted hand where she most wanted it to be, where, indeed, it was most wanted.

She tickled his bollocks with the feather with which he wrote poems.

Now after her visits, the smell of her lingered over the blank pages of the open book, putting some flesh on the dry words of his Chronicle of the plague. "Dry," for he was not an eyewitness and what others told him was second- and third-hand, or more remote from the effluvium that pervaded the City and Southwark. The visitation of the plague had stopped at London Bridge, both sides.

But when she did not come the next day, the next, the next, he imagined that she had been stopped at the staples at the bridge foot and asked her business and that her lie failed to persuade the wardens of the bridge this time that her business was urgent. Then he imagined the worst, as parents and lovers do.

Her maid, going into the street to buy bread, could have been breathed upon, then return with bread under her arm and the taint in her mouth and breathe upon her mistress, who might then take it back out into the streets.

Or her husband, home from urgent business abroad in the streets of Southwark, could mayhap have given Musetta a domestic kiss. "Struck at noon, dead at dark," was the fresh saying. Both may have been carted off to the burying ground and dumped.

Daryl's imagination roamed the streets and achieved expression under his hand, moving across the parchment, even as the printers inked off the mortality bills. In the streets as he had actually in his life walked them, many small fires now burned—fires to smother the plague. He saw their glow and smoke, and smelled the pitch and tar from his high window.

*   *   *

Dragged by the hair of his head, as it were, out of the depths of the dark ages, the building of the Bridge, the Plague Poet, as he began to think of himself, took up his pen, a newly honed one for this new task, as Chronicler of the Plague.

The butcher who sells the meat, the servant who fetches it, the money exchanged for it, those who eat it, then venture abroad in the street, give and receive more money, all transmitted the disease. Necessities and the means of acquiring them, infested, were contagious.

Executions became rare, all the heads aloft on the pikes above the great gate were old now—Thomas Venner the traitor's and that witch woman's and her son's impaled in the memories of historians only, the plague itself having set its teeth into many more prisoners.

The drunk who was taken up from the gutter presumed plague-struck, hoisted by hooks into the dead cart, rolled into a mass grave, awoke two days later under a layer of corpses, pushed himself up into the clear air, took in his face a dashed shovelful of dirt, cursed the man above, who offered the handle to help him up. Will he live to witness many others dead, and then, twenty years later, when plague and fire are only a memory, be struck dead, instantly, by a careening carriage?

*   *   *

Barking Dogs
The barking of dogs on the Bridge
and on the seawall and Within the Gates

and in the seventeen Liberties to each other, at each other,
fell, silent during the plague, 40,000 dogs killed.
Dogs never bark crossing a bridge.
Are animals attracted to bridges?
I don't recall ever seeing
a dog or a cat cross a bridge alone.
There goes a dog across a bridge, across, therefore,
London Bridge—in the house next door, a terrier barks—
and he/she, it looks strange, solitary stroller.
The roadway is deserted. Twilight.
Yes, for this dog to walk this, or any bridge, alone,
twilight must be upon the Bridge. Or else in the morning,
sunlight moves slowly behind the trotting dog
across the Bridge toward Southwark.
The dog is mute from end to end. Off the Bridge, it barks.
Turns and barks? No. At something it thinks it sees.
The Bridge has experienced the dog's crossing.
The first solitary dog crossing since the dawn of Bridge history.
This unique dog loves words, too. He
listens to me read this aloud and repeats it
wherever in the universe he goes,
not looking for a second bridge,
only remembering the first and only one.

Daryl Braintree

*   *   *

What Gilda knew of the plague day by day, her father, having heard
tales in the shop, told her. Customers told her mother, she knew, the
same tales, but her father retold tales to her mother, within earshot of
Gilda, as if she knew them not. But it was all so familiar from the tales
she had overheard of the seven-year-long plague of the 1640s, so vivid
she could have given a stranger a picture of it, she soon mingled details
from the plague twenty-five years ago with daily details of this plague in
her own time, but told no one, as if words might, like the disease, infect.

"They are murthering their own children," her father whispered to her mother, making her weep compassionately, Gilda imagined, for the children, and their parents.

"And some babes are but chrisoms, dying in the first month, before baptism."

"Men and women break in where death has broken in before," her father said, abysmally appalled, "and rifle the houses emptied of its folk only moments before.

"I hear of a great pit in the churchyard outside Moorgate where they dump rich and poor, naked and half-naked, Christians weak and strong, mingling Anglican and Puritan, likely a secret Catholic or two, out of one cart after another and in that pit, friend and foe mingled promiscuously under a common shelf of dirt."

"You have taught me, father, that death and the rapture will reconcile us all."

But the tales Blythe brought to Gilda were not second-hand.

"Blythe, Blythe, how could you of your own free will leave this little Eden on our bridge to venture into very hell?"

"Curiosity, pure and simple, leads me to step foot off the Bridge. Go with me tonight, Gilda, when all the Bridge is asleep, and we will bring comfort to the sick and the dying and together mourn the dead, Gilda."

"I cannot disobey my father and thus my Father."

"Does your father forbid you to visit your suffering Christian brothers and sisters?"

"First, he would have had to imagine I wished to leave the Bridge, and *that* he would never do."

And Blythe said, "Should we be our brother's keeper only when the air is pure? As Saint Paul says, 'God forbid.'"

"I must obey my father, I must, dear Blythe, obey my father. Has not *your* father forbidden you the streets even before this visitation?"

"He has indeed, but you need no reminder that it is our Father in heaven who is the kingdom, the power, and the glory. To serve your brothers and sisters in dire need is a greater commandment than to obey your mere earthly father."

"My father is my Father's delegate."

"Then let us abandon our brothers and sisters and save our own silky skins."

"But what if we carry the plague onto the Bridge and into our homes?"

"'In this world ye shall have tribulations—'"

"'But be of good cheer. I have overcome the world,' saith our Savior."

"Take my hand." Blythe held out her hand. "Will you take my hand?"

"I willingly," she said, laying her right hand over her heart, "and lovingly," she said, laying her left hand over her right breast, "obey my father."

Even so, came to pass one night that Gilda succumbed to Blythe's repeated, alluring entreaties.

As Fleet Ditch was more rammish than the canals of Venice, the cramped streets of London Within were rank, rank, rank. Gilda followed Blythe in her pursuit of the sellers of charm amulets and potions, the rat catchers, the dog and cat killers, the men who painted red crosses on the doors and the men who guarded the houses ordered shut, the walking dead fallen in the streets, the hospitals, the waxed leather–gowned plague-doctors who cared for the sick, their heads encased in leather hoods, vulture beaks attached, the sextons, who rang the church bells, the death knells, the bellmen carrying lanterns calling folks to "Bring out your dead!," the bearers of the dead, the drivers of the dead carts, the plague bells warning of the passing of the carts, the burials by sextons at the Charterhouse, in Shoreditch, in Aldgate, in White Chapel, in Westminster, in Moorfields. And the thieves who broke into houses vacated by the dead or where the dying lay dying, watching, as some act in another world, another life, their own death invading body and mind.

Gilda thought Blythe uncommonly attracted to Solomon Eagle, that sometimes naked enthusiast who denounced the city of London from the parapet of Saint Paul's.

* * *

The Poet was so obsessed with imagining, resurrecting—as he exulted in calling his endeavor—Peter de Colechurch that he was only half aware of, although not insensitive to, the life through which the Bridge dwellers were put by the plague, a life not daily death-dealing for them, however, for each was spared that. As Londoners off the Bridge fell in the narrow streets and were being buried in engorged graveyards, Peter worked steadily at building pillars and arches, the tasks killing at least a man each week, the task the Poet set himself was to kill them, most by drowning. Killed six hundred years ago, he killed them again—heads lying among ancient debris at the bottom of River Thames, aware of heads, now, aloft on pikes above the gate. The exhilaration of the arches! the letdown of the dead, those on the page as he heard or saw those on the streets, lying between thresholds and gutters. The plague scenes he observed got juxtaposed to the grim scenes witnesses described to him and that he contemplated even as he imagined and wrote about Peter directing the erection of yet another pillar.

As witness himself and as listener to other witnesses who crossed his path, the Poet was mindful of the possibility that others might witness his own collapse in the street, that those who told him what they had seen might well be seen by other witnesses in such scenes, scenes seen and told many times each day. Even the newly infected brought into the houses of victims tales of dying in the streets.

Lennox Archer, glover, entered his shop. "They carry torches to guide the dead wagons," Blythe overheard her father telling her mother, "risking general conflagration beyond the daily risk that any fire anywhere poses." Blythe sneered at her father's theatrical expression of shock.

John South, haberdasher, visited Phelan Wood, stationer: "We suffer daily such ninny hammers, simpletons even on this very Bridge, do we not?"

"When I am in the streets, I suck in my lips."

"The pestilential air of the City follows on the wind as we flee."

"Watching the contagion seize so many in a day, the hateful decrease of our population, day by day, is an almost mortal strain on the hearts of some."

"Itinerant dealers in dire necessities have jacked up prices and made hagglers of the most formerly reserved folk."

*   *   *

When the mortality bills told the tale of an increasing number of dead in the neighborhood of the Bridge and Saint Paul's, the Poet-Chronicler dared not set forth in vain search of books and Guildhouse records about Peter de Colechurch and his erection of the Bridge.

Nonesuch House provided such varied vantage points as to make the Poet-Chronicler eagle-eyed. The highest house, six stories, if, like most astonished viewers from elsewhere, one is eager to include the storey depending from under the roadway, it spanned the Bridge's width, so that he walked from his scriptorium on the east side over the gateway arch to the west side, wide views that gave him some prospects north and south on each side so that from the West side of the Bridge, the Poet watched Gilda follow Blythe down Swan Alley to the steps, watched Blythe in peril of her life go down slime-slippery Swan Steps to the surging water's edge and with a driftwood limb snag a wherry and pull it onto the lower step.

Gilda watched Blythe reach into the watercraft to search, she said, the waterman's body for a heartbeat.

"God forbid that he be dead, but dead he be!" Blythe announced, and climbed nimbly but crabwise, as if concealing something, back up the steps and passed by Gilda.

The Poet, not hearing, but seeing, knowing Blythe, was suspicious.

*   *   *

Had you been there in the flesh, you would have seen those men who went before the dead carts ringing hand bells to warn folks of the passing of the cart in their midst. Parish church bells ringing, almost constantly, hoarse voices, not of salvation but of the constancy of death.

You would have seen Blythe watching the sealed lips of grave mouths in churchyards open to receive a second layer of corpses—

strangers who had passed each other on the Bridge might well have been coupled—and then yet another layer, until some churchyards rose three feet higher right up to church walls, and tall men discovered that doorways to vestries were three feet shorter.

Blythe loitered about the hospitals, Saint Mary's of Bethlehem her favorite for an unending pageant of corpse bearers, men going ahead with three-feet-long red sticks.

She wished she were old enough to be given the job of searcher of the dead, women who searched for beating hearts among victims set out for dead.

Dogs and cats searched the dead, too, until dog-catchers and cat-catchers swooped down upon them, bagged them as carriers.

She kicked coffins left in the street for burial later.

Blythe experienced an almost aesthetic appreciation of one scene, so well composed as to resolve itself into a painting: a man lay dead, face up on the pavement in a square before a church, a woman lay face down upon his chest, a sickly child knelt crying beside her, while by their feet passed two men carrying a litter, a body under a sheet, a woman walking alongside, lamenting, thus making of the tableau of the dead parents and child a *tableau vivant,* and into the picture from the opposite direction, as if from the wings of a theatre, came two men, walking together, covering their mouths, one or both mayhap already infected, and liable to die before he reached his home, while coming up behind them was a woman gesturing shock and grief at the sight of the husband she had been seeking, slumped against the column of a building, and, oh, yes, above it all in one window a man draped over the sill, dead, and a woman lifting her hands to the heavens as if to implore God, perhaps to reproach Him.

"God gives us no more suffering than we can bear."

Folks who heard Blythe, shrank from her mocking tone.

*   *   *

Gilda found a stray kitten in the roadway and named it Roadway. She held it up for her father to see and he smiled and nodded, but he was talking, to a young swell. "You are aware, of course, that trade on the Bridge slows day by day," her father lamented, holding a half-made shoe in his hand longer than usually.

* * *

Mister Goodyer, needle maker, huddled with Mister South under the sign of the Fat Lady Made Slender. "Fear is so rampant in London that people show no need of tradesmen, craftsmen, mechanics."

"My brother's job is to take of the dead bodies an exact tale tally."

Rag merchant Upshaw sidled up to the two merchants. "Hordes of beggars, pests, born of the plague, fill the streets. Mountebanks pursue lucre with a passion not unlike that of the disease itself, touching multitudes of both the sick and the sound, thriving also, of course, upon corpses."

"Only sinners have died."

"No, mostly women and children, dregs of society, the poor's plague, the rich having fled."

* * *

Survivors were often dejected, distracted, thinking themselves as surviving only to die later, soon. For such as they, news of abatement was as if they were reborn on the lip of the grave.

The plague conspired to give credence to the supposed foreknowledge of prophets, doom-venders, and those who rejoice to witness the acts of a vengeful god.

* * *

My Previous Life
The plague kept my mistress Musetta
From my bed last night. The Bridge
fades a little from the foreground. But is,

in a strange way, clearly there. It will always
"hang" there. It will never fade. Surely, I lived
on London Bridge in a previous life,
reincarnated to live here differently now.
The Bridge works in mysterious ways,
by a realization that moonlight lies like a grin across
River Thames, a bridge of grinning light.

Daryl Braintree

*   *   *

Blythe "confessed" to Gilda. "I was born and raised and married and had seven children and grew old on this Bridge—in an earlier time."

"Do not jest so, Blythe. If anyone should hear you, they would suspect you of being a witch."

"Jest? God forbid. I know it in my bones, not that I had seven children and died old on the Bridge, but that I was born and grew at least to my present age on this cursed Bridge. Nothing after that."

"I cannot listen."

"And my bones scurried back and forth with the tides from Old Swan Steps to Gravesend over the—"

Gilda covered her ears and closed her eyes and felt Blythe pull her hands away, opened her eyes, witnessed utter belief in Blythe's. "And my bones tell me that after I die, I will return to this Bridge instead of Venice or Rome or Arabia. What sins have I committed to deserve this limbo?"

"God does not punish sinners in such a way. If you lived on the Bridge before, I pray that you shall never return."

"Well, God forbid I *should* return."

*   *   *

Those clergymen who braved the plague, conducted so many funerals, consoled so many who were infected unawares, they too fell and

137

were collected. Out of the selfsame hell-mouth that condemned sinners issued that very day upon several innocents the breath of an infected clergyman—condemned by word and breath in a single hour.

And in the stews, whores served the plague as midwives to the final sperm of many men for whom the prospect of death was occasion for a burst of life.

*   *   *

Like every Londoner and Southwarkian still alive, the Poet woke each morning to another day under a probable sentence of death. Many felt faint at noon and fell by midnight, only to reappear as a fraction of a sum on the mortality bill.

His mistress darkened that cloud when she said, "My husband suspects. He vows to kill my lover when he discovers who he is. He vows to prick my own head either on a pike on the Bridge or at Temple Bar. His is a rather vacillating mind. But I am afraid, dear boy, I am afraid. Are you afraid?"

"God damn me, if I am not."

But we know what the Poet does not yet know—that she is making all this up, that she, going from love to love, is always in love, has never married, is a nurse in Saint Thomas Hospital in Southwark, and carries the plague onto the Bridge and back with every visit to his bed. He will learn only incidentally from John Stow's 1598 *Survey of London* about the hospital itself, "an ospytaly to entertain the poor," originally a part of the priory of Saint Mary Overie, from which, as his mistress had informed him, also derives the Bridge, and that the hospital was moved after the fire of 1212 to where the air was sweeter, intended at first to be a place of hospitality and continued even after it was translated into a hospital (the one word deriving from the other) to devote a night ward to travelers, especially those a-going on pilgrimage to Canterbury. An orphan come of age and wandering the streets of Southwark on the verge of harlotry, she had enjoyed the overnight hospitality of Saint Thomas Spital, so named for the martyr Thomas à Becket after his canonization in the twelfth century, and drifted into the role of nurse in the last years of the Civil War. The nuns told her that she had Dick

Whittington to thank for donating funds to build a "new chamber with eight beds that all things that happened in that chamber would be kept secret . . . for he would not shame no young woman in no wise. . . ."

She read the beloved, blind poet John Gower because she had admired his splendid tomb, his body reclining, his head resting on a few of his books, in Southwark Cathedral even before she saw his poems and later learned that he, who had lived on the grounds of the priory, had donated funds to support each nurse in the hospital. It was not the Poet of the Bridge but Gower, through the Poet, who seduced her in her guise as married woman. Learned though she had managed to become, she had not yet learned that Miles Coverdale's translation of the Bible into English, the first such, was printed on the grounds. Nor that after his visit to the hospital, Thomas Cromwell directed a deputy to visit it, who reported it a bawdy place, causing its closure for a decade. Nor that when it reopened, it was rededicated to Saint Thomas the Apostle because Saint Thomas à Becket had become for Henry VIII a symbol of the clergy's claim to authority over the monarchy's claim in all church disputes pertaining to the criminal acts of clerics.

Not even the Poet's delving will ever reveal all facets of the hospital's history. But the Poet's mistress always thinks of Saint Thomas à Becket when, on the street named for him, she attends services in the decaying chapel once named for him, the tower of which, redolent of herbs being cured for the apothecary, looks down upon the female surgical block of the hospital itself.

Interesting as all this history may or may not be, it did not advance the Poet's research into Peter de Colechurch, although it might gratuitously stimulate his poetic imagination purely for its own sake. It does, however, serve to show that the Poet's mistress had a life not entirely centered upon her weekly stimulation of the Poet's romantic sensibility and his otherwise sedentary body.

*   *   *

Standing at the window with her father, Gilda looked East to the Pool, where several hundred ships were huddled at anchor. "Like this Bridge, each ship is a haven from plague."

"The winds bless us, Father."

"The plague is not yet in the fleet, praise be to God. But the watermen, not so." Not reckoning that on the prison ship *The Black Eagle* nineteen Quaker men and women and many of its sailors perished of the plague, causing ports to turn away "the Plague ship."

She heard the screechings of women and thought she heard Blythe suppress a giggle.

She witnessed men, women, and children run naked into River Thames, thus escaping death by plague into the embrace of death by water.

* * *

Looking over at Southwark, Bridge dwellers saw a town unvisited by infection, but about to feel its fangs.

Fishmonger Brooke and master carpenter Coldiron paused mid-Bridge. "The houses in Southwark have become too clustered together, almost as congested as ours on the Bridge."

"The homeless folk tried to encamp on the Bridge, but most of us shopkeepers fought them back.

"After the fire of 1632, the homeless tried to cross the Bridge on the pretense of going over to friends or relatives in Southwark, but they were discovered crouched in doorways and were driven back into smoldering London."

"The Bridge has been a refuge from plague and fire, to be sure, but only for Bridge dwellers—except for one or two who disappeared into its substructure and lived but their last days—a week, a month, a year— one woman for over a decade, on into the restoration of our Charles II."

* * *

All, sound or sick, experienced the same thoughts, emotions, imaginings, but with differences of which both were acutely aware.

The disease and its widespread consequences in every venue of human need caused extreme disruptions.

A voice. "Ill talk as well as shouts of desperation poisons common discourse."

The general tumult of every type of activity touched so many citizens, confined to their houses or at liberty in the streets, that the populace as a whole may be counted victim of degrees of nervous tension, apprehension, and hysteria.

A voice. "Fifty-two dead in Newgate jail, prisoners sentenced doubly to death, some escaped the one, only to suffer the other."

*　*　*

The Poet stood at the window. 'I shall sit her down and tell Musetta my grand design.'

"Do not move or speak, I pray you, until I have told you. A month or so before the visitation began, a seaman in a tavern, which one I forget, told me—and until now I had forgotten what he told me—told me that he was content to die of the pox that afflicted him, now that he had finally seen the doors of the Baptistry, also called the Basilica de San Giovanni, in Florence, about which he had only heard, but heard often, over many years, and had yearned to see. Let us not forget, as we have done with Peter de Colechurch, the name of the sculptor who decorated the South entrance doors, working only six years, however, starting in 1330, twenty-eight distinct square panels, depicting scenes in bas relief from the life of John the Baptist and of the Virtues—Andrea Pisano. Andrea Pisano. Pisano.

"Almost a century later, Lorenzo Ghiberti, age twenty-three, younger than my own self, was commissioned to sculpt the North door. Twenty-eight panels, fourteen on each of the two doors, depict scenes in bas relief from the New Testament, starting with Our Savior carrying his cross, ending with Saint Augustine. But he, like Peter, labored long, from 1403 to 1424—imagine! One of the small heads affixed between the squares is said to be Ghiberti's own, as Peter De Colechurch is thought to be buried in the undercroft of the Chapel he built to honor Saint Thomas à Becket. Ghiberti then won the competition among the great sculptors of his day to decorate the east door depicting scenes from the Old

Testament, showing the Evangelists and the doctors of the Latin Church in the margins. Imagine him, starting only one year later in 1425, devoting twenty-seven more years of his life to a grand conception, to 1452, giving us not twenty-eight, but ten scenes from the Old Testament, but showing sometimes more than one episode simultaneously in the same square. He starts with Adam and Eve, their fall and expulsion, ends with Solomon and the Queen of Sheba. Michelangelo named the doors 'The Gates of Paradise,' for the work, he said, was not done, he said, on earth, but in heaven, so fine it was.

"We may gaze upon 'The Gates of Paradise' this very day, were we in the heart of Florence, instead of the heart of plaguey hell. As you know, I have written poems about Peter's building of the Bridge as I have labored to reconstruct my father's Chronicle of London Bridge, a Chronicle of plague and fire and blood and glory, traitors and kings. But now as I look down upon and foolishly betimes descend and wander into the streets of London, watching the plague maraud our city, the 'Gates of Paradise,' in this city of seven gates, as in Dekker's *The Seven Deadly Sins of London,* a vision keeps me awake—a vision of a poem, as if in ten panels on a gate, in which, like Spenser's *tableaux vivants, The Faerie Queene,* I capture this hell. 'The Gates of Hell' shall be my masterpiece, once I have brought the Chronicle up to the present, recent entries, and this plague like a lingering tide. My Chronicle entries have already begun to be—even as I deliberately write my nocturnal meditations on the Bridge in a more and more metaphysical vein—a series of poems about the history of the Bridge, Dante nodding approvingly over my shoulder. Am I to become, like Pisano, forgotten, my poems ignored for those of a better poet, or am I to deserve Ghiberti's fame, the poet who is as famous as Dante and Spenser and Milton, whose epic Christian poem has not yet seen the light of day? Am I to labor twenty-eight years, like Peter de Colechurch, my work to be finished by someone else, my son perhaps? Tell me. I want you to tell me right now so that I will know. Stir yourself."

Musetta rose from the bed. "I must walk to loosen my tongue."

* * *

Precautions employed to keep the seamen safe—even watermen were prohibited from contact—finally could not prevail.

Some watermen drifted alone in their wherries as if resting on their oars, their destinations, mockingly, reached several days before.

The seamen had no contact with the river men. Even so, seaman after seaman was stricken.

Out on the river, midstream, adrift on the tides, some watermen and their families or renters sheltered under colorful awnings that made the sail makers richer.

In this seafaring end of town, people were in twists of distraction.

*   *   *

"The air we breathe is full of death." The deep breath Blythe took in puffed out her belly. "I am with child of it." She did not mock. She was in awe.

"And by the Grace of God," said Gilda, "may we exhale death again."

"That," said Blythe, "is the smell of death before death."

At the Bridge foot, just by Saint Magnus the Martyr Church, Blythe and Gilda watched five of the spectators of the rush of desperate people into the water, infected by the hysteria as through the medium of an invisible vapor, follow enthusiastically.

*   *   *

Having wandered around, up and down, the rooms slowly in erratic circles, Gilda went below to her parents to put into words the sum of her wordless meditations. "In the matter of death, we have no say-so. My cat, Roadway, died on my lap in the very dead of night," she told her parents, separately, who looked up from their work. She returned to her room to pray.

Gilda rose from her knees and took the stairs down to the roadway and turned and asked God's blessing upon her father's shoe shop and house and, with a touch, each shop on the Bridge, uttering the name of each shop and of each family living above.

* * *

Solitary Folks

Not only in our four- or five-storey buildings—
like vertical London Bridges—but
in residential neighborhoods, it is true
that you can live next door to a person
fifty years and know him, her, no better
than acquaintances ten miles distant or
around the globe. And so, from wall to wall,
in shops and houses on the Bridge, some people
know only kin, and know them not well.
London Bridge then is composed of isolated
cells, each moons distant from the others.
Generations of solitary folks.

Daryl Braintree

1665, off the Gold Coast of Africa. In the margin of Dante's The Divine
Comedy, *the Italian still beyond Morgan's ability.*

Until I went to sea at the age of thirteen, I smelled char from the
wood of houses that burned on our North end of the Bridge thirteen
years before I was born. On this ship, anything burning—pipes, rope—
the smell of moving water with burning wood, I suppose, reminded me.
Strange word "re-minded." I am of two minds, one on this ship, the
other still on the Bridge.

* * *

A voice. "Plague may nest in cloth coming in bulk from Without
the Walls, so sail on by storefronts that display such as that."

A voice. "I fell into a bit of good hap. My son on a horse showed up
in the nick."

A voice. "And Lord Mayor Lawrence governs still from within a
glass cage."

* * *

From the roadway and along the banks, Thames Street, the Poet watched drunken women hired as searchers, staggering into and staggering out of plague-stricken houses, as if drunk with the disease they had discovered, their demeanor hinting receptivity to bribes to falsify the cause of death so the houses would not be shut up, sealing the fate of all others in the house. Some nurses, he heard, strangled and robbed their patients.

The Poet listened to all who were talking as he approached, to all who, seeing him approach, began to talk, as did this stranger. "I keep, I know not why, a private little archive of the handbills and other memorials of the Great Frosts of 1602, 1625, 1634, but also of the fire of 1633 and the plague of 1636—between April and December, 10,400 dead were buried—for whoever wants to recapture images of those days. When you survive a hell like that, you want to forget, but how *can* you? The images are burned into your brain and nothing that happens afterward can ever compare. You don't ever get over it. My people all say so. I know *I* do. Why do I retrieve these images and pore over them so often? A friend of mine keeps all such, trivial events, too, indiscriminately mixed, all he can find, and he'll pore over them by the hour. Can't get enough. And yet I have little desire to shuffle through them. He, on the other hand, wouldn't walk over two piers to see what I've got to show. Well, neither of us can find many that feel as we do. But you seldom hear anyone say, 'I've forgotten those terrible years.' Here they are. Look at this, won't you?

"Good men who stayed in London during the plague of '36 imbibed so much wine to keep their spirits high, they may become sots all their lives thereafter."

The Poet musing: My old drinking and whore-mongering companions dare not open the door to me, lest the expression "death at the door" prove apt.

From the thicket of spires, the Poet picked out Saint Mary Colechurch and imagined Peter de Colechurch tending to his parishioners. Cold to Anglicanism, the Poet had felt even more estranged from the Catholic mentality, until his imagination had conjured up Peter de Colechurch, as a living, breathing, walking, eating, speaking priest, whose time must have been divided between ministering to spiritual needs at Saint Mary's and building the Bridge to overcome practical needs, but in such a spirit and in such a way as to infuse that fabric with spirit in a sense that moved the Poet, standing highest on Peter's Bridge, to descend and go into the midst of plague to visit Peter's spirit in his church, now four hundred years older.

The cool, dim interior of the little church, situated adjacent to what was once the property, he was keenly aware, of the Becket magnates and was now the site of Mercers' Hall, Ironmonger Lane, realm of the Mercers' Guild in Mercery, made the Poet feel remote from plague. Why would plague seek out this empty narrow nave, as if a haven from humanity? Where was the priest? Was the church here as empty as the chapel Peter built to honor Saint Thomas à Becket, reduced since Henry VIII's desecrations to a warehouse?

Standing in Peter's parish church, where Peter's mind often dwelt upon his Bridge, the Poet saw Father Peter simultaneously standing in Saint Thomas Chapel and felt a full sense of Peter's sensibility, turned slowly as if expecting to see him standing behind him on this sacred site. And did Becket, christened less than an hour after his birth in this place, stand here beside Peter, older than Peter, conversing about Paul's First Corinthians perhaps? Conversing perhaps about his difficult friendship with King Henry II? A question of fact, very little hope of proof. "It is as I imagine," the Poet intoned aloud for the echo.

"I am the author of Peter's story," he said aloud. 'But must be a scholar of Becket's story,' he thought, recounted as fact soon after his murder by five of his friends, one eyewitness, one nearby, and soon after by others and over four centuries many others, on the one hand, every wave of his hand on record. Ancient records kept only a fugitive line or two of Peter, who reappears in the flesh in my imagination, on the other hand. "Thank you, Holy Ghost." The Poet was aware of himself as an agnostic in a church praying, irony his familiar.

In Saint Mary Colechurch's bone yard gaped more graves than the Poet might have imagined possible, in ground no larger than his

Nonesuch bedchamber, tombstones from former graves set aside so that new dead might lie upon the skeletons of old.

Under a fig tree one stone stood up, unmolested. The Poet touched it as he leaned over to read its legend by the rusty light of yet another plaguey evening in its history. In time, weather had made the letters and numbers illegible. The Poet's imagination imposed upon the stone the names and birth and death dates of Peter's mother and father. Thus, here lay the tangible bones of Peter's mother and father, side by side. Saint Thomas à Becket's imagined bones had lain on its side between them for almost a quarter of a century, where now lay their son, Peter. 'The facts fugitive, my imagination takes precedence—Thomas's bones, while still warm at the marrow, vanished into Peter's hands.'

At his back, the Poet felt the existence of a crypt thought to be Peter's, where Saint Thomas's bones reposed instead, just as he had imagined, in the undercroft of Saint Thomas à Becket's Chapel, but with Peter's name carved into the entablature now hidden from view by bales of wool, he had been told, or great stacks of paper, another told him heaps of rags. He decided to look someday, place his palm on the entablature—he already felt it—speak to Becket's bones, missing from the tomb at Canterbury where thousands had touched what they were told were Thomas's relics at the tomb in Canterbury for two centuries before Henry VIII, who tried to destroy all trace of such as Peter and Thomas, strode upon the earth.

*　*　*

At great peril to himself, sniffing an orange filled with spices to ward off the stench, the Poet-Chronicler began to go routinely into the plague-ridden city, moving among the dead-wagons and smudge pots to reach the Exchequer, to inspect the Norman-era Pipe Rolls for financial facts. "Mortmain, mortmain, everywhere." The Poet, too, sought the end of irony, often crossing paths with Blythe, who romped about in search of new sights.

1665, September 19. Bills of Mortality, this week, of the Plague: 1189, in 97 Parishes Within the Walls. 3070, in 16 Parishes

Without the Walls. The horrors are too great and too manifold to record even one of them here. Let Death's simple arithmetic tell.

"Holy Father, I pray that my father is not among that number. I pray that he shall return and shift this burden from the shoulders of an obscure young Poet back upon the shoulders of a venerable Old Chronicler, until Morgan Wood's ship anchors in the Pool."

From the doorway of his father's shop, shut up for the duration of his absence, the Poet observed the darkly lovely child Blythe Archer slipping through the door into the street, and running off the Bridge into hell.

*　*　*

In the Tabard Inn, the Poet found Coldiron, the Bridge's master carpenter, in a more reflective mood than usual, tankard firmly in hand. "Plague and fire alike may keep modestly confined to a single house *or* stray into the house on the right *then* rage promiscuously throughout the parish, circling back to the house on the left. I seem to be talking of women more than of plague and fire, because one dare not, one supposes, touch virgin or whore in these days."

*　*　*

As London Bridge Chronicler, the Poet felt obliged to seek out the facts of this holocaust, fodder, too, perhaps, he was shamefacedly aware, for poems that would assure his fame and immortality. The untainted folk talk. Standing on the wide starling that supports the old Saint Thomas Chapel, now a rag, wool, and paper warehouse, he listened mainly to the watermen. But many watermen had taken their families far up river and tied up all along the seawalls, making tents of their sails for covering during the day, going into their boats to sleep at night.

Alone on the chapel starling, the Poet imagined stacks of paper stored in the undercroft below the waterline, very dry, a mystical place for him, despite its sharing storage space with piles of rags.

The next morning, the Poet relished the irony that amidst plague, he suffered a common cold.

'I have a sore throat and the Bridge. Curative potions muddle my mind. Imagination stagnant. Image-making mechanism slowed. Tomorrow night my imagination will walk this Bridge at a much brisker pace.'

*   *   *

As Peter's resurrector, the Poet felt drawn again to Saint Mary Colechurch to see and know it in the midst of plague. Full of plague orphans, the nave seemed filled with Peter's spirit. No, he felt the Holy Ghost, Peter alive in it as it touched all these and himself.

*   *   *

Feeling that he had neglected Mister Milton for his father's Chronicle and the plague's horrors, the Poet ventured out Moorgate to Artillery Row, found Milton at prayers, and returned to the Bridge empty-handed but not empty-headed.

"I am coming upon the belief, my young fellow, that everyone alive is infected with something contagious."

"I saw Sir Thomas Browne walking on the Bridge alone, coming behind him in a drunken stupor, and pausing in my doorway watched him stand in front of the warehouse that was once Saint Thomas Becket Chapel. A thought seemed to have stopped him or he had gone there intentionally. I expected to find some reference to Peter de Colechurch's crypt as I perused again the pages of *Urn Burial,* but found no trace, merely the faintest allusion to such burial sites. I have marked the place. 'And also agreeable unto Roman practice to bury by highways, whereby their Monuments were under eye; Memorials of themselves, and mementos of mortality unto living passengers.'"

Inspired by being in the presence of Mister Milton, the Poet walked back to Nonesuch House, climbed the five flights of stairs, opened his scriptorium window and looked out, right, at the smokes and spires of Southwark, his cock hard against the sill, his hand on his agitated heart that longed for a visit from Musetta. 'On yonder cloud floating over River Thames, my love, I imagine us fucking all the way to Dover.'

*   *   *

A voice. "The rakers toil in vain to keep the streets clear of the foul refuse of plague."

The sweating sickness without warning springs from within out upon the face and body, itself a warning that in this beginning is the end, with no hope of recovery.

Men carry lanterns, not only as in normal times to light one's search for a child, or a friend gone astray, but to find one such dead.

Some drank water that had filtered through graveyards.

Multitudes sickened fast, died fast. Too late, too late, many fled, many fled, while many died on the escape route and many more in the villages to which some fled failed to escape the embrace of the survivors.

A voice. "It is not fanatical to believe, as many do, that the Hand that sowed the seeds of death would end the harvest of death."

*   *   *

Blythe put on her mask, moist from numerous nights of fervently fitful breathing, and, to conceal it, for the solitary pleasure of conceal-ment, pulled the blanket over her face.

Blythe, inside the tent of her blanket, behind the mask, ventured out each night, spectator of the harvest.

*   *   *

A man stood on one leg outside a house marked with a red cross on its front door, above his shoulder a round cage on a pole full of rats cavorting, an odd entertainment, it seemed to her, until Blythe got up closer and noticed a rat hanging, a noose around its throat, from out-side the cage. Rats breeding at a raging pace, cats being blamed, along with dogs, for spreading the disease, plain to see, as they roamed the streets searching for dwindling food possibilities. Coming round the man, she saw he was one-legged. In a wooden tray hanging from straps over his shoulders, several rats ate pieces of meat. She did not need to ask if he was a rat catcher, rats being only one supposed source of the plague. She supposed he stationed himself outside houses shut up with the plague because the diminishing supply of food and the smoke supposed to discourage the disease would perhaps drive the dogs, cats, and rats out of such houses.

* * *

"Walking this morning, I saw a snake and a rat smashed side by side on the Bridge roadway." Daryl rose from his bed and stepped across the room to his desk.

At the window, Musetta stirred, turned, eyes closed, waited.

My Bed as a Bridge
Tonight, I walked a bedstead up on its end
to turn it, in my room, and it came apart—
the head struck my head. It brained me.
I'm addle-brained.
Beds are bridges
between waking and sleeping,
between life and death, day
dreaming and night dreams.
For me, on this spot, where I
was born in Nonesuch House,
July 25, in 1643, this bed,
where I always sleep well, is a bridge
between past and present. We lie down
upon a bed as we meander upon a bridge
—to cross over in dreams as we cross in daylight.
Beds on London Bridge are bridges.
All beds there are aloft, heads
sleeping like the heads stuck on pikes above the gate.
                                        Daryl Braintree

* * *

A voice spoke to the Poet—out of nowhere—as he lay on the verge of sleep.

"I see a house that burned, abandoned in ruin. The smell of burnt oak rafters lingers from the fire of 1633, over a decade before I was born. In damp weather especially. In the nostrils, pungent, of the famous as they crossed. Who? Call the roll. Oliver Cromwell challenger, Charles II, restored in ceremony, Milton, already pondering Paradise. A procession, from the first Bridge rising out of the mud, spanning light centuries. And they marched from Kent to Southwark and stormed the Bridge.

"But that was in a time before my family went to live on the Bridge."

Out of what he heard, the Poet conjured a poem.

*   *   *

On the Bridge, Blythe heard spectacle-maker George Gill asseverate. "There goes John Locklear, riding high on a new type of business, broker of the dead, who buys up chattels of households in which all die and nobody claims the house's contents and sells at a very low price, contagion suspected at the touch, and this sort sells at a peril to any who buy at a peril, and may all perish in due time."

A dog-catcher cuddled a lap dog.

"How many dogs have you killed?" Blythe imagined almost a hundred.

"Four thousand, thirty-one, exact."

"You think to scare me?"

He cut the throat of the lap dog he was cuddling and held it out to her. She spit upon it and laughed, causing the dog-catcher to cringe.

She sauntered among the shambles in Blowbladder Street, watching the rippling muscles of butchers toiling.

By torchlight, she followed carts to Holywell Lane in Shoreditch, where upended carts let slide their cargo into hasty mass graves, already full almost to the brim with previous unloadings.

She listened to an unbroken stream of cursing from the bearers of the dead and the dead cart men, knowing Gilda was listening to the simultaneous tolling of church bells for funerals, now often without clergy.

A priest vomiting in a narrow alley inspired images of a legion of priests visiting the dying as carriers of the plague from parishioner to parishioner.

A woman passed her, carrying a loaf of bread under her arm. Will "the staff of life" kill her?

Blythe's curiosity made note of amulets. The sight of a man opening his mouth to talk, showing a gold piece on his tongue, made her giggle so musically he looked over at her as she passed and tipped his hat, smiling.

Alerted by the plague bell that warned folk to stand well back, she followed a procession of dead carts, past bakers, brewers, and butcheries that had been visited, to the Charterhouse plague-pits, and from there another procession began to form going to Moorfield's plague pits, pest house within sight of it. Thrilled, she spoke aloud, to an oblivious rat, flea-bitten. "I see it, I see it, I see it all."

A tiny man staggered past her. "Blinding black, shadows, black, blinding light."

Blythe followed him to discover who else might follow him and to what end.

Everywhere she went, she stopped to watch men shutting houses, listening to shrieks of the dying. "I'm on fire!"

Everywhere she strolled, householders were fumigating their houses, lacing the general smog with odors of brimstone, saltpeter, amber, and sometimes frankincense, and folks were tending bonfires on each side of the street every sixth house in every street, and firing guns to shatter the plague-laden air.

"The smoke and the concussions deal with the disease."

"At the risk of setting the City on fire?"

"Child, every fire we mortals set, every day of our lives, risks universal conflagration." Even after he spoke, the man's face was that of a very patient explainer.

"Oh, I see." She bugged her eyes. It satisfied him, as she knew it would.

Smoking pitch stood wavering sentinel before almost every house and shop.

Mesmerized by the bills of mortality, her father, Blythe was certain, was unmindful of her slipping through the door into the street every day.

In pursuit of spectacles of sight and sound, she slipped routinely in human and animal piss and shit in the narrow streets and, almost always, dodged dumpings from upper windows of household slops of the same, mingled with the offal of the kitchen. Where Blythe had walked, she left her footprint in the shit of a dying plague victim.

She watched other dead carts take away servants. One of the dead-cart men threw a corpse into a mass grave, then sank to his knees in the first of the three last hours of this own life.

"How shall we know who is infected from those who are sound?" Blythe heard a man ask another.

Looking inside as a sedan passed her, Blythe saw an old man in re-straining straps. A woman in the street stepped backwards, shaking her head, not only for the old man, but over the general scourge. "Forced off to the pest-house."

Apothecaries took on the duties of the physicians who had fled. One who signed a death certificate fell in the street on his way home. And Blythe was there to see him stripped of his medicine box and his personal valuables by maggoty thieves.

Orphans tended to follow Blythe because she moved about with an air of purpose, but she eluded them, as if they diluted the effect of the spectacles she craved to watch.

*   *   *

What had started up in Drury Lane had spread through Bell Alley, Thieving Alley in Westminster, leaving a littering of corpses, and in Token-house Yard, a mirror image.

Apothecary Tristram West drew in his chin and crossed his thin arms to lend an air of authority to his pronouncement for the benefit of basket maker Robertus Allbritton. "My brother apothecaries are now few. But we are safe because the Bridge is safe. So folks think."

Officials stopped two men carrying a coffin with unseemly haste and, looking inside, found not a corpse but all the household valuables of a family who had all perished.

Out of a cart overloaded with corpses came the cheery-dreary notes of a bagpipe played by a piper who woke dimly out of a drunken sleep among the dead—to whose bourne he might well have followed in the days ahead.

*   *   *

Like a thief in the night, the plague purloined more lives than were newly born.

A voice. "The very ghosts must shift for themselves."

A voice. "The poor suffer more deeply, pervasively, because the sources of charity are dying or dead, or shut down."

The social habits of the laboring poor were little amended, throwing folks together in all the most hazardous menial tasks at low, low pay among the sick and the sound.

A voice. "We are dying in heaps."

Mortality rates lower one week than the previous bred foolish behavior, as when, like sheep, they flock, fearless, back into the still-infected streets.

The leper house became a pest house.

*   *   *

"Nothing's here, nothing." Blythe spoke aloud, awake among her sleeping parents and siblings. "It's all over there in London and over there in Southwark. I must lie here all through the night for fear of them all, the plague too rampant now, even in Southwark, even in Westminster."

*   *   *

"My daughter Blythe tells me, living on the Bridge is like living in a noisy nunnery. As if she knows what a nunnery is, except from books. She craves pictures.

"I forbade her step foot on the North bank. Southwark is another country, but she shows little inclination to venture South, caring neither for what the Bear Garden nor the church over there may offer. No,

Blythe has got Thames Street somehow in her head. Saint Paul's, the Strand, Poultry Street, the Exchange, Temple Bar, Guild Hall, Coventry. I fear I have spoken of that other world overmuch."

Scrivener Thomas Wright sought out necklace maker Burlow Green. "I listened each morning for the voice of my brother, yelling from his window to assure me that he was still among the living, though, like us all, perilously. And then the morning came when . . . It is impossible to know that he lies between two strangers in Charter House yard overflowing already these three hundred years with victims of the Black Death, among other now nameless Londoners."

"Losing my parents in '32, I moved onto the Bridge at the first sign of plague visiting London again, but it was on the North end and so then my house and shop burned in the fire of '33. I must even now struggle to draw breath to keep my shop open and pay rent and my debts."

Fishmonger Brooke visited shoemaker Shadwell at end of day. "The breaches God made upon my family were as sudden as common fires in London households almost daily."

"Many feverishly believe that Heaven sent this distemper as a messenger."

Hearing their conversation as he passed on the roadway, stationer Wood joined Brooke and Shadwell. "I give you Numbers, 11: 33. 'The wrath of the Lord was kindled against the people, and the Lord smote the people with a very great plague.'"

"And *I* give you Jeremiah, 21: 6. 'And I will smite the inhabitants of this City, both man and beast: they shall die of a great pestilence.'"

"And I give you Isaiah: . . . Would, but I have forgot."

"We should not hesitate as they return to reproach with tongue and eye and kicks and jabs those physicians and clergy who fled, expecting their power to have stayed healthy while the subjects of that power limped into eternity, and quacks went quacking about the streets in search of the dying, their open mouths like cesspits."

"The bravery of physicians who have stayed is too often futile, for the contagion dodges all medicines."

"Meditations upon divine subjects are commonplace among the pious and their imitators."

* * *

Gilda's daily meditation ended. 'Nothing but God's mercy can save us.

'Among the victims of plague, Jesus, we must count those dead of sheer grief, whose bodies, twisted in death agony, bore no tokens of the visitation.'

From her window, Gilda watched a squat bulldog of a man, a small dead dog under the right arm, a larger dead dog under the left arm, fling the dogs' carcasses over the bridge rail at an open space into River Thames. Turning and walking ten steps or so, he turned and at a rush thrust his own body over the rail after the dogs.

* * *

And then one morning, the infected, whole families, having sweated out the poison, began to rise up, revived and healed, and rejoice.

News of a decrease in plague deaths inspired not only rejoicing but renewed fears of a return of previous high numbers. Solomon Eagle, the naked Quaker prophet, was among the several who suddenly appeared in public places to keep terror alive, like hot embers, ash on the outside, blowable flame under, ever-present.

The Poet spoke an insight in the solitude of his scriptorium. "If you review the life that went before, each death is a long story, multiplied by over seventy-five thousand, a web of long stories."

And as so and so died of plague, John Milton continued to work on *Paradise Lost.* The Poet found Milton packed to remove his family from Artillery Row in Bunhill, Moorgate, to Chalfont to escape the plague. "But I do wonder, my young friend, whether this line strikes you as true or as too clever for words? 'The Mind is its own place and can make a heaven of hell, a hell of heaven.'"

The tolling of those words rendered the Poet speechless for a moment, but the reverberations followed him, light-footed, out of Moorgate and down through London and onto the Bridge and up into his own scriptorium where he seriously considered burning all his own poems, still only in rough first drafts.

But did not do it.

9

PLAGUE AFTERMATH:
THE BROTHERHOOD OF
THE BRIDGE

Stationer Phelan Wood and fishmonger Kerry Brooke walked together northward toward the stationer's paper warehouse, in former centuries Saint Thomas's Chapel, for the meeting called by goldsmith Clinkenbeard at his shop.

Brooke pointed. "Look! What a deep, inky, and massive shadow the Bridge casts East this evening."

"And West each morning. I fail to take your point."

"Point? There *is* no point. I was simply remarking on the way the Bridge casts its shadow as the sun comes up on the Thames. See how the houses at the London end even shadow the bank-side houses."

"Yes. Indeed. But again, Kerry, is there a point to be made?"

"Point to be made? Damn it, Phelan, must a shadow prove a point to deserve its existence? No. I was simply remarking on—and look yonder, at the shadows the heads on the pikes above the Great Stone Gate cast."

"Why, I never noticed that before, athwart the very steps of the Cathedral."

"Nor have I. What else have we missed? What *else* have we missed?"

They took seats as latecomers.

Mister Clinkenbeard was aware that "pronouncement" was the apt word for what he was about to "intone."

"Our sworn responsibility for saving the Bridge, so to speak, and for the precautions we perforce must take must be kept from the public, secret among our few souls as if we were priests in the remotest monastery."

Observed by any light, solemn and somber was the conclave of elders who meditated and discoursed upon the subject of the plague and its aftermath.

George Gill, spectacle maker, looked askance at Robertus Allbritton. "Why are you quivering, Robertus?"

John South looked at Robertus. "He is not quivering, he is shivering."

Burlow Green looked at John South's necklace—from Saint Paul's yard, not from his own shop—and then at Robertus. "Not at all. He is trembling. I can see a difference."

"I'll tell you why I am quivering, shivering, trembling—quaking, in fact, all at once."

Robertus Allbritton, basket maker, was attending for the first time. "Fear, anxiety, regarding the future of the Bridge, and its basket maker."

George Gill stiffened himself. "I cannot lie. I often tremble in terror."

Tristram West joined in. "Of catastrophe, death. "

Clarke Shadwell, shoemaker, looked at each of the Brotherhood. "God watches the Bridge."

Burlow Green stuck to his word choice. "The Bridge itself trembles."

Master Carpenter Edan Coldiron felt the need to summarize. "The trembling of the Bridge brings us together tonight."

Burlow Green seized upon the word he sensed Coldiron had kept in mind. "We should act *in* this state of trembling, not wait for the earthquake to dismantle us, and the Bridge."

"Yes, we are all trembling." Mister Clinkenbeard was rigid, expectant. "But we must all pledge to act out of a severe and secret sense of responsibility."

Phelan Wood cringed. "Trembling in secrecy seems somehow too circumspect."

"Our dignity runs out with the fluxes."

"The infected air as invisible as wind."

"Strange to see more citizens in the streets down on their maribones than in the churches."

"Which, however, were more crowded maugre the plague than before."

"That in these modern times, this contagion should invade London, the Dog-star, the brightest of the fixed stars of the world's cities, is a calamity as unexpected as a heart attack."

"Fifteen thousand died in Southwark, one needs to remember. Plague must have passed over the only bridge—sparing us."

"Who said that?"

*　　*　　*

A week passed before goldsmith Clinkenbeard announced the urgency of another gathering of the Brotherhood at his shop.

Coming in late, Alfred Goodyer, needles still stuck at the wrist in his left sleeve, sat beside Master Carpenter Coldiron. "One might say bridges are cursed."

Coldiron stood up straight as an ! point. "No one should curse the bridge upon which he crosses safely over."

"I have heard of the Freres Pontiffs, a religious guild that had sole power over the building of bridges throughout Italy and France." Kerry Brooke, fishmonger, felt an obligation as one informed by the Poet-Chronicler in casual conversation to inform his Brothers. "Any bridge built by those who are not of the guild is cursed, he said. We had no such guild here. Consider the story of our architect. Peter, Chaplain of Saint Mary Colechurch. Two archbishops christened there, Thomas à Becket and Edmund Scrope, but mark their several ends—Thomas à Becket murdered in his own cathedral in 1170 and Scrope, Archbishop of York, beheaded for treason in the reign of Henry IV. Mark the end of Peter de Colechurch, Warden of the Brethren of the Bridge, buried in the undercroft of the chapel next door four years before the Bridge was finished. Can we imagine he has rested easy these four and a half centuries, through other plagues and through other fires? And we in the midst of all this water, plagued by fire from one generation to another—in the midst of fire that breaks up our piers. Peter failed, one might venture to imagine, to conduct some necessary ritual that bridges, since man built the first, demand."

Over time, Coldiron's hands had passed over every inch of the Bridge. "I have never seen a sign rituals were ever conducted."

"Ah, but were signs ever actually sought?"

Clarke Shadwell almost did not speak. "Some signs we may read by light, some remain on the back side of dark."

Kerry Brooke looked round as if to discover a sign not yet seen. "We must expose all signs to light and decipher them."

Having paid no attention to what had been said, John South felt the need to say something, anything. "And cursed by water as ice. Freezes and thaws break down the Bridge as frostbite breaks down flesh. The Bridge is an organism." John South had made a leap. "Freezes and thaws break down love in human organisms."

As they told and kept secrets among themselves, each man felt a slight sense of loss of selfhood among the members of the group, present, not present, and perhaps to come, but in the same moment a magnifying of selfhood.

*   *   *

"Everything looks better from the Bridge, don't you think?" Lennox Archer asked his walking companion. Kerry Brooke did not answer. "Well, I do. You've lived here too long. Rather, you haven't lived here at all, ever."

Kerry Brooke turned from the view of ships in the Pool to the defunct drawbridge, where thousands, he knew, had died of warfare and every other kind of peril over the centuries. "I intend, at any rate, to do all I can to avoid dying here."

"I remember in the year 1664, Samuel Pepys told me he stepped in a hole in our dark and dirty street when a constable stationed there to caution nightwalkers was inattentive—almost broke a leg. So even human vigilance is unreliable."

"'Inattentive' is the word we must hold up, Lennox."

"The sound and the sick, the sick and the sound live on London Bridge that has for over these four centuries been sound and is *now* sick."

"Sick ever since the master-builder Colechurch perhaps."

"Perhaps. But now sick indeed."

*　　*　　*

The plague continuing, a few lives each week, the sick continued to breathe death upon the sound, unless the sound held in the mouth in the street.

"I refer you, gentle sirs, to Thomas Dekker." Clarke Shadwell reached up to take *The Wonderful Year*, the year of the plague of 1603, a year full of wonder, down off the shelf.

"Pray, read us from it."

"'Wherein I found one golden twilight at my window— The hardest part to play is a good man, and 'tis rare to see a long part given him to study. . . . Some go hissed off the stage. . . . Some play very long parts (and they are old men), some have done in the midst of the play (and they are young men), some, being but in a scene, before they speak are out and lost (and they are children). . . . The sergeant with the black rod (sickness) arrests us. . . . To our everlasting prison, the grave. . . . we are forced to put off our gay borrowed garments, and, wrapping ourselves in poor winding sheets, hasten to our own homes, and (still) that's the grave.'"

Several felt the urge to chime in, the rest content to savor well-known passages.

"Dekker tells us that a couple fled London to get married in a safe country town. The bride-to-be falls dead at the altar, turning the wedding into a funeral, the wedding coach into a hearse, et cetera."

"Yes, I like that one, but here's one better. A dying woman confessed adultery, but then lived to suffer the consequences."

"I give you from Dekker the man who fled the plague in London, taking his sick friend to the country. Both were struck at a tavern table on their way."

"Nothing has been as it was. Except the heads impaled on Great Gate. They looked a sort of sacrifice to pagan gods to keep the Bridge safe."

All fell silent. One laughed, igniting laughter in all others, except Clinkenbeard, who intoned, "It is an ill wind turns none to good."

* * *

Fishmonger Kerry Brooke visited Phelan Wood, who had sent word he was too sick to come to the meeting. Standing at the foot of the beds of sick folk, Kerry often opened his mouth as a philosopher.

"The truly sick seek solace, but what solace for a sick bridge? Repair workers come—and go. The houses lean against each other like sodden drunks—their balance off, depending upon weak foundations. As the Bridge sways under the staggering feet of bawdy drunks, so houses on London Bridge put their heads together, cheek to cheek, to sing."

Feverish, watching Kerry as he swayed at the foot of his bed, something to say finally came to Phelan. "Bridges seem to sway. I feel underfoot, on stairs, as if, or indeed, they are swaying."

* * *

The brotherhood was meeting now at the same time and place each week.

Dropstitch Upshaw, proud of a recent acquisition of clothes the plague cast off, opened with rare optimism. "If I may turn a phrase, 'Rare is the ill wind that blows no good.'"

"Hear, hear. The good that comes most readily to mind is the mere fact of our coming together to stand between the Bridge and whatever ill wind next visits us." Mister Clinkenbeard outspread his arms, then brought his fingertips together, then dropped his trembling hands to the following lyrics: "From the first dawn of humankind to this moment, Bridges are always being lifted up, trembling, and falling down."

"Words, words." As if alum-tainted, Mister Coldiron's lips pursed. "With all due respect for your words, Misters Upshaw and Clinkenbeard, bridges are just and only wordless bridges."

Needle maker Alfred Goodyer hoped to get a rise out of Apothecary Tristram West. "We too need some anti-pestilence pill, such as mountebanks sold fearful citizens."

Tristram ignored Alfred. "I witnessed merchants like ourselves off the Bridge, the torment of their swellings, wandering, running about so wildly, they appeared to be changing into another creature."

"Those that do wander do finally perish."

John South blinked a close to his withdrawn reverie and was in the room again as a contributor. "The dreams of old women plague our shops."

Alfred retook the center of attention. "We shall be scourged, one and all—all signs declare it."

Kerry Brooke expressed an insight that tingled his very nipples. "The beautiful mistress of the Bear Tavern at the Bridge foot, throwing herself into the Thames, was like a *voluntary* human sacrifice, don't you think?"

Dropstitch Upshaw looked all around at empty tea cups in the hands of the brotherhood. "Have we drunk all the tea then?"

*   *   *

"It's pretty out today, so today I will teach you how to play an old game for a new young girl." The old woman selected one child to serve as Bridge keeper, one on the one side, another child on the other, and positioned them to face each other.

"Raise your arches." She lined up all the other children living on the Bridge. "Now, you all know what to do."

The children filed through the arches, singing,

> "London Bridge is broken down,
> Dance o'er my Lady Lee:
> London Bridge is broken down,
> With a gay lady."

The two guard children lowered their arms, enclosed Gilda as she was passing by.

When a cart or carriage passing came perilously close, the girls jumped to the sides of the open space in the near twilight.

They sang again and again, until all the children were imprisoned in the Tower.

As the last child was thrust into the tower, all the children fled and guards chased after.

The two children the guards tagged became the next pair of good and evil bridge keepers.

*   *   *

The Brotherhood heard it all during their meeting, without being aware that they heard—the voice did not distract them—that voice singing alone today, mayhap Gilda's, or Blythe's, or another girl.

"London Bridge is broken down,
Dance o'er my Lady Lee:
London Bridge is broken down,
With a gay lady.

"How shall we build it up again,
Dance o'er my Lady Lee:
How shall we build
it up again?
With a gay lady.

"Build it up with silver and gold,
Dance o'er my Lady Lee:
Silver and gold will be stolen away
With a gay Lady.

"Build it up with iron and steel,
Dance o'er my Lady Lee.
Build it up with iron and steel,
With a gay lady.

"Iron and steel will bend and bow,
Dance o'er my Lady Lee:
Iron and steel will bend and bow,
With a gay lady.

"Build it up with wood and clay.
Dance o'er my Lady Lee:
Build it up with wood and clay,
With a gay lady.
Wood and clay will wash away.
Dance o'er my Lady Lee:

"Wood and clay will wash away,
With a gay lady.
Built it up with stone so strong,
Dance o'er my lady Lee.
Huzza! 'twill last for ages long,
With a gay lady."

Archer. "I recall variations, especially the one that ends the game with 'Take the keys and lock her up.'"

Brooke. "In the tower of London—so goes the game."

Goldsmith. "Gentlemen, the 'we' to whom she refers in singing is us merchants."

"She has a lovely voice, don't she, John?" Kerry Brooke noticed the singing as the meeting closes, but it stopped before John South could finish this question, "What voice?"

"Didn't you hear her singing 'London Bridge Is Falling Down,' that you and I as children sang?"

John himself heard nothing now.

"Oh. She's stopped."

Phelan Wood had been conjuring up images of his son, Morgan. "Children play this game, I am told, on ships sailing to the New World."

The Brotherhood began to enumerate women living or coming onto the Bridge.

*   *   *

Leaving the Tabard Inn on Tooley, Southwark, the two, Lennox Archer and Kerry Brooke, were walking the length of the Bridge north toward London together.

Both were silently brooding on that song. Lennox spoke first. "That song brings back many, many idyllic scenes of my miserable childhood before my saintly parents chose to enter this paradise."

Kerry clapped Lennox's shoulder. "And my own—only mildly miserable."

"The words and the rhythm are haunting—but the scenes of childhood they evoke are happy. An odd effect. And aren't the words rather grim, if you stop to think about them?"

"They are indeed."

Lennox paused a moment in drawbridge square. "To whom does 'my Lady Lee' refer, anyway?"

"Many of the phrases are a riddle to me—were then, are now."

"Like so many songs and tales of childhood."

"Well, no riddle in the name of the song these days. The iron is rusting, the wood is rotting, the stones are slipping. London Bridge is indeed falling down."

Having crossed the Bridge, they stepped onto Fish Street.

*   *   *

The Poet dipped his quill in ink. "And songs are bridges between peoples." The Poet wrote the first line of a new poem: "Ships are bridges from Waping to Plymouth."

*   *   *

Mister Shadwell realized too late he had not set Mister Clare's shoe down before mounting the stairs to Gilda's room. "I expected, of course, to find you here, gazing out at the river, as if without your gaze it might cease to flow. . . ."

"A river that does not move—the very picture freezes my blood, even when ice covers it." Feeling always her father's presence throughout the shop below and the house above, Gilda knew he felt no disrespect in her not turning from the window. "The *thawings* always seems like the Holy Ghost set in motion again."

"Do you ever wish for wings to carry you out over the river?"

"My gaze moves like a falcon."

"Give me your hand."

Gilda extended her hand to her father, and he led her to the third floor into his bedroom past her mother, who smiled. In the open window hung a new swing, fashioned with a single strand of rope and a round wooden seat, tied back in such a way as to allow Gilda to seat herself safely inside the window and to fly like a bird from the sill. Her father pushed her out over the water.

"Wheeeeee. . . . !"

Looking ahead, she soared as if over the twenty-one towers of the Tower of London, looking left, she soared over Saint Magnus Martyr Church and the water conduits mounted beside its steeple, looking right, she soared out far enough to look right toward the Great Gate and cast a sorrowful gaze into the eyes of the traitor heads mounted there on pikes.

*   *   *

Now and later, the Brotherhood sang the song inside along with Blythe and Gilda out in the roadway and with each when each girl sang alone.

Desiring to unlock the mysteries of the song's allusions and implications, Fishmonger Brooke actively sought explanations. Finally, an old man directed him to a man who lived on the Bridge. "Things arcane—he knows."

Another fishmonger told him, "He has been missing since the early days of the plague."

The fishmonger's wife lifted his mood again. "Perhaps he passed it on to his profligate son, his arcane knowledge. But mind you, he's only a poet."

"I will visit him."

Mister Brooke was glad of this first time opportunity to enter Nonesuch House above stairs.

The Poet seemed preoccupied.

"I visit you today, because I am told right and left of this Bridge that your father, and now you, know more about the history of this Bridge than any of us."

To rid himself of the smelly fishmonger, the Poet tossed him a fact. "The Bridge was often a fort, a barbican, as during the great civil wars of the Stuart era."

"I reached out the window and touched the sleeve of one of General Fairfax's gentlemanly soldiers as they passed by—twenty years ago."

The Poet embraced the fishmonger warmly with a generalization. "This Bridge, which holds us aloft as we talk of it, has played a unique part of great moment in the history of the world, not just four and half centuries of English history."

"May we consider a song as part of our history?"

"Some more than others."

Brooke: "I have in mind 'Lament of London Bridge.'"

"A song someone on the Bridge at this very moment may be singing. We all have sung it."

"But who among us knows its origins?"

"He or she among us whose two thousandth birthday comes round next Tuesday."

"I take your answer to be that its origin is dark. What, however, of its meaning? It, too, often seems dark, as with many sayings we mindlessly mouth. Each stanza ends 'With a gay lady.' Why 'with'?" His spread-out, uplifted arms testified to the vastness of his ignorance.

"In ancient times, dark times indeed, the lore of many peoples is full of child sacrifice, as when a mother promises the gods to sacrifice her firstborn in exchange for an end of her barrenness, but she can avoid paying that price with trickery. A child was often given alive to a creditor, who sometimes pretended to kill the child in front of the parents to test their sincerity. A child was sacrificed to heal leprosy or other illness of the king or of the child's father or father's brother or even his friend. To protect themselves from leprosy, Egyptian kings covered their seats in the baths with the blood of children. Constantine the Great was told that to cure his leprosy, he should bathe in the blood of children, but the grief of the parents moved him so deeply, he refused to have the children killed and resolved to die, but it is believed that that act of compassion miraculously cured him." The Poet as historian felt his time with the fishmonger was being well spent. "I have steeped you in centuries of the blood of children to lend credulity to this: In Europe and perhaps in Saxon or Viking England, and even during the Roman occupation, the building of bridges was thought to have been— perhaps—an affront to the gods, so to appease the jealous gods and to ward off sundry other evils, such as enemy attacks upon the bridge and thus upon the towns the bridge served, the builders of bridges some-times sacrificed a fair virgin of about thirteen, mewing her up alive in the pier next the shore on the side opposite the town."

"I had no idea."

"Of course you didn't. What monster first had it, I wonder?"

"Mind the greater good, young man."

"Mind the 'gay' suffocating child."

"Well, she's long gone—the whole legion of them—and the song, the song is on everyone's lips, lovely to listen to. *And* can anyone say bridges so sanctified have fallen over the centuries? Not I."

The Poet was beginning to feel a little exasperated. "One can imag-ine. Mortmain, dead hand, mortmain of history."

"Facts. Give me facts."

Two hours later, the Poet noticed with dismay that the eyes of this gentleman fishmonger who had called for facts had glazed over, for facts—even though they were the Poet's own figments—about the builder of the Bridge could not compete with the legend of the gay vir-gin children mewed up in thousands of bridges across the known world.

After his caller had gone but not his effluvium, the Poet returned to his mélange of facts and fancies, totally ignorant—as was the fishmon-ger as of *that* moment—of the fact that his recital had placed his life in a sort of danger for which only the word "grave" will serve.

Brushing shoulders with the fishmonger as he descended, Musetta ascended the stairs carrying, she was certain, the stink of him faintly in her clothes, which she soon cast upon the bed. The Poet drenched her in words about the fishmonger's visit, igniting a summary shrug. "The spectrum of superstitions is indeed wide and wild on the Bridge. They say that if you say goodbye to a friend on a bridge you will never see each other again. So, let us kiss and wave but never say . . ."

*   *   *

Bridge to Nowhere
To people who feared London, it was a bridge
to nowhere, especially in times of plague and fire.
To the Puritans a bridge to sin.
"Bridge to Nowhere" is a good title until
you stop and think about it. "Nowhere" always
turns out to be *somewhere*—somewhere bizarre,
unique. So maybe this Bridge—this writing—takes
my reader across time and space *to* London Bridge.

For crossers who don't come back
—those whose heads were cut off
and who returned to the Bridge dead—
this is a Bridge to nowhere. Or
missing people, seen crossing, but never
seen again. People using the Bridge to cross over
into a nowhere of their own choosing
or creation somehow, like that girl,
Blythe, who walks into plaguey London, oblivious.

Daryl Braintree

*   *   *

"I told him that shooting the Bridge is impossible at high floodtide. 'If *I* fail,' said he, '*then* say it's impossible.'"
"And did he fail, Mister Shadwell?"

"It's not known. After that declaration he was never seen again upon the Bridge."

Mister Upshaw contributed conjectures. "Then the plague took him off, or he fell through a hole in the Bridge roadway, perhaps simply vanished, as those known to have vanished vanish."

"Exactly. Just so."

Coldiron hammered a practical point into the wavering conversation. "Shooting through the arches, the tidewater caused a fall of five to six feet."

Fishmonger Brooke felt brimming with the information the Poet conveyed a few days before. "And also bear in mind, bear in mind, gentlemen, that this future Bridge also has a part of great moment in the history of the world, and if it falls, with it goes six centuries of English history. We have *that* burden also."

"Gentlemen, there is somebody in the room who has the plague."

These blessed but fearful Bridge survivors and those surviving creatures in the streets of London and environs never imagined that fire would visit London houses within the plague year and that with that fire would end all the great plagues and great fires that have contaminated and singed the pages of London's history.

10

LUCIEN TORMENTS MORGAN
AT SEA

While the plague was dying out in London, Morgan at sea whispered to Lucien, "A child's voice singing 'London bridge is broken down, broken down,' drew me out of my father's shop on the Bridge at twilight, but as I followed the sound, it dwindled and faded, gone. I heard it a few days later in the morning, not knowing whether it was a boy's or a girl's voice, and went out of my house again and found the singer in front of the House of Many Windows—a girl of about three or four, all alone, whirling as she sang. Out of her mouth, the song soared up across the windows, sad-sounding, not a play song, but strangely beautiful, not beautiful as a song sung by a child playing, but unforgettable, as you can see, and all these years, she has been the muse of my memory as I meditate and often write about the Bridge. My spiritual sister, Blythe."

That night, Lucien dreamed he was a child again, before the first shot was fired in the Civil War, playing with Morgan's "spiritual sister," singing, dancing on London Bridge. Morgan's "sister" was, by his intention to seek her out, now already Lucien's sister too—the Lucien of this moment—exposed to his lust, to the Luciferian pride that kept him beating his wings at a great height above the petty struggles of men.

The next night, Lucien took Morgan by the hand, speaking in a voice he had not heard before. "I have seen the girl as she is now, thirteen years old, still singing and dancing, not just sad-sounding now, but distracted, mad, savage, almost screaming the song, like Cassandra in Troy. This girl child, I claim as my own, *my* spiritual sister. Although, who knows, she may be a boy, dressed as a girl."

*   *   *

Early August, ashore in Lisbon, Morgan sat down beside a seaman, a stranger, sunning on a wrought-iron bench in a public garden. Without opening his eyes, his head tilted back to catch sunrays full face, the seaman spoke to him. "Imagine, this same sunlight on London, where the plague is killing every poor soul it touches, thousands, they say, more since months ago."

"They?"

"Seamen whose ships were turned away and escaped the lurking Dutch. And now I'm telling you. Don't go home, lad."

"How do you know I'm English? And a lad? Eyes shut."

"I can smell the difference, youth in general and English in particular, and overall, the sea."

Roaming the streets of Lisbon, Morgan sought out seamen from other ships until he had gathered a fuller, traumatic story, that the plague had diminished, wondering whether Lucien had come from London with the plague in his clothes.

Lucien gorged himself on onions, scallions, and beans to torment Morgan.

Morgan was on the verge of sleep when sickening fumes pulled him back to clear consciousness. "Every man, woman, and child on the Bridge, I fear, is dead of the plague." Lucien's words came out of black dark, seeming to Morgan like cold water, drop by drop, off a roof onto the neck.

"Not so. Everybody on the Bridge was spared, as they were in earlier plagues."

"You can know only what you are told, and I was told the Bridge is bereft of people."

Lucien's tone was not the lulling voice it had been for weeks.

"They told me all on the Bridge were spared."

"They? The plague still visits the City. The men who lived who tell about it left before the plague came onto the Bridge."

Even as it seemed to abate, the foul fumes sank into his nostrils.

"Why are you telling me?"

"If you go home to the Bridge, everyone will be rank strangers."

"Why do you want me to imagine that?" Lucien did not answer. "Lucien? Are you asleep?"

As they rose for night watch, Morgan hoped Lucien would speak to him out of the dark in his earlier lulling voice.

As they stood watch in the moonlight, Morgan looked at him, expectant, but either Lucien's back was turned or his profile was immobile.

Every night the smell returned, not from something dead, or someone sick or dying. Morgan fixed upon Lucien, even though his health seemed better than ever.

Feeling his way about in the dark to go on deck for the morning watch, Morgan felt hot, sleep-fetid breath in his ear and a mouth grazing his cheek. He reached out, but took hold of nothing.

On deck, Morgan watched Lucien's every muscle-move.

Taking a moment from work on the rigging to lean over the rail at noon, Morgan felt someone coming up close behind, turned, and looked up, into Lucien's face in full sunlight. "One of these nights, would you like to be Blythe?"

"What?" When Lucien said nothing, Morgan asked again, then again, and again, but Lucien did not move. His eyes stared down at Morgan, but as if looking into the night sky for the farthest star. "No," Morgan replied, finally. "No. No. No."

He returned to his work on the rigging.

All day and off and on during each night for a week, he imagined why Lucien had asked him that question. He asked Lucien again, why, but got no answer, only the stare. He knew what other men meant by that. He had fought off many men who told him he was beautiful, lovely, sweet, a tasty morsel, that his ass was home port, his mouth was a sea cunny, his eyes were girlish, his voice was alluring, his pissing prick was worth hell twice over, and some even begged, eyes tear-swollen. He knew what they wanted, craved, and might at any moment take by force, he knew because he knew what he alone had discovered before he could ejaculate, that friction alone was delicious in the way hitting your crazy bone would be if it didn't also hurt. Older men and young men had come and gone and some remained aboard who had grabbed his buttocks, his cock, who had, in passing behind him, licked his neck.

"Pretend I am a priest. Then later you can confess."

Morgan did not reply, and Lucien said no more, but left that smell in the dark for Morgan to suffer.

The next night came too soon, sudden as Lucien's voice. "No, you are not a girl, but you are not a man either, you are a boy trying to become a young man, and left alone you can become very much a man, but one night you will be a girl, and then you will never be the man you are now trying to be. I know. You are afraid. I know. Be merely afraid now, because as you are being a girl for me, you will be terrified, or you will be thrilled, but imagining it now, you are afraid. I will wait. You will come to me. To kill me or to surrender to me. Killing me will make you a man, if I don't kill you first, but then you will be a man who is a killer, like me. Being a girl for me will make you either a girl forever or a man who has once been a girl. Think about it. Imagine it. Curse me. Pray to resist me. Pray *to* me. Or avoid me. Try to sneak up on me and push me overboard—take that risk. But even now, you are not the same. You will never be the same, even if lightning strikes me on the midnight watch. You are already becoming a girl. Dream about *us.* Lie awake and go over and over it. Linger in a limbo between waking and sleeping and toss and turn in *it,* so that *it* will happen many times before it happens."

No, no, Morgan told himself, no, and returned to inscribing his memories of the Bridge in the margins of the books his father had given him for his self-education. Being between the covers of books, inside the folds of memory, on the Bridge, strolling on the Bridge, was as if he had a solitary room on the ship, door unlocked, but admissible to no one. "The Sinful Seaman hangs above me, perfectly still." Naming him gave Morgan a sense of power over him.

*   *   *

As Morgan opened pages of Tyndale's translation of the *New Testament* looking for clean margins in which to write, the Poet wrote a draft of a new poem:

One and Only
I have set out upon these nocturnal walks
on London Bridge every night but a few
for the past several months.
The Bridge is *in* my unconscious
and *on* my mind each day. How unique in the known and
unknown universe does that make me? One other person
—my double, as John Donne saw his wife's double in Paris—
is, in time, contemplating a book
of poems on the Bridge perhaps, but how improbable is it
that even one person, who has ever lived or ever will live,
thinks and writes of the Bridge every day and night,
coming daily into a room where a print or painting
of the Bridge hangs. A drudge, at least, in some great hall
where Holbein's painting of a view
from a window on the Bridge hangs?
So am I, possibly, the *only* creature in all creation
who steps onto a page, onto the London Bridge
of past eras each night? If so, "it is
a consummation devoutly to be wished."
To love one of a kind. To be
he who walked on the Bridge, who
stood out of the rain in a doorway, whose
shoe soles mayhap kept two spots dry.
Almost reason enough
to have been—to be—a consciousness.
For, even though I have walked many bridges,
these nocturnal strolls on London Bridge
are excursions of consciousness.
Do I step toward God?
                                                   Daryl Braintree

*   *   *

In the margin of *The Canterbury Tales,* Morgan wrote:

"On the Bridge now, it is dark for me, on my Bridge, London Bridge. Mine because it is not a street, it is unlike anywhere else men have set up abode. So for each of us, it is 'my' Bridge, with others living by on each side, and across the way, tight together. Where, when it is not dark, they, the heads on pikes above, cast down shadows, across my path. They, now, cast no shadows. No moon. Except by an inner light, that spiritual light that flows through all ever alive and now living, their shadows, the shadows of only transient, ferociously reluctant residents, guests fall across my consciousness tonight, as I stand at the Bridge foot, in times of plague. But not tomorrow in the moonlight. Then I am free of them, unless I look up, against the light, standing firm on my London Bridge."

"I open my window just as a woman opens hers over at Southwark," wrote the Poet, even as Morgan was writing. "We see each other's arm flung wide with finger tips pressing back the shutters till the wall stops them, and aren't we sensible of waking up to two very different ways of life—ways of feeling about, experiencing our domiciles, habitats on this Bridge?"

*   *   *

"Malcontent." Morgan blushed for choosing a weak word.

"*I,* a malcontent? Shame on you for a flagrant euphemism. A malcontent is to me as a gnat is to a vulture. Say the word. Is it hideous enough to put *me* in your mouth?"

"Sinful Seaman." Morgan hissed at him.

Derisively, Lucien's arms flailed at him, his legs gyrating as if they, too, were arms.

Lucien whispered to him at every possible opportunity. When Morgan was aware that Lucien sometimes caught him writing in the margin of one of his books, he stopped, pretended only to read. Telling Lucien about the Bridge had given him an even finer solace than writing about it had given him before Lucien came aboard, and he knew that writing now was not as good as telling Lucien had been. But Lucien was now a different man, replacing the man who had listened to his nocturnal memories of the Bridge.

Evil farts silently, Morgan thought, tears stinging his eyes.

Reaching into its hiding place in the hold of *The Rocket* for Plato's *Republic,* his hand felt splintery wood only. Chaucer's place was empty. Tyndale's *New Testament* was gone, and *The Canterbury Tales.* None of his books were in their several hiding places, in the cargo and other places about the ship.

"Where did you hide my books?"

"I didn't hide your books. I ate them. Listen for me to expel them in an endless series of silent rhetorical farts."

"You are the very cesspool of evil."

"You are a boy, no match for a man who kills for pleasure as often as he can freely, secretly, safely do it. Even so, you flatter me. I have not yet achieved evil so pure that I am its very cesspool. I so aspire."

"I'll find them, each one of them."

"Unless I flung them into the sea."

"Did you? Tell me, so I won't—"

"Ah, you know torment is my aim."

"If you hid them, I will find them. If you flung them into the sea, I will triumph by taking the sea as metaphor of my memory."

"I hid them. Find them if you can."

On the second dog watch, Lucien whispered, as he passed behind Morgan so swoopingly that he was not there when he turned, "After your books, comes your virginity, little girl, little girl, little girl."

Alert, Morgan remembered the Bridge as shield and solace, down to its very stones. He prayed, alert. Even his sleep had a quality of alertness. "Stay alert. Watch," he told himself, sometimes aloud, he realized, when Lucien, unseen, shouted into the wind, "Stay alert! Watch!"

"Did you hear the news?" The voice was yet another of an expanding repertoire of voices at Lucien's command, each quite natural, none really theatrical except in effect.

Morgan hoped his blank look would make Lucien hold his tongue.

"I didn't see you on deck. All hands on deck, except for yours. Would you like to hear the news you missed then?" Morgan turned away. "No good, turning your back on me, Mistress Morgana. The captain called us all on deck to tell us, through the first mate, of course, that your Plato, your Chaucer, your Shakespeare, your Dekker, your Bible, your handwritten marginal memories have been destroyed. How, he refused to say, despite my fervent pleas. And he declared that someone will go to your Bridge one day and burn it, leaving naked piers of stone like grave stones in River Thames, like cathedral spires, like Stonehenge."

Believing him, Morgan turned for deliverance to silent prayer. As the Holy Ghost pervaded his soul, he was pushed forward, crushed under a great weight that lifted an instant, in which cold air and a rod smacked his buttocks. Bucking, he put air between his back and the weight and the thrusting rod that failed to penetrate, again and again, until Lucien lay sprawled on the deck, and began to roll, laughing, in a fit.

"In time." Lucien got up, twice naked in the dawn light: his cock— his rapier body.

Morgan expended his anger and outrage, running around and around the deck, shocked that his own cock was erect.

Morgan so compulsively steeped his mind in memory that the same fewer and fewer memories came to him in almost regular cycles, monotonous, predictable, but bright and clear, and finally compulsively, but with less and less power to solace.

Joining Morgan at the rail, the cook clapped his hands. "The captain says we are taking on a cargo of coffee and sailing home, Morgan."

Never certain whether Lucien only seemed to be out of sight and earshot, Morgan risked speaking to Master's Mate Chriswell. "I want to go home. Please convey to the Captain my desperate wish to sign off and take another ship bound for London."

"I must give him a reason." He sounded as if he knew the reason, but only wanted to hear it from Morgan's own mouth.

"Fear for my life" was what came out of his mouth.

"You must stop persecuting poor Lucien." The Master's Mate shook his fist in Morgan's face. "A man with a fatal disease. A man who always thinks first of his friends."

"I have never seen you near Lucien."

"Oh, but I see *you*—*at* him, at every turn."

Morgan shut up and eased away from Master's Mate Chriswell.

He decided to jump ship in the next port. Imagining how he would do it and the adventures and misadventures he would have between the ends of the earth and finally his home on the Bridge, he thought better of it and nerved himself to go directly to the Captain, an act he knew was seldom justified, without the intercession of the Master's Mate. About to lose his life in saving his soul, he knocked on the Captain's door, confident that he had nothing more to risk.

"Before you speak to me, young man, think of the consequences of coming directly to me."

"It is a matter, captain, worse than life or death."

"A rehearsed speech is usually a sign of desperation, and I heed all such signs. Tell your story—skip the long of it, go to the short of it."

Morgan told it, as if with short, blunt strokes of a quill.

"Indeed. Indeed. I have noticed that man. He strikes me as more inscrutable than the usual inscrutable seaman and therefore is something of a worry to me. I will instruct Master's Mate Chriswell to watch him."

"Master's Mate Chriswell *has* been watching him, Captain, but in such a way that he sees me as the tormentor."

"Indeed. I will watch them both then, with some interest. And you, too, Master Wood. Now you have given me more than enough to watch—but after my nap, if indeed I am *able* to nap. Out."

Morgan left the Captain's cabin uneasy, and walked on a deck that seemed it would turn, with a single misstep, into quicksand.

That night, no voice came down from the bunk above. *He* knows, too. Master's Mate Chriswell told him before I was told. Homeward bound, Lucien will act again now, draw back, or attack.

Morgan waited. After six days and nights not only of silence but of few glimpses of Lucien, Morgan impulsively spoke his name, "Radford," Lucien's childhood name, "Radford," again and waited, hoping to appeal as if child to child, tormented to tormented. "Radford, have you turned?" Into the third silence, he dropped off to sleep.

After the first dogwatch, he returned to his hammock. Upon it, Plato, Chaucer, the Bible, and his several other books lay, as if casually, not in anger, tossed.

"Thank you, Radford," he whispered that night, up into the pitch dark, as if to a new-found friend.

A pain at his bunghole woke him, flat on his stomach, a weight on his back. A strength his body had never before exerted thrust the weight and the blunt battering ram off and into the abyss.

Lucien was not above in his hammock.

"The quick and the dead." A voice at his back at high noon was new. Morgan turned and looked up at Lucien. He did not move, fixed like a furled mast, eyes like a rook just alighted. "Now you are quick, now you are dead."

After three nights of wakeful watchfulness, Morgan went again to see the Captain.

"I know the gold merchant Clinkenbeard to whom your father is indebted, and several of the other merchants he has indentured you to, keeping you at sea from ship to ship for half your young life, homeless. But a man in the making. I like this man who stands now before me. Let me think on it. Tomorrow night we take on the pilot. Stay awake one more night. 'The quick and the dead, indeed.' What does he think *he* is?"

Morgan stayed awake, but his hammock swung empty. Moving from place to place about the ship, he kept out of sight. Under a sky full of stars and moonlight, he watched the pilot come aboard. He had never seen a pilot come aboard in the night. "The Pilot came aboard in the night," the cook had told him that first time, seven years ago, a mysterious saying that he sometimes repeated to himself at night in reverie on the verge of sleep, out of his feeling about Christ as being his Pilot.

Having unloaded the cargo, the men went ashore at Tangier. Tomorrow they would take on new cargo and set sail at last for London.

Morgan was happy not to have to jump ship.

"Good," said Master's Mate Chriswell, seeing Morgan on deck reading Tyndale's translation of the New Testament. "Lucien needs to be free of you for a time. But, say, what are you doing with Lucien's favorite book?"

"It belongs to me. See the inscription. That's my father's hand-writing."

"Back talk. Lucien always says you're a master of back talk. Best not to give *me* any of your back talk. Mimicking him, are you? The same books? Go off on your own and leave the poor man alone, hell-born babe."

* * *

At twilight, Morgan came upon Lucien, nude, bent over the rail. Looking down into the sea, watching dolphins, exposing to Morgan his torn up, hemorrhoid-ridden bunghole. Hell Mouth?

* * *

Going ashore with the Second Mate, an unusual situation, the Captain turned at the gangway and tossed his head, winking, at Morgan.

Morgan did not witness Lucien's going ashore nor his return to the ship. He did not look for him. The Captain's parting wink reassured him enough to return to his hammock that night.

"I said my name's Phillip. . . ." A new voice above in Lucien's hammock woke Morgan.

He felt his way out of the dark onto the deck and stayed until his watch.

A new man appeared on deck to keep the watch with him. At first light, they were relieved and went below.

The new man climbed up into Lucien's hammock and sunk into it.

"What's your name?"

Morgan got the answer he expected. "My name's Phillip, what's yours?"

"Call me Morgan, but not for long. I'm signing off in London Pool and taking a walk on London Bridge."

"London Bridge, aye? Never clapped eyes on it, but it's one of the wonders of the world, they tell me."

On the morning watch, a new Master's Mate asked Morgan for a report. "All's well."

"Yes, well, not quite. You see me instead of Mister Chriswell—and why is that?"

"I don't know, sir."

"Dead ashore of a cutthroat."

Lucien, he was certain, did it. His own friend. No, Lucien had no friends. Put off the ship by the captain, at Morgan's request, the Master's Mate, Morgan's substitute? No. No, reason. Purely out of sheer perversity.

Cargo in the hold, mooring ropes slipped, Morgan took a last look at the last country not his own.

On the dock, looking up, hands in his pockets, stood Lucien, looking forlorn, like a boy named Radford Croft.

Morgan called his name, "Radford!" and pointed at him, "'In the world, ye shall have tribulations. But be of good cheer. I have overcome the world.'"

Radford-Lucien merely turned and walked away.

Among the hammocks, the men were all talking, profoundly shaken with disappointment.

"The ship has been diverted to take on more cargo that will make us dangerously over-laden."

"But then, at last, we shall indeed set about for England."

"Or so they say."

11

THE POET BUILDS LONDON BRIDGE OF STONE

With great delight, the Poet told Musetta that he was at last deep into writing the story of Peter's epic task of rebuilding the Bridge, considering elm as of old, when suddenly—

"Or make the Bridge itself of stone, Holy Spirit?"

A roving knife sharpener, looking over at Peter, stepped smack in a puddle, and stomped and skipped on.

"Peter, you will build a stone Bridge from London across River Thames to Southwark," he commanded himself, "and it will last until the last trump reconciles the north and south shores—now divided by the turbulence of the river—to each other."

After Mass, Peter took his master-builder out upon the Bridge again. "Make the Bridge itself of stone, for the people's sake, to serve them long after you and I molder in our graves."

That possibility struck George dumb, his face giving Peter the impression that he already felt he was standing on a Bridge of stone that he had built himself. Peter felt it with him. Without a word, awe-struck, they embraced, as if consecrating a mutual pledge.

* * *

Looking into his eyes, Mark reached up and put his arm around Peter's shoulder. "As God said, 'Let there be light.' As John said, 'In the beginning was the word and the word was made flesh.' Lo, Peter says, 'Let the Bridge be made of stone.'"

* * *

1173, February 21. Archbishop Thomas à Becket was canonized.
When Barbra took the drawing from Peter with one hand and looked at it and dropped the fingers of her other hand lightly upon her breast, and said, "Do it, Peter," he knew how much she believed in him and wanted to see a Bridge of stone and walk upon it.

"'Christians see the invisible, hear the inaudible, attempt the impossible, believe the incredible.'"

"I simply see you at work on it." Barbra discreetly covered her bare leg.

Peter turned the conversation from the chapel and the Bridge to Saint Thomas himself. "Tell me everything you know about Saint Thomas."

"I knew him as I know them all, and his cock was not outstanding."

Looking at her, Peter saw a body visited by a Saint. Odd. But he remembered libertine Augustine confessing that 'In those days I kept a mistress not joined to me in lawful marriage; but one found out by wandering lust empty of understanding.'

Peter wagged his finger. "Jesting was far, far from my mind."

Her body sweetly convulsed into a posture of serious remembrance. "I knew him first as Thomas of London, then less as Chancellor, as Archbishop not at all. All personages I knew knew him, though none knew him well. But enough, I fear, to tell me more than enough to require me to play Scheherazade. Night the first. . . ."

* * *

Having read aloud one of his favorite scenes between Peter and Barbra, the Poet-Chronicler looked Musetta full in the face. "Am I not clever?"

"No disputing."

"It suddenly occurs to me, however, that of all the words in the English language, neither I nor anyone I know of, not even Shakespeare or Milton, certainly not Dryden, speaks all the words on which we might draw, or writes them. Were one to turn to a book of words and hold it in one's hand, one must admit that one cannot lay hold from memory and make use of more than perhaps twenty percent of them."

"Let us turn to that very book."

"What book?"

"The one whose ponderousness you invoked."

"Are you saying there is no such book?'

"I pause."

"There is no such book!"

"Then you must *omnium gatherum* the words of our language."

"Perhaps I shall. Perhaps I shall. Someday . . ."

*   *   *

To begin building the London side bridgehead frame of oak, Edan, master carpenter, reached for his hammer, grasped it firmly, bent his elbow several times to feel the hammer's heft, and plucked from his leathern apron a nail and pounded it into the deck plank. This event altered the way the universe as we now know it is set up.

The sound of the hammer penetrated distance and took up places in thirty consciousnesses. Almost five hundred years later, we gaze upon the nail and know the event of its penetration into the frame of the bridgehead.

*   *   *

Christopher Wren, renowned architect, scrutinized the Poet's drawing of a pier. "What Peter needs is to come up with the concept of the starling, the outwork that surrounds the piers, projecting in front, to protect against the force of the stream, reduce the flow of the water, to prevent the tides shifting the rubble, running out from under the pier, an extension of the pier resembling the bow of a boat. Starlings—well, look out the window, down there at the closest pier—resemble a wherry even more. They also help prevent damage from impact of vessels. Peter must drive piles close together, creating the shape of the starling, drain the water, build each pier, and fill each starling with loose rubble stones to stabilize each pier. This drawing of the Bridge as you have conceived it—well, you, Daryl, dear poet, should be an architect."

"I *must* be, if I am to be Peter de Colechurch, for a while."

* * *

On the Nature of Bridge Building
The erection of a bridge is an act
of defiance, against Nature,
against Death, an act
like the Tower of Babel, an act
of mastery. But the act
of erecting a bridge
produces a mystery
—and consilience with God.
The trembling
of bridges. Bridges
always tremble,
as working clocks
always tick, as
blood beats.
A finished bridge poses a question.
Will it fall? Does anyone,
Bridge builder or crosser, ever cross
without a twinge, at least, of fear?
Gephyrophobia: fear of crossing bridges,
like the fear that the rope by which one dangles
will suddenly snap.

Daryl Braintree

* * *

Eager to tell Barbra what he had enthusiastically told Mark, Peter visited her earlier than usual.

"Are you aware, Madam, of the animal fact that you are stark, raving naked?" 'Her veins are blue, a very map of London's Lanes."

"I am the devil herself incarnate, come to tempt and torment you, Father."

"No, Madam, you are from God, who delights in my faithfulness. Drape thyself. . . . For Lent, I affirm my intention to finish the new Bridge by Easter. And—"

"The wagons carrying elm for the framework into the town wake me each morning." Barbra pretended a drawn-out yawn.

"—and I have resolved, you will kindly note, to give up lust."

"Prick of conscience!" Shocked, Barbra seemed to imagine all London following Peter's example.

*   *   *

Picking a gristle from between her teeth, Barbra broke their pause with this: "From what you are telling me, I gather that your Bridge—"

"Our Bridge—that is to say, God's Bridge."

"—is mired in language."

"So it seems, so in practice it is. My assistant, Allen, tallied for me this morning the toll language has taken in time—misspent labor, and human suffering, accidents, even death. For want of a word."

"You see before you, draped on this couch from Paris, a perfect example of the convergence of languages. I am of Viking extraction from the eastern Highlands of Scotland. I speak only the language of the Franks, I write only Latin, and to speak any one of the mongrel tongues of this island would be like fucking a lawyer after fucking a prince without washing."

"You cannot speak the Saxon or any other tongue at all?"

"Painful sounds. What in this world did you just ask me?"

"I can speak Saxon, though haltingly, only because I am myself at times face to face with a worker and an immediate problem and must muster words to tell him how, do not, or why not. Words I keep like keepsakes from my father, son of a Jutland warrior from Kent and my mother a Norman from north of London."

"Your assistant Allen should indeed feel sheepish caught speaking Saxon and, did you say, the garbled tongue of the Danish or Norse Kentish dialects as well?"

"Yes, poor man, and neither of them very well, because he feels tongue-tied. I give him an order in Frankish and he hangs about until I leave and then passes it on to the men in Saxon or whatever other language he has garnered for practical use."

"As a saving grace, can he write Latin?"

"He has learned a few terms which he employs on his sketches and plans—for my eyes, I suspect."

"Tell me again, in Norman, why this tangle torments you so?"

"I am building—we, O Lord, are building—a Bridge for our people, from the lowest peddler, even beggar, to the King himself. They will all have daily use of the Bridge as a common experience, and yet crossing, on it, they, men and women of England, setting foreigners aside for the moment, speak an assortment of languages—"

"Is the Frankish tongue then part of a mere assortment and not the sky over all?"

"—and cannot therefore communicate, except in a kind of dumb show of gestures that hark back to eras before language. As nature impedes our progress in building the Bridge, so language interferes with and will or may impede commerce on the Bridge when it comes alive with our people."

"And yet you speak Latin in church."

"And the Frankish tongue when I converse with churchmen and magnates and the court. But Latin in church is in harmony with Latin in scriptures."

"Originally Greek. Latin is a sublime improvement. Worry such as yours produces, in time, change. Do you see that this line of reason—"

"I do not reason, I merely worry, and only just today."

"But do you not see that this line of 'worrying' could lead, in you and others, such as your friend Mark, for only one instance, to the most lamentable step imaginable?"

"And what, pray tell, is that?"

"Translation of Latin—"

"Do not speak it. Into the vernacular tongue?"

"What in your experience moves you to the thought that a common language would enable men to understand each other, when those who speak French and write in Latin dispute quite readily? That the men who build the Bridge from the bottom up do not understand the Frankish tongue is one thing, because knowing it affects in no way how they lift stone or timber, but that they should one day come to read and understand scripture can lead to questions such as you and Mark often torment yourselves with."

"I come here to you, Madam, for the consolation that comes from the contemplation of the beauty of God's handiwork, none other than yourself."

"And, poor Peter, what I sometimes give you is a piece of my mind."

"Setting aside with a kind of secular piety, that youthful night in the Garden of Eden with you, it may now very well *be* for your mind that I crave your company more than for the spectacle of your beauty, Madam."

"Let us dwell upon that thought, as I become haggard with age and snaggle-toothed."

"Ah, you see, you can't help yourself, you are come here through your grandfather of the Danish Isles, and snaggle-toothed will out, confounding your Frankish speech."

"I have fouled my nest. Forgive me, King Henry."

*   *   *

"My dear Musetta, did you hear about the couple that fled the London plague to get married in a safe country town?"

"Pray tell."

"She fell dead at the altar. . . ."

"Don't tell me that!"

"The wedding became a funeral."

"Not another word, please."

"The wedding coach became a hearse."

"I have seen with my own eyes more than I shall ever tell."

"Not even me?"

"Especially not you."

"Not even if I tell you one more?"

"No more, I beg you."

"A woman at death's door confesses adultery to her husband, but she wakes up not dead."

"Some things interest young poets more than normal people."

"Who would not want to hear about the man who fled London, leaving his plague-stricken friend behind, to seek the crystalline air of the country, and was struck dead at a tavern table just outside Moorgate?"

"I, for one, refuse to hear more."

*   *   *

"Do you like music?" Barbra uttered her most musical tones.

"You know, building the Bridge, rowing up close to the work done and the work being done, I have come to prefer, above even liturgical music, the music of the air and the wind among the pilings and the fluting through the two finished piers."

"I know. I try to hear what you hear, but I hear only the bells."

"Tolling, tolling . . . tolling. A sad and melancholy music after the death of my workmen."

"I know, dear friend, that the drownings and the accidents plague your dreams."

"Especially the drownings. And haunt me when I return to the bank in the twilight to review the day's work."

"They lie among the swords ancient warriors tossed into River Thames."

"Oh, don't let's be poetic. The poor sinners sank slowly as their lungs filled up with River Thames, and we always find them, along the south bank usually, below Southwark, and further downstream than you would suppose. . . ."

"Yes, but a few never found?"

"Snatched by wild dogs or boars, on the Isle of Dogs or wandering in from the forests. I wish I might bury them all in Saint Mary's yard."

'With our saintly Archbishop Thomas. I hear, Holy Spirit, music I can never follow to the source.'

*   *   *

Peter is in a cove, close-woven trees, feels, God is here, then feels he is in Barbra's curving cunny. The juxtaposition, the contrast bewilders him.

*   *   *

"It is another sign that our love is not physical, Father." Barbra stroked his healed, naked wound.

"A mangled arm does not—"

"A sign only. Not a prevention. We still could, if we would."

"We could, but we won't?"

"Unless someday we do."

"Fucking you again now after all these decades would be rather anticlimactic." Peter turned from the view of London that made her window famous throughout the realm. "The Bridge work will not suffer delay because my arm is mangled."

"Yes, and perhaps the men will work with even greater dedication."

"Even so, one of my hardest workers has only one arm."

"But did he not come to the work one-armed?"

"Yes, that is a difference. And he has a woman he could not lift with two good arms."

"I've devoted this afternoon to musing." Barbra covered more of her body with a fold of her chemise.

"Is that an invitation to ask about *what* you have been pondering?"

"Not pondering exactly. More precisely, musing. Here's what. We had no choice when we were born human. But it is we who choose to be reborn Christian. You know the story of the boy who was raised as a dog and resisted becoming human a long time, but finally chose to be reborn human, and who then discovered sin and chose to be born a third time as a Christian."

1188. Year 13, arch 3 finished, pier 5 started.

While Daryl was still captive inside Musetta, she changed the subject. "What progress on the Bridge, my love? Why the look of utter surprise?"

"You never asked about it before."

"That's neither here nor there. Tell me."

"I think not."

"Rather, show me. You never offer to show me."

"No, I think not. Somehow, I feel, I must—"

"Inarticulate?" Her body began, as if on its own, to move again.

"Yes, I must confess. Kiss me."

"I think not. I will only say that I am a bridge you may not cross tonight."

*   *   *

"I must put aside the tormenting thought that I who made the Bridge will have been dead long, long before the Bridge itself falls."

Barbra set before him a dish of berries picked without Moorgate.

"Peter, watching your men at work, I feel you are yourself the one workman doing all the work and I am elated—though by increments of inches, for it is, you know, very, very slow."

Peter remembered his mother saying that to his father about the building of Saint Paul's, even now still unfinished, the stones his father laid snugly in place though.

1189. Year 14, pier 5 finished, arch 4 started.

*   *   *

Peter sank into Barbra's new chair, gift of a Bishop whose name she was not inclined to utter. "The hours pass heavy as stone. I look at the unfinished Bridge and I see my life thus far in each stone, most of them under water, under the riverbed. I felt more lifted up as we built the first three piers than I do now with this twelfth. The fourteenth will only remind me that I cannot stop there, but must go on into a new century until the nineteenth or twentieth pier—I know not how many the river will demand— is finished."

'I am tired, Lord. I suffer the sin of taking pleasure only fitfully now in the sight of work on the Bridge.'

* * *

1192. Year 17, pier 7 finished, arch finished.

"Each day you watch the work become a Bridge and you come here and watch me become nothing." Barbra lay in a posture in which he had never seen her. "When I am gone, you can look at the Bridge, but you cannot look at me. Gone is gone. Remember me. And pray for my soul in purgatory."

'As out of the stink and filth of the river we raise this holy and beautiful fabric, Holy Spirit, I watch a beautiful woman sink deeper and deeper into the decay and stink of her own body.'

"Put it out of your mind, if you can, Peter."

"Out of my mind? My mind is *in* it, you, in you and whatever it is that is killing you, dear lady."

"I'm sorry, but now I must go. I am very nearly in the mind of God."

Barbra, now about 80 and afraid of English as of disease or death, spoke to him on her deathbed in French and all Peter's words to her were in French.

* * *

Peter walked alone to the middle of the Bridge, unfinished on the South side, into the unfinished Saint Thomas Chapel where he was eager to conduct masses.

'And then, God, she was gone. You took her. She is not here to say to you, Here I am, Lord.

'But how can I cry woe? You blessed me with her presence all those years and I should be grateful and I *am* grateful. You know I am. Is missing her an act of ingratitude? I incline not to think so, Jesus. She is here in the work. She was there, you remember, when I conceived it, and she said, "Do it, Peter." When she took the drawing from me with one hand and looked at it and dropped the fingers of her other hand lightly upon her breast, I knew how much she believed in my capability to do it and wanted to see it, to be able to say, "Behold, the Bridge."

'Now, God, she is gone and the Bridge is still a-building and I may be gone before the first footsteps sound upon the Bridge.

'Peter's Memorial: *Barbra, who imagined the Bridge and watched the work.*'

1201. Year 26, Bishop Foliot died. Barbra, beloved courtesan, died.

*   *   *

Bridges Are Falling
Bridges must first support
their own weight. Then yours and mine.
For if ever a construction's purpose lay clearly before us,
a bridge's *does*. And any other half-hearted, tentative
use contradicts that purpose.
Between this bank and that bank.
From North to South. Bridges
are demarcations. And the bridge's elements
must resist the elements: wind, earthquake, ice,
snow, rain, flood, sleet, hail, the rising
and falling of temperature, as
the sun rises and goes down. Timber bridges
—a few feet to several miles long,
from covered to suspended—are rising
and falling all over the world.

Daryl Braintree

*   *   *

After an absence longer than ever before, Mark, a wandering scholar, someone told Peter, had gone northwest into the Hebrides.

*   *   *

"Into thy hands I commend my spirit, O Lord. Into thy hands I commend my soul, O Lord. For we must die unto ourselves in loving thee, O Lord. Into thy hands, I commend my soul, O Lord."

*   *   *

As Peter was dying in pain that made him cry out again, again and again, "The stones, the stones, like knives!" he was trapped on the burning Bridge. His father took him up in his arms and ran with him, but they were still on the Bridge when Peter suffocated, in time.

1205. Peter de Colechurch, architect of London Bridge, died, leaving the Bridge unfinished, and over a hundred workers dead.

*   *   *

"What, Edmund, were his last words?" Bishop William of Ste Mere l'Eglise held both Edmund's hands, looking directly, deeply into his eyes.

"'Light is God's shadow. It is finished.'"

*   *   *

Peter's clerk, Edmund of Lewes, opened Peter's letter: "By the west wall under the fig tree in Saint Mary's bone yard, between the graves of my mother and my father, you will find a narrow grave, as one for a child, sunken, unmarked. Dig up the bones. They are the mortal remains of Saint Thomas à Becket, whose family house once stood next that wall. Secretly and without ceremony, bury the bones of the Blessed

Martyr Saint Thomas à Becket, Archbishop of Canterbury, as if they were my own, in the undercroft of Saint Thomas Chapel, in a tomb of black and white marble, under the stairway leading down from the upper chapel, going down to the water. No monument, no inscription, explaining that I wanted only the Bridge and the chapel as sufficient memorial to the memory of their builder.

"Then bury my own body, secretly, in the unmarked grave where Thomas has so long lain at Saint Mary's between my parents' graves by the wall under the fig tree."

* * *

In a crowd that almost crushed him, Edmund led the burial cortege from Saint Mary Colechurch on Poultry, out of Old Jewry, down Fish Street, across the Bridge, still unfinished on the Southwark side, to the burial ceremony for Peter de Colechurch, master-builder of London Bridge, in the not yet finished Saint Thomas Chapel.

That night, solitary Edmund dug up the remains of Saint Thomas à Becket in Saint Mary's graveyard, carried them onto the Bridge and into the chapel, broke into the tomb in the undercroft, removed the body of his former master, Peter, replaced it in the tomb with the body of Saint Thomas, and conveyed Peter's body to the churchyard, where he buried it in the open grave, lying on his side, as Thomas had lain, to fit in the narrow space, between Peter's mother and father. At Peter's earthen grave, a stone bore, for disguise, the name Mark.

By order of William of Ste Mere l'Eglise, Bishop of London, this inscription was graven on the eighth pier, under the north side of the chapel: 1205 *Obiit Petrus Capellanus de Colechirche, qui inchoavit pontem lapideum Londoniensem, et sepultus est in capella super pontem.* The same is recorded in the Annals of Waverley Abbey, *Annales Monastici,* volume II, page 256. Go see.

* * *

"Peter's friend Mark vanished without a trace. It is said that as he departed he said what Rabelais is rumored to have said on his deathbed. 'I go to seek a Great Perhaps.'"

Musetta was shocked. "So soon after—And are you absolutely certain?"

"It is an indisputable literary fact."

* * *

The Poet, loitering drunk on Old Swan Steps—[Do you know that your father slipped here into River Thames? No, you do not.]—penciled a note by moonlight, "To stay: domestic. To go: aspire/to transcend: religious."

* * *

The Bridge hangs like a moustache from the moon's face,
complete. The dogs roll, crookedly, in the camel's excrement.
My lifted foot aches, my word-horde shivers.
Descending Fish Street, I smell Musetta's fuckery,
laugh, wonder if I tell her, will she, won't she laugh?
Peter de Colechurch's heart stopped, he fell, with the Bridge,
into the arms of God, Saint Thomas's bones
settled a fraction deeper into the swampy grave.

Stone upon stone, anger upon irritation, dirt upon clouds,
I labor, while in Labrador the reindeer raise their teeth
to the berries in the bush. Rainwater in the broken teacup
on the windowsill is a week old, frozen and thawed thrice.
My hand lies open to the sun, its canals full of swamp slime.
We do not sneeze. We do not run. We stampede
the caravan, our necks stretched, our throats vibrant with
     adulation.

I must make even dates express my passion. Somehow
a connection must be made. Do not misdate. Date
each day properly. Failure can run sparks up one's spine. Sparks
of shame and discomfort—sense of stupidity. Missing dates hurt
To the quick, like a hangnail. Do not go there on the wrong night.
It will have happened the night before. What do you say?
What do you do? Life does not forgive misdating. A date missed
is a future in your face suddenly. Past achievements are for naught.

Daryl Braintree

The Poet, drunk on words from his word-horde, is convinced in his
bones that this poem, scrawled in the margin of his Chronicle, will live,
once it is set to meter and rhyme, longer than the Bridge itself.

* * *

Having entered the death of Peter de Colechurch, architect of London Bridge, the Poet as Chronicler, working the Chronicle from both ends—past and present— felt more guilty than usual for lacing his Chronicle with vivid traces of the emotions, imagination, and intellect of the Poet.

But Daryl told himself, and Musetta, to whom he always read his entries in full, hoping her reactions would give flight to his ego, that once he has brought the Chronicle up to the present moment in the Bridge's history, he will go back and perhaps transcribe the bare dates and facts into a new record book, trim Peter's narrative to the terseness of a legend, and copy his own varied poetic asides and musings onto separate leaves for further transmutation into poems or perhaps a philosophical miscellany or a book of aphorisms and religious maxims. They will make him, he is profoundly convinced, more famous than Gower, Sidney, Donne or, in his own time, Milton, Butler, or Dryden.

"'God's will be done,' Musetta retorts, with a sarcasm that seems to pervade every line I have entered into my Chronicle," he writes. "Now I take my nocturnal walks on the Bridge with a noticeable limp."

The clear source of the Poet-Chronicler's guilt is his keen awareness that his father, should he re-emerge from out of that nowhere into
which missing people, we are told, go, will be shocked by the liberties
he has taken with that venerable form of history, the humble Chronicle,
now in his own time seldom practiced. A vaguer source of guilt is his
uncertainty as to how Peter de Colechurch, not even the actual priest
engineer about whom a mere mouthful of facts was known, but the
man he has imagined and created himself, might feel about this hybrid
of Chronicle, narrative, poetry, and unnamables that he has been con-
cocting through a year of plague. The Poet has kept up his Chronicle as
an act of filial piety and as a memorial to the actual and his own imagined Peter de Colechurch on whose Bridge he has lived and written and
for a while fornicated with a woman he has taken to be adulterous.

*   *   *

"I walked up to Saint Mary's today and stood on the very spot
where a few plague victims are buried on top of Peter's mother's and
father's graves, and, if you believe my imagination, Peter's grave, among
the smoldering ruins and ate a dried fig." The Poet licked his lips as if
offering evidence.

"A figment of your imagination?" Musetta tossed her hand as if to
dismiss the bad pun. "And did you perhaps wonder whether you are
not yourself the figment of a poet's imagination?"

1209. London Bridge opened to the people.

**1212. Fire started up in Southwark and spread across the Bridge,
killing some 3,000.**

12

VOICES IN THE GREAT FIRE
OF LONDON

In states of mild dementia, aggravated by frequent heavy drinking and hangovers, in obsessive fulfillment of his conception of his mission as Chronicler and out of his skewed compulsion as poet, the Poet-Chronicler employed his "method" in his account of the fire, even more often than when he wrote his account of the plague, still in flux, sometimes putting phrases and sentences from eyewitness accounts, published and unpublished, into the mouths of merchants and others, sometimes quoting Pepys and Evelyn, old friends of his family, and other eyewitnesses with intense fidelity by name. But as he made other mouths utter the testimony of Evelyn and various others, the sheer sound of the words inspired him sometimes to modify their expressions and to weave into their words expressions of his own, feeling an exquisite kinship with all writers and his neighbors in the same moment.

Supposing, then assuming, then certain no one would ever publish his accounts, now and then, even so, hoping some one would, referring to himself in the third person, here is the elderly Poet-Chronicler's bizarre account of the Great Fire of London:

The question was: "And where did it start, may I inquire?"

Most said one place, some said another, and another, and another, and Fire said, "Here!" Here where plague struck, as fire had often started before. Folks on the Bridge and in the City were still mindful of the recent plague rampant, knowing that it still visited a few throats now and then even now.

The fire began, as later charged, in the mind of an Irish papist, but a papist did not actually set the fire, nor did Hubert of Ruen, the man called a papist and hanged for the crime, set the fire, nor did others charged in rumor and misprision, the gypsies passing in caravan across the Bridge, the Jews in old Jewry, readmitted to London by Cromwell in 1655, nor even the French nor the Dutch residing in London, the wars with Holland and France still raging, rumors started early with the first viewers of the fire that it was the success of Dutch or French espionage and sabotage.

The fire started in the minds of many of these sets of folks, but not in the mind of the man upon whom history's heavy hand is laid, the King's Baker, Thomas Farynor. The live coals' origin in his bake house in Pudding Lane was late coming into the consciousness of Londoners, joining the array of causes that rumor had spread out to test and tax the credulity of the Parliamentary Investigation Committee. The fact of the baker's fire must compete still with causes imagined, each of which has, as the Poet would contend in his writings and until the end of his days, a life of its own.

While the plague's numbers were still a grim presence, though much diminished, on the mortality bills, Mister Clinkenbeard flicked a tidy bird-turd off the sill of his bedchamber into the Thames.

The Poet sneezed, spraying the room, pinched his nose, wiped his fingertips on his trousers, and again on the tapestry that hot, humid winds through his open window blew along the wall, flapping in his face as he stepped down the stairs.

Kerry Brooke, fishmonger, sharpening the blade, did not hear the rush of the tide, the creaking of the mill wheel.

By lamplight, using one fingernail to clean the others, flicking the black into the black water, John South, haberdasher, admired his work, his nails reflecting the light like polished horn.

Walking upon the tooth-picked pickings of a hundred teeth of the evening in Tabard Inn, Dropstitch Upshaw, rag merchant, stabbed between his teeth, speared mutton, spat.

Blythe heard the roar over water of bears tearing furred flesh and men cheering, wanting to hear the actors as clearly as she heard the human-like cries of rage and pain from the throats of the bears baited in the pit.

Blythe's mother felt the mill wheels below the Bridge in her chair, in her bum.

Edan Coldiron, master carpenter, was almost aware that farting pleasure is keenest where atmospherics favor echoes.

Musetta scraped her shoes at the front door, left tracks anyway where she paused on the turning staircase, rising to meet Daryl, Poet-Chronicler.

Gilda's mother stared into the eyelet of a needle.

Phelan Wood, Morgan's father, spewed a bitter potion into a handy pot, tossed it window-ward, took it, windborne, back in his face.

Hiccoughs made solitude even more unbearable for Blythe's father, Lennox Archer, glover.

Reverend Thomas Vincent may or may not have been calling that very night upon God to punish with more than plague the citizens of London for committing all the sins enumerated by prophets in the Old Testament.

Drunk, Mister so-and-so crookedly crossed London Bridge from Southwark, aiming his body, if not his mind, at Fish Street hill that would give onto Pudding Lane where his bed set, patient.

Pulling it up, Gilda caught her neck and arms in her own dress. Came near strangling. "Strange, my little drama, rooms above the Bridge. No one to hear me gasp and groan and at last—sigh." She looked down at her knees, shiny as the lids of ginger jars.

The Poet in his Cupola. ". . . that life can be this—only this— *awareness* of life—and be enough. Death so near, plague now becalmed but still hovering to touch us."

The bake house was in dark, nasty, dank Pudding Lane, so named, some said, for the hogs that passed up that narrow, steep Lane from ships on the river to Fish Street and East to Leadenhall, leaving pudding plops of shit behind, and thus its name, others saying the puddings of entrails of animals butchered along the lane named it. At 10 p.m. on Saturday, September first, Baker Farynor "drew" his oven, and, following routine, left a bundle of bavins beside it to rekindle the morning fire.

Round about midnight, needing to relight his candle, Farynor went into the bake-house for a final look. The oven fire was out. He crawled into bed.

Born of a spark in a heap of bavins, kindling wood, the fire started.

Near-about 2 a.m. Sunday morning, Farynor's servant Teagh woke up choking on smoke. The house full of it, he ran from room to room, raising the alarm.

Like most of London's houses and shops, Baker Farynor's was old and dry, made of pitch-coated timber, and, in this extremely hot and dry summer, combustible at the slightest provocation. Like many others, his house was built out over the street, close enough to the houses opposite that the fleeing inhabitants opened a garret window and climbed over the hautepas through the window of a neighbor.

Farynor's maid-servant Rose, fearful of falling to the cobblestones, turned to stone. Unable to move or budge her, Farynor was forced in sorrow to leave her to perish.

Farynor and his neighbors failed to douse the fire with water brimming in the leather buckets stored in Saint Margaret's.

He and his daughter fled to safety—and then fled again to safety, and then fled again for three days and nights, the fire following.

The bake-house was within only ten houses of River Thames.

A strong east-northeast wind that had disturbed city streets for a week worked its will upon the sparks, the fire seizing upon timber and rubbish, sowing them all around. The next street alight, the wind fanned flames down Pudding Lane and Fish Street Hill, separately, to converge at Thames Street and flow on down to the river where distressed folks, on the one hand, expected it to extinguish itself. Fire, on the other hand of fate, has a life, a will, a way of its own, and it worked its will among the wharves and the goods in sheds and warehouses, where tallow, wines, hemp, and oil, and brandy were stored, and along the open wharves laden with hay, crept up upon a lot full of stacked timber and piled up coal. Spreading as the plague had spread, from house to house, but more swiftly, lethal to homes and other buildings that the plague had left untouched.

The fire that marched down Fish Street divided at the Bridge, West along Thames Street and East along Thames Street, then into Tower Street up to the moat, burning on its way Saint Magnus Martyr, there at the north end of the Bridge. By eight in the morning, the sixteen shops and houses on the London end of London Bridge were ablaze, but about a third of the way across the Bridge, a small space still left open by the fire of 1633 kept the blaze from seizing upon the rest of the Bridge. But merchants trembled to know that the heat weakened stones and arches along the rest of the Bridge over to Southwark.

Blythe called melodramatically from the roadway, "London is on fire, Gilda! Wake up and save yourself!"

A voice. "The spoiling flames quickly grew powerful enough to shrug off our use of buckets."

A voice. "The fire burnt down to the very moat of the Tower, where it was feared the gunpowder in stores there would explode."

By ordering the demolition of the houses by the moat, His Majesty saved the Tower, although sparks, soon suppressed, whirled, rising and falling. From her window, Blythe was delighted to see the fire get to the vicinity of the White Tower, because her mother at her elbow said it was so full of military powder magazines as to blow up the Bridge and all vessels anchored in the Pool.

Victory over the fire was now only a few hours hence, many believed in abject terror.

John Evelyn wrote in his diary: "The lane is so close built with wooden pitched houses, the fire spreads itself so far before day, with such distraction to the inhabitants and neighbors, that care is not taken for the timely preventing the further diffusion of it, by pulling down houses. It fell out most unhappily too, that a violent easterly wind fomented it."

To folk for forty miles around, the fire was a bright fierce glow in the night, but then the sun rose blood red in a thick pall of heavy yellow smoke, laden with the smell of burning spices and all the other odoriferous combustibles that filled the City.

A strange consternation about them, the people were so astonished by the dismal spectacle of a great fire, they were not, for a long while, moved to save their possessions, they hardly stirred to quench the fire, running about, creatures of a town now strange to their eyes.

A voice. "We put in at Paul's wharf and were sorry to see Saint Paul's afire in the most fearful way."

From aloft in Nonesuch, the Poet watched King Charles draw near the Bridge in his royal barge to view and assess.

The sight of the Thames covered with goods, floating, barges overladen put a spring in Blythe's steps on the hot pavement. "I did all that!" She talked to herself, aloud, but in whispers.

Edan Coldiron, master carpenter, went out in search of an owing customer. "The people, all classes mingled together, fled into the suburbs about the City."

Fire in one house, fire started up again far from where it was seen burning, kindled another fire of combustible rumors in the breasts of men, almost as dangerous as that within their houses.

The fire like a monstrous storm spread out two miles long, one mile wide, generating moiling clouds fifty miles in length. The sound of crackling timbers and of stones cracking rent air heavy as the thickest drapes and tapestries.

Men fighting the fires with their fire-hooks and pump engines ran past running looters on a rampage.

Dropstitch Upshaw, rag merchant. "Sweating, struggling to get over mountains of smoking rubbish, lost, the ground burnt the soles of my shoes, don't you know?"

As if the fire were taking a view before devouring the structure below, it set the tall-spired steeple of Saint Laurence Pountney afire, melting the lead.

Escaped Londoners who could cross the river in wherries joined Southwarkians to watch the spectacle, their role in the fire merely as spectators, but they played it with diligence.

News of the fire's stages reached the Poet in his scriptorium, where he was starting a hasty rough draft of a new poem.

Dreams Create

How can I see the views and perspectives
from a roof I've never walked? I dreamed
I did, and also dreamed,
moments before I woke and realized I had missed
my nocturnal walk on London Bridge,
dreamed of a group—thirty at most—of men, lunatic,
staring—and *not* staring—into my eyes,
not at all aware of my eyes. Distinct
facial expressions. Proof again—
I could swear with a pure heart before any Holy Tribunal—
since I've never seen such men—that the human imagination
is *creative* or that a single consciousness breathes
the world's one breathing, so that somewhere
such men exist and that my consciousness partook
of a consciousness that took them in with a gaze.

Daryl Braintree

As he might tell you himself, Daryl Braintree craved his poems in everyone's mouth, reciting all over London, even amidst the smoke.

Joseph Cartwright, returned from a voyage to Lisbon, ignorant that his friend, the Poet's father, was missing, appeared in the doorway, ready to convey the sad news of the death of their mutual friend, the seventy-year-old playwright James Shirley, and his wife, fleeing the fire, dead from fatigue, fear, exposure in Saint Giles in the Field.

"The second news must be then that my beloved father and your good friend is missing."

Alone again, disconsolate, for he always wanted to like Shirley's plays more than he had done, the Poet watched from aloft a man reach down into a smoking chimney to rescue a cat, its fur burned down to its skin, and hand it as a natural instinct across the broken water pipe to a child, oh, yes, her, Blythe, who cuddled it, pacified its shock, in her arms. 'What will she do with it? Kill it? Eat it? Set it afire? Pet it?'

A voice. "We witnessed fire make a leap over twenty houses upon the turret of a house in Thames Street. It was, I assure you, a melancholy dinner."

Almost every street barricaded with goods, carts, and coaches, and people running in contrary spurts here, no, there, no, go there, back, turn, stop, cry out, set out again for—where?—past many landmarks, charred, made anonymous.

As she had followed the plague wagons to the great burial craters, Blythe followed a ways the carts going to the gates and out into the fields, where goods were strewn for miles, as if left behind by a monstrous receding flood, tents erected among it all, all the fields filled up with women and children.

A voice. "Cradles were rocked in every field."

A voice. "We paused at the Three Cranes, near the Bridge, hoping to see it again anon."

Blythe felt uneasy as she walked, responding to the allure of yet another chaos in the night that was dreadfully like the light of day.

"For ten miles around . . ." she overheard Mister Pepys say, as she passed the Three Cranes in the Vintry, where wine was stored and sold.

Now Blythe was unable to tread on the pavements, both man and horses backing out, or turning off into byways not yet so scorched.

Kerry Brooke, fishmonger, brought news to Lennox Archer. "The fire on the Bridge has burned down all sixteen houses that we erected on it after the last great fire in 1633 that started on the Bridge, to which I was a child witness, no more able now to cope than then. But it can go no further on the Bridge."

The fire having grown to a great Medusa head in Cripplegate, the sudden appearance of whiny Lord Mayor Bludworth lifted no spirits.

A voice. "Oh, yes, I saw him too passing through our Parish, the Lord Mayor on horseback with a few attendants, looking like one frighted out of his wits and into his trousers, all the privies burning."

A voice. "The weakness of Alderman Sir Richard Browne, joined with the Mayor's exhibited failings, was ugly to witness."

The Poet wrote, "I now have in my possession, *Holinshed's Chronicles,* 1578. Less than a century ago, but he looks back as if on ancient times. Paradoxical that at twenty-seven years old, I look back upon it with no such sense of a far past time."

'Had you, Father, not gone astray, I would never have had these wonderful experiences, writing about the life of Peter de Colechurch and the building of our bridge, and even the plague and fire, eventually.'

The thought that his Father had been sacrificed by providence for raw material of his poems made him cringe. Benevolent irony?

Published in the *London Gazette,* the first English newspaper, the only one in London, the licensed mouthpiece of the royal court, a royal proclamation urged citizens to go to friends in the suburbs and the King urged the country folk to take them in.

A voice. "I was exceedingly astonished and sad, watching this detestable fire take hold of Guildhall."

A voice. "I saw Pudding Lane today. Ironically, not three houses burnt on north side of where the fire began."

Clinkenbeard reported to Bridge Wardens Scarlett and Hussey. "The stones in the piers are unstable. The Bridge is unsafe. Stop the wagons and horses at the bridgehead."

A voice. "Our minds are terribly shattered, witnessing the progress of the destruction of our private property and of our city."

Clarke Shadwell, shoemaker, went out in search of a friend, but found him not. "I found many wretches about to perish from wrenching fear."

Standing at her window the evening of the fire, Gilda told herself, "Christ is there." She wondered how He saw everything and how it made Him feel.

"After this death, death is no more." That was what Gilda had been moved to say that time she watched the baptism of a neighbor in Saint Magnus Martyr at the end of the Bridge. Looking out the window, fire light on her face, smoke in her nostrils, she did not recall those words consciously, but it was there in her contemplative mind as the essence of baptism, the old life of the flesh dead, the new life of the spirit born.

"Nothing can be like unto the Day of Judgment than this." Blythe heard severely panicked people uttering such sentiments everywhere she ventured.

*   *   *

1666, September 4, Monday. A fire storm is sweeping over London.

"We are here, gentlemen," began Mister Clinkenbeard, "saints and sinners alike, to determine how we shall deal in fire with the same problems that vexed us in plague—with the added threat of destruction to property as well as person."

Dropstitch Upshaw, rag merchant, raised an urgent question. "How may we keep off the Bridge those who flee the fire, as we beat back those who would flee the plague onto the Bridge?"

Mister Clinkenbeard was glad of the occasion to clarify their immediate purpose. "We cannot, nor do we wish to prevent fire refugees— our erstwhile customers, after all—from crossing the Bridge. It is fire itself we must beat back."

Any of the merchants could have made the next point, but it was Kerry Brooke who made it. "We know from '33 how fire goes where we do not expect it and how the wind has a will of its own, to fan fire to any point on the compass, following its capricious nature, as when it returned to do again yesterday what it did in '33 to shops on the north end."

Phelan Wood, stationer, was happy to agree. "Yes, yes, quite an open space that, quite enough to stop the fire from crossing the Bridge."

Lennox Archer, glover, expanded on that subject. "Wind, sir, as Mister Clinkenbeard said, may carry live sparks as far over the Thames as the rooftops of Southwark."

Burlow Green, beads and necklace maker, enhanced his voice with a tone of awe. "Little pieces of scorched silk and paper were picked up in very many places distant, near Windsor, Henley, Beaconsfield, and beyond."

Another explosion interrupted the meeting, as the imagination of each pictured a house somewhere collapse.

Mister Clinkenbeard stood up, sat down. "We mourn the burning of the houses built on the London end—"

Tristram West, apothecary, interrupted with his favorite theme. "And our beloved gate-tower by Magnus Martyr, itself first church to burn down to ashes."

"—after the fire of '33, which stopped at the open space that has stopped the fire this time also, thanks be to God. The rooms overhanging the Bridge fell into River Thames but the foundations collapsed, blocking entry to the City except for brave souls who insist on threading themselves as through the eye of a smoking needle."

George Gill knew his contribution was off the mark but felt moved to make it anyway. "We are blessed, mark you, in that the traitor Thomas Venner's piked head and his companion's noggins look down unblemished upon London burning. An omen, perchance?"

Thomas Wright, scrivener, wanted none of that. "And hang your morbid sensibility on an occasion such as this."

Mister Coldiron scanned the faces around the room. "Is our task not clear? We must create immediately a company of fire watchers to keep watch from midnight to midnight."

John South wanted to be heard behind that point. "Yes, yes, hear, hear."

Robertus Allbritton, basket maker, ranked himself beside Coldiron and South. "And appoint others to stand by with buckets."

Burlow Green saw the need to veer away from that line of thought. "The water conduits and pipes have been broken open in many streets to release water to fight the fire. The King himself, fighting the fire his very self, ordered it, making the pressure too low."

Edan Coldiron hoped to lay that idea to the side. "Pertinent point, because the waterwheels at the Bridge cannot keep the pressure up. Much of the force is diminished as the water is jetted up through the pipes, conduits over Saint Magnus Martyr's steeple, now ashes. And fire may yet come in on the West side and set its teeth into the wheel itself."

Kerry Brooke suspected the weakness in his suggestion. "Fetch it in water buckets from the Thames then."

Phelan Wood, stationer, brought to consciousness what he sensed was deep down in everyone's fearful minds. "And will the King or the Duke order the blowing up of the Bridge to thwart the will of the flames?"

Clarke Shadwell, shoemaker, felt the absence of God in the discussion. "Not to mention God's will working in the flames."

Piece-meal solutions proposed, action postponed, the meeting broke up in a room into which smoke over the river was seeping through cracks.

The wind continued in the same excess all night Monday and all day Tuesday, and slung and scattered burning brands into all quarters, the nights more terrifying than the days, the light of the fire supplying that of the sun.

Sparks on the wind had set alight most of ancient London, from the Tower, which escaped the flames, westward to Chancery Lane, North to the Old Roman Wall. "All was consumed."

Providence was no respecter of class, leaving the meanest here and there untouched, serving the richest here and there with ruin.

Prisoners for debt, in Fleet, Ludgate, and Compter prisons were freed. Those in Newgate were sent with a guard to the Clink in Southwark, but the guard was not strong enough to keep the most notorious from escaping on the way, Blythe a delighted witness. Passing the Poet with a flurry of her dress, she followed one of the fugitives and watched him rob folks as they rolled, afire, on the cobblestones.

Watching Newgate Prison, emptied of its folk, burn, the Poet wondered what kind of mind conceived of a city gate, through which the world's work passed everyday, as the proper place for a prison. Perhaps the same minds who first decided to place the severed heads of traitors and murderers over the gate on London Bridge combined the very image of safe passage into the City by road with punishment of some of those who passed through.

In the mouths of many, God was the hero whose warnings had gone unheeded; in the mouths of others, God was the villain who tormented the survivors of the plague with fire.

The rank, the middle sort, and the poorer, all, repeated the prophet Mother Shipton's prophecy "that London in '66 will be burnt to ashes. . . . A judgment upon the City for their former sins."

Thomas Vincent, who gave himself up to Jeremiads on Sunday, gave no thought to sermons on Monday, so appalled was he by the spectacle of a fire that ran through ten streets at once, screeching, rattling, snorting, bellowing, deafening the voices of Londoners. Witnessing, Reverend Thomas Vincent, but for bucked teeth a handsome man, meditated, already seeing his thoughts in print, in a pamphlet. "God with his great bellows blows upon London, fanning a fire of such raging force, it invades the City like an enemy, enters the doors of every house, breaks into every room, looks out every casement with a threatening countenance." But he can't help suspecting another source of these 'furious flames.'

'This doth smell of a Popish design, hatched'—here Reverend Vincent reached for pen and paper—"hatched in the same place where the Gunpowder plot was contrived."

That thought reverted his mind to the finger of God. "The time of London's fall is come: the fire hath received its commission from God to burn down the City, therefore all attempts to hinder it are in vain." A sermon—and perhaps a pamphlet following—under way, Thomas Vincent hoped God would spare one of the churches in which he, as a fanatical Nonconformist, preached from time to time.

Acting upon rumor that the Dutch or the French ignited what they intended to be the fate of London, many took whatever weapons they could come at, the clamor and peril grew so excessive, the whole Court was amazed at the impetuosity of the crowds, which rose up inflamed and then declined into scattered smoldering groups, mimicking the moods of the fire itself. They were persuaded to return to the field again, where, watching all night, they became fairly quiet.

A universal conclusion was that this fire came not by chance, but by conspiracy and combination of all the Dutch and all the French in the town. Even in the best company, that was believed, thus whosoever said the contrary was suspected to be a conspirator, or to favor the incendiaries.

When this rage spread as far as the fire, and every hour brought reports of some bloody effects of it, the King suppressed such acts.

These rumors dismayed Phelan Wood. "Nor did there want, in this woeful distemper, the testimony of witnesses who saw this villainy committed and apprehended men who they were ready to swear threw fireballs into houses, which were presently burning."

To Lord Hollis and Lord Ashley near Newgate Market many were brought in custody for such crimes, but most were innocent, as was a man who found a piece of bread in the street and put it on the window ledge and was accused of firing the house. The Lords went there, found the bread.

A voice. "After all the ill usage that can consist in words, and some blows and kicks, they were thrown into prison, including many of the Roman Catholics."

Many went willingly to jail for safety, the Lords convinced they were not guilty.

So terrified men were with their own apprehensions and anger, the inhabitants of one street, believing all the French were marching at the end of their street, ran in a great tumult the other way, often into the fire's zigzag path.

Blythe lent a hand in spreading rumors through the thick veils of smoke. Some few screamed at her for being a child on the loose in an inferno. "Go home to your poor mother and father!"

With more speed and panic than good sense, a hot-headed fellow rode through the streets, crying, "Arm! We must arm ourselves!" frightening a multitude out of churches that fire would soon consume.

The fire conspired with a fierce wind in that exceedingly dry season.

A voice. "As the wind lifted the fire on its wings forward, the flames kindled back against the wind."

The violence of the wind contended with the violence of the flames until, allied, they redoubled their forces.

Relentless lamentations everywhere she turned made Blythe giddy.

Wind stirred the fire thoroughly through four hundred acres of ground.

The wind changed, its irresistible violence kept the English and Dutch fleets, so near each other, from grappling.

A voice. "The Duke was caught in a circle of fire, the wind high, blowed great flakes, far and wide, finally forcing the Duke to fly for it, almost stifled with the heat."

Everywhere he ventured, Blythe his witness, the Duke of York bestirred himself very much, to good effect.

Edan Coldiron shared what he knew with Clinkenbeard. "'Pull down houses!' We implored the Lord Mayor, but he neglected that prudent advice in favor of a paralyzing consternation that in another world would have provoked laughter."

A voice. "Most orders declared to the people signified nothing, but for the Duke's being active on the scene, forcing all people to submit. The result would have been that not a house would be left standing near Whitehall."

The Duke beat reluctant people, men, women and children, to work in places away from the site of their selfishness.

The pulling down houses with engines proving ineffectual, firefighters blew up many houses with gunpowder.

Round about Whitehall, the banquet hall of which had burned once before, in 1619, the pulling down of houses with grappling hooks included some newly built, some hardly finished.

Men pulling down houses, worked often too near the fire, hoping to save more houses, but they had to abandon the task, realizing at last that they should have started work further away from the fire.

The Lords Manchester, Hollis, and others came into Fleet Street and ordered and executed the pulling down of some houses in Whitefriars, as others urged pulling down houses on each side of River Fleet from the Thames northward to Holborne Bridge.

Blythe watched the Duke with a guard, as he sat on horseback at Lombard Street.

Wind. Sandys wrote: "The King's brother James, Duke of York, was suddenly there among us in Lombard Street. Being constant with the Duke of York, I presume to believe none have seen more of the fire than

I have, he being so active and stirring in his business, he being all the day long, from five in the morning till eleven or twelve at night, using all means possible to save the rest of the City and suburbs."

A voice. "The King's Privy Council assisted the Duke, overruling in the King's name the common law that whosoever pulleth down a house shall build it up again."

Like King Charles, persons of quality in the Strand had access to the River, as the Poet-Chronicler witnessed from his window, and so sent choice goods upriver to Hampton Court.

A voice. "The King was in the City two or three times, preserving the remaining parts, exposing himself among all persons, lending his ear to the advice of the lowest."

Companies of the King's regiments arrived, inspiring confidence, the fire itself declaring itself inattentive to authority.

John Evelyn wrote in his diary. "Some stout seamen proposed early enough to have saved the whole City, the blowing up of so many houses as to make a wider gap than the selective pulling down of houses in places that achieved a lesser effect, but tenaciously avaricious men, al-dermen, *et cetera,* would not allow it, knowing their own houses would have been first."

Hearing that the Duke of York had ordered another hundred houses blown up, Blythe sought out the scene.

Watching the explosions, feeling them shake her body, feeling fi-nally as if they originated in her guts, Blythe whirled around, to see all the fire from all the angles, even climbing up on the Great Gate among the heads impaled on pikes for the most commanding view.

Dancing, she stomped so hard she wished her feet could jolt the Bridge off its foundations and that she would, with a heart brimming with spiteful joy, sing "London Bridge is burning up," even as she (who never sang the song without conviction that she—ignorant of the meaning of the name, mewed in the tower, not the Bridge—was the Fair Lady) fell with the Bridge, her hateful mother and father roaring down after her. She sang the words ferociously, stressing each syllable, feeling that they were more vibrant than her feet and just might do the work of her heart's desire. Hate was not what she felt so much as the thrill of destruction, clear and cold as frost's teeth in stone, her father glover Archer witnessing.

*   *   *

Another Voice, Musetta's Recalled

"Don't forget the fog and plagues
and fires in our time, how they affected
all our sufferings and fears, the look of things.
Fog as the watery grave of the dying,
a street stream, London as Venice,
carrying off the night's dead. Fog settling
into charred ruins—walking among that. Seeing
fog and fire from varied angles through
windows on the Bridge. "A favoring wind."
Whose voice is that? "To see what
I have seen, see what I *see*," eyes lidded.

Daryl Braintree

*   *   *

Blowing up houses and shops did not prevent the diffusion of fire.

The descendants of the Knights Templar of the Crusades were careless, refused to open to the gates to the temple and other structures and let people in to quench the fire there, which all knew desired to leap out of there and into the next westward venue.

The Duke turned his back upon the Templars' objection to the use of gunpowder to blast a firebreak.

The Duke blew up the Paper House in the court by the Temple Chapel and the Hall by the Chapel. Blythe felt triumphant, as if it were an exhalation of her own will.

That fire quenched, the Temple Chapel and Hall were saved.

Blowing up houses at first seemed to many citizens a desperate cure, but gradually achieved some success.

A voice. "We were glad to see forty horse of the Lifeguard in Cornhill."

The King, in Thames Street on horseback, a knight approached him. "We have not mastered it, your Majesty."

The fire had labored like a willful slave all day.

Having labored continually, the soldiers were slumped, sprawling, staggering, bent over, hands on knees, leaning tired.

George Gill sought the ear of Kerry Brooke to augment the intensity of his awareness of the fire's range. "I was there delivering repaired spectacles when the fire burst out afresh at the Temple, by the falling of some sparks, some say, upon a pile of wooden buildings, a lurking spark that had lain concealed ever since the morning. The fire defeated two engines."

The Temple on fire again, a new alarm went up. Fifty thousand French and Dutch were shouted to be in arms against London.

A voice. "Can you countenance those who would settle for calling this holocaust merely a calamitous accident?"

A voice. "Trained Bands marching into the City were a gladsome sight indeed, sir."

Blythe darted ahead of each outbreak, sustaining the feeling that she was the motive power and leader of each.

King Charles came down on his royal barge, with entourage, as he had the night before, soberly surveying the widespread chaos of fire, then returned to Whitehall in Westminster.

Blythe rushed toward, as if to embrace, but couldn't stand near the burning and glowing ruins.

Musetta, waiting by an open window for Daryl to return home, blew wood ash from the open book's gutter, the question as to its origin not quite over the threshold of consciousness.

A voice. "Our streets are too narrow to allow the engines to assault the impetuous flames."

A voice. "The heaviest strokes of bad fortune that ever fell upon England, or any other great nation, invasion by a barbarian horde not excepted."

A brick house, unusual in this city, slowed here and there the fire's advance. While all wood burned inside, the brick walls stood still, proving superior to stone. Brick is, mind, child of fire.

Left were but pieces of walls and some pillars standing.

The fire nearing, a man in Bread Street got his stuff out, and into his friend's house in Holborne, where fire followed and brought it down, as some who escaped the plague to another town embraced it there.

Many on the water in wherries afire and overloaded with household possessions sank, in which fiery deluge, envisioning plate, jewels, even money and cloth, some men were ready enough to fish.

A voice. "Westminster Abbey is endangered."

Saint Paul's, that had burned from time to time over the centuries—961 and 1136, the Chronicles show—at noon was safe. Soon after, given up. Saint Paul's, one of the most ancient churches of early piety in the Christian world, and a hundred other churches, were in ruins, as was—sad sight—Saint Paul's beloved portico. The augering fire split many stones. But an inscription in the architrave still showed the name of the man who built it, Inigo Jones, not one letter defaced.

Blythe returned again and again to the Bridge to tell Gilda what she had seen and done and had wanted to do and now intended to do, her father catching mere glimpses of her.

Blythe wandered north into another parish. There was Lord Craven, sole hero among the noblemen during the plague, setting himself the task to frustrate the fire from Holborne Bridge to Fleet Bridge.

On Nonesuch's fifth floor, the Poet, looking down from his study window, asked himself, "Do not fires of another sort burn inside sick, angry, panicked people?"

The roadway lured the Poet out of his scriptorium.

"Not only is food scarce, it's overcooked," a man standing beside the Poet joked, to himself, then wept.

The Poet turned and went back inside Nonesuch House.

But he felt that as a poet, he ought to descend and move among them, feel the heat of the fire, although he ought to be able to imagine it, imagine anything he chose, as his imagination had resurrected Peter de Colechurch.

The Poet wrote, "The plague continued, so that danger, too, kept one in doors."

Even so, worried about its fate in fire, the Poet-Chronicler went to see Saint Mary Colechurch as the site sacred in his imagined memory of Peter's church and he wanted to see what fate might have befallen

Mercers Hall, Thomas à Becket's home place, occupying the entire block between Old Jewry and Ironmonger's Lane, except for Saint Mary Colechurch.

He found the fire's gnawing teeth in Saint Mary Colechurch, spewing up clouds of ashes that rained down on the graves of Peter de Colechurch's mother and father, and, in fact or imagination, is that Peter's or Archbishop Becket's grave between? Neither his intellect as Chronicler nor his imagination as Poet was clear enough to answer. He conjured up his memories of it, willed it rebuilt in memory, and went away weeping.

"I will not see this place again," said a stranger, passing a man who carried all his worldly goods on his back, both heading for Moorgate, "but in cold ashes."

The Poet watched three hunchbacks toiling toward him through the smoke who the light of a house afire metamorphosed gradually into two men and a woman carrying on their backs all that the fire allowed them of their possessions.

The demolitions of houses stopped up the Poet's passage through one street after another, locking other houses into the fire's eager embrace. Was that Blythe he saw, breaking through where he had feared to go?

Resenting yet another distraction in the present, the Poet, lost in the past history of the Bridge and its master architect, had resisted recording the fire, oddly, he thought, knowing fire was an ongoing story in the history of London, and so he finally fixed his attention again upon this minor event and its potentially major effect.

September 5, 1666: Saint Mary Colechurch was, but is no more, and ever shall be.

Blythe took only some notice of people coming out of cellars, as books and papers belonging to the stationers around Saint Paul's were carried off to yet another place of safety.

Blythe ducked the stones of Saint Paul's as they flew like cannonballs, sidestepped a foot-wide stream of melted lead that flowed from Saint Paul's down into the streets.

Blythe was among the spectators when the ruins of the vaulted roof of Saint Paul's collapsed and fell into Saint Faith's chapel. Blythe dared stand in the midst.

Of the monuments, "the shrouded effigy" of Dean John Donne remained entire.

A voice. "I never expected ever to see fire in the steelyard."

The heat ignited the congested air, full of combustible dust, causing the fire to make prodigious leaps from house to house, street to street, parish to parish, from zones of sanity to new zones of insanity dear to Blythe's heart. "This is my will at work," she declared, repeatedly.

Mister Clinkenbeard patrolled the Bridge with Kerry Brooke, whose fish stock the fire had kept low. "Amazed at with what rage and greediness it marched up Fleet Street, I took umbrage as if it were a loud, disorderly bully, drunk on bad beer."

Fire and fumes drove off those working at leveling the houses along River Fleet. Flames advanced as high as Fleet Bridge water conduit.

The torrent of fire rushed down Ludgate-hill like giddy girls holding hands, feet flickering, dresses flapping, hair flying, screaming as do girls running down hill—"ut, ut, ut!"

Blythe was contemptuous of the fire, a force that had no selfish purpose in mind. But watching three thieves, two men and a woman, plunder a house from which the decrepit owners had just fled, lifted her spirits. One dropped a silver goblet but, overburdened, could not stoop low enough to pick it up.

The better to advise the King, Lords of the Privy Council rode to every place, to order pipes opened for water, but that caused less pressure in other places.

The King in person, setting an example, exhorted his good subjects to resist the fire more aggressively. A fresh spirit of work lifted hands to the task and the fury of the conflagration began to abate, lifting hearts and hopes as high as the flames had roared previously. The courage of the multitude persisted until hissing embers lay where most flames had cackled like the toothless bawd who plagued the Bridge, spent much time in the cage on the south end.

The work spirit of the people was finally a match for the fire, the ambition of which was to consume them.

Lord Clarendon wrote in his *Life of Edward Earl of Clarendon, Written by Himself,* "The King and the Duke of York, who rode from one place to another, and put themselves into great dangers amongst the burning and falling houses, to give advice and direction what was to be done, underwent much fatigue as the meanest, and had as little sleep or rest; and the faces of all men appeared ghastly and in the highest confusion."

Biscuit out of the sea stores were sent into the City, but the poor didn't know how to eat it, so it was returned to the stores.

A voice. "We packed our books into a barge and went to an unknown house upriver."

Proclamations of Charles II, September 5: "that all churches, chapels, schools, and other like public places, shall be free and open to receive the goods people bring to store, and all towns admit all refugees."

Thomas Wright, scrivener, back home from writing an inventory of a wine merchant's fire-threatened stock, told his wife, Nan, the saga of his journey through smoke, fire, and the noise of fire and falling houses. "I knew where I was solely by some tower or pinnacle miraculously still standing after the incendium."

A voice. "We fetched our movables home and have remained here without disturbance."

A voice. "Since then I've seen one or two enticing drawings, represented as the first ever done, remarking on the strange circumstance that for the Bridge's first three centuries no drawings were made—or preserved. But I must confess to you, my children, that the drawing I hereby bequeath to you in the packet you hold in your hands, I, I alone, rescued from the Great Fire."

Listening, Blythe remembered a drawing she had seen floating above her head as she raced through the narrow streets.

Samuel Pepys picked up a piece of melted colored glass from a heap in the street and pocketed it as a curious souvenir of the Mercers Chapel. He wrote in his diary, "Our feet ready to burn, walking through the town among the hot coals."

A voice. "That night we got into a bed in a house in—"

Upshaw, rag merchant, testified to Clinkenbeard. "I say this as a survivor of the plague, that the fire exhibited all the dread horror imaginable."

A voice. "I tried to get to you, but an abundance of high-piled goods and over-laden carts stopped up Cannon Street."

The Poet described the fire to Musetta, allowed on bridge more often, at least to his house, even though she had seen the fire herself from upper Tooley Street.

"The fire lit up the dead of night, and up there, too, the moon offered her light as a sort of cosmic non sequitur."

Musetta teased him out of her own poetic sensibility. "The fire melted smaller bells down, warped larger bells, forever mute."

"I don't want to talk about it. Fire on the Bridge is like an eclipse of the sun—the world suddenly disrupted. No sun, no Bridge—there is a shadow, there is fire in place of the sun and Bridge. The Bridge is where fire, except for warmth and cooking, is *not*. Where fire is, there is nothing else, no room, house, field, Bridge. Plague, on the other deadly hand, is very different. There is plague *in* London, not plague *replacing* London. And for the Bridge, the plague is what *may* come on, and cross. If plague comes onto the Bridge, the Bridge is a place where the plague has come."

"Let us turn now to fucking."

"Tonight, all over this globe from our London Bridge to the Ponte Vecchio to the Pont aux Changes to the Bridge of Sighs, to Mostar Bridge, men and boys are pissing off bridges. Only one woman, Dolores, aims between the slats of a swinging Bridge over a gorge in Andalusia."

Daryl never saw Musetta again.

The Poet wrote, "The noise of the fire broke into the naves of each of London's hundred churches. Hissing smoke, fire insinuated from steeples and towers downward, through the tiniest openings ground level, rose to pulpits, roaring infernal sermons in mocking polysyllables, then exploded, burning voices loud and raucous as spectators in the bear-baiting gardens, melted down or broke open windows, looked out over the City, assaulted massive doors, and stood up in the doorways to greet fleeing parishioners as they passed. Clergymen fled the unfamiliar, unrepentant visitors who brought into the naves mimics of hell."

On Pye Corner, north, near Newgate Prison, men finally extinguished the fire. Quenched at last, the flames seemed to heave one long, but faint sigh, then expire. The Poet-Chronicler wrote, "The fire inhaled-exhaled first in narrow Pudding Lane and ended at the Fat Boy at Pye Corner. Pye Corner shall ever be known as the spot where the Great Fire of London breathed its last."

But the ashes that had risen settled into smoldering heaps. Among the ashes blown over the City and over the countryside for many miles were leaves of valuable books and etchings and scraps of paintings.

Fire extinguished the conditions in which plague thrives so that it may never return.

Beat down and extinguished, the fire lurked in unopened cellars for over six months, even after Lucien came to the Bridge and Blythe and Gilda disappeared and Morgan stepped onto the Bridge.

Friday, September 7, 1666: The Great Fire of London, nearly defunct.

Faithful to his diary, Samuel Pepys wrote, "London is no longer a city."

John Evelyn wrote that London resembled Sodom, or the Last Day, or the ruins of Troy. "London was, but is no more."

The Poet wrote, "Fall is icumen in. What do they smell in the air? Change of season is *distinct,* unprotected as they were, compared with folk in these last years of the sixteenth century. But Bridge weather is the Bridge, more so than London weather is London, despite the fog that set in a thousand years ago, and is so constant."

Because John Evelyn and Samuel Pepys in their diaries and others tell of the pestilence abating in late October, that a ten-day deluge of rain failed to stop smokes and fires from the Great Fire starting suddenly up, that even as late as March 16 of the following year, rain water coursed through streets where fire had raced and River Thames iced over, and that March 7th, the coldest day in London memory, I, and so, you, see what they saw. Hear it. Smell it. Taste London, too, on the tips of our tongues. And voices kept on talking:

"Because composed of brick, arched cellars held up, so we must arch all convenient places."

"In future, streets notoriously narrow must be of a breadth as to prevent the mischief of fire run amok. None shall be so narrow as to make the passage uneasy, especially towards the waterside, nor will we suffer any lanes or alleys to be erected if not absolutely necessary."

"For years after the fire of '33, the Bridge was down or in disrepair most of that time. Idyllic in the Dark Ages, compared with the same ground flattened, in ashes."

"Sad to see the mere shell of Saint Paul's, the fourth church built on that site since 604, as I read in the Anglo-Saxon Chronicle. Or did I? Maybe not."

"At the center of world trade, and thus as the center of English power, merchants are ruined."

The Poet-Chronicler: "But Newgate Prison, on the site since the time of Peter de Colechurch, is, as one would expect, to be rebuilt."

Like plague, like fire visiting the City, Lucien Redd had visited the mind and body of Morgan Wood, to sicken it, to incinerate it.

13

THE BROTHERHOOD OF THE
BRIDGE: CABALISTIC MEETINGS

Growing daily more feeble, never quite hallucinatory, the Poet-Chronicler continued his bizarre account of the Great Fire of London and the meetings of the Brotherhood of Merchants, drawing upon the besotted memory of his drinking companion, rag merchant Dropstitch Upshaw. "Like the river," he was once heard to pontificate, warm ale in hand uplifted, "facts are simply there; imaginings are newborn forever."

So that he could enjoy listening to phrases and passages he found in published and unpublished accounts coming sometimes from the mouths of the Bridge merchants in their meetings, the Poet continued to put the words of published accounts and the unpublished words of John Evelyn, Samuel Pepys, and others in the mouths of the Bridge merchants. Listening now and then to their words speak, as if aloud, in different attitudes and tones, he made of the merchants a chorus, singing, for instance, parts of a long passage by Evelyn.

Still referring to himself in the third person, the ancient Poet-Chronicler wrote:

Having inspected damage to the Bridge each day of the fire, the Brotherhood made an urgent overall assessment in their meeting after supper on Friday, the first day of the aftermath of the fire.

Goldsmith Clinkenbeard opened the meeting of fifteen merchants. "Once more, we have very grave business—"

"Yes, yes," all averred.

"To conduct, very—"

"Yes. Yes," all assented.

"—grave business indeed."

"Yes, yes . . . quite so, quite so. . . ."

Eldon South, haberdasher, saw his chance. "The bawdy woman still vexes the Bridge."

"Have mercy, Mister South. Fire, sir. It is fire that vexes us."

"But we are safe."

"And so we are. And so are all those outside the City, within the Minories just outside Aldgate and most in the Liberties who have not yet at the moment felt the sting of fire on their cheeks and in their nostrils."

Phelan Wood stood up and plucked at his clothing. "The smell of the smoldering ruins is in our own bedrooms. Sniff, in fact, the clothes you are wearing now."

Clarke Shadwell struck his characteristic note. "Once again, God's voice speaks in the City, as Reverend Thomas Vincent relishes saying each day."

"Sometimes I feel we are looked at." All turned to look at Mister South, who, someone once remarked, habitually, ritualistically, sat as far over on the North side of any room, as if to make of his very body a non sequitur. "Spyglasses are turned upon us here. We are, of course, defenseless. Where do they stand to look? From windows and roof-tops on London side and Southwark side. From the banks. From ships. From the Tower. From Saint Paul's, though she in ruins. From steeples, though far fewer they now are."

"If," Mister Clinkenbeard trebled, "we may proceed."

Heedlessly, Mister South continued. "Into our shop and house windows. Peering straight across the roadways. Like ravens above and cats below, not to mention woodworms within. It unnerves one to imagine this spying. This constant spying. Always someone raising a spyglass, extending his—or her—eye to see the very iris in mine. A mystery that I have never caught such a one in the act? And yet it *must* be so."

"Time enough for all that, Mister South, once we are safe from the fires of hell."

"Who here on the Bridge looks back at them? With a spyglass?"

"Not I!" declared all in the room but Mister Clinkenbeard, who hung his head, succumbed to the inevitable straying of minds, even when immediate crisis dictated deliberation and deliberate action.

Edan Coldiron, master carpenter, present as advisor only, hoped his voice would bring simple reason to the gathering. "Let us form our own permanent squads of fire wardens and fire quenchers and thus prepare for the future, for fire will come again, rise up, perhaps, as in '33, from one of our own hearths here on the bridge."

Dropstitch Upshaw was athirst. "Have we drunk all the tea then?"

Clarke Shadwell too felt a compulsion not to shut up. "Gentlemen, I sing for your midnight contemplation 'London Mourning in Ashes,' which many of you had for a penny on the Bridge last evening, the fire only just then abated. But only the relevant part, for you all will seek it out, I trust.

> 'Although the fire be fully quenched
> yet if our sins remain,
> and that in them we still are drench'd,
> the fire will rage again;
> Or what is worse,
> a heavier curse. . . .'"

Lurching on, Shadwell concluded.

> "'If this do not reform our lives,
> a worse thing will succeed,
> Our kindred, children, and our wives,
> will die for want of bread. . . .
> But if we mend,
> we never shall come to't.'"

"The moral is clear as fire itself in these times uncertain as plague." Mister Clinkenbeard stood up. "We must mend the Bridge, or sing a very different tune, to wit,

'London Bridge is falling down,
falling down, falling down,
London Bridge is falling down,
my fair lady.'"

Necklace maker Green provided a bit of well-known information. "Versified news-stories, a penny a copy, are hawked about the streets."

Basket maker Allbritton enjoyed sharing experiences. "I got a poem from that drunken poet whose father is missing."

Leader Clinkenbeard endeavored to keep the focus on fires to come. "Bestir the ashes and this wild fire may flare upon again, as that time when we thought fire on the Bridge had been thoroughly extinguished."

Lennox Archer, Blythe's father, took the theme of purification as somewhat his own. "The filth of this great City is purified by wind and fire."

Mister Shadwell felt a compulsion to keep on ringing the bells of doom. "The fire has been quenched at last but not our appetite for sin."

Goldsmith Clinkenbeard clearly cleared his throat. "And we do well to meet as we do to recite all points of damage and possible remedies to the ills of the Bridge that we have inspected and the ills we dare yet imagine. Let us all be prayerfully mindful of the fact that we are among many thousands who, having survived plague, now have survived tempest and fire, and that thousands who are alive are, unlike ourselves, without houses in which to be blissfully mindful of this fact. Refugees live in camps outside the walls, in Moorgate fields, in the seventeen Liberties, north and westward, very like Gypsies.

"No fertile imagination has given us a description of the old City during the dark ages, after the Saxon invasion, to provide comparison. But this we do know, that for centuries only sixty or so Saxons lived within the Roman Walls among Roman ruins, among trees, grass, shaws, vines, serpents, rats, while most Londoners lived westward outside the walls in what we now know as the town of Westminster."

Hatmaker South had nothing urgent to say, but spoke. "Am I to deduce from the length of your preamble that we are met in no state of urgency?"

Clinkenbeard had begun the day resolved to show forth as a paragon of patience. "If I may. Only a few met the fate of Thomas Farynor's maidservant. The report so far is that only six people burnt to death, two or three, searching ruins of their houses, sank into vaults the fire opened—as *we* might fall should this Bridge break down—and a hundred other folk of secondary causes during this fire."

Glover Archer was eager to be spoken of as an active participant. "The forced hasty removal of the sick and of women lying-in caused their death, one of my young nieces among them, wearing the gloves I lovingly made for her, I like to imagine."

Clinkenbeard reasserted his leadership role. "We must perforce take stock. London's losses are our losses, our losses theirs. We are like an island, but, in fact, we are not an island. First, the plague took a fifth of our city population, about a hundred thousand, and now within the walls and without the walls, within the freedom and the liberty of London, about fourteen thousand houses consumed in fire, making over fifty thousand folk homeless. Eighty-seven parish churches, six consecrated chapels, the Royal Exchange, the Custom House, fifty-two halls of Companies, three city gates, Newgate Gaol and three others, four stone Bridges within the gates, Sessions House, Guildhall, its courts and offices, Blackwell Hall, Bridewell Gaol, debtor prisons in Poultry Street and Wood Street, Saint Paul's, the scaffolding for renovation of which lately in progress fed the fire, as did books and paper, wine, tobacco, sugar, plums—the list is long. Cruel abbreviation for such vast and thorough destruction. Only a sixth of what stood within the walls remain.

"More commodities and household goods are preserved than perished, especially those of least weight and most worth. The financial reckoning for loss and for dealing with fire and ashes and the long, desolate aftermath is, if I may hazard a guess, twelve million pounds.

"The extent of the fire's fury is estimated by many to be about four hundred acres within the walls, eighty acres yet standing, unburnt. About seventy acres without the walls. Around nine hundred parish churches, not counting chapels burnt. Do I hear any contradictions?"

Necklace maker Green raised a finger as if it were a token of identification. "I, I say, I watched efforts to save Saint Bartholomew hospital near Smithfield and another hospital in Savoy."

Master Carpenter Coldiron felt the need for a voice of experience. "I toured Cripplegate, Fenchurch Street, and Grace Church Street and High Holborne and Holborne Bridge. London must never again build of wood."

Stationer Wood rose, sat down, delivered. "Mister Pepys declared to me that none have suffered so deeply as the booksellers, principally those in Paul's churchyard. If they lost so much, as small businesses, imagine the larger losses."

Rag merchant Upshaw did not speak of the new crop of rags the fire would turn up. "One cannot imagine the spectacle of the general astonishment and confusion, everyone running up and down, like a strange breed hidden in our midst that only fire would smoke out."

Fishmonger Brooke knew what Upshaw had very much in mind. "Many attired, I happened to notice, in the rags they had cast off and that you resold to others, not despising one class over another."

Upshaw leaned forward, thumbing forth his own lapels. "I see in that, a sort of gutter-fashion charm."

Spectacle maker Gill wanted to add to the survey. "Those who fled densely populated the open fields in Moorgate, where they are forced to stay snug by their goods night after night."

Mister Brooke could not resist the opportunity. "Picked clean to the bone by rag pickers in the night. Only teasing our prince of rags here."

Mister Gill was proud of his status as eyewitness. "The King ordered bread sent into Moorfields for the relief of the poor, and I watched them bring it in."

Shoemaker Shadwell wished he had been an eyewitness but had good information to add. "The King, seeing Moorfields filled with goods and people, assured them that the fire was direct from the hand of God, and no popish plot, and commanded them to raise no more alarms against Catholics, French, and Dutch. 'I will by the grace of God,' he declared, 'live and die with you if we are attacked.'"

Glover Archer wanted to be certain he was to be regarded as knowledgeable. "I know some of the wealthy who employed city coaches and carts that swarmed in from the country. Some removed their goods four or five times to safer houses, of friends and relatives, or hired houses, others went into the countryside, some in hired carts from hell hellbound. For want of a cart, some lost all, but in the dashing about of so many carts, each hindered the other."

Mister Brooke pointed at spectacle-maker Gill, smiling. "And some for want of a needle . . ."

Mister Gill asserted his status compared with that of fishmonger. "As a gentleman, I disdain to reproach those of dim wit."

"I am haunted by the bookman who died of grief after the fire destroyed his rare books. All was safe in the vault under Saint Paul, until the book dealers opened it to the air, and fire took it all in one great instant swallow." Scrivener Wright bowed his head, looked up, eyes shining. "Stationers are hit hardest of all trades. I do not want to die of grief. But should this Bridge be the scene of a major catastrophe, I can well imagine myself dying of grief. Can't you? Each of you?"

Mister Wood elaborated on what he heard Mister Shadwell to say. "The fervent belief that the fire was the design of our enemies kindled such a rage in the multitude that I witnessed the killing of one poor woman who had something in her apron that the mob imagined to be fire-balls. They cut off her breast. Do you hear me, they cut— And they sadly wounded and maimed many others, especially French and Dutch, condemned by very birth."

Mister Brooke called more attention to fishmongers. "Mobs set fire to an honest Dutch fishmonger in High Street. I shudder to imagine it."

Mister Clinkenbeard raised his finger. "But in the end, in the end, gentlemen, good government preserved those of other nations from a massacre. Good government, allow me to stress, is our own charge as a duly appointed committee of the Wardens of the Bridge."

Apothecary West pounded his fist on his knee. "When we speak of good government, we may not speak of the Lord Mayor, a person delighting more in drinking and dancing than is acceptable for such a magistrate."

Mister Gill pounded his fist on his knee. "Universally condemned."

Mister Green splayed the fingers of his hands, darted them at the floor. "His authority and the aldermen were little more than piss in the smoke."

Mister South whirled in his chair to second Mister Green. "Piss, by all means, yes. I saw a man try to douse the fire on his sill by pissing at it."

Glover Archer offered a fresh subject. "The Lord Mayor was not as bad as some men of the Inner-Temple, who would not save the goods of absent persons, nor allow others to do it, using the excuse that it 'is against the law to break up any man's chamber.'"

Mister Clinkenbeard knew he could use the Mayor to bring the Brotherhood to their purpose this evening. "An otherwise very honest man, the Lord Mayor was blamed for want of sagacity. He came with great diligence as soon as he had notice of the fire, and was present with the first officials, yet as he had never been exposed to such spectacles, his agitated fear was equal to that of the men he led, nor did he know how to apply his authority. His is a cautionary tale."

Rag merchant Upshaw felt the need of a metaphor. "As a rainbow is a sign of peace and blissful tranquility, smoke made an arch in the heavens as a sign of wrath, a hell mouth, if you will."

Lennox Archer kept his presence known. "Fire nearly mastered our minds even as it mastered the City."

Mister Shadwell returned to his theme. "I was not one of the few who viewed the fire as a natural and bare accident, but one of the many who shrank from it as a judgment of God."

Mister West agreed. "Pride, greed, whore-mongering, gluttony, and more." Thus, he enhanced the theme. "I have been privy to a letter Dural wrote, during the plague, around August 23, as if prefiguring, to a minister of the French church in London, that a fire from heaven is fallen upon a city called Belke, where a world of people have been killed and burned, which seemed a work of cabal, cast out by some that were knowing, others that might be ignorant."

Mister Clinkenbeard, rousing the Brotherhood of the Bridge from gossip to the business at hand, bulked forward in his chair. "Are we to take the very fact that the Bridge escaped plague and much of the fire to be a sign of catastrophe to come, to us alone, separate here, isolated, even though we are that centuries' old paradox—the life-line to the greatest city on earth and yet always apart, exempt from some laws and regulations, subject to others unique to our unique function in the scheme of things? And even man-made actions, clear as sunlight on the river, threaten us, the fire-born prospect of a second bridge, probably at Westminster, as Mister Coldiron may well agree. We therefore cannot—"

"No, we cannot!" Master Carpenter Coldiron stood up, an exclamation mark to his declaration. "Therefore, let us forestall, henceforth prepare ourselves—"

Mister Upshaw thought his fellow merchants would do well to revisit the prophecies in anticipation of worse to come. "Most of our last year's almanacs talk of fire in London."

Fishmonger Brooke reminded the committee of a prophecy more dire. "The very last in Mother Shipton's book of prophecies, in 1641, 'That London in 'sixty-six should be burnt to ashes' is not rooted in religion, but some region between religion and superstition. Mark, even so, it is so."

Mister Clinkenbeard regained the lead. "Reach it on yonder shelf, Kerry, for I have it marked with a broom straw. Hark: 'A ship come sailing up the Thames to London—and the master of the ship shall weep, and the mariners shall ask him why he weepeth, being he hath made so good a voyage, and he shall say 'Ah, what a goodly city this was, none in the world comparable to it; and now there is scarcely left any house that can let us have drink for our money.' Mother Shipton sees us thus, twenty-five years into the future, to this day."

Mister Wood often assured himself that prophecies were more harmful than helpful. "Thousands of stories fly up and down. I confess some are shrewd ones, but I shall suspend my judgment till time make a more perfect discovery. . . . I must profess myself unsatisfied."

Mister Brooke returned to an immediate question. "As we have often said, some blamed loathsome Papists and loathsome Quakers more than God our Father. Some blamed vicious fanatics of various factions. A fanatic act of revenge upon us Londoners for the murder of Charles I is one rumor still current."

Spectacle maker Gill talked with his mouth full of dates. "In his proclamation for a general repentant fast, I thought the King most eloquent."

Mister South heard little of that. "Hear, hear."

Mister Gill felt playful. "The King's men brought out all the gold-smiths' money to Whitehall."

All somber faces refrained from turning toward Clinkenbeard.

Rag merchant Upshaw was thinking of his own trade. "Most of the cloth burnt, so the wool trade will benefit later, and the poor working in wool."

Goldsmith Clinkenbeard tried another steering strategy. "Too many saved their personal goods instead of early working for the common good, which had they done would have benefited them as well. Some such purpose brings us together tonight, as you may have surmised."

Haberdasher South stared at the wall. "The suddenness. Imagine, being in your bed—the fire suddenly in your house, in your bed. Time to save nothing but yourself. Imagine."

Mister Shadwell harped on his theme, as if reciting. "O the miserable and calamitous spectacle, such as haply the whole world has not seen the like since the foundation of the world, nor till the coming universal conflagration of it in the Last Days. God grant mine eyes may never behold the like. Three days, London was an inferno, a literal metaphor of Hell, especially for the majority who saw God's hand raised again against the City, in a time when plague deaths are still reported and are even today. Almost two thousand more this year so far, one or two near Pudding Lane, origin of our present damnation."

Mister Coldiron surrendered to Mister Shadwell's preoccupation. "Yes, yes, a visitation so dreadful, that scarce any age or nation has ever seen or felt the like. Although the afflicting hand of God fell more immediately upon the inhabitants of this City, yet all men ought to look on it as a judgment upon the whole nation."

Mister Shadwell enjoyed linking with Mister Coldiron when he could. "The ruins bear a resemblance to the Sodom of my imagination."

Aware of Mister Clinkenbeard's dismay at not marshalling all minds to the common task, Mister Brooke wanted to come to his aid, but could not resist adding to the fiery rhetoric. "The ruins resemble the pictures I loved as a child to see of burning Troy or Rome, Nero's harp strident behind the curtain of fire, now silent."

Mister Shadwell sounded yet another note on the same theme. "This severe judgment cries out for atonement."

Mister Green saw a positive side. "Or to speak better, the punishing hand of God upon us sinners shows us the terror of his judgment. But let us be mindful of his mercy, in putting a stop to it, when we were in the last despair, a memorable deliverance."

Mister West was thankful for the good effect upon the war. "Hear, hear. Let us give God thanks that the naval stores are safe, as though it pleased God not to deliver us to our enemies."

The war brought in, Mister Clinkenbeard seized the opportunity. "Let it not be lost on any one of us that a war, a war is, in fact, exactly what our King and his soldier citizens have conducted, the fire targeting our houses, our shops, the concussions felt in the very soles of our feet, making our hair stand on end, the heat as the fires of war on land and sea just as scorching, the smoke smothering, the fire winds hot and unbalancing. And what wars are to come? Invasions, armadas of sin and retribution?"

Mister Shadwell felt obliged to add a positive note to the outcome of God's anger. "Hear, hear. Since it pleased God to lay this heavy judgment upon us, let us comfort our selves with some hope that he will, upon our due humiliation before him, give us a new life that we may see the foundations laid, the buildings finished, of a much more beautiful city than we see now consumed."

Mister Brooke summed up. "I lost hundreds of customers."

The others followed his lead with personal lamentations. Mister Wright. "I lost many who have no immediate need for pen and paper."

Mister Gill. "Many are as if looking for a needle in a haystack."

Mister Green. "Dim wits all. None of whom crave a necklace above all."

Mister South. "The winds of the firestorm blew many a hat to the four corners of the earth. So to speak."

Mister Green. "More dim wits."

Basket maker Allbritton. "Multiply the number of horses burned up in the fire or sent crazed into the countryside by four and you may calculate my loss. Whereas you, Shadwell, lost by half and by many less those two-footed creatures whose—"

Shoemaker Shadwell. "Whose sins bring us to this grim accounting. On the bright side, of course, all those burned soles may wander back to my shop for repair."

Mister Wood brought them back the more general account of losses. "The Bridge was not entirely spared. As in the fire of '33, houses on the north end, and Saint Magnus are but ashes, and the waterwheels are a shambles."

But Master Carpenter Coldiron felt he had to admit a personal advantage. "Had I not the task of repairing the Bridge on which we now sit, I would suffer the least loss of us all, for houses and other buildings must very soon begin to rise out of the ashes."

Mister Wood. "And I lost—"

Deliberately making his chair scrape noisily, Mister Clinkenbeard stood up and walked about the room. "Losses, losses, and losses! Acts of God!" Then he sat again behind the table behind which he would now preside more forcefully. "We are here to prevent the loss of everything in the future, perhaps the all too near future."

Mister Brooke chimed in with Mister Clinkenbeard. "Yes, prospects of the future. We of the North end know what it is to catch fire, recovering still from '33, and now new ashes, and what of the future for us at the North end? All of you of the other shops take heed, think of us, pray for us, help us now and help us prepare for what is surely to come."

Mister Upshaw heard only the word "future." "This may show the way. I am in possession of a rumor that the king intends a proclamation declaring that the rebuilding this famous city will be with brick and arches which frustrate fire."

Mister Clinkenbeard, exhausted, made a final point, weakly. "We are already built on stone and arches, and yet . . ."

*   *   *

Shoemaker Shadwell opened the next meeting with a question. "Should we not wait for the others?"

Goldsmith Clinkenbeard sat straight in his chair, consciously try-ing to appear statuesque. "We are all present. I have selected you six to plan some drastic course to ensure the future of the Bridge.

"To begin. We *seem* to have been spared such horrors as they tell of during the plague and fire, and that we have witnessed from the Bridge with our own eyes, as when infected unfortunates in fever wrapped themselves in blankets and ran into the great pits and waited for the dirt to bury them over."

Haberdasher South was in a first-meeting frame of mind. "In my own humble opinion, I think I can assert with confidence that this was a deplorable fire."

Mister Shadwell's duty was to keep the others mindful of God's plan. "Prognostications for the year to come threaten the like ruin to the remaining parts, amid God's greater judgment on the whole land."

Mister Clinkenbeard posed the question. "Have we been spared? Has our fate been only postponed, delayed?"

Mister Wood wanted very much to know. "Can we *know?*"

Glover Archer laid a path. "Or prevent somehow."

Mister Shadwell was skeptical. "How?"

Mister Clinkenbeard took a step, firmly, his voice clarion. "Fire following plague has persuaded us to meet again in secret, as a select few, and recommence deliberations, each man putting forth possible measures."

One by one, all obeyed.

Mister Brooke followed Mister Clinkenbeard's lead. "This has been a decade of infection and contagion—not just fire and plague."

Mister Wood. "Greed."

Mister Upshaw. "Crime."

Mister Shadwell. "War."

Mister South. "Credulity."

Mister Clinkenbeard raised the forefinger of his right hand. "I took the comet to be an ill-omen only after the plague set in and—" here he raised the forefinger of his left hand—"the second comet as an omen only after the fire followed so soon upon the plague—"

"Don't neglect—" Mister South raised both forefingers as if in absentminded mockery—"to speak of the tempest before and during the fire."

"—and I resisted the import of dreams and visions and half-naked prophets on the Bridge. But now, looking back, I cannot deny the verity of numerous signs and intimations."

Mister Upshaw sensed he was reaching backward, but spoke nonetheless. "I am moved to invoke once again but not for the last time Mother Shipton's prophecy, so familiar to all of you that I need not recite it."

Fishmonger Brooke. "Merely invoke it."

Mister South. "Precisely."

Mister Wood. "Michael Nostradamus predicted this very year— more than a century ago."

Mister Brooke mindfully served Mister Clinkenbeard's purpose. "Commerce cannot rely on the logic of trade either. Should we not then take *everything* into account? Ignore nothing as irrelevant?"

"Even though we are finally ignorant," said Mister Clinkenbeard, "of cause and effect."

Mister Wood was growing more skeptical. "It is undeniable that we cannot say of any one way that it will lead us into a bright, predictable, reliable future."

Mister Brooke persevered. "All things must be given due consideration. Dark signs alongside bright prospects."

"Our road across the Bridge is often called narrow, congested, dangerous." Mister Upshaw felt that what he had said would raise a question that would distress him.

Mister Brooke took his cue from Mister Upshaw. "Perhaps, some will say, a new London Bridge is called for."

Sensing that Mister Shadwell's obsession was drawing him into an uncertain, unstable frame of mind, Mister Clinkenbeard alluded to his role as God's voice. "As we have been told, as Shadwell at our last meeting often repeated, all bridges are affronts to God and the gods, and so, in some sense, cursed."

Mister South was suddenly attentive. "Is that so? Who then told us?"

"Shadwell himself told us, and now I am myself telling us that—"

Mister Shadwell. "Not I. 'Twas *you* said that, Mister Clinkenbeard. But 'tis true. We are not safe."

Mister Clinkenbeard. "Let us say it often amongst ourselves—we are not safe."

"We," all said, "are not safe."

Mister South. "Hear, hear. Hear."

Mister Clinkenbeard felt the mood was right enough to take another major step. "Saint Thomas Chapel was renamed Chapel of Our Lady. I take this name change to suggest that perhaps the name change has kept the Bridge for ten years before the chapel's demolition by man, to wit Henry VIII, not God from more harm than *she* would otherwise have suffered. A fair lady may now, again, be needed to save us from future harm."

Fishmonger Brooke. "That song?"

Mister South. "What song?"

Mister Brooke. "'London Bridge Is Falling Down,' and the Fair Lady in the tower."

Momentum was building in Mister Clinkenbeard's mind. "There is a pagan quality in a bridge, or in a bridge's nature, that reverses God's geography. A river divides, separates more emphatically that any other topographical feature. You can cross most hills and mountains more easily than you can swim a wide river. A river is like a commandment from God—thou shalt not cross—which bridge builders and crossers violate. So the act of building a bridge is in itself both a defiance of, and a protracted prayer to, pagan gods. Perhaps they must be appeased, retribution must be paid. A bridge is a community service—mayhap a sacrifice must be offered by the community.

"Indeed, primitives believed that to erect a bridge was to trespass on the powers of the gods of land and water. A bridge negatively symbolized those powers. To appease the wrath of those gods, a human sacrifice—alive, in the anchor pier at the Bridge foot opposite the City, facing possible enemies, bands of traitors, and to guard against malevolent pagan gods or spirits or random forces. In the song, the possible materials are enumerated, as we all know, and found too weak without human sacrifice. Something so primitive must have risen up in the human heart all over the world from the beginning. A girl child was buried alive in a pillar under one of the bridges in ancient Paris, I once heard, or read, or imagined. Perhaps Peter de Colechurch built the chapel in the middle of the Bridge out of some awareness of what the ancients did.

"In the Dark Ages, the belief crossers carried onto the Bridge was that one side represented good, the other side evil, making crossing a daily psychic ordeal. In the song, 'cabbage' alludes to evil, 'rose' alludes to good—"

Mister South had been waiting for an opening to speak his mind. "But do not forget the rosette of the plague, the red token on the neck or chest. 'Red Rover.'"

Mister Upshaw felt that he had been silent too long. "A tug of war between good side, evil side ends this elaborate game."

Mister Clinkenbeard raised his voice an octave. "Mindful of the deep-seated belief that if the Tower ravens ever leave the Tower, the Tower will fall—recall King Edward's solution, trimming their wings, now a tradition, a ritual—I suggest we take seriously the legend that a bridge requires, if it is to stand, a sacrifice of some kind.

"Both may be mere superstitions, but both may arise from dark regions of the spirit world. We must not gamble. The risk, the loss may be too great. From this window above this Bridge, look, see the Tower ravens, see the Tower still stands, amidst fire ruins, while the entire North, London, side of this Bridge gapes in the stark sunlight. Houses still standing lean like old women over a laundry tub. For over a century, the drawbridge has been too weak to repair. The rush of tides along the river bottom scour the stones away from under the piers and starlings are crumbling." Goldsmith Clinkenbeard, having set himself somewhat atremble, thrust himself forward an inch, then pushed himself against the high back of his chair, and said not another word on that occasion.

* * *

"Mister Shadwell, what were you saying in your sleep last night?"

"How should *I* know? You were the one who was awake, my dear. You tell me." But he hoped she couldn't. Her face showed she couldn't. He was relieved.

"When you talk, Mister Shadwell, I *always* listen."

'But will she tell me what I say? Maybe she'll use it against me when she sees an advantage. She fears what she will hear will be of women. I can rest easy on *that*. But. . . .'

Shadwell, alone, read aloud from Romans 3: 11–18.

> There is none righteous, no, not one:
> There is none that understandeth, there is none that seeketh after
>   God.
> They are all gone out of the way, they are together become un-
>   profitable;
> there is none that doeth good, no, not one.
> Their throat is an open sepulcher; with their tongues they have
>   used deceit;
> the poison of asps is under their lips:
> Whose mouth is full of cursing and bitterness:
> Their feet are swift to shed blood:
> Destruction and misery are in their ways:
> And the way of peace have they not known:
> There is no fear of God before their eyes.

*   *   *

Goldsmith Clinkenbeard opened the second meeting of the committee of seven. "Mister Shadwell pleads illness for his absence."

Fishmonger Brooke noticed that Mister Clinkenbeard was introducing the idea he had rehearsed with him a few nights before. "We try to tell ourselves we have left all that behind—centuries ago. But the whole world seems to have slid back down into the bog. It makes sense in these times. Civil War, tempest, fire, and plague are passed, but we know they could return—and more—and worse. Be ready. Take measures."

The six present were now all of one mind, and spoke with a single voice:

Mister Brooke. "If Mister Coldiron were among us, he would say that the stone Bridge itself is solid enough, if repaired. But look at how precariously our houses lean together upon it."

Mister Wood. "We need help that no carpenter or Bridge Master can even know to give. It's a gamble. Maybe no dark force is out there to see our offering. It's a gamble. We must do *something*—if only to throw the dice—Pascal's wager."

Mister Brooke. "The plague may be among us in this very room, gathering strength from the weakness of our resolve. Fire is daily common among us, and some one—even among us here—may be unmindful of its desire to consume us as we sleep—as in '33."

Mister Clinkenbeard. "Add to all these shapes of doom our own several secret sins, and God or the gods of chance may drown us all."

Mister Brooke. "Hesitation, delay are our enemies. Strike them down and act!"

Mister South. "But how?"

"We must not budge from here until we are of one mind." Mister Clinkenbeard raised his hands, fingers knitted. "A mind bent on mending. We have been given the sign—two signs—plague and fire—"

Mister South. "Three—tempest!"

"—from God, or the gods, as some would say. But no written record until 963 or so exists. No mention of a bridge or ferry even. Sometime around 970 AD, a widow and her son, found guilty of witchcraft, by sticking iron pins in a figure representing the victim—a practice still in darker regions of Yorkshire—were taken to River Thames at the Bridge and drowned, a sacrifice of sorts, was it not?"

Mister Brooke. "The next allusion to the existence of the Bridge is to the tolls. From the sinister to the mundane."

Mister Clinkenbeard. "Ah, the Anglo-Saxon Chronicle of London is a chronicle of fires. The years' toll. And to that is added tempest, ice, flood, plague."

Mister Brooke. "The isolated Bridge then was always caught up in the events on both sides. Everything is connected somehow with everything else. They drowned the widow but not her son, or, therefore, her craft."

Mister South. "A curse on the Bridge?"

Mister Brooke. "Or on those who use the Bridge?"

Mister Wood. "Or both? The one is, in fact, the other."

Mister Clinkenbeard. "And how, I ask you, do we remove this curse or forfend yet another curse we know not of?"

Mister Brooke. "And also bear in mind, bear in mind, gentlemen, that this Bridge in the future, as the young Chronicler at Nonesuch told me, also has a past of great moment in the history of the world, and if it falls, if it falls, with it go six centuries of English history. We have *that* burden also. He assures me that sacrifices at bridges—"

Mister Wood. "You asked him?"

Mister Brooke. "Yes."

Mister Clinkenbeard. "We must remember and beware of the fact that he has been drawn into our conversations."

Stationer Wood. "The talk here tonight disturbs me deeply. Six bridge merchants I have known all my life are sorting through a nasty bag of solutions to a problem to which we have not even given a name. Fear and fears. As if fear had a monster life of its own. We would bar the door and set fire to the house to destroy the monster. We forget to leave the room. We perish with it. Behind that locked door, we talk of plague and fire as survivors, and yet we sound like victims beyond hope. Oh, yes, there is the future. It *may* be dark. Let us go out and meet it and take extreme measures against it. But what is it? Where does it lie in wait? On the parapet of the Great Stone Gate, among the severed heads?"

Mister South. "Perhaps inside one of the piers."

Mister Clinkenbeard. "*God* gave. *You* give."

Mister Brooke. "Abraham did not know God himself would later sacrifice his own son, but he obeyed God *anyway.* We know about both sacrifices."

*   *   *

To recount the particulars, the drift of the meeting, nervously aware of Gilda Shadwell in the bedroom above, fishmonger Brooke, sent by goldsmith Clinkenbeard, visited shoemaker Clarke Shadwell, who had not attended the meeting. Having declared himself ill, he lay abed.

Mister Shadwell heard himself sounding like Mister Clinkenbeard. "The net of business acquaintances has *changed* into a web of business transactions. 'Honeycomb' is of course a better word than 'web.' Rather, one suits now, the other better suits later. Within days, within an hour."

Mister Brooke told Mister Shadwell that there was more talk of the old ritual of a sacrifice of some nature.

When Mister Shadwell, father of Gilda and an older daughter, protested the mere mention, Mister Brooke asked him repeatedly, insistently, "The challenging question before the seven of us is this: Is the Bridge safe?"

"Is it safe?" Mister Shadwell, incredulous, covered his face for a moment. "Well, if you recall the plague dead, the fire dead, and forget the Tempest dead, and don't count the shoot-the-Bridge dead. Because by 'safe,' I take you to mean living on the Bridge itself, not sealing your fate by wrecking yourself against its piers and starlings, or throwing yourself, *throwing* yourself over the rail, or losing your footing, losing your *footing* whilst building up or tearing down these four- and five-storey buildings, or repairing them, sweeping their chimneys—or surely one or two Keepers of the Heads have fallen while hoisting the pikes with the heads, the shafts slippery with blood draining out of the brain and neck. Battles, I mustn't forget. And ice undermining the foundations. Safe, certainly. Until now. When a child can't play on it, singing games, without putting ideas into the heads of pale and trembling merchants. Unsafe for a child, however seductive in her burnished innocence, to sing and dance and laugh and cavort? Taken off, the dust settling slowly where she struggled to resist?"

Mister Brooke, having ended his visit with, "Your allusions rush beyond any solutions posed at the meeting," duly appeared in the goldsmith shop at the sign London Bridge Gold to report to Clinkenbeard.

"He wanted to kill me, but I could see it in his face—he would think it over, in fear perhaps. Soon. Because he knows it must be done quickly. Each man in the Brotherhood sees the necessity to do something—and this is really the *only* thing any of us can imagine. It goes deep. It's dark."

Mister Brooke left the goldsmith shop, feeling, as usual, that time spent in Mister Clinkenbeard's company was always edifying.

*   *   *

As the members of the Brotherhood deliberated, the Poet wrote:

Never Curse the Bridge
In a brangle on the Bridge, a captain
whose objective was to cross it in force,
cursed the Bridge—its drawbridge obstructed
his progress. My father heard him,
and what he said to me, at the end
of the story, has haunted me
for over a decade, haunts me now,
as I reluctantly pursue his task as Chronicler.
"Never curse the Bridge by which you cross
safely from shore to shore." The captain's head,
hoisted on his own spear, my father cautioned me,
still adorned the Great Stone Gate the day I was born.
Something evil loiters about this Bridge. Godless,
despite Peter de Colechurch, because look at this drawing
of Sir Thomas More's head on a pike.
What kind of people
would live where severed heads look down on neighbors
and on strangers entering the Bridge Gate from the South end,
gazing all around and behind them, then up at the heads?

                                            Daryl Braintree

*   *   *

At the next meeting, Eldon South spoke first. "Listen to the voices of the past, of those who have perished on the Bridge in plague and fire and ice and tempest and accidents and illness. They *will* speak. That you listen triggers them. Listen. Don't make a sound. Hush. Attend. *Pay* attention and get your money's worth. We merchants can grasp that."

Having learned from Mister Brooke that Mister Clinkenbeard had chosen five from the seven to constitute a secret committee, Mister

Archer had persuaded the leader to include him, with the stipulation that Archer would serve only as an alternate. Mister Shadwell's continued service in doubt, Mister Archer was now vividly present. "God will provide a lamb."

Brooke waved his forefinger before the other four faces. "*One* for us all—sacrifice."

"In fear and trembling," Archer insisted. "Was not Moses ready to sacrifice Isaac and did not God give his only son?" Archer held out his hands, palms up. "So we can give our daughter's death that we and 'she' might live, we on the Bridge, she with our father in heaven."

"Remember Robert Hubert," asked Mister Clinkenbeard, "hanged in October for setting fire to London, thus to our Bridge? Some say agents of France or the Dutch or Popish terrorists, Jews, gypsies. That feeble-minded young man was, of course, innocent. A scapegoat, but also a sacrifice. The prevailing conviction, held by our King, and Samuel Pepys, and John Evelyn, and perhaps Richard Baxter as well, and which I share, was that the cause was the finger of God.

"The majority see God's judgment, as do most of us here in this room. And yet the courts, the state, hanged Robert Hubert, a twenty-five-year-old son of a Rouen watchmaker. Why? Because civilized men and women must punish one person, at least, for so grave a crime. Only six lives lost in fire by official count, but twelve million pounds in damage. I cannot but believe that many more perished in the flimsy wooden tenements, especially the very young and the very old, incinerated, chosen by God as sacrifice for the sins of us all.

"There is something almost mystic—I will not go so far as to say religious—about this need to fix upon *one* person—an example set by Pilate—if possible, blame for an effect to which many people may have contributed some cause. We know now that poor Robert Hubert was not even in England at that time, that he was feeble-minded, telling contradictory tales that any sane judge—a few there were, but were ignored—should have recognized as a sign of enthusiasm crossed with feebleness of mind. Perhaps acts committed in that spirit *after* the fact, upon the innocent, may affect causes before they can have effect.

"I knew when he was tried, I knew when they led him through the street to point out where he threw the fireball, that he was innocent. I was already nearby on some business and saw him coming. I realized that my knowing could have no consequence. There is no legal, social, or religious means of testifying to such knowledge of the heart. Strange. Something left out. No means. But the feeling is as real as prison stone."

Archer avoided Clinkenbeard's eyes. "I feel now that innocence is our salvation—our means of prevention."

Mister Wood had innocence in mind. "Our sign to God."

Mister Clinkenbeard clarified. "Or the gods. . . . I often think innocent people die or suffer *after* every great assault by war, plague, or fire or famine or act of God in tempest or ice. Men judge. Men misjudge. As after the plague. Only last month was Robert Hubert hanged, that already seems a tale of distant times. The ice will form upon us. Visitations of ice each year. The Bridge is weak. Time. The fires. Tempest. Rust has set its teeth into the iron, termites into the wood."

Mister Archer wanted to keep it simple and easy. "The Keeper of the Heads who risks his worthless life to hang the severed heads over the gate. We may hope to buy his services."

Mister Brooke half-liked that suggestion. "I hear he has a dark past, prison and escapes from prison and worse crimes since. Only temporarily keeper of the heads."

Mister South felt a narrative impulse. "No, that one is gone, don't you remember? He reached out to pinch the cheeks of the piked head of a nobleman—Venner perhaps—among the impaled heads he had placed there himself and lost his balance and fell into the roadway and mayhap was dead before the horses and carts trampled him."

Mister Clinkenbeard asserted that "the pike is reserved for noblemen and traitors, not gutter-born kidnappers."

Mister Archer stood up to speak.

Here the Poet-Chronicler's account of plague and fire ended.

In time, his pleasure in reading again and again his mingling of voices diminished until the time came when he could no longer distinguish what he had written out of his own imagination and what he had taken from published works that had become more and more famous, and then when his sense of time became vague, he read his accounts of plague and fire and merchant meetings as not his own, and wondered, scrutinizing the handwriting, who might have written those pages.

Always, even at eighty-six, more convinced than hoping that his father would call to him from the stairs, he was unmindful of the fact that the old man would have been one hundred and twenty-six years old.

When Nonesuch House, then woefully derelict, was dismantled in 1757, the Poet-Chronicler's bones were discovered, as if hidden, but neither his father's Chronicle nor his own were found, nor his imagined account of the life of Peter de Colechurch, based on a single paragraph of information, nor his imagined account of the murder of Archbishop Thomas à Becket, based on eyewitness accounts of five Becket biographers, nor his fact-imagination fabricated accounts of the Great Fire and the Great Plague of London and of the meetings of the Brotherhood of the Bridge, nor his never-published poems.

*   *   *

Mister South joined Mister Wood on the walk home from the meeting. "I will go with you a while, across the Bridge perhaps, but you must promise me not to talk of things that may disturb my sleep, *our* sleep. Oh, beautiful is the moon, almost full, and how quiet the water, now that the fire has stopped the mill wheels from whining, disturbing the peace."

"Not whining. Grinding? Well, creaking. Rusty. Slightly askew. The foundations infirm? I allude to nothing."

"Whine? Infirm? Why do you pick at my choice of words? You are like Kerry Brooke. Agitation. You can't be still. We made a decision together, you know. We are all—we—I won't say 'to blame.' Not the word."

"What's the word?"

"Better no word at all."

"Silence."

"We are sworn to silence, aren't we?"

"But there you go again, grunting. I'd rather you stood stock still and delivered a sermon—a speech—than utter expressive grunts."

*   *   *

An hour after all had left, goldsmith Clinkenbeard alone with his thoughts, a tentative knock lifted him out of his chair and to the door.

On his threshold stood Glover Lennox Archer, heavy with purpose. "Mention of Abraham's sacrifice this evening prompts me to put forth a proposal that has tormented me since our previous meeting."

Mister Clinkenbeard had imagined this visit. "Torment is our daily bread these last two years."

"Mine is Biblical."

"As was Christ's."

Mister Archer raised his hand to ward off such talk. "Let us not speak of Christ in the same room with the devil."

"Let us leave a room the devil has entered."

Mister Archer regained control of his mission. "No, not the devil. Only seems so, I suppose. No, a true sacrifice. One will be chosen from among us. I choose to take that torment upon myself."

"I dimly perceive . . ."

"If Abraham could . . ."

"I will not allow you the luxury of comparison with Abraham, Mister Archer. Do but stand on your own feet."

"Very well. I stand here to tell you that mine is offered."

"Literally? Blythe?"

"Hearing her name in this room weakens my resolve."

"Pray tell me why you are—"

"Each of us has declared that we stand ready to make the offering. I want to spare . . ."

"You are not such a man, Archer. You are as good a man as any of us by reputation, but no better. All good men need money."

"I will forgo the money."

"Then your motive . . . ?"

"Is. . . . No. Is. No, not money but. No, I mean, yes, I must confess. I need it. A debt I must pay."

Aware that his body embodied authority, Mister Clinkenbeard turned aside. "I must decline."

"You are horrified?"

"That word is a third party in this room, in a red hat. Good night, Mister Archer."

*   *   *

Near the end of the next meeting of the cabal, Mister Clinkenbeard spoke the truth as clearly as he could. "We sacrifice ourselves also—to hell, for this act. We are, before the act, mad. We are, in the act, murderers. We aspire but to be humans, after all."

Before the vote began, shoemaker Shadwell backed out of the room, and fled to his shop, where he stood behind the counter, among his tools and materials. He went through the process of starting a new shoe, staring out into the dark street, where a sliver of moonlight cut the dark roadway.

Clarke Shadwell woke his wife to confess that from meeting to meeting in the past year, he had traveled a dark, rocky road and that he had chosen his own solitary peril over a peril to be endured in common with the other men.

"To pay the kidnapper, we were all given today as the deadline to pay each our share. I did not. I do not know the consequences. Perhaps someone will be hired to put a fireball into my shop—no, that might ignite the very catastrophe all here feared. If the solution works, I will be marked as one who refused to fund it. If it fails, I will be accused of casting bad luck upon the scheme by failure to participate. But I have stated my conviction that the sacrifice would fail to protect us. Why then should I pay? They will say I was part of the chosen group, a cabal, that met to find a solution, that I had to go with the majority."

*   *   *

Mister Clinkenbeard saw the necessity for visiting Clarke Shadwell alone, and acted upon it.

Having made his argument, he waited to see its effect emerge in Shadwell's face.

"And now I must insist, sir, that you remove your damned self from my bedchamber. Your evil proposal will foul the air I breathe long after you are yourself asleep in your own bed. Your voice will keep me awake while your innocent dreams refresh you. A nightmare is all *I* may hope for. At least it won't be a living nightmare for my daughter."

"I named thee, sir."

"Do not dare repeat the names in this room."

"Dare I offer you myself double the compensation should your name be drawn? Mind, yours may escape the lottery."

"Your mother's son may escape thrashing if he comes to his senses and quits these quarters before I fling back these bedclothes and—"

"I go reluctantly to report to the Brotherhood that not only do you refuse to be counted in this matter, but that you have refused double the price, and that, sir, may prove very worrisome for all of us. But not tonight. I will wait to convey your decision. Hence, should you recon—"

"I'm at your throat."

Goldsmith Clinkenbeard fled the room, the shop.

Mister Shadwell embraced his wife. "I must hide. You must watch over Gilda. Tell her I have gone on a long journey into Kent."

He kissed his wife and fled into the night, bound for Scotland.

*   *   *

When her mother told her that her father was missing, had perhaps fallen into River Thames, Gilda went into London, searching for her father, and into Southwark, and back and forth along London Bridge roadway, calling his name, "Father!" And whispering God's fatherly name, "Abba . . ."

In her father's absence, Gilda, attendant at the counter, aroused men to while away the afternoon in desultory talk.

"Sometimes the stink from Within the Gates and the surrounding liberties is straight from Hell. That's not a manner of speaking. Take it literally. In the nose, it's literal. On the tip of the tongue, it's precise. Stinging the eyes, it's actual. When the stink invades you, you don't think of words, you think of wind or a brisk walk to the other end of the Bridge. Of course, stinks originate on the Bridge itself. This morning, I wanted to stick my head in a barrel and shut the lid over me. But there's no escape. I live and work here and the stink is intimate. And now this everlasting smell of things burnt and still smoldering."

The customer's very words began to smell as foul as his feet. As her mother descended, Gilda faded politely, backward, up the stairs.

As Gilda entered her room to finish drawing a ship in the pool, a bird fluttered its wings against her breasts, darted against the ceiling, then a wall, perched on her bed, and she ducked as it flew toward her. Her bedroom window was open to soft but still smoke-laden air. She spoke to the bird, ushering it toward the open window. Finally, it flew out, and she looked out to see where it had gone, saw it falling, not flying, onto the starling.

She went down to the street to look for it between the houses where they leaned slightly away from each other. There it lay on the starling. Then it walked. Then it tried to fly. Then it flew.

Light-footed with happiness, she walked along the roadway, singing, not "London Bridge Is Broken," but a song about birds.

"Flow my tears, fall from your springs,

Exil'd for ever let me mourn;

Where night's black bird her sad infamy sings,

There let me live forlorn."

*   *   *

The five merchants meeting for the sixth time as a cabal knew the song Gilda sang as it came through their open window, and knew who sang it, and wondered if she, her father missing, would be chosen. But chosen how, the father missing, his consent mandatory?

Mister Clinkenbeard with a heavy heart and a mind less filled with rhetoric, opened his mouth to begin the meeting. "Mindful of what we are about to commission one of us to do on our behalf, we do well to take note of the encouraging fact that throughout London rebuilding has already begun, and in that spirit, Master Carpenter Coldiron began work on the erection of the safety palisades this very day.

"The woeful experience in this late heavy visitation has taught us that building with timber and even on stone foundations exposes us to the wrath of fire, but we saw brick resist and even extinguish the fire in places.

"Next to the hand of God in the terrible wind, plague and fire have been our worst fate. London Bridge, though it was built of stone, is narrow, all wood above the roadway—the hautepas. Our wood will burn, for bricks are too heavy for the patience of the Bridge. We must change.

"The King calls on the magnanimity of the people to restore the churches defaced by this lamentable fire. Saint Magnus Martyr burned centuries ago and rose from its ashes. Let us begin immediately on this very day, when we do this thing no Christian ever did before."

"This dismal year of 1666—people almost as dead from hellfire, their sudden neighbor, as from the ruins they sustained."

"The burning wall of a house afire fell on Miss Maudy, and there she goes, disfigured, crossing, whose loveliness we all daily had admired as she passed."

"Do not hesitate. He who hesitates is lost. Lost opportunities. The opportunity eludes me. The elusive night stalker shall look down on us from a pike."

Goldsmith Clinkenbeard reached into Mister South's hat that he made himself and pulled out and held aloft a ticket, South written on it. "Mister South."

"No. I cannot. I cannot. No. Draw again."

Clinkenbeard declared, "That would be unfair."

Each of the five merchants so vividly brought the image of Mister South's child to mind that she stood amongst them five times over, each image slightly different from the others, one skipping, one standing, arms akimbo, another stooping to gaze at her reflection in a puddle exposed to fast-moving carts, another giggling as she ran, another singing, all five Mister South's daughter, too many to mew up in a single pillar.

Sadness made Phelan Wood's voice almost inaudible, and seemed as if only he heard it. "I heard her say as she passed me one evening, 'Have you seen my father looking for me?'"

Mister Clinkenbeard declared, "We must be deaf to such remembrances."

To the others, Eldon South seemed a stranger. "No. No. No. Will no one say 'no' with me? No. No." He repeatedly pointed at each of the cabal, including himself, repeating the word he desired would triumph, "rescue."

Lennox Archer's body drooped as if mimicking Mister South's emotion. "Mister South is too stricken, as we can all see." He looked at Mister Clinkenbeard.

Mister Clinkenbeard turned away from Mister Archer, who had replaced Mister Shadwell. "Who will stand for Mister South?"

No one stepped forward. Mister Clinkenbeard looked at Archer, who had turned his back, thinking that might influence Mister Clinkenbeard's thinking.

Mister Archer turned to face Clinkenbeard and thus the other three.

Mister Clinkenbeard looked up at the ceiling. "You, Mister Archer?"

Mister Archer did not look at Mister Clinkenbeard, but moved his gaze from face to face of the other three. "Mister South cannot endure it. He is not as strong as the rest of us."

Mister Clinkenbeard looked Mister Archer full in the face. "You then, Mister Archer?"

Mister Archer lowered and nodded his head.

What difference might it have made had Lennox Archer known that Blythe had deliberately tempted him that night, had known that she loved it—the power and the sex together—known that that evil streak in her ran through most of the streets of London and a few in Southwark? He donated his own daughter because having raped, as he supposed, his own daughter, he hoped to shut her up before she could tell the world, so to speak, never considering, until later, that his act might come out somehow anyway at some point in the years to come. No, not the money. The silence. He did not know that two of the other four secretly refused and together bought out a third, putting Mister South's child in peril, until Mister Archer saved her by offering his own. Saving Mister South's child gave him a deep-felt sense of redemption.

Human nature had subtly woven a web among them. Ready to respond, the others in the cabal tossed their money pouches onto the table, one loud thud after another.

14

THE BROTHERHOOD HIRES LUCIEN AS KIDNAPPER

From his ship far downstream near Gravesend, Lucien stared at the smoke rising and hovering over London.

When his ship anchored in the Pool, he dove into River Thames close enough to a crossing wherry to hail it and board it.

On shore, passing the site of Saint Magnus Martyr, Lucien stepped through the blackened arch to the west side of the church onto the Bridge and delighted in seeing houses East side, West side, ten or so, burned down to the roadbed, smoke persisting. "Lucifer, you have been here before me."

He thought of the year in which he was steeped, 1666—666 the mark of Lucifer.

Glad that the fire that had destroyed the heart of one of the greatest cities of the world, as he had known them, had not raged across London Bridge entire, the smoldering fires in a house on the London End of the Bridge next to one unburnt house inspired him to re-ignite the fire so that it might spread across the entire Bridge. Parting ashes with a stick, he uncovered embers that he could have forcefully breathed into flame. An obscure sense that a greater destruction, desecration, was possible moved him to piss-quench the revivified fire, grind the embers underfoot.

Looking up at each sign and into the windows of each shop, East side, West side, and at the entrance to the warehouse he had learned from Morgan to have been in ancient times Saint Thomas à Becket Chapel, he moved as slowly as a statue faintly animated.

Gazing up at the heads impaled on pikes above the gate, he remembered thinking for a moment as Morgan vividly described them that one of them was his father's, saw now in memory starker than those heads above him his father's head on a stob in their field, and he knew, without clearly remembering yet, that he had a few years later walked onto this Bridge, when he was a wandering child.

Stepping off the Bridge onto Tooley Street in Southwark, Lucien felt that his desire to burn the Bridge made it his property.

Eating and drinking among the low life, Lucien overheard rumors that a kidnapper-for-hire was sought. To give himself something to do, something a little different, until he could imagine some shocking, unfamiliar way to devastate Morgan's little urban Acadia, he set about finding the client, not only by asking likely men and whores but by cannily scrutinizing the demeanor of men moving about on the Bridge and in the still hot, smoking ruins of the town.

Tracing a web of connections, he found a beggar woman who pointed out the portly spider in Saint Paul's Yard pretending to browse among book stalls the fire had not reduced to ashes.

"I seek work you will not do yourself."

Glover Lennox Archer was alert. "I had my eye on you as you came into the yard from Ludgate."

"We have found each other. The work of the Lord? Or the work of the devil?"

"I would rather speak of it in some middle fashion. Necessary work, but necessarily—"

"Secret?"

"Do you seek secret work?"

"It is for that I am come here from the ends of the earth." Lucien opened his coat to reveal his outlandish seafaring garb.

"I took your walk instantly for a seaman."

"You seek a man who comes and goes?'

"Aye, aye, as they say. Newly landed?"

"So newly landed solid ground gives me pause."

"My good sir, may I ask, have you lain in jail more than once?"

"Too many times to give a perfect accounting."

"Jailed not for murder, else you would have been hanged."

"Caught often, but not for that. Is the job murder?"

"Kidnapping and killing."

"Then you know a kidnapper when you see him. Now to the fine details. How rich will you make me?"

"I will meet you over there by that smoking tree, inside Saint Paul's Cross tomorrow at nine with all the details and half the money. Step carefully, for the old church continues to rain fire debris."

Having parted with the man, Lucien doubled back to Cheapside Street and followed his man through the heaps of rubble, thrilled to see him step onto the surviving London Bridge, hoping he would turn in at one of the shops as its owner. In you go, my devout gentleman. Ah, under the sign of the Hand and Glove.

Lucien paused at an angle that gave him a view of a glover's shop and of the gentleman slipping as a master would behind the counter.

The next evening, five hours before he was to meet the man by Saint Paul's Cross, among the ruins of the still smoking church, Lucien waited close by the man's shop to be the last customer before closing.

As the fat, agitated glover gathered his motions into the rigid shape of an effigy, a piddling version of the giant Gogmagog came to Lucien's mind, a mind ignorant of the fact that Gog and Magog were the two giant guardians of London, paraded every year across the Bridge in the Lord Mayor's show each November.

"You were to meet me, sir, in one of the rooms in Saint Paul's Cross by yonder smoking tree."

"I build trust on mistrust. What am I to do?"

"Meet me *here* at nine. I will unlock the door and we will talk in the dark."

When Lucien returned that night, the man was standing behind the door. He unlocked it, and Lucien flashed like a pane of glass inside.

"Quickly, I will tell you, and demand that you leave before you are seen. I will pay you well to take my daughter, Blythe, from her bed and mew her up alive in a pier closest to Southwark supporting this Bridge."

265

"Which pier?"

"Bankside, South, Rock Lock, Eighth, Gateway pier."

"Point at it."

"Come to the back of the shop." The glover opened a window and leaned out. Lucien leaned out over the merchant's shoulder, inhaling the odor of the Pool mingled with fear and guilt. "There, after the House of Many Mirrors and the square under the Great Stone Gateway." So he could keep an eye on her.

"East or West side?"

"West, of course."

"Naturally.

"I will show you what must be done. Follow me."

Past the House of Many Mirrors next door, Lucien followed the merchant to Rock Lock pier, the Gateway pier, severed heads above, the Corn Mill still smoking.

"When?"

"Three days from today."

"Where?"

"In her bed or in the street in London among the ruins. She is wayward and wanders there often."

"I must see her."

"You will see her here behind the counter with me tomorrow morning at seven o'clock. I will go upstairs, and she will slip away, as she does every day no matter how vigilant I am. I made sure she was in her bed tonight before coming down to meet you. Even so, she may even now be out there in the night somewhere."

"You are not alone?"

"No."

"Your own daughter?"

"I am a good man, God knows. A good husband. A good father. But to the point, I must choose to be the chosen one."

"You do a good act, though you profit. Why I am to commit this crime?"

"'Why' is my province. *What* is yours."

"I am the original 'why,' sir. I am no 'what.' How, yes, but no 'what.' And you are nothing, today and tomorrow."

"Riddle as you will. But we must stop. You must go. Go quickly."

*   *   *

Lennox Archer reported to Clinkenbeard. "I expected him at nine at Paul's Cross. But he darkened the door of my shop five hours early, dressed as a merchant. I gave him the instructions you instructed me to give to him and gave him half his fee and pointed out, from my window, the two of us leaning out over the river, the exact pier, South, Rock Lock, Gateway pier, the eighth. Having assured me that he would obey our wishes as expressed by myself, he left my house, and I wish to God I did not have to see him again. Respectfully submitted, your servant." No signature. "In the year of our Lord, September 15, 1666."

Mister Clinkenbeard prayed for forgiveness and then he prayed for Blythe's soul.

Others prayed on the Bridge that night.

"Forgive me, Lord, for I have sinned," prayed Clinkenbeard's wife. "I coveted my neighbor's flower garden. To atone, I am starting a garden of my own, tomorrow, in Christ's name. Amen."

"I pray the birds will return when the smoke dwindles down."

"Our Father, who art in heaven."

"Now I lay me down to sleep." The last word out of her mouth, Gilda sank into sleep.

"Yea, though I walk through the shadow of death, I will fear no evil, for thou art with me . . ."

"Hail, Mary, full of grace." He is not yet known on the Bridge to be a strict Catholic.

In an attitude of prayer, Blythe intoned: "London Bridge is broken down, floating down River Thames to the Nile."

Her father Lennox Archer dared not begin a dialogue with God.

*   *   *

Having, like Blythe when the Poet was writing about the murder of Becket, slipped in, Lucien was reading the rough drafts of poems when the Poet returned to his scriptorium.

Lucien saw the response in the Poet's face and body that he had expected, an easeful acceptance. "I saw you standing up here at this window and was jealous of your view. Standing here beside you, I see what you see, but you are blind to what I see."

Receptive to entertaining uninvited strangers, this one more than most, Daryl responded as if to a friend found waiting for him. "Had I not this house from father, I would restore—someday I may anyway— the Chapel midway on the Bridge, where Chaucer and other pilgrims paused to pray safe journey to Canterbury. History records, you may know, that the master-builder Peter de Colechurch is buried in the undercroft. The sacredness of the Chapel has kept the Bridge safe from total destruction by fire, tempest, and great frosts, even though it is now a warehouse above for rags and below for paper. I see my life's work, as Chronicler and as epic Poet. May I know your life's work?"

"I am pregnant with it, and my water will break at any moment."

"Now I have met yet another London poet."

"If I could burn every poem ever written in the history of mankind, I would do it in an instant."

"Why do you hate poetry?"

"Hate must hate."

"You are a rank stranger to all I have ever known."

"So well said, I am eager to thank you. I am eager next to know from this Bridge's historian—so I have been told—the origin of that song yon children are singing, even in the midst of plague and fire."

"You mistake me for my father, who is missing, thus I am the historian until he mayhap returns. The words of the song, like the houses on the Bridge, obscure the legend that in ancient times, when a bridge is built, a virgin girl child must be mewed up in the pillar—variants are told, of course—next to the alien shore, the bank facing strangers crossing into the town."

"I came to London with that story in my head. I assume then that the architect of the Bridge performed that ceremony."

"Unlikely. The master architect of the Bridge, Peter de Colechurch, was a priest. But not impossible five hundred years ago. They must sacrifice a thirteen-year-old-virgin girl to keep the Bridge safe from evil forces. A virgin buried alive in a pier facing the enemy may ward off evil, they believed, in those dark centuries. A pagan practice we have willfully forgotten."

Lucien tried to suppress a tone of mockery. "But God is greater, it is said, and may burn the Bridge in his wrath or let it stand on a mere whim. Our dark ignorance of the past makes men fearful—of what may still linger after the death of pagan gods, do you not think so?"

"And would the fleshy word 'enemy' embrace plague and fire as well as armed men?"

"Having seen what my eyes have seen and my ears have heard and my nose has smelled, I am inclined to imagine that that is so. But the Bridge is presently safe from plague and fire?"

"Throughout its history, except for the open space you passed on the city end where forty houses burned three decades ago, before I was born, and the ten rebuilt that were among the first to burn several days ago."

Lucien turned sideways, aware his thin frame would startle the Poet. "We are told that God moves in mysterious ways, so that he may have held back his hand, poised for a time when the blow would be least expected and far more destructive and lasting."

"As a poet imagining his life story, I have imputed such fears even to the master architect himself."

"You have answered my questions." 'And now I, who am the how, know the why. And that I am on this Bridge to fulfill the ancient legend.'

Lucien took a last look at a young man whom he was certain would soon die at the hands of the men who hired him to kidnap the very virgin of whom they were hypothetically speaking, for knowing the legend about to be played out on the modern stage, and turned away to descend the five flights of stairs to the Bridge roadway.

'It is not impossible that for over four centuries a virgin has been standing in one of the piers facing the enemy.'

Lucien sought, watched many girls. 'Is it you? Is it you? Maybe you. You? No, not you. You, certainly. But maybe not.'

He watched a girl go in at the door under the sign of the Green Hat. 'Which sign up ahead calls *that* girl child to go in? The Golden Needle or the Telescope and Star or the Three Burning Leaves or the Open Book? No, it will be what will be.

'Only a few more and then she will be off the Bridge. She lives on the Bridge. She is stepping off the Bridge, setting off westward through the smoking ruins. I will wait for her return.

'The dark comes on. She will return perhaps in the dark, fewer people on the Bridge.'

His wait was futile.

When Lucien returned the next morning in the role of an innocent customer, the father had to confess. "She has eluded me and may be anywhere on the Bridge or wandering among the ruins. . . . My wife is at her loom in the attic. Follow me quietly up the stairs, and I will show you her bed. We can only hope you will find her deep in sleep tonight."

Looking at the bed, Lucien imagined a sleeping virgin child and felt Lucifer-blessed at such an opportunity for damnation.

On Lucien's way out to search for sight of her, the Father showed him how to get into the shop noiselessly. He would leave the door unlocked, closed upon a red handkerchief, signal that he had seen her in bed and heard no sounds of her venturing into the night.

"Walk behind me as we go."

They had not left the Bridge on the London side when the father turned and pointed.

"There she goes!"

"You are pointing at two girls who look alike."

"The one who walks more assertively than the other."

"The one on the left."

"No."

"The one on the right."

'I shove off, he stays leaning against his shop.

'I follow them to fix upon her.

'Innocent virgin? I see little difference. Why that one and not that one? One will escape. The other one stops at the bridge foot, my virgin waves and goes on into Southwark out of sight.

'The hand of God at play again. Lucifer's choice. My life's mission is soon fulfilled.'

*   *   *

Counterpointing Gilda's compassionate seeing, contrasting Blythe's very selective seeing, Lucien's eyes, like mirrors, reflected every detail of swarming life on the Bridge. The Poet thought Lucien hated poetry, but as he walked, late at night and into the early dark hours, Lucien recited several of the Poet's poems, weaving into them his own phrases, thus to taint them.

'I move back and forth across the Bridge under the false colors of a chimney sweep, faring well by my false face. Wearing a false face, I will—or perhaps I won't—approach her on the Bridge, not in her bed-chamber, under false pretense. By telling her a falsehood, I will succeed in false imprisonment. "One false step," I will tell her, in a voice slightly falsetto, "and I will falsify your very existence."

'Falsity becomes me, I am proud to own. False-hearted, I place my hand over my false rib and swear not to reduce her to false work. In a few days, an alarm will go up—in no way false. I will never cry false arrest, because I will never get arrested.

'Will those rain-laden blossoms bending down the limbs of trees growing between the stones finally break the Bridge?

'*I* will. I have been "rain-laden"—in the crow's nest, on watch. I broke no Bridges at sea, mindful of my own skin. But tonight I, hired to save the Bridge by smothering the child, will break it, spirit by spirit! Whether I do as they hire me to do or lie that I did it but do it not, the command has already set teeth in the Bridge that will rot—gnaw it slowly and perhaps not these men but the others, children and descendants of these men will feel it give—well, yes, as I felt the ship give at sea—under foot.

'I come against the Bridge like a tempest, infect it like a plague, set it afire.

'I want to be the agent, but I know I am not, I know I am not sin. Sin is in the thought, not the deed. In the men who thought it, and in the spoken command, the offer of silver, bless Judas. Whether I do what I am hired to do and take the pay does not matter. The matter, like plague spores, is in the very air these men will breathe. My sin? Or yes—greed—no, not greed, but the compulsion to do and be evil, the thrill of snatching her, her body writhing, her heart suddenly beating against my monster chest, the thrill of knowing God's hatred for me is certain. No, not even that, but the—Oh, God, what of this deed *is* mine? It is theirs already, in thought. The deed eludes the doer.

'Why *is* love—or illusion of love—in this world? It is a fly in the ointment. Evil is the universe. Love is only an aberration. An irritant. It keeps evil from being complete. No, not evil. I am not *evil*, and the child Morgan, *good.* I am the true agent and they are the false agents of whatever force created us all, set the first stone in this Bridge over which we have moved all our lives toward each other. One misbehaving ember and the Bridge burns. The keystone dislodged, the arch falls. I am the Bridge—they are the ember, the unmoored stone. *I* will survive fire and rot. I *am* the Bridge. I will shout it from the Great Stone Gate among the impaled severed heads.'

In the first light, he climbed, stone by stone to the top of the Great Stone Gate, west side, and stood among the heads on pikes.

'I am the Bridge. Bridge dwellers will wake, the tower prisoners below will wake, hearing my voice upon the waters, declaring.'

From among the severed heads, he shouted his declaration: "I *am* the Bridge! Love will not tear *me* down!"

Windows all along the Bridge seemed to sprout heads that turned upward, left, right, downward, seeking the source of the clarion voice.

Before the Keeper of the Heads showed up on the roof among the pikes and heads, Lucien, master diver off seaside cliffs and master swimmer from ships to islands around the world, dove like a spear into River Thames, missing upward jagging rocks on either side of his plunge.

15

LUCIEN KIDNAPS BLYTHE, DARK LADY OF THE BRIDGE

Having let the night in which he was hired to take the child pass, imagining with delight the consciences of the father and his co-conspirators in the throes of anguish, Lucien waited for the most inspired moment.

'The face of every child into which I peer is as if a mirror showing her face.

'Here she comes. It is late. Pitch dark. Where have you been, innocent little girl? To church? All churches not ashes are far off beyond the Wall, west. Perhaps. But after that? To your grandmother's house in the suburbs and on the fringes or in one of the slapped up shacks among the ruins of the fire. Even so, alone, late?

'She goes in under the sign of the red gloves.

'I will return tomorrow and hope to find you dancing and singing with other girls because to pluck and snatch you where little girls are playing makes the shock greater.

'No, I am eager, I will follow you. I will pause and then follow you. Intrude like the plague, silently, like the live ember under the gray mantle of ashes, and take you out. Your father knows. Your mother knows? Who may hear and resist? Whoever does confront me will in an instant become nobody.

'All those years at sea and in seaports were but a rehearsal for this moment. I have never *taken* anyone before, never taken the *last* step into perdition. This is the single most hideous opportunity, the one for which there can be no redemption. Of all men, I despise the redeemed most of all, the so-called saints. I long for separation from God, the ultimate state of sinners.

'How easy to break into a shop, as I have been forced to do all over the navigable world, when in desperate need, and you walk up the stairs unaware of the breathing of a stranger behind you, not a squeaking stair, not a rusty door latch. I may as well be a ghost. And now I walk silently in *your* house, and which door, that door, yes, she is sleeping, I am drawn to the innocent, the good, the Christian saintly ones.

'Look at her face. I hope she is in fact an angel. One less to contend with.

'Her breath against the back of my hand, stirring the hairs. Her nostrils flare. Not natural. She *knows* me. She is pretending. She heard me coming. Her body is taut to spring against my force. Her heart, swollen, beats, wild against her ribs. Good. Good. I taste terror. Delicious if she would die now of fright. I will prolong her fear until I see her bosom heave, betraying her. She smells me.

'Smell me, child. Foul fish breath. Am I fish or fowl? Tobacco stale in my sea-tainted clothes. From my asshole, sulphur from hell. Her nose quivers. Open your eyes, see the knife, and if you scream before my hand clamps over your mouth that has never tasted a kiss, I will kill each and every one who comes to your rescue. Your pretense persists.

'My knife is at your ear. Do not scream. Open your eyes and look at me.

'She opens her eyes. Black mirror my face, my face mirrors all the faces I have broken.'

"Come slowly out of your bed, lass, and come with me."

'She comes, she does not shrink. To protect her mother and father. I hold out my hand. She takes it. Her hand is not cold in fear, it is warm. Down the narrow stairs we go. I reach back to keep hold of her hand. She is being very quiet, mimicking my movements. How obedient she must always be. As if I am her father. We pass a mirror and I, and she, in one motion, turn back to look at our faces in a wall mirror, startled, she, too, that our faces look somewhat alike. We rush on, down.

'Her white gown may stand out in the dark. I wrap her in my cloak.

"Think of my knife puncturing your eardrum."

'She nods. Why is she smiling?

'This wherry rocks too easily. Why does she look at me? I took her from her safe harbor bed. She seems to know what is happening, but she does not shiver. She does not seem to be imagining what is going to happen to her. Perhaps a child virgin of thirteen is this way. I do not get close to virgins of thirteen, until tonight. She does not know what I am paid to do, that she has less than an hour to live.

'I tie up at the chapel warehouse and pull her up onto the starling. We pass the pool in the starling where men were fishing yesterday. Is she stepping ahead of me, pulling at my hand?

'We enter the warehouse by the old fisherman's door, carrying her up the ladder into the room of the old chapel just below the decking.

'The lock on the door is still broken, not discovered. I bar the door from inside.

'Is that Peter de Colechurch's crypt?

'We are here. Where I want us to be.'

"Sit."

'She sits on a shorter stack of paper, among surrounding stacks that reach almost to the ceiling. She does not take her eyes off me. I will stare her down. I want to feel her shiver.'

"What do you think I am going to do to you?"

"Slit my throat?"

"No."

"Strangle me?"

"No. Guess until you get it."

"Do what men do to young girls?"

"Yes. First."

"And then?"

"Smother that fire in you."

"With a sheet of paper? It will combust."

"I have broken open a place for you inside one of the piers." 'Not the one her father chose.' "I will mew you up, and after three or four hours of sheer agony, you will suffocate. You will scream, but no one can hear you."

"Why?"

"Are you not afraid?"

"I'm no fool."

"Do you hope to fight me off?"

"We shall see."

"Oh. I see. You have a mind of your own."

"Oh, yes. Oh, yes, Mister . . ."

"Lucien."

"French?"

"An Englishman, with all the vices also of the French and the Dutch. . . . I feel a faint premonition I have been on the Bridge before."

"I go out, day and night, onto the Bridge and into London to seek what is interesting, but this is only the second time something interesting has come to my own bed."

"You do not show your terror."

"Terror is not all I feel."

"You are not what I expected."

"You *are* what *I* expected."

"Explain."

"I have dreamed that such as you would come to my bed."

"Afflicted with nightmares?"

"No, I mean dreamed with my eyes open, lying at night in my bed."

'Is she my his spiritual sister?'

"These words give me no satisfaction because they are on the lips of most people every day. Don't you regret that we have no profane words original to such as we?"

'"We" chills my spine, the keel of my existence.'

"Before I mew you up in the pier, I am going to violate you."

"Why do you tell me these things?

"I want you to suffer, not in body alone, more in mind than in body."

"Why?"

"You are in the presence of evil incarnate. If you know one who is more evil than I am, point him out to me and I will kill him so that I may be who I say I am, and kill you only *then*."

"I know no one who is that evil—until now. I have known many who do what the world calls evil, but on such a small scale, no one need fear them. Are you going to do all this to me out of pure evil?"

"Yes, but those who hired me paid me, not knowing that I would do this for nothing, that the doing is my pay. Violating and suffocating you, a child innocent of evil, is the fulfillment of my mission on earth."

"Surely there are worse things to do."

"What can be worse in Christ's eyes than to violate and murder a child?"

"To steal a gentleman's handkerchief, for which they hang a child."

"There is more evil to your death than what I have told you. Can you imagine who paid me and why?"

"My father."

"You do not think like a child."

"I am a woman trapped in a child's body, a woman unlike any other I have ever seen. One day I will escape."

"Why would your father pay me to murder you?

"Because he is afraid I will tell."

"Tell?"

"That he fucks me. First to come to my bed, you the second, others other places. You look surprised. Or shocked."

"I—I am not shocked, little girl. I am surprised that he would rape his own daughter. The domestic world is alien to me."

"Oh, he didn't rape me. He is terrified that, if I tell, the Brotherhood of the Bridge will *think* he raped me."

"Because—?"

"Because they would never believe that *I* enticed *him*. That is a look of shock on your face, not surprise. He doesn't realize that I tempted him."

"You are not—"

"No, I am not what you take me to be. There was once a bawd who lived nigh the Bridge who mocked me. She mocks me no more."

"You are not the virgin they paid me to sacrifice."

"Sacrifice? Sacrifice?"

"Now it is *you* who looks shocked."

"I am not shocked, I am outraged! I will not be a sacrifice! I will not be a scapegoat! I will not be used without my consent! I choose to do whatever I do. I am not a victim! That contradicts my very being. Sacrifice for what?"

"Their agent, your father, did not tell me, but I think I know. That song you children sing about London Bridge has come down to you from a time when men mewed up alive a thirteen-year-old virgin girl in the pier facing invaders and traitors or other threats to the common good—to appease the gods, make the Bridge safe. I think your father and other men fear a catastrophe so strong they do not trust their prayers alone. So they must have chosen you, thinking you to be not just a thirteen-year-old girl, but one who is pure and innocent.

"Do not laugh so loud. Someone in the goldsmith's shop next door may hear. Do you want to die laughing?"

"You have taken the wrong girl. You were meant to take Gilda, my friend."

"Your father said 'Blythe' and pointed you out. You were walking on the Bridge with another girl."

"Yes, and she is Gilda, the purest virgin in all the world, in mind and body. Seeing us together, could you, evil incarnate, not see that I am not as she is and never was and can and never want to be like her?"

"I sensed something was amiss."

"Very, very amiss, Lucien. I run with her, when I can persuade or entice her to run, because she is good and innocent and pure and clean speaking and clean thinking and loves her parents and keeps all the commandments, so that I can enjoy what I do by contrast to her. And deceiving her gives me almost as much pleasure as deceiving my parents and every other human being, and animal, who crosses my path, and my path, Lucien, goes, like a web, everywhere, in all directions, all day and all night long. I sleep little at night and nod now and then during the day, but I am too eager to do things, things some men call evil, that I never would think to call evil, because I don't know what evil is, I don't feel it, I don't think it, I may do it, but I don't set out to do what you might call evil."

"Everything I do is evil. I know evil. I can tell you what evil is."

"Why waste your breath, Lucien, when you could be doing everything possible under the sun? I went into the streets to bring the plague back to the Bridge in my tainted clothes so my family would have to move. I lured the fire onto the Bridge, but it stopped at this old chapel. I want to do everything possible under the sun—and moon. So please don't smother the fire in me. Fuck it, fuck me, oh, do, yes, fuck me, but don't cut short a life already more full of experiences than any seaman you ever saw, or were."

"You *want* me to violate you?"

"I can hear it in your voice, if I want to, you don't want to. Well, no, I don't want you to fuck me, *I* want to fuck *you,* you can't violate *me.* Can *I* violate *you?* Nobody ever fucked me before. It was I, always I who said, I want to fuck you, suck you, lick you, murder you, infect you, steal from you, lie to you, cheat you, curse you, set you afire, I am a witch, I am a killer, I am a rapist, I am a thief, and I want to watch the innocent become in a single act corrupt. Pure pleasure. No, I am not evil. I am good, I am good at everything I do. You, you, too, see me coming and think me innocent, good, and then I take you, you one way, him, her another way, by whim, and never, never, never, without pure pleasure. Evil sounds dull to me, even duller than good. Good I can violate. Evil just stands there on the Bridge acting a fool."

Lucien perceived that the rhythmic speed and pitch of her talking had reached orgasmic force.

"Those men, my father, their agent, they are evil and they are dull witted, without pure pleasure in what they do, what they do, they do only for money, I can get money from men, I can get money from women, or steal it. Do evil for money? I don't understand. I do what I do only for my own pure pleasure, sometimes with men, women, and children, male and female, who get pleasure with me. But part of my pleasure is to take more from them than they give willingly or unwillingly to me. No, not me, Lucien, it is she, Gilda, my best friend, they meant. Take her."

"And violate her?"

"Yes, yes, yes! We can do it together. There are things it would thrill me to do to her. I will point her out—do you remember what she looks like?"

"No."

"I will point her out and you take her and bring her down here and between us we can fuck her to very death. I have been saving her for another time, but now I am bored with her. I always wanted to lure her into something far more dangerous than I have ever done and—my favorite dream is ten seamen raping her, ripping her hymen, ramming her asshole, filling her mouth with cocks, the last so huge it chokes her. You see the difference between her kind and you and me?

"I took possession of four men once, behind Saint Paul's, lured them, almost against their will, or their better judgment, and took the hugest cock in my mouth with ease, while one of them sat beside her, kept her unaware and innocent on the cathedral steps. The little fool thought they were hurting me somehow, she heard my moans, behind the Cathedral. It would give me pleasure pure as rain from heaven to see her innocent face suddenly shocked into terror, to see her turn at the last moment to evil, embrace evil with you and me, because evil is twin to her goodness, she is not, she cannot be good without evil for contrast. Wouldn't you love that, you who are already the most evil man on earth—or so you tell me?"

"I see that I am no longer the most evil person on earth."

"But think of the ways we can pleasure ourselves with her and then after you have mewed her up as a sacrifice, a scapegoat, in the pier, you will be what you want to be."

"She's your friend!"

"Lucien, as evil incarnate, haven't you violated your own friend for the pure evil of it? Greater love of evil hath no man than to take the life of his friend. What makes her my friend is that when I compare what I do in my life with what she does in her life, my pleasure becomes greater, but now I am only bored by the comparison. Now you come into my life to take my life, but I will show you how we can do famous things together, starting with her."

"Alive, you will always be more evil than I am."

"I see tears in your eyes, Lucien. No, no, that is not so. I will not let you call me evil. You are evil because you think so and you want to be even more evil. I am not evil because evil is only a word to me, as empty as a condemned man's pocket. I will suck your cock now."

'She kneels at my feet, her hands lie lightly upon my hips, as one who loves truly.'

"No one has ever given you the pure pleasure my mouth will give your cock."

"No one has ever given it pleasure, little girl. Do you believe in God?"

"Certainly."

'Slitting her throat opens her mouth in pain, astonishment, and horror. She falls at my feet, a pile of bones and rags. I am stepping back from the flow of blood among the stacks of raw paper and old rags. I step in her blood, violate the sanctity of this place, and walk it about the warehouse, the undercroft of a fabric that was once a chapel erected to honor a saint.

'Lift her up.

'And there is the crypt of the master architect of the Bridge, the saintly Peter de Colechurch. Has she ever walked here among these nether pillars, passed and pondered that tomb? This is my first murder in a church, my first slaughter of an "innocent." Even so, this is not an act of evil. I do not know what it is. It is not an act of pleasure, pure or impure. What is it?

'I am rowing her out on River Thames, slipping a noose around her neck, pushing her over, tying the noose to the stern and dragging her and shooting the Bridge on the raging tide of her tears. No, no tears. Has she ever wept?

'I am mewing her up in the burned waterwheel pier, north end, east side, tying her, so water washes over her—Why did you do *that*, Lucien?—The water, I mean. To mock baptism, the death, cycling repeatedly, never the rebirth?'

16

MORGAN WOOD, A CHILD OF THE BRIDGE, RETURNS

Morgan wrote, "Rapidly approaching—the day of our arrival in the Pool. Will I walk home from Katherine's Dock or hire a waterman to take me to Old Swan Steps?"

On the verge of sleep, Morgan decided he would take his very first step on the Bridge from Saint Magnus Martyr Church at the North end, the sacred place from which he had set out to sea. From the Pool where *London Rocket* docked to discharge cargo, he imagined first going ashore west of the White Tower and enter Thames Street, pass by the Custom House, go on past Botolph Lane, Pudding Lane, then down New Fish Street to Saint Magnus Martyr. Every street was as real in memory and imagination as the deck of his ship.

Imagining walking on the Bridge, dodging death by horse or wheel, set his blood pounding. A stroll on Thames Street, he expected, would be something *between*. After seven years at sea, he was returning to walk again where memory had often taken him—upon London Bridge.

But finally, he decided, 'By water I left, by water I shall return to the Bridge.'

"Well, I have lived a cloistered life indeed on this ship. Farewell."

Having written, in Thomas Dekker's *The Seven Deadly Sins of London*, his final marginalia, Morgan intended his farewell gesture to his life at sea as an exile from the Bridge would be to throw, as ancient victorious warriors threw their spears into River Thames, his first spear, Sir Philip Sidney's *Arcadia*; his second spear, Plato's *Republic*; his third spear, Dante's *Divine Comedy*; his fourth spear, Chaucer's *Canterbury Tales*; his fifth spear, after some hesitation, William Tyndale's translation of the *New Testament*; his sixth spear, Shakespeare's *The Merchant of Venice*; his seventh spear, John of Salisbury's *Vita S. Thomae*; his eighth spear, Thomas Nashe's *The Unfortunate Traveler, or the Life of Jack Wilton*; and his last spear, his Thomas Dekker. *The Seven Deadly Sins of London* overboard, all his memories, his thoughts would be inscribed now only on the moving stream of his mind, the actual bridge underfoot day by day.

As Morgan slept, the pilot came aboard and brought the ship into the Pool. Morgan opened the porthole onto a view not of London but of Southwark where more autumn fire smoke than he remembered drifted over the rooftops. When he went on deck and turned smiling toward London bank, a frown of bewilderment began in a second, turned to a frown of shock the next: London was on fire, from the White Tower to Temple Bar. No flames. Only smoke and morning mist in tortured entanglement. Black structures, steeples, like broken spears stuck straight up. The remembered image of the Bridge whirled him around West. London Bridge stretched from bank to bank intact, except for a few blackened structures and the open space the fire of 1633 left at the North End. He stared, as late dawn defined all structures along the bank, and gradually up on Thames Street and around Saint Paul's and Ludgate Hill and Cripplegate. None on fire, many still smoking, few standing intact. Ashes. Black holes. Black spaces. A few houses and taverns and great Halls here and there starkly standing out for being whole amid the black ruins. Many brick chimneys. From where he stood, he could not see, but expected that he soon would, the tower of Saint Magnus Martyr.

He assumed, of course, that the waterman would put him ashore at the London end, but suddenly he cut toward the rapids, to shoot the Bridge!

"A rousing homecoming, my lad!"

Morgan suspected the waterman wanted to give him at the end of his travels an adventure far greater than any Morgan may have experienced at sea—a matter of personal pride in *his* own profession.

"I aim my craft as I aim my cock—straight between the piers. Shoot the Bridge, fuck the wife. My cock in my hand all day long—my steering shaft. I feel it like flesh and the water like fast fucking. It's all in fun. Get on your mark. Ready. Set. Go!"

'To a watery grave—after all those near fatal accidents and nautical misfortunes—virtually at my own hearth!'

The waterman moved Morgan closer to the seaman's entrance to Saint Thomas's Chapel turned warehouse on the starling.

From his window high above in Nonesuch House, the Poet, gazing northward, happened to see this stranger, this seaman, and watched him coming, disappear between piers.

The waterman and Morgan shot the rapids between the chapel and the square.

The waterman brought Morgan out on the West side still breathing and deposited him and his sea chest on Old Swan Steps. [Where the Poet's father, the old Chronicler, had slipped out of the plague, into River Thames.]

Morgan's memories, at sea—never in port, but sometimes on a bridge in a foreign city—were always visual, light falling in slanting shafts upon the congested roadway at a distance, oriented North usually. Listening to the organ and the singing of the race of River Thames between the piers, seemed to Morgan, who had sailed around the world, music rare on this earth.

Approaching the Bridge foot, he saw that a covered palisade had replaced the houses burned in 1633, that he had forgotten, where ten or so houses had been built, some of those still smoldering from this fire, houses he had not remembered. Dismayed that no scenes of his memories immediately greeted him, he stopped dead in his tracks. Something was amiss. He knew not what. Foreboding made his footsteps heavier and heavier and heavier.

After all the good-feeling memories that kept his spirits high at sea, after nearly a decade of yearning for home on the Bridge, he felt a powerful urge that moved him to go into the Bridge from Southwark, to see first the heads above the Great Stone Gate.

He hailed another waterman, who rowed him over to the South bank.

"Are you searching for *her*?"

"For whom?"

"For the little girl who disappeared from the Bridge?"

"I have just returned from a long voyage at sea." Seven years missing from the Bridge and come home to this news, a girl missing. "How long?"

"Three days. Little Blythe Archer." This was a greater blow than all the rest. "I can't bring myself to join the search, but somehow I have never felt so good as I have these past few days when not only everybody on the Bridge but many of my passengers out of London as well, seems to me, have thought, talked, and done nothing else. Not since plague and the fire have I witnessed such extreme concentration on a single crisis, the stark difference being that it is *one* person, not thousands, in peril. Some tell me in the crossing over of loss of family or homes or both and then they lament Blythe Archer and ask me do I have news to share. As if that single child is yourself, or could be, and so people seem to feel elated, exhilarated to be in search, buoyed up on compassion."

'Maybe Blythe will show up the very day *I* am showing up.'

And the Old Chronicler would have made an entry about the missing girl in that huge book. Morgan resolved to visit him soon.

As he watched people, round Southwark Church and Tooley Street, racing off in all directions, imaging all were searching for the missing girl whom he had remembered all his days at sea, he felt so sluggish he could scarcely move.

Standing at the Westside staple, he willfully conjured up and surrendered to the enchantment of the Bridge. As he passed Boar's Head's dead ashes and entered the Great Stone Gate, eager to look up and see the heads, he wondered whether the fact that Blythe was missing had made him stop dead in his tracks. Had they taken down the heads as finally too barbaric?

Feeling watched from behind and above, he turned on his heels and looked up and saw eighteen heads on pikes above, and felt as if his memories at sea had turned into a nightmare Bridge of the future, for as he remembered it, the heads had faced South toward Southwark, but turning from the heads, looking at the House of Many Windows across the little square northward toward London, he now remembered his father telling him that in the previous century the heads were mounted looking South on the Old Drawbridge Gate, torn down for the building of Nonesuch House, where the Old Chronicler lived.

He remembered his thrilling anticipation that morning seven years ago, to see perhaps a new head being placed—is it still up there, is that one it, or that one, maybe that one, no, maybe none, all new—whisked away by his father's hirelings, kicking and screaming, to the ship. He had remembered that scene over the years, almost as a single dark star in a bright sky of childhood, but now he knew that the head was to have been his bright morning star and that all else was dark.

Walking across the long defunct drawbridge, he felt Lucien's presence, and wondered why.

Standing in the morning shadow of the rag merchant's shop, he gazed across the Bridge road upon the façade of his father's stationery shop, which seemed somehow unlike his memories of it.

The opening door revealed the face not of his father or mother or a brother or a sister but of his Uncle Rafe, little more than a rank stranger.

"The stationer's business had failed, your father told me, but I have rescued it, my boy. Your parents left with your thirteen-year-old sister, Anne—suddenly. Your family lives on the border now, near Hadrian's Wall, but we are not to let that be known on the Bridge, why, he did not tell me. Come in, sailor, and stay with *me*—for a while."

'The day we moved into our home above our stationery shop on the northwest end of London Bridge near the clearing the fire of '33 made was the happiest day of our lives. We each of us said that. I recall the precise sensations of placing the ball of my foot on the second step, and climbing those narrow stairs made me feel I was rising much higher than I really was. I know because a few days later I felt the contrast—habit or hesitation had set in.

'I am climbing above the roadway of London Bridge into a high room like the ones I often admired and coveted from Old Swan Steps. Climbing stairs elsewhere even now that I am habituated never seems the same. I turn and gaze upon the lower steps in the lamplight and anticipate planting my foot on the next step *up.*'

* * *

Commanded by Clinkenbeard, the Brotherhood of the Bridge, eager to see an increase of Christian behavior, a decline in the kind of conduct that provoked God's Thunder over the City, began to monitor the inhabitants of the Bridge, men, women, and children, to point index fingers, to whisper admonitions, to shout accusations, to write anonymous letters of reproach, to sow seeds of suspicion, as Venetians spoke into La Bocca di Leone (Mouth of the Lion, accusing people of treason), with the effect of stiffening necks, lowering eyes, softening voices, making gestures tentative.

When Glover Lennox Archer, having paid Lucien half his fee, sent up the alarm that his daughter Blythe had been abducted, Goldsmith Arthur Clinkenbeard called the cabal of five together.

Mister South was simply curious. "What if she was tainted with plague when he mewed her up?"

Mister Brooke felt safe. "Wise decision to mew her up in Rock Lock, at the Great Stone Gate, below where heads hang, double deterrent, primitive and modern. Rock is easily broken into."

As the other fathers remaining of the cabal of five talked, Mister South thought. 'What if a vessel strikes the pier and stones pile up and water rushes with greater force, undermining the pier, and one morning a boatman sees her standing there, the early morning sun upon her face?'

Dark possibilities haunted Mister Archer. "We feared so many things could afflict, assault, the Bridge. But perhaps many things could destroy our solution. Imagine."

Clinkenbeard rather weakly asserted leadership confidence. "God's hand at work is not seen. Our hand at work is not seen. God's *working* is unseen; we behold the work. And so our neighbors will behold our good work."

Mister Brooke had faint fears. "My, *our,* thinking process is mysterious. That those merchants left out of our secret have not participated will cause demoralization."

Mister Archer wanted to give the others the impression that he was not at peace for the first time in some time. "From the moment he told me, 'She's in,' I have never had a moment's peace."

Mister South expressed intimations he had sensed in the speech of the others. "The most haunting sound is footsteps late at night or very early in the morning heard through a fourth story open window.

Wondering, who's *that*? Who *was* that? Waiting, half awake, for familiar footsteps below on the roadway, to come under the window. They come. They go. The peculiar silence after, very unlike the silence that prevails throughout the night. The silence just before and just after a disturbance of the silence. The silence is mother to the sound of footsteps. Strange, slow footsteps, hesitant, suddenly fast. You are safe above, but who or what *may* be unsafe below?"

Mister Archer gave no thought to what he said next. "Screams in the night. Weeping."

Mister Brooke's choice of words was deliberate, for effect. "Farting, great roaring farting."

Mister South conveyed compassion for the father. "Disappearances are hard to take. Even of enemies. Though, of course, of loved ones."

Mister Clinkenbeard suppressed an inclination to tremble. "Our hireling is now our enemy. Find him. Mister Archer, send your shadow to find him. Then we must deal with the young Chronicler's likely suspicions."

*　　*　　*

Openly, Clinkenbeard called together at the Bridge house all the merchants to organize a thorough search throughout London, declaring the Bridge already had been searched.

Secretly, Clinkenbeard called the cabal together to organize a search for the abductor. "We see no sign he has broken into the Bridge. He has wronged us severely. We must find him and demand to know where he has put her."

*　　*　　*

Lucien was suddenly in Mister Archer's glove shop. "Father, I have come for my other glove."

"My wife is nearby. I will meet you on Saint Botolph's wharf tonight at nine."

Prepared, from the shadows of stacks of wool set for export, Lucien kept watch on his double, whom he hired to dress in his clothes, a near perfect physical choice.

Once Archer's agent had slit Lucien's double's throat, Lucien flashed out of the shadows and slit the glover's throat, sorry to discover by the light of the moon a face not remotely like Blythe's father—*Archer's* own double.

*   *   *

Unable to find Saint Thomas Chapel, Morgan felt severely disoriented. "Where's Saint Thomas Chapel?"

He asked many people crossing, until one told him. "The Chapel was deconsecrated, desecrated in the dissolution by Henry VIII—and everything else to do with Archbishop Thomas à Becket. Where have you been these one hundred and twenty some years past? It's there, right behind you, degraded to a rag and paper warehouse next to the goldsmith shop."

Morgan realized that for a decade he had remembered as real what his father had only described to him as history.

Morgan noticed the contrast between the demeanor of those living and working on the Bridge and those crossing the Bridge from London to Southwark, Southwark to London. "Even in plague and fire," a merchant not of the cabal told him, "we are more at ease with ourselves, except, naturally, for the disappearance of Blythe Archer."

"Was any sign of blood found?"

"Blood on the Bridge has always been a daily sight—causes varying. Accidents. Fights. Wounds? Let by night. Let by day. She left none. Or we found none the day she disappeared, no trace. If only she had somehow left some trace, we would feel closer to discovery. No clues. That spot there, she sang and danced there that very day—a void by twilight time."

'The world is a strange place when you're in it—how strange when someone you look for *isn't*. Some sense of death.'

Morgan saw Blythe step into the doorway of a shop, and stand still for a moment. "There she is!"

"No, no. That's the Shadwell child, Gilda, I think they call her. Blythe's bosom friend. Her father's recently disappeared."

Morgan waited for her to walk by him, stopped her. "Are you look-ing for Blythe?"

"Yes, I have searched all over London. It is a foul and evil place, I have learned in my wandering. Forbidden to go into the City, I have not known it. If I go to hell for disobeying my father, it will look like London. I do not speak of the smoldering ravages of fire, the broken mucky ground of plague burials."

"I've been at sea for seven years, and every day it was her face on this Bridge I longed to return to. And now I seek her face among the missing."

"Did you know her when she was a very little girl, then?"

"I never knew her, I simply watched her sing and dance, and the memory was very much alive all those years."

"I came to the Bridge only a few years ago, and we sang and danced together."

"Did she ever speak of me? My name is Morgan."

"No."

"I promise to keep looking for her."

"My name is Gilda. I am glad you will keep looking. Some are giv-ing up the search. I have disobeyed my father and gone off on my own solitary search among the smoldering ruins of this burned down city. During the plague, she was drawn to the spectacle, and during the fire, she rushed in, as if to feed the flames with herself. Horrors I have seen, looking for her, shall make me restless in heaven."

"I have forgotten where she lived. I wish to talk with her mother."

"There, behind you."

Morgan talked to Blythe's mother.

"She was not in her bedchamber, so I went out upon the roadway looking for her. Hoping to hear her singing before I saw her. I did hear singing, but she was not among the dancing children.

"Listen, the bear-baiting has begun! The screams of the ferocious and wounded bears biting bears affrighted my other children but not her. She is not like the other children. Perhaps that will help her survive.

"Find her, boy, before she takes her last breath. Save her life and her father's, for if you fail, Mister Archer will drown his broken heart in River Thames, myself not far behind."

Walking among the smoldering ruins, Morgan interrogated everyone who would give up time to him.

Sifting among the ashes where his house once stood, a man stopped just long enough to bemuse himself, overheard by Morgan. "We are remarkable creatures, are we not? To go through plague and thousands die, lying in the streets, heaped into open graves, and soon, after three days of fire, and now we lie awake three nights worrying about the fate of a single child, and rushing out sleepless, into the streets of London searching for her as if the fate of all London depended upon finding her safe and sound. Are we not remarkable creatures, we humans?"

*   *   *

The Clock Maker
The ghostly, ghastly, work-a-day
million-footed beast slouched,
in leaden day-time and sodden night-time, across
this Bridge, over and over, again
and again and again, century upon century.
I cannot keep time, on the Bridge, clock maker,
time repairman, here, at the end of a long,
long line of training, generations.
The feet keep time, the same soles,
flesh and leather, under Romans,
under Angivins, Tudors, Stuarts, Hapsburgs.
River traffic up to the Pool, over Thames Street
and then over the Bridge to Southwark.
Time in the trudging tread of tireless, tormented feet.
Wheels of the King turn on the axle of the poor,
the grease of the dead. We do not *keep* time,
not with one machine or the thousands
this shop has heard. Crushed together
in one thunder clapped second—the sound
would not be *time,* but *loss,* what's lost.

Pulse in the wrist that writes is time
trying to record, stay, or keep Time.

This newly discovered first draft of a poem by clock maker–clock repairer Coyle Stamper, Daryl Braintree never saw.

*   *   *

Climbing up on one of the highest perches on the Bridge, the Great Stone Gate, Morgan felt as if he were climbing into a ship's Crow's Nest, the sky red from still spiraling smoke across the horizon. He screamed to wake the Bridge to hunt for her.

A man came to a window on the top floor of Nonesuch House across the square at the drawbridge, in severe disrepair, not raised in centuries, and looked down at Morgan, who wondered if he were the Old Chronicler's son, the dissolute poet.

A lace shopkeeper would not stop shaking Morgan's hand. "Oh, she'll turn up, lad. Never fear. They go astray, some kind person discovers them lost, takes them by the hand, and you'll look up—just you wait and see—and she'll be skipping on the Bridge ahead of her earthly angel Gilda toward her good, worrying family, singing. Never fear."

"She is not really my sister. Not yet. She was to *become* really my sister, I mean I wanted to become a sort of big brother to her on my return as we walked the Bridge together. I imagined every step the ocean aroused under my feet. She would tell me everything. Who lives *here*. Who once lived over *there* in that house but died or moved away. The strange events of her short life. I have listened to her for seven years. It would have been all very familiar."

A bridge guard by the staples at Southwark looped his arm around Morgan. "I have decided to keep a diary, suspect the hunt for the missing girl will go on a long time, and at the end I will make this a story deserving of some sort of record to hand on. Would you not agree?"

Morgan followed searches that went on through that night, throughout both London and Southwark sides of the Thames. The searchers used the Bridge roadway to go from bank to bank, town to town, none imagining, naturally, that the Bridge itself might imprison the child.

Alfred Goodyer took hold of both Morgan's forearms and looked him piercingly in the eyes. "When I first heard about the missing girl, I thought, as others around me everywhere I went did, that she was a London girl. A Bridge dweller did not seem likely, so I looked across the water to London bankside—over there awful things happen. Suddenly missing was the Bridge itself, with a new girl living on it, my neighbor."

"She is on the Bridge." Morgan was certain of his intuition. "She is alive and breathing."

Mister Goodyer released his hold on Morgan's arms, averted his eyes. "How can you know, you a stranger?"

'Bridge deck and ship deck, I have moved about upon water all my life.'

A Southwark merchant felt drawn to the strange young man passing and repassing his needle shop. "I have known many disappearances in my many years on this Bridge and witnessed one with my own eyes. A needle maker, like myself a long time resident. Last I saw of him he was crossing from London to Southwark. Nobody over there saw him come off, or go out into the town. Never seen again."

"All London is but a suburb of this Bridge, and Southwark is merely a way station."

"So be it."

Evening fallen, the soles of his shoes feeling lead-soled, Morgan stepped onto the Bridge, swaying as if he were at sea, so weary, bone weary he was, from searching the streets of London for signs, the Liberties and the Minories, and Within the Walls. He had met many who were searching as *he* was, but saw no signs, nor did they report any. The empty look of the Bridge roadway was the empty look of a road empty of Blythe. And yet, from meeting and speaking to so many people, whose eyes expressed a desire to find her, to look upon her safe and sound, some for the first time, he was full of a vibrant sense of her.

Morgan eavesdropped on two men talking on the Bridge, one saying, "Sadness on any bridge is deeper than the water running under it. Sadness weighs any bridge down. When word went forth that she was missing, we Bridge dwellers were *all* sad for days on end. We shuffle from end to end, searching, despondent. London Bridge feels the weight."

A basket maker was eager to talk to this young stranger. "And it occurred to someone to search the Bridge itself. Magistrates know so well what the everyday person never could know—that often the criminal leads the chase. The inclination, sometimes compulsion, is native to the criminal mind. The question arises then, Who first suggested that she might be on the Bridge?"

Morgan hoped it was not himself.

"We merchants must inquire—discreetly. We must know who this person is and clap him in the clink."

Another merchant happened by as Morgan and the basket maker were talking. "Looking everywhere for a child victim can stand you up in some strange places, under, above, beside the most familiar places of your life. I had never been under the old chapel, nor in the home of a bookbinder, in that particular shop, in the Nonesuch Tower. So that as we searched for our neighbor child, our Christian sister, snatched by Satan's emissaries, I have become much more familiar with the Bridge itself."

Morgan decided to ask whether he could go to work temporarily for his uncle the stationer, uncertain whether he would live on the Bridge or sign articles on a ship again. He wanted a steady home. The Bridge was like a ship—actual ships were close by in the Pool and below the Bridge, many others downstream unable to enter the Pool—so that he stood with a foot in both worlds. He enjoyed the cart food and two taverns, the Bear at the Bridge Foot and the Three Neats' Tongues at the northern end, which were only singed badly in upper Tooley Street, Southwark.

Morgan got to know all the trades people, merchants on the Bridge as he did business with them, but mainly as he asked them whether they knew his parents and what they imagined might have happened to them, trusting his uncle well enough, but desperate to know, to dispel the mystery entirely. He began to pick up hints something was wrong. A few were suspicious of his questions, the new merchants who only vaguely knew of his parents. Searching for Blythe in the flesh, he sought the facts concerning his missing parents and sisters.

*　*　*

Morgan wanted desperately now to seek out the Old Chronicler, as if in need of a father, his uncle, preoccupied, distant. He stood in front of Nonesuch House preparing his mind.

Morgan met the Poet staggering in the roadway just as he was about to cross the threshold to enter Nonesuch House.

"I am Morgan Wood. Your father is expecting me—from seven years ago."

"Yes. Yes, indeed. Welcome. Follow me up."

Morgan wondered why the Poet was so delighted to see him.

Full of a conviction of the Old Chronicler's knowing everything, not just the history of the Bridge, Morgan climbed the stairs to the top floor of Nonesuch House.

"Up these narrow stairs, five flights, and here you are on top of the world. From here, you look out and feel what 'the four points of the compass' means. My roof is the highest, so you're able to look out and down on the rooftops of the Bridge dwellings. I sometimes forget, for a moment only, of course, the Bridge itself. It's as if I am still living in London in my garret, from which I could look out and all around, too, even see from the city parts of these houses, but no part of the Bridge itself in view, except the drawbridge."

"So you can be high over the Bridge and not *see* it all or think, 'I'm on the Bridge.'"

"But to feel you are on the Bridge, do you need to *see* it? Daily knowing you live on the Bridge is more than enough."

"Is your father at home?"

"My father is missing. The Chronicle is missing, but I have reconstructed it—in a way— mingling fact and fancy, as poets will, I suppose, but clearly I am unfit, though faithful in my fashion.

"Looking at you now, I see before me the true successor, found at last. My missing father found in you, I may now turn to my epic poem about the Bridge, Peter de Colechurch my ghostly muse. And you are now in my scriptorium."

Daryl read to Morgan the rough draft of Canto 52 of his Spenserian epic of London Bridge in progress.

As Birds

We—rather, I, and, consequently you—can move at will,
not only over the Bridge and in and out of the shops
and domiciles, but above and below and out a ways,
East and West of the Bridge, as a bird,
a moth, a waterman, anyone brave enough
to shoot the Bridge between two piers,
but also we may hover—as if a humming bird,
just outside this window, then that window,
and look in, lingeringly—vantage points, perspectives
impossible even to conceive centuries before new
inventions that displace us in order to *re*place us.
So that I may imagine for myself, and so for us, above the water
peering into each and every window, thousands.
Holbein caught only one view
from inside looking out—at a house leaning
like the tower of Pisa over the water, Westside.
A unique, unsettling, but welcome view.
Who would have been moved to imagine other views
from the outside of windows, each a little proscenium
through which to glimpse dramas, comedies, farces,
melodramas, one tragedy every half century in that hot bed
of lower upper class life perhaps? The image of life
as a play, of people as actors is prevalent in our literature,
mostly from, say, 1550 to now. Shakespeare's plays
West in Southwark behind the bear baiting amphitheatre
going on, speaking sometimes of the Bridge,
perhaps actor's voices muffled, carried over the water,
mingled with vicious cries of fighting bears, coming
through the open windows of rooms where men and women
toss, each alone, or together on humid summer nights, conceiving.

The Bridge is an image so charged,
it illumines all human experience.

'This poet and this young man can move only as far as the rush moves the pier under me each hour or so.'

The Poet suddenly became conscious of the fact that he was speaking to the boy his father chose seven years ago over himself. 'I must enlist this young man home from the sea to aid me.'

"The old man at the window—I could see him only when I stood on Botolph's Wharf and looked back Westward upon the Bridge. I used to wonder, Is it to me he motions so frantically or is his frantic gesture perpetual, as a sign of witlessness?

"I have returned with every intention of accepting the task from your father, but accepting it from his son at a time when the event to be recorded this very day is the search for the missing girl makes my mind list precariously."

"I almost hung my head and cried, but when I learned that the girl was Blythe Archer, I thought better of it."

"Why do you speak so?"

"If Blythe Archer is found alive, you will know from her own mouth. But you must have other questions about other things, having been so long at sea."

"Where are the dogs and cats? Well, more than that, much more, but that struck me."

"In the plague, thousands were executed as suspected proliferators of the disease. Came a day when none were seen in the streets. All the dead dogs and cats and their executioners and those who carted them away were soon branded with the red rose themselves and carted to the churchyard pits. The fire found only some few, evasive ones."

"The few cats I've seen do seem oddly pampered."

"Yes, they're coming back. And so are the rats. In ships such as yours, no offense, lad."

"I remember everything, the cats and dogs, but I misremembered as real what is now no more, Saint Thomas Chapel."

"Well, as facts would have it—though not one's imagination, perhaps—Peter de Colechurch, the master-builder, is still buried there, warehoused, so to speak, with old rags and new paper. Perhaps his spirit set you sailing back in time, as it did mine, God knows."

"I try to see that master architect as he might have looked, but have no picture whatsoever."

The Chronicler in the Poet was delighted to teach. "I see Peter de Colechurch like Atlas holding the Bridge's key arch, the Chapel Lock, up on his shoulders, but for him, Saint Christopher is perhaps the better figure, Peter lifting each of us, daily, up and carrying us over the Bridge on his back.

"I feel that the Bridge lives continuous from epoch to epoch in the minds of its dwellers. When someone on the Bridge dies, I always feel as if some part of the Bridge itself dies, with one less mind to see it, touch, hear, taste it, it is less alive, less complete.

"And then, even now I hear my father calling out to me sometimes from a room nearby, 'Father, come put me on the potty,' and I showed myself in the door frame to bring him back to the present day and he said again, looking me in the eye, 'Father, put me on the potty,' and when I, hesitating, repeated it, who had done that often in recent weeks, I felt the Bridge give way ever so faintly under my feet and steadied myself in the door jamb, and shut my eyes, and, feeling strange to be called father by my own father, said, 'All right, son.'"

Seeing Morgan Wood again, now as a young man, descending the stairs, made Daryl feel old.

September 16, 1666. Seven years at sea, Morgan Wood returned to London Bridge.

Ignorant of the history of his own house, except in fragments that once held no appeal, the Poet-Chronicler fit together, as he researched the history of the Bridge itself, the story of Nonesuch House, learning that it was constructed in Holland, taken apart, shipped to London in 1578, and reassembled, replacing Drawbridge Gate also called New Stone Gate, begun in 1426. Display of the severed heads was moved from the Drawbridge Gate to the Great Stone Gate, the faces facing not Southwark as before, but London. Why? The Poet wondered. Opposite the Great Stone Gate, across a square, stood Gateway House or the House of Many Windows, reflecting, when the light was right, the spiked heads.

* * *

When Morgan came into the cupola scriptorium the next morning, the Poet was yawning. "As I was yawning just as you entered, the bones in my jaw crackling, the air rushing out of my mouth, my ears popping, I felt what the Bridge must feel sometimes as it braces against some assault—and relaxes after. The Bridge is like the human body lying down, stretching, shoulders squinting, ankles twisting, chest heaving. We lie in space as the Bridge does, content in blissful sleep, or tense in nightmare, the Bridge too, surely. Don't you imagine that's so?"

"I can remember more clearly than I can imagine."

"There, my boy, there it is, the very first record." Lying, the Chronicler passed his reconstructed Chronicle off as the original that his father had promised to pass on to Morgan. "First record that there ever was a London Bridge—all the centuries, the tides that marked the days on the hoary piers are for *me* to imagine, I may *do* that at my leisure and in my own way, and so, my boy, may you—I see in your eyes that it begins. . . ."

Morgan recalled reading that nothing is in the mind that did not begin in the body. "Nothing that passes before the mirror of the mind may be, without peril, cast aside. What the mind, like a mirror, reflects exists in the flesh. Imagine the thing itself, and then search for it until you can hold it in your hand, if you dare."

"The temperament of Bridge-dwelling affects one's view of mankind, the universe."

'Is he listening to me?' Morgan spoke what had been on his mind. "There is, I have read, nothing in the mind that did not start in the body."

"The night of the fire of 1633 more died by drowning, driven by fear of the fire, by panic into River Thames, than by fire. To go onto the Bridge to watch fire, then to die by fire for watching fire? The death of spectators! Imagine this, sailor, as you search for *one* lost soul, how your search fits into a much vaster, older picture. I am spectator to *all* events, minor and colossal, on the Bridge, each event, like yours, seeming to the actors the sole reason for the universe's existence. We see no further than our toenails. We never see our own faces unless we deliberately seek and find a mirror. Never see the soles of our feet when we're walking nor the backs of our necks as we fade from view. Nor our assholes. We need help. A mirror provides such help. So do I, the Chronicler, if you crave a view larger than your own interests at the moment. And now your face is a mirror in which I gaze upon myself."

"Strange to remember and imagine a childhood elsewhere, then start an adult life of work on the Bridge."

"Yes. I, too, feel I am not of the same breed. Even so, I like Bridge folks and others like them well enough. And you."

"And I *you*. But I feel that my own long voyage makes me different from both my parents and from you—now that I have your extraordinary answer to my ordinary question, which has slipped my mind."

"I feel the double difference myself, and look upon you as another breed. Almost another species."

"But we have this in common—on the Bridge and at sea, one breathes pure air laden with salt water."

"As those Within the Gates do not."

"Let's drink to Bridge *air*."

"The millions of aliens over the Bridge's history take away its image in the brain, scattering, sending this pen flying, broadcasting.

"You are in the very midst, but what you see up ahead looks remote, another world, not even one you are moving into, a world forever up ahead. And there, among bobbing heads, I see *his*."

"Your father's. Yes, as I have seen mine. He, too, is missing, in a way I have not yet discovered."

"Meditation walks on the Bridge are negotiations in language, each word is its own peculiar step, sentence gait, paragraphical epiphany— sprint across. See here what over the years I have by nightly compulsion writ—the whole story of the Bridge from the laying of the first stone. I am the latest, quite likely last, of a secret Brethren." He scrutinized this Morgan Wood significantly. "I take down everything I see and hear. I naturally seek out, dig for, anything that pertains to the history of the Bridge, eyewitnesses and I-witlesses, even hearsay, not despising dreams, partial to nightmares. I sometimes, in my nocturnal rambles, hear children put out on the Strand, shoved off as mud-larks, stranded in nightmares. Watermen, pulled up at the steps along the bank, murmuring."

'The Poet has it all writ down. Amazingly. During my decade at sea, scrubbing down the deck, painting the ship, freezing on watches, *he* was collecting and recording fine details about the Bridge. Wonderful. This Poet has never been confined to *this* Bridge, life-span, rather he has lived in all the Bridge's avatars. Something holy in that.'

"I am chosen to chronicle, an unbroken secret society of scriveners, in my scriptorium."

'The son is telling me what his father told me a decade ago.'

Morgan wished he could let the Poet read his marginalia, but they lay among the ancient spears upon the bed of River Thames.

"All the other chronicle books are hidden somewhere on the Bridge. I don't look for those—all are hidden to be found, I am convinced, as mine will be. So the one that is missing torments me. Will you help? So many rooms in this house, east and west, and under the Bridge."

"Yes. Will *you* help *me* find *her*?"

"Disappearances. In those five hundred years, the Bridge was the scene of all kinds of disappearances, enough to populate a small village. In fire and tempest and frost and war and stampede, of course, but also solitary mishaps, un-witnessed, and suicides by Bridge jumpers—and watermen never found. Your look is of a boy who craves sleep."

"Sleeping on the Bridge again, I feel as though I am still at sea, though the water here makes constant commotion, of a kind never heard and felt at sea."

Morgan wished the Poet good sleep. As Morgan descended the five flights of stairs to the roadway, the Poet wrote:

"Sleep as a flow of negative energy, sleepy heads, producing great psychic storms on the Bridge in times of calamity crises, chaos. Or sleep as a fluid pervading the body, activating imagination and memory. Or one. *Which* one? Imagination involuntary? Or only willed? Or awake, does imagination work by *allowing* it to? And asleep, is totally free. Mixing with memory? Is memory mainly an act or involuntary? They do not remember asleep, do they? Plague. The earlier fire that *started* on the Bridge, 1633.

"Dreams seem neither, or a very dynamic co-operation of imagination and memory which create something else? Dream. Or a better,
more descriptive word is needed.

"One night—linked to some dramatic or melodramatic incident—
we enter their collective dreams. Hints of past history and presages of
the future emerge."

*   *   *

Walking North on the Bridge, looking left and right, hoping for a
glimpse of Blythe, to his uncle's shop and house above, Morgan medi-
tates: The sadness, melancholy of being confined to the Bridge after a
decade of freedom of movement at sea. But confined to the ship, the
deck, as on the Bridge. At sea, moving on water, here, water moving
under me. The perversity of the human spirit—change itself the in-
stigation, I suppose. After delight in returning, curiosity in learning
about the Bridge's changes—north end rebuilt, now burned away again,
the waterwheels drenched in fire—and this terrible change—Blythe
missing—and the sense of change as confinement, the sadness. End
of an era. I do not have to stay here. I could live Within the Gates, or
Without the Gates, somewhere in the Liberties. The Minories. But that,
too, would be changed after the newness wore thin. Why not change?
Life at sea? No, no, a thousand times, no. Nor even an entire life on
the Bridge. A time here, and then perhaps America. Funds my uncle
may provide. In 1492 this Bridge was—what? I must inquire of the
Chronicler.

*   *   *

"1491 nothing happened."
"And then what?"
"The Bridge seemed unmindful of the discovery of America. And
then what? My father always used to prod me. 'And *then* what?'
"'Nothing. I've told it.'
"'Nothing? Is that *all*?'

"'Yes, sir.'

"'Get out of my sight and don't come back until you can *tell* me *then what?*' He was a great wag. But it always left me walking on the Bridge uneasy. *What?* Something. Inevitably. But what?

"After plague and fire, the child abducted."

17

MORGAN AND LUCIEN ON THE BRIDGE

Glimpsing the Sinful Sailor on the Bridge, dressed in the weird costume of a violent tribe they had encountered in their travels, shocked
Morgan as if he had looked up from his own bed in his father's strange
house and seen him standing at the foot.

Chasing after him ended in arm-flailing disappointment. Perhaps
the man was not the Sinful Sailor, Lucien.

Morgan sought out Mister Clinkenbeard, the man to whom his
father owed the debt he devoted his childhood to paying in full, unaware of his role as leader of the Brotherhood of the Bridge which had
become the cabal.

"I saw you off as a lad who would return in a year, but your father
darkened my doorway time and time again in need. I sent orders then
to keep you on board and go on to another port with another cargo and
yet another, as your eyes tell me you know all too well."

"What my eyes have seen, good sir, is not what a gentleman such as
yourself should suffer seeing."

Morgan decided to tell him about the coming of Lucien onto
Mister Clinkenbeard's ship and the general thrust of what followed, but
in brief.

"The Sinful Sailor, as I have reason to call him, is somewhere in London. I caught only a glimpse of him on the Bridge. He will come looking for me. I *know* he will. He ridiculed my love of the Bridge. He said, many times, 'One night, I will grab you out of your bunk and toss you over the side, and when I return to London, I will burn the Bridge.' He tormented me to death. I believed him then and I believe him now. But I could tell no one what I am telling *you* now. They would all have laughed at me. I am not yet old enough to forget how long they laughed at me when I was a child on your ship."

"Yes, I *know* them."

"So, I was watchful. I have glimpsed him a time or two. Or thought I did. Now—he wants to inflict more than pure malicious torment. He wants revenge for what I did to him."

"What, may I presume to inquire of you, did you do to him?"

"Caused him to get put ashore. From rail to dock, we looked each other in the eye, so he knows, he knows. And I had told him often that I love this Bridge and how much and in what numerous ways."

"You pose a danger—to him." 'And to the cabal.' "Oh, certainly, you do, my young friend."

'We are forced by this circumstance to resolve to have this fine young man killed.' Clinkenbeard sighed. 'Whoever knows, outside the cabal, must not live. For the sake of what we have committed for the Bridge.'

*   *   *

High, on the third floor of his father's house that the expenditure of his youth at sea helped purchase, above the roar of the tides rushing through the piers, the roadway silent, except for a late coach crossing into London, Morgan did not feel he slept on the Bridge quite, more that he was in his old home, snug up under the roof, closer to moon and stars, window-framed, than to piers, mill wheels, waterwheels, drawbridge, but it was the Bridge that kept him turning in his bed, his awareness of its demands in broad daylight, inescapable, never beyond the reach of dreams, nightmares.

He flung back the covers, arose, and descended, past the doors to his uncle and his aunt's, their son's and their daughter's rooms, down the narrow stairs, to the stationer's shop, the still heart of the building. Now he felt the vibrations of the water against the piers and heard the traffic as if about to rush out, North and South, upon the Bridge, the people emerge, the voices mingling with water and wheels and gulls. He held his breath. Exhaled. He felt drawn out into the roadway. He stood just onto the roadway, listening, stepped into the middle of the it, stood stock still, expectant, as on watch at sea, for signs of peril, icebergs, tempest, derelict ships or crafts adrift, all hands dead on deck and below, the Bridge's near five hundred years beneath his feet, made so by the old man's memory by way of his son the poet, his words.

*   *   *

The Anglican Priest burned out of Saint Mary de Colechurch, awaiting assignment to another church, walked down Fish Street toward the Bridge, praying, "Holy Ghost, I have rattling around in my noggin over forty years of confessions. When I consider that other priests have heard altogether a million or more since Peter de Colechurch heard the first one on the Bridge—not Romish confessions, just the urge to confess, spilling into the proffered ear—I am even more oppressed, my daily progress toward the grave—let it be River Thames, I beg you—is sluggish, sluggish, oh, it is sluggish. And now it comes to me that not only men of the church are burdened with the sins of Bridge dwellers, Bridge dwellers themselves bear witness to the sins others tell them, over their lifetimes, too. The mouths. Oh, the way mouths that confess, breath the odor of tarnished silver, are different mouths from kissing or cursing mouths! Confessions are the sad burden of the Bridge itself. How easy to pity *me,* when a child of God is missing, and how does man, how dare man pity a bridge? And so, Peter de Colechurch's Bridge must bear its traffic of confessions without pity—or compassion."

*   *   *

1666. Shoemaker Clarke Shadwell disappeared from the Bridge. Date unknown. Robert Hubert of Rouen, Normandy, hanged, his head impaled among the others above the Great Gate.

*   *   *

Fishmonger Brooke agreed with goldsmith Clinkenbeard. "Can we not so affect the thinking of our Bridge dwellers and beyond throughout London that this newcomer, Morgan Wood—who *is* a newcomer of sorts—is the abductor, much as one person began what thousands have taken up as the truth in the case of Hubert the incendiary?"

Mister South. "We could—and we shall, shall we not, gentlemen?"

Mister Brooke. "Let us resolve—though perhaps for the nonce not as gentlemen—to broadcast this newly minted fact."

Mister Upshaw. "Hear, hear."

Mister Archer. "We are then as bonded men of one mind?"

Unanimity usurped the room, the cabal vacated the room, resolved, ill at ease with life as they had known it.

To no purpose, however, given that the rumor failed to take root in the minds of Bridge dwellers, fertile though they were, and among Londoners proper, as smoke, ashes, and loss of a child took precedent over vengeance. Morgan was taken, questioned, and released, to the ways of the world a wiser young man.

*   *   *

"You see now," Lucien called to Morgan from a safe distance, "what ill they intend to do you?"

"I see what you say you see, but no assassin, and for what cause?"

"I see even more clearly, having my own ill-intended shadow." He pointed at a man very badly pretending not to stalk him.

"They suspect you, too?"

"Oh, yes. Their weapon is not mere rumor, but my own weapon shall prevail, as I am sure you can believe."

Morgan believed.

"Look you to your own." Lucien pointed to a point behind Morgan.

Morgan turned and saw a short, wild boar of a man turn to pick up a book in a bookshop window open to the roadway, as if he could read it.

"They have now turned to the dirk." Lucien made a dash at his own stalker among the ruins.

Playing Lucien's game to see toward what end it might tend, Morgan had turned to point at the wild boar, nose in book, before he realized he was taking Lucien's lead. No, no, it is Lucien's own malicious spirit that brands that mild man perusing *The Gull's Hornbook*.

Even so, Morgan henceforth did not make a move without consulting the darkness, alert to a sudden appearance of Lucien in one guise or another, or some stranger as satanic as Lucien.

When a man who lived in Tooley Street was reported missing, folks began to think he might have taken Blythe himself and absconded with her, alive, or transported her body south into Kentwold. But Morgan suspected he was Lucien's assassin assassinated by Lucien.

*   *   *

"We met," Clarke Shadwell, who had fled to Wales, not knowing Blythe had been chosen and taken, wrote in his confession, concealed for later discovery and revelation, "We met, and we met, and went over and over long lists of possible preventatives, striking each one off as we agreed it wouldn't help, one proposal after another. We did not, I am stating here, simply meet and say, yes, that is what we must do. And even when the solution was presented, half in jest, we dropped it as impossible, and went on to others and to others, but it kept coming back in some new guise, and finally it was that game song about the breaking down of the Bridge coming through the window like an omen no longer a play song, that moved us to take it up as a serious proposal and examine it from all sides, until the plan, set down point by point, was adopted.

"I refused to endorse it. I swore silence and left the room, and in the middle of night, got up and abandoned my family, left the Bridge forever, cheating so far the assassin I am convinced they will have hired and set upon me, who searches for me now, this very night, as I set aside my quill to listen."

∗   ∗   ∗

In his shop, Eldon South, haberdasher, who had refused to surrender his daughter, fell to talking to Lucien—ignorant that he was the abductor his profits had helped to hire—reminisced, darkly. "The man who always wore the black hat too far down over his brows, pouching out his ears, was going to murther someone someday, so my parents told each other. I overheard. As a child, I watched him walk across, to and fro, year after year, until he was decrepit, until he vanished from the Bridge. And yet he walks there still. Even now. Perhaps even as I tell you about him, he is out there, crossing over to Southwark on his nocturnal business. But if I get up and you follow me to that door and we look out, we will never see him." The cherished daughter flounced down the stairs and skipped out into the congested roadway. "The spirit of such a man never vanishes because he lives in the hearts of the likes of me as a stark image, bereft of any other life than that of the man whose hat sat too far down."

Having bought a newly shaped hat from Mister South and crammed it down on his head to his ear, Lucien fixed Mister South in his eyes. "I will see you another time when you see me not, and you shall by these stained hands *be* not."

Lucien haunted the Bridge at unpredictable times of the day and night, stopping, naming aloud, each pier, each shop's motto, collecting tokens of each guild, speaking in shop or in street or standing at the foot of each brother's bed, making a promise to relieve each brother of his burden of guilt, to take his guilt upon himself in their moment of dying, a declared mockery of Christ, for no gain, for pure pleasure only.

∗   ∗   ∗

Stalking Gilda, Lucien became mirror-conscious. 'Jews cover mirrors when death snatches a loved one. Mirrors reflect everywhere. From

River Thames—waiting, jutting shadows on walls, ceilings, the water-fronts, windows in the shops and houses here on the Bridge, vacuous mirrors, window glass carried on crouched bodies crossing, mirrors, ac-tual, deliberately crafted, variously shaped mirrors on walls. Mirrors, glass, water reflected, flash, turn dark, grow bright, faces swim by, bare shoulders, bald heads, eyes, cat's eyes, in the dark, child's eyes, sleep-walkers, brass buttons go by, and ornaments that never move. Nonesuch House windows, and the windows of the House of Many Windows. A plague of mirrors. We do carry, don't we, mirrors as we live and breathe—eyes, spectacles from which to borrow vision power? Mirrors and Bridges. London Bridge and its myriad mirrors in time, starting from the day Peter de Colechurch peered into the water and cast upon it from the fount of his knowledge a Bridge centuries would embrace. Am I remembering the Poet-Chronicler telling me this?'

* * *

"If we work together, we can dismantle their satanic design."

"You are the Sinful Sailor yourself."

"No longer. I am now a Christian. Do you not remember what you said to me as we parted at the dock? Satan can overcome this man and that man, here and there, now and then. Only Christ can overcome the world. The Lord through you has worked his will upon me. I came to the Bridge to tell you that."

Standing, almost touching him, in the crowds of pedestrians avoid-ing roadway hazards, Lucien had succeeded, for a moment, in convinc-ing Morgan that he had, perhaps, modified his character.

Having looked at the Bridge from the Pool and climbed high on tower hill where executions were often done, but not so he could look all around, Lucien was transfixed for a moment, leaning against the needle shop he had passed many times over the past few days, under the sign of The Golden Needle as if about to remember something.

Nabbed on the Bridge as a wandering child, thinking ever since that in fog and darkness, it was a street, and taken to sea, he felt as if he were standing on the very spot. As if the spot itself moved up over his feet and up his legs and up to his navel and up to his chest, up his neck, his mouth, his nostrils, his eyes, making his hair stand on end, he felt "as if" no longer, *was* and *is* stabbed his guts, his heart.

"All those years, I was missing from the Bridge."

*   *   *

"Forgetfulness," said Mister Clinkenbeard to Mister Archer, Mister South, and Mister Brooke, his remaining three co-conspirators meeting secretly on the Isle of dogs. "A quality we will never know again. Unable to forget the darkest act of our lives, will we ever be able to forget other evils we do hereafter? We are doomed to remember everything. We can never mew anything up, out of sight. The friendly dark that creeps over the Bridge, step by step, will bring peace to others, but for us the glare of noonday light falls every hour until death falls upon our eyelids. Close your eyes in vain. Darkness is the alien. Stark light forevermore our familiar. We have sacrificed our very souls for the good of our fellow Bridge dwellers. We are parodies of both Christ and Judas in one."

In the shadow of Saint Magnus Martyr ruins, Clinkenbeard prayed. "I must not be held accountable, be made to explain. Lest God forget me."

*   *   *

Having asked hundreds of Londoners before, Morgan stopped a beggar to ask him whether he had seen the missing girl.

"The evil bastards that rot—no, not live—on this fucked-up Bridge they call London Bridge dare to look me in the face as they elbow me into the gutter where *they* belong and fart at me as they piss past me, the High and Mighty lowlife that breed like lice and Canton rats and raise their eyes to heaven and knock their wives onto the bed and their maid servants up against the wall, whose skirts up over their bawling heads expose raw arses in the stairway dark for all the world to see and who cheat and steal and give bad weight and serve up watered beer and bad pork and walk the way they do, how can they then walk like that, up and down the roadway cross and crisscross the Bridge—and as if their heads didn't belong aloft with all the others—to sicken the very ravens of the Tower who turn away from such mockery of God, no, I'll not bow, not I, even though I beg up and down, crisscross and crosscriss this Bridge, my nose too will point up or down at will, at sight of me own kind daring to come two inches, breath stinking close to me or knocking me by hips and shoulder and elbow and once a month or so by aiming a kick where Cromwell got me first after the battle of Cropredy Bridge—it was Waller who wallered. Ah, life on London Bridge! Goes better there in spite, than in Newgate prison or the galleys or as last visit to Tower Hill gallows. I'm free, ain't I? Free to hate all these bloody Bridgers equally.

"I alone hear rats sigh, content, as me, or saddened by the spectacle."

*   *   *

Folks searching became resigned.

Then the idea took hold among the Cabal that God wanted Blythe indeed and would not harm the Bridge. They reverted to the primitive. They felt better, until imagine! Corpulent goldsmith Clinkenbeard lugged a jar of flammable liquid up onto the Great Stone Gate, no mean feat for a young man, much less this old man, and standing among the pikes whose severed heads rose up around him, called out, "Beloved!" and lit the torch and then touched the torch to his oiled coat and, all-enveloped in fire, jumped screaming into River Thames, knowingly extinguishing his deeds as chief co-conspirator, bearing witness to God's promise to bring down those who raise themselves up by bloody deeds, especially in the name of the Public Good.

1666. Arthur Clinkenbeard, goldsmith, committed suicide by fire, while smokes were still rising from the ruins of Old London.

Light Is the Shadow of God
But even if light were still my ally against the dark,

death, my hand trembles. Worse. I have exhausted
the possibilities. Nothing remains to see. Those stacks,
towers, of unfinished poems contain a complete record,
so people centuries from now may see,
long after my sockets are fleshless. My
father's Chronicle has its story to tell.
And what will *this* record show?

Daryl Braintree

18

LUCIEN KIDNAPS GILDA,
FAIR LADY OF THE BRIDGE

Gilda lay awake watching the shadows and lights change on her ceiling like clouds passing over the moon in the dome of night, feeling the rhythm in her own pulse. She stared hard, aware that simple blinking interrupted the flow.

Hearing a creak in the staircase, she thought for a moment the very lights and shadows had made sounds, hoping to see Blythe face to face, that awful word "missing" obliterated.

*   *   *

'This night is darker than the night I came for Blythe. The backside of darkness. Gilda's household will be more vigilant than Blythe's. I must be invisible. I have earned my pay. This one is for me. To achieve what I set out to achieve for my own glory. In my own eyes. And Lucifer's.

'She has said her prayers. She sleeps the sleep of the truly innocent, unless she has fooled others, even Blythe, as Blythe fooled her. No, she is perfect.

'Did she have premonitions, dreams, nightmares? Did she long to see her savior step onto the Bridge, but saw the rank stranger instead, or saw me but didn't really notice me?

'The light on the bed. Where does it come from? No moon. She is asleep, not a fake.'

Into the gentle flow of light and shadows an almost winged dark shape spread like a stain, as if absorbing the lights, the shadows, bloating itself, pulsing where light still defined its shape, until the dome of night above Gilda's bed was night only, and she turned her head slowly as if it weighed one hundred pounds. 'Holy Spirit, illumine me.'

'A drawing on the foot of the bed. Blythe, looking perfect, innocent. Gilda recalls, memorializes her friend who is missing. Forever. No one will find her. Not even if my employers confess. They may break open Rock Lock, but they shall not find her.

· 'But this one I will not mew up either, but leave her splayed out in the middle of the roadway or ram her head down on a pike above it.

'Her eyes open. She has been waiting.'

"Take me to Blythe."

A shape bent over her, light flowed back over her ceiling and illuminated the smiling face of a saint.

"Come, my fair lady. London Bridge is falling down." These words out of his own mouth surprised Lucien.

Other children—never she again, Gilda knew—would sing that song. The palm of his hand clapped over her mouth—she tasted it, rancid cabbage, moldy tobacco?

'Can I tempt her?' "I will let you live, if you will help me set fire to the Bridge, right here, your bed the bed of fire."

'She is rising, she is reaching out to me.

'Take her hand.

'We go down quietly, four flights, to the shop, and out into the black, blank roadbed.

'She does not speak, as if not to break a spell she has willed over herself and—she seems to think—me. She will speak, she thinks, when she sees Blythe. Expecting to die with her? My sister's keeper?'

'Something in his grip is lacking. As if, even as he grabbed me, he would let me go. And in his eyes, as if he saw more deeply into my eyes than he meant to do.'

'I, we, are on Old Swan Steps, going in my stolen boat to the chapel starling.

'The consternation will be agony for the cabal.'

As Lucien carried Gilda through the fishermen's entrance to old Saint Thomas à Becket Chapel, yet another fire still latent in the undercroft at Saint Paul's exploded.

'In the rag and paper warehouse, Saint Thomas à Becket Chapel, I feel at home where Henry VIII committed the desecration, Gilda's white gown trails in Blythe's damp-dry blood. Yes, look down and scream. No one will hear you.

'She does not scream. She turns, looks at me.

'I do not turn my eyes away.

'We stand face to face, our eyes mirror each other's face, eyes, mouth.

'I tell her every detail, Blythe's father hiring me to kidnap Blythe, the creature Blythe really was, and what this moment means.'

"I knew, but I always believed she would remember, repent, and return."

'I give her a questioning look.'

"Remember her innocence, her christening, repent of her life, and return to the forgiveness and grace of Christ. I pray that as you dragged her by her hair, shooting the Bridge, she remembered, she repented, and that she now abides in the Holy Ghost."

"You are not afraid of me either, are you?"

"'Betwixt the stirrup and the ground, mercy I asked, mercy I found.' No. I pray for you. I forgive you, as Christ has forgiven you since the foundation of the world."

"You compete with God. It was God's will and Lucifer's pleasure— and mine—that I slaughter Blythe. Against God's will and for Lucifer's greater pleasure, you attempt to bring her back by drawing her to the life. You compete with Him."

"No, it was God's will that you see her face again before you saw mine."

"And there Blythe's face lay, at the foot of your bed. But I was not moved."

"You say it."

"You deny me your fear. But you are, nevertheless, the pure girl I seek, because in the act of slaughtering you, I do the great evil act I have always dreamed of committing."

"Do you know why?"

"So I will be free. Are you good or are you false?"

"I am not false."

He looked at her, searching her face, wishing it were not a surface, but deep, like a stream, something moving over a river bottom landscape.

Gilda looked so directly into his eyes that he lidded them for a moment. "See, Lucien, the darkness denies your shadow, but look! how God's shadow, light, casts your shadow."

"I want to wear my sins on my skin as a leper wears his sores. Evil, I come and I go, but good remains."

"On faces, in voices of Jesus in plague and fire."

"What do you see, looking over my face as if it were a landscape?"

"I see resemblances to God."

"Have you ever seen his face?"

"We can see his face only in faces such as yours—and mine."

"You shut your eyes."

"Your voice is His."

"Shut up! Did God make me what I am?"

"Yes, as he made me."

"That's no answer."

"It is, if you linger upon it. Your hands are pierced. Remember, Jesus included Judas, *knowing*, at the Lord's Supper."

"I would have chosen Judas as my name, but I do not intend to end as a suicide."

"Imagine, as Londoners are looking for me, Christ is looking for you."

"Lord, how could you let me come to this?"

"To save you. To set you free. Is your spirit not mewed up in a cramped space, shut off from the sound of living water?"

"You Puritans are sin itself, because you are so obsessed with sin."

'I do not rape her.

'I prepare her for the sacrifice, tearing off her dress.

'I rape her. She does not resist. She does not respond.

'I cross the room, lean against a stack of paper and look away from her.'

"I raped you!"

"No, I am Christ's. You raped only the body God made. You can't rape the Holy Ghost who was not made but *is,* in me."

"Have you ever turned your back upon Jesus?"

"Never."

"I have. Often. With great deliberation and sheer delight. Do I horrify you?"

"No. Jesus looked upon your back, patiently, waiting for you to turn. And I have faith that you will."

"I never had a chance *to* turn to Jesus. So I have not turned *away* from him."

"Then turn. Be blessed. Live in the mind of Christ."

'Now she merely talks to me.'

"I was always dancing. Dancing. Not with my feet, but in my— heart? No. In my head. I felt the dance of ideas in my head, and I call it dancing because the movement of an idea through my mind I felt in rhythm with the flow of water between the piers below my house and all the piers as I crossed and re-crossed, pacing, thinking, trailing after ideas. The music was the rush of water, the machine racket, the beat of the waterwheels, the sound of feet and wheels and hooves over the roadway, the chiming of glass or tin among the cart peddler wares. I *saw* dancing often, but in my head, dancing always."

"Never look back. Lot's wife, you know. Nor to the future. Live or die in this instant. I have no recollection of the War. That time when my guts were on fire. Nor of the horror. I know it happened. I feel its hand in my guts, at my throat. But only that—a sense of choking. I cannot vomit it. I can look at an axe now and not shudder and drop what mayhap be in my hand. When I first went aboard a ship, I was always dropping things. As if taking something into my hand. . . . I became like Satan so that I would not have to go on being human, like those others."

"Jesus became like us so that we—all humanity—could become like Jesus."

'She is no longer a virgin. Mewing *her* up where I promised will be the epitome of spite. They wanted her virginal, alive, to suffocate behind the stones. They do not get what they want.

'I want to hear you say it.'

"I want to hear you say it again. Do you believe in God?"

"Yes."

'At her throat without thinking. Shut your eyes, child. Die fast. Don't linger. My hands are strong, and work faster than an airless tomb.

'I am blessed. A greater blessing would be if child Morgan, searching for her among all the other searchers, were to find her, too late, *now,* and for me to rape him, alienate his head from his body and then ram his head down on a pike above the gate.'

19

THE SEARCH FOR GILDA

That night, having just learned that Gilda too was missing, the 599 Bridge dwellers prayed to God, with Thanksgiving for who she is and pleas for the safe rescue of "this child of God."

As a pebble dropped—or dislodged and fallen—into a stagnant pond sends ripples over the surface, the sneezing rat gets ripples of response from Upshaw, the rag merchant, lying awake, stiff, in fear of starting to tremble and not being able to stop, who, listening to his own heart beat, heard the sneeze and thought it the cat and strange, and said to his wife, "You know, I don't think I ever heard a cat sneeze in the night," to the neighbor, to whom the wife said, "Your cat got out again, I hear, and set up a commotion outside me husband's bedroom—and me own window, keeping him awake so that there he stands behind the counter red-eyed and his head full of stuffing," to the friend of the neighbor at the butcher's, "I'll drop it off me selve—if you like," who spit on the meat, so the dry goods merchant's wife, suspected poison and tossed it to a dog that dragged it bloody across a gentleman's boots who cursed the dog and stopped to wipe off the blood and saw a man trying to duck, who owed him.

"When on a community scale, the routine of one's daily life is suddenly disrupted, one becomes, ever so slightly, at the very least, a different person among different persons, and so when plague came, followed by fire, and then the two children disappeared, causing the great search, the Bridge itself looked, even, one might venture to say, *behaved* differently. The leaning houses leaned more precipitously, the waterwheels screeched louder, the millstones sounded like giants grinding their teeth in nightmare sweats, and the heads over the Great Gate seemed they would speak, if they could, or perhaps would. A simple glass of water had the taste of plague-rotten flesh or scorched wood or the taste in the mouth of a child dying of thirst—and fear."

The Poet meditated. 'Throughout the years of plague and fire, Gilda sang and danced 'London Bridge Is Broken Down' alone and played the game with other children on the Bridge, but who can say whether the child singing now in the street in the dark is Gilda or fair Blythe?'

Panicked by news "Gilda has been kidnapped," the surviving three of the cabal, Brooke, South, and Archer, met again well out of sight and discovery on the Isle of Dogs.

They decided, in sincere and manifold anguish, that they must themselves—"no more hired assassins!"—must find and kill the kidnapper, the betrayer, waylay and kill Morgan where he walks, searching, and the reclusive Poet-Chronicler in his scriptorium, all three knowing the legend of mewing up a virgin in a bridge pillar.

Mister Archer indulged wearily in solace of a sort. "Hundreds crossing would have seen her. And as they forget seeing each other, forgot seeing *her.*"

Fishmonger Brooke. "Blamed momentarily, as in plague and fire, now this kidnap, those who live in Old Jewry, the Jews or a Jew, the Dutch or a Dutchman, the French, or a Frenchman, those who prophesy in the streets, those who are mad and were harmless are now out to do harm. But let us look to the Jews. Expelled in the Thirteenth Century. England was free of Jews, until King Henry VIII opened to them, our King Charles promised protection, but the Bridge did not want Jews. I mean, the very Bridge itself. The dwellers, too, of course. And, of course, Londoners and Southwarkians, and even strangers, foreigners, aliens crossing. We suspected something sinister afoot. Jewry in London was tolerable, but on the Bridge, it seemed, when you saw a Jew crossing, a risk to let him. But they did. And we have let them. No law forbade it. No man stood at the Bridge foot and blocked the roadway. Few people cursed or hissed them. That *I* know of. *I* didn't. I'm telling you about a feeling. A feeling that started with the Bridge itself and that you—*I*—felt in the soles of my feet. Let us pray people will think of the Jews in this."

As the cabal was meeting, Alfred Goodyer, needle maker, told Thomas Wright, scrivener, a story. "The kind old man who came onto the Bridge each night to feed the cats—we were glad, they ate the rats— was discovered last night roasting one of his fat cats over a flotsam fire. Only weeks before the first virgin was missed, he confessed he neither loved nor hated cats alive, but preferred cat meat to any other. Like most of the cats, he had no home. Cats staved off starvation. As we searched for the girls, we talked. The cat man became a possible cannibal. We cornered him and put him in the cage for safekeeping. A hundred cats rubbed up against his cage all day for two days. They dwindled, one by one, down to one and then none. He died this morning of starvation."

Brooke, fishmonger. "It is a dread sound. Footsteps that cross the Bridge between nocturnal reverie—light sleep—awakening. Hesitate a moment just out of earshot, then resume. I cannot bear it. Sometimes I cannot bear it. . . . You, too, have had that self-same experience, and you also? Footsteps that wake you, pass on beyond earshot, then hesitate?"

"And resume."

"And resume. But going on *with* what, and to where, and why? Unnerving."

"To lie awake trying to imagine."

"Reason naught availeth, so to speak."

"I'm never satisfied that, well, it was only—"

"Nor I. Oh, eventually I fall asleep."

"And do *you,* too, pass the night in fitful dreams?"

"Yes, and all day long on the Bridge the dread sound lingers, hovers, that all day long other Bridge walkers in broad daylight mimic."

"Well, I, for one, heard it last night."

"The dread sound?"

"Let us talk of pleasant things."

"Not possible on the Isle of Dogs."

Each of the three had begun to see that no one can die in his place.

Mister South felt a severe need to speak plainly. "Once I planned to break into Rock Lock and let Blythe out. I did no more than visit the stones of Rock Lock in the dead of night, lay my hands upon them, in fear God would cast me down into the rush of water, uttered only half a prayer."

Alone again on the Bridge, Mister South prayed for forgiveness and then he prayed for Blythe's soul and for Gilda, only missing, the cabal not having hired anyone to take *her*.

*   *   *

The Poet told Morgan the full story of Peter de Colechurch's building the Bridge until his death left it unfinished in 1205. Morgan was not very interested. The immediate Bridge was his interest and concern.

Morgan prayed amid the still warm ruins of Saint Magnus Martyr.

"The Bridge is an altar to several churches close by on either side of the Bridge on both banks."

Morgan overheard the priest say to a woman praying on her knees in the open ruins, "Our peak point fallen afire, we are a malformed star." He wrote it down to pass on to the Poet.

Moved by Gilda's spirit, the Poet wrote:

> As once we saw her, we see her still.
> Dancing. To search for the missing
> is to see one as one once saw one,
> reiteratively, always expectant, to see,
> when found, in the flesh what we saw
> so often in the flesh before and, missing,
> in memory. So Gilda before she was
> missing is always the image we
> best knew and so, she is *never* missing,
> and, if not dancing when found, shall dance still.

London Bridge is falling down, Prague's Old Stone Bridge, Pont d'Avignon, Ponte Vecchio, Pont Neuf, Ponte Rialto, the Bridge of Sighs are falling down. The Bridge at Mostar, the Bridge over the River Drina, Three Arched Bridge in the Balkans, the bridges all over the earth are burning, burning, falling into the rivers, agitated, chased by gravity below.

We move across, the river moves beneath, while the Bridge stands still, or seems to, but it, too, moves, falls slowly, crossing by crossing. Swinging bridges move, sway, swing, fall, down.

*   *   *

"We seek Shadwell," Mister Brooke is writing in his confession, hoping he and the Brotherhood have saved the Bridge and that his descendants will show this document. "We sent agents out into the towns and villages, the country-side. He was as if *vanished*—not a trace, and so always a worry to us. That he might speak of us. That he might confess. Return and point us out, now his daughter is taken, even though he was gone before we put our plan—even before we laid out the plan in detail—into effect. As much as any of us whom we saw in the course of daily business, he who was most absent was most present. In our shops, in the roadway, in our bedrooms. I often quit the Bridge to put Shadwell behind me. Once away from the Bridge, I no longer feel his presence. I am left *alone* with my own conscience. And that, of course, was hell's fire.

"Daryl Braintree will know in time. In time, we will be forced to deal with him. Perhaps from the open window of his scriptorium."

*   *   *

Shadows, Light
On the Bridge now, it is dark for me,
on my Bridge, London Bridge. Mine
because it is not a street, a road, it is
unlike anywhere else men have set up abode.

So for each of us, it is 'my' Bridge,
with others living by on each side,
and across the way, tight together.
Where, when it is not dark, they,
the heads on pikes above, cast down shadows,
across my path. They, now, cast no shadows. No
moon. Except by an inner light, that spiritual light
that flows through all ever alive and now living,
their shadows, the shadows of only transient,
ferociously reluctant residents, guests, fall across
my consciousness tonight, as I stand at the Bridge foot,
in this time of plague and fire and kidnapping.
But not tomorrow in the moonlight.
Then I am free of them, unless I look up,
against the light, standing firm on my London Bridge.

Daryl Braintree

*   *   *

"The rumor, sir, is that Gilda came to the Bridge a year before I went to sea, seven years ago."

"No, no, no." Morgan's uncle shook his head emphatically. "Those rumors are false. She was not born on the Bridge. She was brought here to live when her parents moved into the house on pier twelve, Pedler's Lock, east, at the sign of The Buckled Shoe, so recently no one quite remembers. Gilda was seen dancing and singing alone in the roadway in the evening by only one or two who remember her. *I* never saw her, and *I* see every one. So viewed as a resident on the Bridge known to others, there wasn't very much of her to vanish—for us, don't you know? I would have noticed, by habit, and remembered, don't you know? Making one wonder, was she ever really there?"

Mister South to Mister Brooke, who were standing by, overhearing. "Pig pudding! *I* saw Gilda dance once. I remember her swirling hair, her haunted voice, as if she knew she was in peril, being watched mayhap as she danced and sang. Or not to put too fine a point on it—the child I saw, I see no more."

Overhearing the two men, Morgan turned to his uncle. "I fear that one or the other or both are one false step away from madness."

"I share your sense of it."

*   *   *

In his scriptorium, the Poet distilled all the talk he had heard. "She is simultaneously and ever was and always will be all the aspects she has enacted of herself and that diverse others have perceived, imagined."

*   *   *

Mister Goodyer. "Thomas, I beheld Satan as lightning fall from Heaven. Luke 10:18."

*   *   *

"Terror overwhelms." Eldon South spoke, aloud, working alone among his hats. "When one supposes there is, in all the universe, only one spoon, among an infinite number of knives and forks."

A year later, a rootless wanderer in the streets of London, all he wanted to say, or would, or might, or could was, "Only one spoon."

*   *   *

Having despoiled Gilda, Lucien was inspired to desecrate, by mock, the chapel.

Having buried her deep inside the highest pile of rags, Lucien set a tier of paper afire, stamped it out, wondering why.

Having stolen tools from Master Carpenter Coldiron, he cast aside the rags, carried her out of the undercroft through the ancient door fishermen used to use to enter the Chapel from the water, broke into the chapel starling, stronger and longer than the others, the one that broke the tide most sharply, dug a place for her and laid her more gently than he intended in the grave.

'I will tell one who will tell the others that I did not bury Blythe or Gilda in Rock Lock Pier, but swear I buried her on the Bridge, and not say where she may someday be found.'

*   *   *

'In this shop of harps only, I strum the largest one, setting up among all the smaller harps responses melodious. I am the arch disharmonium.

'There goes the Poet-Chronicler, sauntering through a superfluity of obliviousness.

'I intend to call my autobiography "Don't Remember."

'I will visit each member of the cabal, hatless, as I visited Mister South, hatmaker.'

Taking on with a bundle of rags the false identify of a rag merchant, Lucien approached the warehouse below the former chapel.

He startled Rag Merchant Upshaw. "I did not see you come in."

"I merely happen. Do you feel the spirit of Peter de Colechurch down there when you sort your rags?"

"You know then that he built a chapel for Saint Thomas here."

"Do you know his cast off garment to lie at the bottom of a heap there?"

"You will kill me one day, will you not?"

"Kill you? You are already so moribund the effort to kill you is hardly worthwhile."

'I am a demolitioner. The dark subtractor.'

*   *   *

The Poet wrote: "Tonight makes a year that I have been taking these nocturnal meditations or walks on Ancient London Bridge. This year of our Lord 1665–1666 has been a terrible year indeed. A wonderful year, full of wonder, as Thomas Dekker in *The Wonderful Year,* meant that word to mean. One catastrophe after another. But the solitary walks have been a simultaneous journey toward the end of the year, and all these walks have kept my imagination fertile. It is amazing how readily words and images and insights come to the point of these quills. I never wrack my brains. I merely begin. And tomorrow night I will allow myself the delight of starting to reread these three hundred and twenty nine sheaves of paper. And now I crawl into bed."

20

LIGHT IS GOD'S SHADOW

'When my captain forced me off the ship, I stood on the dock, and Morgan pointed his finger at me, saying, "In the world ye shall have tribulations. But be of good cheer. I have overcome the world." Did he refer to me or to himself? But an acoustic shadow must have been in effect—as when quite close we see the smoke of a ship's cannon but hear nothing—so that I could not clearly hear, and I assumed it was an accusation. Perhaps not.

'God, name the sin in lightning on the dark sky over the Bridge so that I may know it is written that I do what I do. That You willed it. Not Satan. I don't love Satan in spite. I hate God. I hate you, God, for allowing such as Satan—*me*—to live. I am happy only when I am Darkness—Darkness in the night, Darkness in broad daylight, undistinguishable, ever undiminished.

'In the swaying hammock above Morgan, listening to his murmuring voice, I saw Blythe before they paid me to sacrifice her. In a dream we were children playing together, singing, dancing on the Bridge. I remember her only in the dream now, but I mock it, I sneer.

'Morgan writing, remembering, often in the margins of his books. The Chronicler, his history of the Bridge, and, as poet, forging words to capture the spirit of the Bridge.

'Look at the goodness my heinous act, like Judas's, has wrought. Without Judas, Christ is not. The evil act is always double, as evil and as inspiration to good. The war, the plague, a malicious action of nature, and fire, a malicious act of providence, brought out both the best and the worst in mankind, but *my* act, but *my* act brings out only goodness and mercy, while only *I,* all the days of my life, must suffer evil. The good to whom evil is done do not *suffer* evil, they suffer harm, loss, grief, but it is only the evil-doer who is condemned to suffer evil itself. My suffering is in the Word (In the beginning, Lucien, was the Word). I must put into words all day and all night long, talking silently, how I think and feel about my enormous act, my act more intense than any ordinary man's daily act. I am unique.

'Before I die, mayhap I will write a confession—to Lucifer—my failure to do even greater evil than I have done.'

"Lucifer, you above all, more than Judas, suffer evil. Compassion! Forgive me."

'I am a ship with a false keel. My soul has a false bottom.

'Even when I make music my pitch is false.

'Words are armament.

'I am half-asleep. The night air over the Bridge chills, to the bone.

'Half-asleep, with the water roaring in my ears, a fine rain, whispering rain, struck up against the starling in my face stinging my eyes. And now curl back my imaginary covers and roll myself up in a thick blanket of deep sleep.'

An inspiration stopped Lucien dead.

'I will remove her from the starling of the desecrated Chapel and bury her in the arms of Peter de Colechurch in his crypt in the undercroft of Saint Thomas Chapel, among the stacks of paper and the multitude of rags.'

"Lucifer, do you look upon this act as re-consecrating that ancient fabric into a chapel again? Turn your head."

Under cover of the inky shadows of midnight, Lucien used his bare fingertips to locate the cracks, his fingers to dislodge, his hands to remove the stones and pull her body out of the tomb he had made into his arms, the exertion of stealth, the stone heavier this time. Lifting up his burden again, he carried Gilda through the fishermen's door to the chapel, to desecrate it, Henry VIII having failed.

'For I feel the spirit of this place.'

He handled hammer and spike to break into the wall and then into the tomb and open the arm bones of what he assumed to be the almost four-centuries-old skeleton of Peter de Colechurch and with a slowness he had never felt in his body placed Gilda's body, speaking to it all the while, up against the breast bones of the master architect of the Bridge, and then he folded Peter's bones over her rigid body, never having read the Poet's imagined version that put Saint Thomas à Becket's bones there instead. Repairing the cracks, like streaks of lightning, and restoring the concealing wall was faster work that drenched him in sweat. Wanting to say 'Gilda,' he said aloud, "Gilda," almost bowing.

Up on the Bridge again, he set himself out as lure.

'I see him following me, the man who has been following me. Is he, too, a seaman? He doesn't know why he has been hired to kill me. If he did, they would have to kill the member of the cabal who hired him too, and another and another. When they hear of his death, it will strike them as a very bad omen indeed.

'You do not know that here where I stop is the very spot where you stop breathing.'

'I put the words in your mouths, repeated from mouth to mouth, until your mouths are so dry you cannot spit.'

Lucien imagined two merchants of the cabal talking.

"Did you hear they found Mister South mangled in the burnt waterwheel turned by the tide?"

Mister Brooke. "A bad omen, if I do say so."

Mister Archer. "A very bad omen indeed."

'I shall stand on the highest point and look out over my creation, because this Bridge will never be the same now, this Bridge that has survived visitations of wars, great frosts, famous gales, plagues, and fires, but will not survive my visitation. I have put a human face on their misery that they can never forget. I will not burn it. *They* will destroy it. God will punish. God punishes those who fear He will.'

He climbed up to the top of the Great Stone Gate.

'There are the faces. Eighteen faces. The oldest, how long ago, and the newest still dripping blood.'

Lucien watched the Keeper of the Heads climb the tower, a bag greasy-blackened of blood hanging heavy by a strap from his lopsided shoulder and remove a head from a pike, take the head from the bag and jam it down on the pike, then put the discarded head in the empty bag, and climb down again into Lucien's waiting arms, taking the blade in his ribs, into his heart and sink down, thrice heavier, dead, in his arms. He tossed the head from the bag into River Thames, hacked off the head of the Keeper of the Heads, climbed up the tower, and replaced the most recent head with the headsman's head.

'What crimes? Let me look into your face, old man. Let me? You cannot stop me. Now you, young man. Now you, woman. Why do you not resemble Blythe? And you, why do you not resemble *me*? And you, I am eager to hear you confess your crime. And you, why are you, you, not the mastermind of this plot?

'What made that black burnt spot? The man they said set himself on fire and leapt into River Thames? A conspirator's solution?

'Oh, I know you all. I saw you first the day you murdered my mother, my father, my brothers and sisters, my relatives, my friends, my neighbors, and violated me throughout four years of daily death. I see the faces of all you men, Puritans, enslaved to sin, and Royalists, Cavaliers, enslaved to the king, and that seaman on my first ship who failed to become the last in the legions assaulting my asshole, and then never again. I baptized myself in a sea of hatred and cunning.

'I must leave you now, ladies and gentlemen.

'The wind is sudden and cold, and I see a curtain of gentle rain, wavery, over the Pool, the masts of ships, furled, and the river curving and curling fast toward the Bridge.

'Maybe I will sail to America. But save a pike for me, in case they catch me.

'The wind is harsh and cold on my face. My black heart burns.'

"There he is!" 'I look down.

'Morgan, looking up, pointing at me.'

"Radford, in this world, ye shall have tribulations!"

334

'He is not accusing me.'

"Lucifer, I beg you—ask God's forgiveness—for *my* sake!"

The rain becomes a deluge.

"But be of good cheer! I have overcome the world!"

'I no longer see Morgan in the roadway below. The tempest is for me. Thunder. Lucifer contending? Fallen angels falling?'

"Remember, repent, return."

'Whose mouth speaks? Gilda's?

'Lightning, like a shadow, falls across me alone, the heads on pikes in the outer darkness.'

Lux umbra dei—light is God's shadow.

"It is me, O, Lord! Radford! Christ, forgive me!"

In an instant, as forgiveness enflames Lucien-Radford's heart, he lifts his foot and brings it down on the rain-slick roof of the Great Gate, a wordless declaration: 'God loves me!'

Lucien dances joyously for twenty-three seconds exactly, slips in the rain-reliquefied blood of the headsman's severed head, and so, mind full of the living Christ, falls upon a pike, his body and mind falling into pain. Alive a few seconds more, he could have stared directly into the face of the woman, but he was too close, face to face.

His soul abides, as Gilda envisioned, in the mind of God.

SELECTED READING

Listed here are books I read or delved into over three decades. The first book was *London in Plague and Fire, 1665–1666: Selected Source Material for College Research Papers,* a textbook I used at Centre College in 1960, my second year of teaching. It includes writers listed on page 120 of this novel.

Among other books, the most useful were:

Gordon Home, *Old London Bridge* (the second book I read and the best)

Frank Barlow, *Thomas Becket*

William Urry, *Thomas Becket: His Last Days*

Robert Speaight, *Thomas Becket*

Michael Staunton, editor, translator, *The Lives of Thomas Becket*

Walter George Bell, *The Great Plague in London in 1665* and *The Great Fire of London in 1666*

Samuel Pepys, *Diary*

John Evelyn, *Diary* and *Sylva*

The Autobiography of Richard Baxter

Roland Bartel, *London in Plague and Fire: 1655–1666*

Daniel Defoe, *A Journal of the Plague Year*

Other useful books included:

Patricia Pierce, *Old London Bridge: The Story of the Longest Inhabited Bridge in Europe*

Richard Thomson, *Chronicles of London Bridge*

John E. N. Hearsey, *Bridge Church and Palace in Old London*

Peter Jackson, *London Bridge: A Visual History*

John Stow, *A Survey of London*

James Leasor, *The Plague and the Fire*

Stephen Porter, *The Great Plague*

Leonard W. Cowie, *Plague and Fire, London 1665–66*

Gustav Milne, *The Great Fire of London*

Neil Hanson, *The Great Fire of London: In That Apocalyptic Year, 1666*

Adrian Tinniswood, *By Permission of Heaven: The True Story of the Great Fire of London*

The Anglo-Saxon Chronicle

Thomas B. Costain, *The Conquering Family*

Liza Picard, *Restoration London: Everyday Life in the 1660s*

Ross King, *Brunichelli's Dome*

Eileen Power, *Medieval People*

Christopher Brooke, *From Alfred to Henry III, 871–1272*

Doris Mary Stenton, *English Society in the Early Middle Ages (1066–1307)*

John Butler, *The Quest for Becket's Bones: The Mystery of the Relics of St. Thomas Becket of Canterbury*

Peter Marsden, *Roman London*

John Burke, *Roman England*

The London Encyclopedia

Bruce Watson, Trevor Brigham, and Tony Dyson, *London Bridge: 2000 Years of a River Crossing*

A. L. Rowse, *The England of Elizabeth: The Structure of Society*

John Richardson, *The Annals of London: A Year-by-Year Record of a Thousand Years of History*

C. V. Wedgewood, *The Life of Cromwell*

Barbara A. Hanawalt, *Growing up in Medieval London: The Experience of Childhood in History*

J. J. Bagley, *Life in Medieval England*

Donald Hill, *A History of Engineering In Classical and Medieval Times*

Christopher Dyer, *Making a Living in The Middle Ages: The People of Britain, 850–1520*

Maureen Waller, *1700: Scenes from London Life*

John Boswell, *The Kindness of Strangers: The Abandonment of Children in Western Europe from Late Antiquity to the Renaissance*

W. L. Warren, *Henry II*

Helen Waddell, *Peter Abelard*

Urban Tigner Holmes Jr., *Daily Living in the Twelfth Century*

J. J. Jusserand, *English Wayfaring Life in the Middle Ages*

Chris Given-Wilson, *Chronicles: The Writing of History in Medieval England*

Charles Pendrill, *London Life in the 14th Century*

Johan Huizinga, *The Autumn of the Middle Ages (The Waning of the Middle Ages)*

Norman F. Cantor, general editor, *The Encyclopedia of the Middle Ages*

Norman F. Cantor, *Inventing the Middle Ages*

Jacques Derrida, *The Gift of Death*

Miles Richardson, *Being-in-Christ and Putting Death in Its Place*

G. G. Coulton, *Medieval Panorama: The English Scene from Conquest to Reformation*

LONDON BRIDGE IN PLAGUE AND FIRE was designed and typeset on a Macintosh computer system using InDesign software. The body text is set in 11/15 Adobe Garmond Pro. This book was designed and typeset by Chad Pelton, and manufactured by Thomson-Shore, Inc.